Stoker & Bash: T

When will She open Rebecca Northcote's box?

Finding lost poodles and retrieving stolen baubles is not how DI Tim Stoker envisioned his partnership with his lover, Hieronymus Bash. So when the police commissioner's son goes missing, he's determined to help, no matter what secrets he has to keep, or from whom.

When a family member is kidnapped, Hiero moves heaven and earth to rescue them. Even if that means infiltrating the Daughters of Eden, a cult of wealthy widows devoted to the teachings of Rebecca Northcote and the mysterious contents of her box. The Daughters' goodwill toward London's fallen women has given them a saintly reputation, but Hiero has a nose for sniffing out a fraud. He will need to draw on some divine inspiration to rattle the pious Daughters.

Like weeds gnarling the roots of Eden's fabled tree, Tim and Hiero's cases intertwine. Serpents, secrets, and echoes from Hiero's past lurk behind every branch. Giving in to temptation could bind them closer together—or sever their partnership forever.

Praise for Stoker & Bash #1: The Fangs of Scavo

"*Stoker & Bash: The Fangs of Scavo* is a witty, thrilling romp through Victorian London I couldn't help but fall in love with. If you enjoy paranormal historical, go ahead and clear a space on your keeper shelf for this book."

—Jordan L. Hawk
Author, *Whyborne & Griffin* series

"I adore the outrageously sexy Hieronymus Bash! If you love sexy Victorians solving mind-boggling mysteries, you'll love *Stoker & Bash*."

—Joanna Chambers
Author, *Enlightenment* series

Stoker & Bash: The Fruit of the Poisonous Tree
Copyright © 2018 by Selina Kray
Cover Art: Tiferet Design (www.TiferetDesign.com)
Editor: Nancy-Anne Davies
ISBN: 978-0-9959925-5-9
eBook ISBN: 978-0-9959925-4-2

First Edition
October 2018

STOKER & BASH

The Fruit of the
Poisonous Tree

SELINA KRAY

You snake, you crawled between my legs
Said, "Want it all?
It's yours. You bet
I'll make you queen of everything
No need for God
No need for him

Just take my hand
You'll be my bride
Just take that fruit, put it inside"
You snake, you dog, you fake, you liar
I've burned my hands
I'm in the fire

You salty dog, you filthy liar
My heart it aches
I'm in the fire
You snake, I ate a true belief
Your rotten fruit inside of me
Oh, Adam, please you must believe
That snake put it in front of me

—Polly Jean Harvey, "Snake"

Dramatis Personae

THE DETECTIVES
Detective Inspector Timothy Kipling Stoker, Scotland Yard
Hieronymus Bash, a consulting detective of growing renown
Calliope "Callie" Pankhurst, Bash's ward, pistol aficionado
Han Tak Hai, fixer, confidant, sculptor

THE CLIENT
Colonel Sir Hugh Winterbourne, Commissioner of the Police of the
Metropolis, widower

THE DAUGHTERS OF EDEN
Juliet Tattersale, spiritual leader and current prophetess
Norah Hawfinch, right-hand woman
Zanna Lawless, midwife
Emerald "Merry" Scaggs, head gardener and chief gossip
Amos Scaggs, her brother
also, Rebecca Northcote, founding prophetess, arisen

BERKELEY SQUARE HOUSEHOLD
Lillian Pankhurst, Callie's mother, indisposed
Shahida Kala, her companion
Aldridge, the butler
Minnie, the cook
Angus Fotheringham, the chauffeur
Yu-Jie Fotheringham, the ladies' maid
Ting, their daughter
also Admiral The Viscount Apollonius "Apollo" Pankhurst, Callie's
uncle and Bash's former lover, deceased.

Chapter 1

MAY 9TH, 1874

When will She open Rebecca Northcote's box?

Hieronymus Bash contemplated the question posed by the long, red-lettered banner that blazoned over the otherwise quaint fruit and vegetable stall. A sharp tug of the arm from Callie, his ward, brought him to heel. He'd already been struggling to match her brisk pace, having been dragged from his early afternoon repose in the cozy climes of his study into, of all things, the sunshine, or what passed for it on this weak-tea day.

Rays of piss-yellow sun trickled down over the city, tinting the fumes that oozed up from the Thames. Clouds of smog blurred the distant Albert Bridge into an impressionist's nightmare. A growing crowd choked the small stage erected just before the river's edge, scuttling in from both directions of Cheyne Walk like ants over a carcass. A bald man with a white mustache that flapped out to his ears checked his pocket watch for the fourth time since Hiero and his companions descended from their carriage.

At the far end of the stage, a squad of low-rank militia struggled to keep a path clear for the Duke of Edinburgh and his bride, Grand Duchess Maria Alexandrovna of Russia, only beloved daughter of Tsar Alexander II. The newlyweds were, in the timeless tradition of royals everywhere, unfashionably late to the opening of the Chelsea Embankment, the third and final stage of the sewage system that had

1

transformed London's riverside.

"Look, it's Bazalgette!" Callie tugged him forward, doing a fine impression of an excitable hound.

"While I admire your enthusiasm, I do wonder if it's not a tad misplaced."

Callie scoffed. "Only you would prefer the arrival of some dippy duke over the architect of this entire endeavor." She threw her free arm out wide. "Can you not spare a moment to admire this feat of engineering? In the place of muddy banks, pavement has been laid, a fence with lampposts erected, with gardens and greenery to come. And running beneath it, the waste of London, and soon an underground train! How can you be so trout-mouthed in the face of such marvels?"

"Not your most persuasive argument, comparing the face that dropped a thousand trousers to a fishmonger's wares."

Callie sighed, relinquishing his arm to chase after her muttonchopped idol. Hiero watched her go, marveling at how much she resembled her Uncle Apollo, Hiero's long-deceased lover who had charged him with her care in character and spirit. Theirs was an unconventional household, where the lady moonlighted as a detective, the servants were part of the family, and the lord of the manor—Hiero himself—was neither a lord nor owned the manor.

"Come now." Han, his friend and self-appointed keeper, fell into step beside him. The rhythmic taps of his lotus-headed walking stick slowed their pace to a stroll. "You're no longer catch of the day with Mr. Stoker about."

"Perhaps if he *were* about, someone would defend my honor." Hiero bristled at the mention of his fair-weather paramour, Timothy Kipling Stoker, a detective inspector with Scotland Yard who shadowed them when there was a mystery to solve but otherwise preoccupied himself with... well, finding them another mystery. His dedication to duty exasperated.

"Not likely."

"No, I rather thought not." Hiero pressed a lavender handkerchief to his mouth and nose. Mr. Bazalgette's innovations would have to work much harder to filter out nearly a millennia of filth, the river being a cesspit into which the city had poured every conceivable kind of rubbish, from human to animal to otherwise. A place where sins had been cast off and bodies buried. A few of Hiero's personal acquaintance.

"Where has your Mr. Stoker taken himself off to this—" Han considered the urinal murk of the embankment and found himself at a loss of an adjective. "—afternoon?"

"I do not presume to know what impulses rule that man."

"And yet you are the one who rides his... coattails."

"Only when he deigns to undress for the occasion. Otherwise..." Hiero huffed, his mood irretrievably spoilt by this line of conversation. "I cannot think where I've gone wrong with him."

"No?" Han evidenced something close to a smirk. "It wouldn't have something to do with meddling in his work affairs, compromising his relationship with his superiors, forcing him into our fellowship, risking everything he holds dear, and then sharing nothing of consequence about yourself, now would it?"

Hiero peered at him out of the corner of his eye. "Nothing of the sort, I'm sure."

"Ah. Well, then, it is a mystery."

"Coo-coo! Mr. Han!" a voice trilled at them from behind.

With a pair of heavy sighs, they turned to heed an all-too-familiar call. A hand waving a white handkerchief fluttered up and down amidst a dense crowd. A grunt from Han parted the sea of surging revelers to reveal Shahida Kala, the latest of Hiero's charity cases, hopping with the vigor of a spring hare. Her compact figure contained a carnival of personality.

The instant this bright light had beamed into his study on the arm of her father—who served under Apollo in Her Majesty's Navy—Hiero recognized her for one of the rare people who could steal his spotlight. So he had relegated her to the least enviable position in the household, that of nurse to Mrs. Lillian Pankhurst, Callie's permanently indisposed mother. But the long days of attic dwelling and reading Richardson's *Pamela* ad nauseam had not snuffed a single spark.

Instead Lillian had transformed from bed-ridden depressive into a semifunctional member of the family. Every morning she and Shahida took a two-hour stroll. They cultivated a rooftop garden. Shahida had imposed an afternoon tea regimen on their household, always leading the conversation as Hiero, Callie, and Han plotted ways to return to their preferred solitary occupations. Dinners were always a family affair, but Shahida's insistence on more healthful, nourishing fare that conformed to Lillian's new diet had Minnie, their cook, weekly threatening to resign. Callie was the only other member of the household resistant to her charms.

Even Han, cynical, monkish, seen-it-all Han, danced to whichever melody she played. Hiero watched as he bounded over to her, biting his lip at the comical sight of a surly giant bowing to the whims of a pretty imp, but also to keep from emitting a growl of frustration. He glanced back to search for Callie, but the crowd had swallowed her. By now she'd likely clawed her way to the front of the stage and barked questions at a baffled, bewhiskered Mr. Bazalgette, which Hiero thought should be his formal title.

Schooling his features, he joined Han and Shahida's conversation in medias res and was somewhat aghast to discover them talking about produce.

"... the plumpest, juiciest berries. Artichokes the size of a fist. Fat aubergines and cabbages and cauliflowers, and cucumbers as long as..." Shahida pressed two fingers to her mouth. Hiero didn't miss how her eyes flickered down. "Well."

Shameless, that was the trouble. As if she'd snipped the best pages from his playbook and then had the temerity to improve on his notes.

Han chuckled. Chuckled! Hiero hadn't seen his friend so much as shrug in all the time he'd known him.

"A religious order, you say?" Han asked.

"The Daughters of Eden." Shahida leaned in, gave him her most conspiratorial smirk. "And I think they might be." She didn't even have the grace to straighten when she spotted Hiero. "Oh, Mr. Bash! Mrs. Pankhurst and I don't mean to spoil your fun. But if you wouldn't mind, we'll stay here for a while. We've discovered the most—"

"Impressive cucumbers. So I heard."

"Mrs. Pankhurst is just beside herself. We've big ideas for our garden, but this..."

Hiero was unmoved. "And what is it you want?"

"We've done our third crate and could fill two more. The crowd is bit much for Mrs. Pankhurst, so I thought Mr. Han might take us back to Berkeley Square? We'll send the carriage back for you."

"As it is my carriage, I rather think it will return for me regardless."

That got her attention. "Of course. If you'd like us to stay—"

"Let us see these berries from heaven." With a sweep of his hand, Hiero directed them back toward the stall that had earlier piqued his interest. "Their Majesties will wait upon *our* leisure."

A long line of enterprising vendors hawked their wares along the edge of Cheyne Walk, hoping to entice royal watchers to purchase a bit of refinement for their life. One stall lined up its dainty little bottles of oils and perfumes like Russian nesting dolls. A mini royal portrait gallery sold likenesses of Queen Victoria, Prince Albert, and their progeny in a variety of poses. The gentleman scooping iced lollies for the children had his work cut out for him on such a tepid day, Hiero thought. The pub with a street-side stand offering hot tea and cider already did brisk business. A few watercress girls fought against the crowd's undertow, but their wares looked shriveled as seaweed compared to the glorious bushels of the Daughters of Eden.

Even Hiero had to admit, upon inspection, the quality of their produce astounded. Fat and luscious, their fruit allured like the bosom of an opera diva, ready to smother and enthrall. Their vegetable stalks evidenced a virility that would put most molly-houses out of business. Little wonder their customers meandered around the baskets like lovestruck swains. Their bounty conjured images of orgies culinary and carnal. Hiero didn't doubt there were more than a few serpents lurking about this tiny Eden, eager to defile a peach or two.

All of this was overseen by a trio of women dressed in immaculate white uniforms that somehow defied the city's grime. Hiero drifted away from his companions to better observe these wyrd sisters. The tallest was also the least remarkable, a stout but cheery woman with farm-worn hands and hard-earned streaks of gray in her brown hair. She milled through the customers, answering questions and nudging reluctant buyers toward the register.

A skittish dove of a girl dutifully kept the ledger and the cash box, cooing her thanks before slipping some sort of pamphlet into people's baskets. Her crinkly hair had been woven into two winglike braids that perfectly framed her heart-shaped face. A sprinkling of dark freckles contrasted with her pale-brown skin, all but disappearing when she blushed.

Which she did whenever the third sister glanced her way. "Willowy" did not do this petite, flopsy woman justice. A willow branch would look as leathery and stiff as a whip compared to her wispiness. Near-translucent skin and stringy cornsilk hair completed the otherworldly effect. Hiero almost questioned whether she was really there, such was the nothing of her regard. She appeared to have no occupation other than to pose under the sign in a demure attitude. The crowds gave her a wide berth, and little wonder. Nobody wanted to mingle with a possessed scarecrow.

Except possibly meddlesome not-detectives stuck on a boring outing with friends who had abandoned him for some phallic parsnips and a walrus architect.

Just as Hiero made to pounce, the waif leapt as if lightning struck. Eyes ravenous, mouth agape, hair billowing in an invisible breeze, she stared into the buzzing hive of customers. Transformed in an instant from trinket to spear, her astonishment gave color to her cheeks and heft to her bearing. She appeared somehow taller, bolder, a colossal spirit crammed into a compact package: a genie unleashed from its lamp.

All the better to bedazzle you with, my dear, Hiero thought.

Hieronymus Bash, professional cynic, knew a performance when he saw one. He read again the red sign that screamed above her head: *When will She open Rebecca Northcote's box?* But there was no box he could see, and if this woodland sprite was Mrs. Northcote, he'd eat Han's walking stick. These Daughters had lured in quite a crowd with their sensuous produce. Was she the serpent come to tempt them? And if so, to what end?

Hiero shuttered his natural radiance to watch the spectacle unfold. The pale sister glided, arms outstretched, into the maze of crates, eyes fixed on her prey. Hiero hissed under his breath when she stopped at Lillian Pankhurst. In a state of docile confusion at the best of times, Lillian continued sorting out a mess of string beans, oblivious to this starry-eyed suitor. Han, ever protective, moved to Lillian's side just as the sister shrieked...

"Daughter! You are found!"

The woman at the ledger jumped to her feet. "Juliet?"

"I've heard your spirit call to us these long nights, and now you have come home!" Juliet continued at eardrum-splitting pitch, making herself heard to all in the vicinity and probably those across the Thames. "Welcome, Daughter, into Her grace and light! Welcome home!" She hugged a startled Lillian with impressive fervor for one so slender. Lillian, looking to Shahida for a cue, patted her on the back.

A frowning Han caught his gaze from across the way, but Hiero signaled he would play Polonius behind the curtain. Hopefully without the knife in his gut.

"Don't fear, Daughter. You are among friends," Juliet nattered on. "We have come to shepherd Her back to Eden through our good works, and, by your pallid cheeks and trembling hands, I can see that you are eager to play a part."

"Oi!" Shahida hollered, shoving her way between Juliet and Lillian. "Mrs. Pankhurst gets three square a day, and her arthritis is much improved. I dare anyone here to say otherwise."

"But her spirit, dear girl, droops like a flower too long out of the sun." Juliet backed away a step to address the customers, every one of which stood rapt. "*She* knows how this frail woman has struggled. She has heard her prayers and her anguish. She has shone Her glorious light into her, lit her like a beacon for her sisters to find. She is a Daughter, called upon to continue Her good work and bring about a second Eden!"

Shahida let out a trill of laughter three octaves too high. It effectively pierced the balloon of hot air Juliet had been huffing and puffing.

"Angel with a flaming sword you're not, ma'am. Sorry." Shahida locked an arm around Lillian. "Stick to the fruit and veg." A pointed look directed Han to escort their charge away.

"But I haven't finished the beans…" Lillian muttered as they disappeared into the gaggle of onlookers.

"Shame!" Juliet bellowed, beseeching the yellow sky. "Shame! It is the burden of womankind." The customers moved into the space vacated by his friends, and Hiero followed, curious as to how she would spin such a public defeat. "The prophet Rebecca Northcote warned against it in her great bible, *The Coming of the Holiest Spirit.* Too often we ladies wait upon the actions of others. Are made to feel shame and guilt and worthless when we do act. Allow others to lead us astray, away from the truth in our hearts. We pay the price for the sins of our fathers and brothers and husbands. But She… oh, She is coming to deliver us from these injustices, from our fears and torments. As our Holy Mother Rebecca divined, if we join together, Daughters, and build the garden, She will come to save us all. She will gift us with her light!"

"Amen!" the ledger-keeper cried, having abandoned her post to shove pamphlets into the hands of any who would take them.

"Thank you, Mother!" the other sister seconded, lifting a basket of golden pears for all to see.

Juliet scanned the crowd. "You reap of the bounty we offer, but you do not know of how we labor in Her name. To prepare for Her coming, our prophet Rebecca chose each of Her Daughters with care. And though a shame-filled few will deny Her, everyone is welcome to hear Her message and to contribute however they can." Hiero swallowed a snicker as she gestured to the donation tin. So transparent. "If you are committed to peace and prosperity, if you would see heaven retake the Earth, then I invite you to heed our prophet Rebecca's call. And She will shine Her light upon you for all the days of your life."

Juliet seemed to resist taking a bow, but only just. She gave each customer a final angelic smile, then returned to her perch beneath the red sign. A few of the curious chased her with questions; a ragdoll sag and a vacant stare shut them out. Instead the ledger-keeper, who introduced herself as Sister Nora, gathered them around the donation tin before addressing any queries.

"And?" Han appeared beside him, sudden as Banquo's ghost. "Showstopper or second-rate?"

Hiero rubbed a thumb over his knuckles. "Better than a pair of poncy royals cutting a ribbon, but only just."

"Fit for a return engagement?"

"Perhaps. Their setup is commonplace, but she does have a certain je ne sais quoi."

"Enough to *en savoir plus?*"

"Time will tell. You know how religion turns my stomach. But their focus on Lillian was…"

"Agreed. That Sister Juliet read her too easily."

Hiero nodded. "Could have been instinct."

"Or she saw a mark."

They shared a look weighted by their years of friendship and experience, a partnership of equals who knew, without another word, how to protect their own.

DI Timothy Kipling Stoker turned the card in his hand over and again, flicking the edge with his index finger as he considered the townhouse before him. Wedged amidst a row of houses in the same porridge-brown brick, there was nothing to distinguish it save a withered Christmas wreath that drooped off a nail in the front door. An overgrown strip of lawn had overtaken the walk some time ago, such that a half-decent tracker could probably tell Tim about the recent comings and goings. Tim, an avowed city man, could only make the most basic assumptions about the inhabitants based on the state of the place.

Which brought him back to the card. Blank except for a cryptic summons—*718 Dodger's Way, eight o'clock. Wait for the candle. Come alone*—and the stamp of a coat of arms he could not place. He was fortunate to be at his lodgings when it arrived with his breakfast, or perhaps not so fortunate, depending on the result of this evening's adventure. Tim shifted against the lamppost he leaned on, reassured by the press of the truncheon concealed in the inseam of his coat. He should have enlisted Han's assistance as lookout, he knew, but there was no way to do so without alerting Hiero and Miss Pankhurst, and thus their circus of a household.

After months searching for missing baubles, chasing down absconded servants, and once, not so memorably, a lost python, Tim's desperation for a real case had reached fever pitch. The eccentricities of his new colleagues he'd been prepared for; the tedium of their routine investigations had left him longing to be demoted back to constable. Tim now had a better understanding of why they were so eager to chase down the thieves who stole the Fangs of Scavo. He'd rather have launched himself back into a cage of man-eating lions than tracked down Mrs. Minniver's cherished poodle, Dumpling. Found behind the butcher's, raiding the bone bins, a conclusion Tim was certain her butler might have come to, given half the chance.

The mystery of Hiero's true identity helped Tim endure these elementary cases. For the occasional peek behind the masterwork that was Hiero's persona, he would persevere. Tim suffered a twinge of guilt at not having invited him on this adventure—certainly the two hours' wait would have been more agreeably passed in his company—but some matters called for stealth, not spectacle. And to Tim's mind, there was no greater show on Earth than the life of Hieronymus Bash.

A candle sparked to life in one of the front windows. A pair of spectral hands slipped back behind heavy curtains. Tim straightened, on the scent. Slipping the card into his pocket, he forced himself to count to fifty before he mounted the steps and knocked.

The door creaked open. It had been left unlocked. Tim unsheathed his truncheon before pushing the door all the way in. Its clang against the back wall announced his arrival. The dark void of the entranceway tunneled in to a solitary lantern, hung as if in midair far down a long, black hallway. Cursing his naivety, Tim took a few hesitant steps into the house. He stopped before the entryway became the corridor, glanced back in time to see the door slam shut.

"Hello?" Tim straightened his posture and his resolve, truncheon poised to strike. "You summoned; I have come. If you want my assistance, you'd best show yourself."

Tim listened into the silence for too many heartbeats. Lantern fumes and a thick layer of dust conspired to choke his panic. He stood his ground, unwilling to venture farther into a house of who-knew-what horrors without some sign this was more than an elaborate prank. He refused to even consider the other scenarios racing through his mind. He'd ruffled his share of feathers in his time, from the criminals he helped convict to the vengeful lord still clamoring for his head to, unfortunately, his fellow detectives at Scotland Yard. Let alone the fiend who'd murdered his parents, who might have gotten wind of his latest inquiries into their deaths. Only one person, if he really thought about it, preferred him alive.

The one he'd failed to tell about this little excursion.

Footsteps. A silhouette merged into the lantern light, face obscured. The man's dress gave nothing away save for his wealth. Under Hiero's tutelage, Tim had learned of cuts and colors and quality of cloth, enough to distinguish Savile Row from a lesser tailor. This man had means, a fact not immediately reassuring.

"Mercy's sake, Stoker, come in, come in!" a familiar voice called out. The rip of a match against the wall revealed Colonel Sir Hugh Winterbourne, Commissioner of the Police of the Metropolis, Tim's indirect superior and sometimes ally.

Stunned, Tim hurried to catch up as Sir Hugh disappeared around a corner. He followed him into a musty room that may have once been a study but now housed only two wingbacked chairs and a small table, on which sat a bottle of top-shelf Scotch and two tumblers. One, Tim noted, glistened with amber liquid. A growing fire had been kindled in the hearth, which cast only enough light to skirt the edges of the chairs. Darkness blurred the corners of the hollow room, teasing Tim's peripheral vision with half glimpses of movement.

"Apologies, Sir Hugh. I thought—"

Sir Hugh tutted. "It is I who should beg pardon for all the cloak and dagger. I do hope you're not too disappointed?"

"Disappointed? How so?"

"That I'm no despondent widow possessed by a demonic cat or

nervy lord plagued by a hellhound."

Tim stifled a frustrated grunt. "You can forgive me making assumptions, given your choice of rendezvous."

"Ah, yes. You must be wondering." Sir Hugh gestured toward one of the chairs. "My brother's old pile. He fell in the Crimea, and so the house fell to me. Never could bring myself to part with it, though as you can see…" Tim traced the line of his gaze to the stone above the mantel, where the faintest outline of a missing portrait could be discerned. No doubt the subject had been Sir Hugh's fallen brother, perhaps in his military reds. "Drink?"

"If you would be so kind."

Tim eased into the chair and the silence as Sir Hugh poured him a double shot and refreshed his own. Sir Hugh had always been a strict but convivial sort. Himself a decorated veteran of the Crimea, he was the antidote to the previous commissioner, Sir Richard Mayne, who crossed the Home Secretary over the Clerkenwell bombings of 1867 and lost favor with the peelers over his increasing rigidity. By contrast, Sir Hugh's support of the 1872 police strike made his name among government officials and officers alike. While not exactly beloved, he'd earned the respect of both parties.

Doubly so for Tim, who owed his career to Sir Hugh, as he'd twice now overruled Tim's superintendent, Julian Quayle, to keep him with the Yard. Given his tendency to embroil himself in cases that resulted in major solves but aggravated his superiors, Tim would forever be in Sir Hugh's debt.

One he expected was about to be repaid, in part if never in full. Tim scented something like melancholy on the air in this abandoned place that housed so many of Sir Hugh's memories. Any detective worth his salt would have by now deduced they'd be discussing a matter to be kept well away from official police business. That Tim was chosen not just for what he owed, but his position as an outsider. He worried a finger around the rim of his glass as he waited Sir Hugh out, praying he was not about to be trapped between the proverbial rock and a hard place. While Tim indulged in certain freedoms as Hiero and the team's minder, he drew the line at committing any criminal acts. Any major ones, at least.

"How are you getting on with this Bash fellow? I'm afraid Superintendent Quayle is more of a glass-half-empty sort when it comes to reports. I take it no news is, for lack of a better word, good news?"

"Mr. Bash is"—*Wonderful, infuriating, delectable, maddening*—"unique. His chief talent lies in assembling a team around him that make up for his deficiencies as an amateur."

"And you feel you've been collected?"

"Precisely so."

"Your exploits have garnered a certain renown. Not something, I think, you are accustomed to."

"Mr. Bash earns most of the attention, but…" Tim inhaled deeply, dove in. "If I may be frank, sir, it's the quality of the cases that concerns. I don't expect every villain to live up to Lord Blackwood's infamy, but petty criminals and thieving servants…"

"Not quite the challenge you were hoping for?"

Tim shook his head. "I'm grateful, sir, for all your efforts on my behalf."

"But you'd prefer something with more meat on the bone." His lips curled into a thoughtful smile that didn't quite meet his eyes. "Well, Stoker, I hope you've brought your appetite."

It took everything Tim had not to leap on his chair and perform a celebratory jig. "Haven't eaten for weeks."

"Good." Sir Hugh settled into his seat with what should have been a magisterial air but looked more like hugging into himself. His sheep in sheep's clothing looks little helped convey an attitude of strength. Sir Hugh was of a classic beauty more suited to the heroes of romance than stern military men. Chestnut curls now streaked with gray, cherub cheeks, petal-plump lips—an English rose by any other name. The divot in his pronounced chin only added to his poetic air. His melodious voice should recite poetry, not bark orders.

Tim had quickly understood two things upon their first acquaintance. First, that any attraction he might feel should be strangled in the crib, for survival's sake. Second and most vital, that the great battle of Sir Hugh's life wasn't the Crimea, but to be taken seriously: his greatest victory being that he was. Even now his soft brown eyes scrutinized Tim the way a stag might a dozing hunter, curious, but wary of being wounded.

"First, some preliminaries."

"Not a word," Tim assured him. "To anyone."

This earned him a soft chuckle. "I'd almost forgot who I was conversing with. Perhaps you should list my conditions."

"With pleasure." Tim straightened in his seat, excited to finally—finally!—exercise his detective skills. But for all his enthusiasm, he tread lightly. If Sir Hugh was to be his newest client, it wouldn't do to scare him off before he even learned the facts of the case. "The matter is a private one, not to be shared with anyone at the Yard or in police circles. I must pose as a personal investigator; I'm not to let anyone I interview know I'm a detective unless absolutely necessary. I'm to continue my work with Mr. Bash while devoting myself to this matter in my own time. I'm not to make my reports to you in any official capacity or at any recognizable location with which either of us are associated. This house, I imagine, is the only safe spot. To request a meeting, I'm to send an encoded note to your… valet? Head butler?"

"That would be telling."

"No. The porter at your club." Tim fought to sober himself when Sir Hugh nodded. The commissioner was right—he was bone starved with need of this. "How can I be of service to you, sir?"

His smile fell. All the rosy beauty drained from his face until he looked as gaunt and ghostly as one of the forgotten inhabitants of the house.

"My child is missing."

Stunned, Tim let the silence stretch to impossible lengths. A million questions buzzed through his mind, but he would listen to Sir Hugh's story before jumping to any conclusions about his life, the same consideration he would show any other client. He would ignore the stinging knowledge that his wife had died of consumption some five years past, their marriage childless.

"I have not behaved honorably in this affair. I cannot but admit to that. I have done a great deal of wrong to several persons and to my mortal soul. But he... My son is an innocent. And so I ask you to do this for him."

Tim met his eyes with confidence. "I see no harm in helping you both. What are the circumstances? And please, spare no detail."

Sir Hugh let out a blustery breath. "If you must take notes, make sure to burn them."

"No need." Tim tapped his temple.

"Astounding." Sir Hugh downed the last of his Scotch and, with a shaking hand, refilled their tumblers. Tim had mostly ignored his but took a quick sip in solidarity. "It was never my ambition to marry. My father was a kind but pious man who valued honesty above all. He urged us to examine our deepest selves: our motives, our flaws, our desires. My weakness has ever been that of the flesh. I knew myself and sought to spare any decent woman the burden of having me as a husband. But after the war, I wanted stability. Thinking I could devote myself entirely to Laura may have been my first mistake.

"I was always careful. A man of purpose must be. And in truth she seemed relieved when it was clear she could not carry a child. Ours became a marriage of the minds. But once she passed, in my grief... I indulged. Too many, too recklessly. One in my household." Sir Hugh forced his chin up, having bowed it during his recitation. "Maude Mulligan is her name. Laura's ladies' maid, whom I kept on. She was four months along before she even realized... or so she said. I'm not proud to say I encouraged her to be rid of it, but she insisted."

"Did she mention marriage?"

"Insinuated. As if that would ever have been possible. I found a lying-in house that would care for her, a society of sorts for fallen women, the Daughters of Eden. She was furious at first, but after a few weeks, her letters were much less angry. Eventually she birthed a son. It gives me no pleasure to report I do not know his name. I could not claim him as my own, not with... The Daughters arrange for the child and the mother to be placed in a proper situation, once she's recovered."

"Did you pay a one-time fee or a monthly stipend?"

"I assure you it was not a Margaret Waters-type affair."

Tim stifled a shudder at the mention of such a villain's name. He'd attended many a trial in his time, but the case of the infamous baby farmer still haunted him. Servants and other working women of the lower classes were often forced to send their children to live with caretakers, seeing them but once or twice a year, if at all. Some of the more devil-minded of these starved their innocent charges, feeding them nothing but laudanum, all the while continuing to extort money from their mothers. Margaret Waters, the most demonic of these baby farmers, was hanged for the murder and neglect of nineteen children.

The faintest echo of that case resonated here.

"Sir Hugh." Tim leaned forward, arms on his legs. "Everything."

He clenched his jaw, bit out, "A fee. Four installments. Upon arrival, when her confinement began, after the birth, and once they'd found her a position."

"But she fled."

A low growl reverberated through the room. "Yes. But without the child."

"Stole the money from the Daughters?"

"All of it, yes, or its equivalent."

Tim considered this a moment. "You don't want her found?"

"Payment for services rendered." Sir Hugh struggled to collect himself. "I've no real quarrel with her other than abandoning the boy."

"But he is also missing?"

"The root of the matter."

Tim reclined back in his seat, absorbing. Sir Hugh's predicament, while not uncommon, did raise a few concerns.

"You are aware of the most likely outcome?"

Again Sir Hugh locked his eyes on the empty space above the mantel. Here in the house where his family once thrived before everything went to ruin. Tim well understood how desperate such a man—professionally prosperous, personally isolated—might be to offer an olive branch to an offshoot of his family tree. But Tim knew there was little glory to be found in investigations involving lost children.

"I'm no fool." Sir Hugh's stare, back with a vengeance, pinned Tim to his chair. "I've also no heir. Find my son, Stoker, and you'll have your pick of posts at the Yard."

Chapter 2

"The rest..." Hiero pried the dagger out of his heart and cut the rope that restrained the blade of the guillotine. "... is silence."

Clutching his chest as his shirt ran red, he artfully collapsed beside Henry Irving's severed head, which he gave a little tap so it fell upright. Applause rumbled the floor of the stage as the curtains swept closed, whisking dust up his nose. Hiero had enough presence of mind, despite his coughing fit, to tuck the fake bust of Irving's head under his arm as he rose to bow. Devil eyed, Irving made a grab for it as the cast scrambled into position, but Hiero proved, as ever, more nimble. When the curtain opened, he petted the coarse-haired death mask to uproarious effect, leaving the audience—*his* audience—thoroughly entertained.

Hiero briefly considered kicking the head into the crowd, but he knew it would be a step too far. Though if not on the closing night of their French Revolution-inspired *Hamlet* burlesque, *Let 'em Eat Ham*, when? Then he spied The Gaiety's former owner, Mr. Webster, at the back of the stalls and decided a game of catch was in order. Hiero tossed the head up into the left-side boxes, ensuring thunderous cheers as he moved to take his final bow.

The crowd showered him with roses. And other lesser blooms, but that couldn't be helped. The Gaiety was a prestige establishment, which was how Hiero—or rather, his stage persona, Horace

Beastly—preferred it. A haven for those whose predilections fell outside of society's norms, The Gaiety was as much flesh market as temple of high art. As he scanned the crowd, Hiero picked out the Mary-Anns, sisters of Lesbos, and fine ladies who were not ladies at all, each of whom had found leisure and acceptance here. These people, his people, were being cast out by the vile new owner Mr. Tumnus and his Society for the Moral Preservation of the Arts, or some such grandiose title. Irving, Tumnus's creature, craved respectability and wealthier patrons. "Strict" interpretations of the classics, cleansed of any questionable plot points, would replace the bawdy burlesques.

And so Horace Beastly must take his final bow. Hiero milked the attention for as long as the crowd cheered for him, blowing kisses and clapping at them in return. Though his vision clouded at the edges, he refused to blink. He would shed no tears before that bilge bog Webster or give Irving the satisfaction of his sadness. Instead Hiero looked to box number five, where a pair of shining green eyes wept for him.

Later, in his dressing room, as a battering ram's worth of knocks almost splintered his door, Hiero stared at his face in the mirror. The room behind him, once his sanctum, was as hollow and brittle as an eggshell. Pocked walls exposed beams that playbills shouting of Horace Beastly's triumphs once covered. His armoire, his costume chests, his shrine to the Muses had all been packed away to Berkeley Square. Only his chartreuse fainting couch, scene of many an entanglement, waited in the center of the room, an empress without a retinue.

He couldn't quite bring himself to wash the last of the makeup from his face. The pale patch over his eye gave him a piratical air, or perhaps that of a villainous mime. Though he had shed a number of skins in his time, Beastly proved... well, something of a beast to molt. Performing was the only honest trade he'd ever undertaken. The only profession he'd chosen not out of fear or desperation, but for himself. And though the growing popularity of Hieronymus Bash, consulting detective, risked exposure every time he tread the boards, Hiero chafed at conceding to a pant-twist like Tumnus and his familiar Irving. Hiero loathed religious fanaticism in all its forms, but especially when it invaded his theater.

A commotion beyond the door heralded DI Tim Stoker's arrival. Or "Kip," as Hiero dubbed him when their professional relationship turned personal. *His* Kip, specifically. Hiero hurried to scrub away his white eye patch as Kip inched into the dressing room, shoving and booting back Hiero's more zealous admirers. A dab of rejuvenating cream and a quick brush of his mustache later, Hiero was ready to receive his most ardent fan. He could do with a spot of devotion, and Kip knew just how best to worship him.

Hiero waited, eyes at half-mast, for the snug of Kip's arms around his neck. And waited. And waited. When he finally glanced back, he found Kip glaring quizzically at the fainting couch.

"Looking for someone?"

"Hmm?" Hiero would never tire of how the slightest insinuation pinked his cheeks. "Oh!"

Even after seven months, they were still hesitant around each other, as if waiting for the other to say "when." Though born of conflict, the strange alchemy of their relationship enhanced their passion, which burned ever-hot. Unlike any fire he had felt before. Not even with his dear, dead Apollo. It occurred to Hiero that, just like performing, Kip was his choice. In a world so often against them, they had chosen each other, and that made all the difference.

"I'm searching for something to bar the door," Kip explained. Given their tendency to be interrupted midcoitus, a fair preoccupation. "You appear to be sitting on it."

"As I'm unlikely to move without reason, perhaps you should come greet me."

"Ah, yes, manners." Kip hastened over, pecked Hiero on the temple, and purred in his ear, "Hazelnut?"

"Almond."

"Mmm." Kip stroked a hand down Hiero's chest as he knelt beside him, settling it on his thigh. He traced teasing circles on its inner aspect with his thumb, his freckled face turned up like a flower to the sun. A twinkle in his fern-green eyes hinted at his meeting having gone well. "You were magnificent."

"Go on."

"I'd dreamt of your Hamlet, and you surpassed even my wildest imaginings. Except for the clothes."

Hiero huffed. "You dare criticize my costume?"

"Only that you wore one." They shared a chuckle as Kip slid onto his lap and wrapped lean, muscled arms around him. "How are you?"

Hiero opened his mouth but could only sigh. Not just a detective by trade, but a sometime codebreaker, Kip read all the things Hiero couldn't say in his expression.

"Must this truly be the end of my beloved Mr. Beastly?" Kip asked. "Every theatre manager in the city would hire him on the spot."

"And well I know it. But would they let him cancel at a moment's notice or conduct his *affairs* backstage? Part of The Gaiety's charm under Webster was its flexibility." Hiero cupped Kip's firm buttocks to force himself out of his dour mood. "Much like your own."

Kip smirked, inched closer. "It's just rather unlike you to roll over so easily."

"If there's one thing I've learned in my years of adventure, dear Kip, it's when to bow out gracefully."

"I think you mean cut and run."

"That too."

Hiero stopped further protests with a kiss, slow but greedy, feeding off Kip's arousal to nourish his own. He still didn't understand what drew him to such an honorable, average man, other than how deliciously pliable he became after enjoying a bit of theater. Hiero had expected, once the thrill of their first case wore off, to find his attentions flitting elsewhere. His was never the most focused of minds. But that very solidity and dependability, which Hiero once would have mocked, touched something in him. When Kip gave himself, he gave everything. He possessed such a deep well of character that Hiero could drink and drink and drink—ever greedy, like his kisses—and Kip would never fail to replenish.

But though his desire was bottomless, Kip's patience was not. And so Hiero had begun to dread the day when Kip would discover all of his secrets. When his sterling detective would know the truth of him, and his affections would run dry.

Kip licked under his tongue as he broke off their kiss to explore, nipping at an earlobe before dragging the tip of his teeth down the side Hiero's neck, through reemergent stubble. Hiero shut his eyes, more to blot out the empty room than to concentrate on Kip's ministrations. The pinch of his nipple through his robe proved inspiring, the worry of silken fabric over the hard nub more so. Kip gnawed playfully at his neck, careful not to leave marks above the collar. With his free hand, he caught up Hiero's, twining their fingers and rubbing a naughty thumb over the inside of Hiero's wrist. Kip guided his hand to the buttons of his waistcoat, where Hiero made quick business of freeing him.

Hiero heard more than saw it fall to the floor in the wake of Kip's jacket, leaving only one white, straining shirt between him and his prize. Kip's daily visits to the gymnasium at his policeman's club, as well as three decent meals a day, had primed his physique into a devastating weapon. It certainly vanquished Hiero every time he admired it. Hiero made a mental note to have Kip's suits recut to accommodate his latest muscles as he unsheathed them, exposing pale but taut skin and an explosion of freckles. Hiero had made it his mission to account for each and every one, and he set himself to the task with ardor.

"How do you want me?" Kip panted. "Astride the couch? On my k-knees? I could... I could suck..."

Hiero spun them around on his stool, hoisting Kip onto the makeup table. His pots and potions skittered and clattered, but Hiero didn't care. He couldn't face the vacuous room; the punters still beating at his door; his lonely couch, waiting to be packed away with all the rest. He narrowed his worldview down to the thing that mattered most, the huge, vital cock smothered by Kip's trousers. Time for some resuscitation.

"Mmm, yes," Kip moaned. "Let's finish as we started."

"I thought the symmetry beguiling."

"Not so much as your mouth..."

Kip pawed his thumb across Hiero's plush bottom lip, spread his legs even wider. He towered over Hiero, sweating, panting, flush cheeked and fierce eyed, a vengeful woodland god. Kip moved to undo his trousers, but Hiero batted his hands away. He nuzzled his face into Kip's groin, drank deep of his fresh, mossy essence. Kip gripped his hair, need cresting. His senses saturated by his lover, Hiero could have devoured him whole. Instead he tugged Kip's trousers down and swallowed his thick, red cock.

Kip hissed, whispering, "Beautiful, beautiful," as Hiero took him to the root. He worked his throat around Kip's massive length until stars burst behind his eyes, retreating only when the sear of his lungs became too impossible. Barely a breath's respite before Hiero set about his real work, licking him from balls to tip, then circling his tongue under the ridged edge of the head, teasing his slit until rewarded with a salty pearl. Ever attracted to shiny things, Hiero palmed and pumped him for bead after bead, Kip's cock diving deeper and deeper into the tight shell of his throat.

Hiero gripped Kip's hips as he gave himself over to the rhythm, encouraging him to thrust. Kip swept back a curtain of hair and cupped Hiero's jaw, gaze rapt. When Hiero dared look up, he saw only adoration in Kip's blown-out eyes. But would it be enough to satisfy him over the coming weeks, months, years? Could his audience of one be his everything?

A shudder ripped through Kip. He released his cradling hands from Hiero's hair, fisting them around the table's edge. Kip bit his bottom lip, stifled a curse. His thrusts came quick and shallow, angling down against Hiero's indecent bottom lip.

Hiero shuttered his eyes and his concerns, opening himself to everything Kip had to give. There was only this man, this moment. The pulse of his prick and the tang of his come. The muffled howl of his end and the climactic burst down Hiero's throat. The echoing throb in Hiero's groin that didn't quite pop, no matter how he savored every last lick and suckle of his Kip's softening member.

Dazed Kip collapsed back against the mirror, a portrait of debauchery. He petted Hiero's head where it rested on his thigh, shivering as tremors of pleasure continued to quake through him.

"Come home with me?" Hiero hated the quaver in his voice, the question as soon as he asked it. That even after seven months, he still had to ask.

Kip raised his head, instantly alert. "Of course." He slid off the makeup table into Hiero's embrace, found his lips as if the seduction had only just begun. Hiero lost himself anew in the silk of his tongue and the strength of his arms, how pliant and eager and easy Kip was, as if he lived to fuck. "Shall we slip away, or do you want me here?"

Only Hiero was permitted to see this side of him. Had seen Kip for what he was from the start: a man who had been ignored and overlooked his entire life, who with a little polish would shine only for him. He enjoyed submitting to Hiero's whims, craved his ingenuity almost as much as his command. Yet when Kip played his fingers along the fringe of his robe, the short *V* of chest hair that was all Hiero dared reveal of his chest, seeking a permission Hiero could never give, he knew he couldn't equal Kip's abandon. Not without shedding the last of his skins, exposing the raw, vulnerable flesh beneath. Exposing the man Hiero had vowed he would never be again.

"Let me see you," Kip whispered as he nipped at the end of Hiero's mustache, skirting his fingertips beneath the fringe without pushing it back. "I've wanted to touch you, really touch you, for so long, my lovely one…"

Hiero caught him by the wrists, pried his hands off him. They hovered between them, palms soft, fingers spread, a gesture of surrender.

"As I've said before"—Hiero struggled for a nonchalance he didn't feel—"I don't care to be disrobed. Ruins the mystery."

"Pity you're bedding a detective."

"A tragic error I don't particularly care to correct."

Kip clicked his tongue but smiled. "Always so contrary."

"But see how my garden grows." With a magician's flick, he released Kip's wrists so they fell within inches of his cockle shells. Instead Kip wove his arms around him, hugging him in.

"I won't look." Kip gazed at him with such kindness, such affection that Hiero wanted to scream. "Just touch. Just let you feel something of what I feel when you touch me. It's all I can think about most nights. Mapping the plains of your skin. Following the trail of your dark hair down, down, down…" Hiero wished he could admire the blush that stained Kip's cheeks a violent crimson. "I never thought to say such things to anyone, never thought to have someone like you in my life."

"Am I? In your life?" Even Hiero didn't know where such a wellspring of resentment was sourced, only that it spurted forth at surprising and unexpected volume. As if it had been rising in him all this time, surging against the dam that held his emotions in check. He thrilled at its release. "I didn't fail to notice this is the first we've seen of each other in over a week."

Kip started. "If you have word of a case, you've only to send a note."

"As nothing else dares interrupt your boxing and brooding regimen?"

His look of dismay almost stirred a sense of guilt in Hiero. Almost.

"Forgive me if I've been too long absent." That Kip wrestled with something within himself did not go unmissed by someone of Hiero's less than heroic background. "If you've need of me, for *any* reason—" He drew his hands around to Hiero's front, massaged them over his abdomen. "—you've only to send a note."

"So you've said." Gently but firmly, Hiero removed Kip's hands from his person once again. "Perhaps it was too much to hope you might call just to see me. That you might find my company reason enough for a visit."

Kip let out a blustery sigh. "I don't recall you ever setting foot in my rooms, if we're tallying."

"Only you would insist we huddle on some poky mattress in a frigid closet when we could be taking our leisure in perfect comfort."

"I don't see what difference location makes when you're so well insulated." Kip dismounted him with a small shove and snatched his shirt off the table. "My rooms may not be the equal of your rococo fantasia of a pile, but they are mine." He yanked on his waistcoat over his tight-tucked shirt, not bothering to button up. "A man must have something of his own."

Hiero let out a bitter laugh. "You'd be astonished at how much nothing a man can live on when needs must."

"Oh?" Kip spun Hiero around on his stool, sauntered over to the couch, and sat himself down, a look of mock intimacy distorting his features. "Do tell. Have you an anecdote from your past to share?" Hiero firmed his mouth, glowered. "No, certainly not. Must maintain that cunning air of mystery."

Seething inwardly, Hiero smirked. "Happy to share, if you'd care to tell me what's preoccupied you these past weeks?" The alarm that flared in his green eyes confirmed Hiero's suspicions. He found himself wishing Kip were a bit more skilled in the art of deception.

"No? Then it's as I thought."

"Hardly," Kip stammered.

"I very much doubt that. I tend to think of myself as an excellent judge of character, which is why I would have believed the reassurances you've failed to give as to the state of our arrangement. In fact, I've given you every chance to fabricate some reason why you've been so absent. But you cannot because you are you, the redoubtable DI Stoker. A man so honest he cannot lie to his lover, even when he must keep a secret from him at all costs. That he has taken a case in which said lover and sometimes partner cannot be involved."

Kip shook his head. "Hiero—"

"Save your reasons." Hiero raised a hand, half command, half benediction. "You cannot lie, and I don't care to know the truth. Only this: are you breaking from the team, or do you wish to break from me?"

Despite his bravado, Hiero couldn't quite catch his breath as he awaited the response.

"Never from you," Kip insisted with a look so ardent and earnest Hiero almost shied away from it. "But it's vital I finish this preoccupation of mine alone. It's a delicate business."

Hiero shivered, suddenly too aware of the emptiness of the room. Of the one thing of priceless value left in it. Of how he would be rid of all of his mementos forever, if only he could keep the man sitting too far from him.

"I suppose, if you must. But we'll delay none of our adventures."

A soft exhale gave Hiero hope. "I couldn't ask it of you."

"We managed perfectly well before you happened along."

Kip dared a smile. "As I recall."

"Now as to your earlier question..." Hiero stood, fetched Kip's jacket from the floor, and held it open for him. "I'd prefer you in my bed."

A drop of water trickled down Calliope Pankhurst's spine as she cocked her pistol and took aim—a distraction she could ill afford. She'd taken refuge in the tunnel beneath the house at 23 Berkeley Square in order to test the range of her new MAS French army revolver, whose double-action system allowed the shooter to unload all six cartridges without pulling back the hammer between each shot. The manufacturer claimed a maximum range of one thousand feet with diminished accuracy. She'd plotted out five hundred in the tunnel, which burrowed under three adjacent houses but took a sharp right turn to merge with the sewers under the square.

A full-range test would have to wait on their next visit to Hiero's hunting lodge. Not that her guardian had ever fired a pistol, let alone at an animal. A creature of the city, he floundered on their infrequent escapes to the country, as if suffocated by all that fresh air. Callie had spent several years of her late childhood at the lodge and missed it dearly. Especially given the space required to perform most of her experiments.

She'd chosen the dank, smelly tunnel after nearly decapitating poor Aldridge, who'd reminded her of the dangers firearms presented to the household staff. A string of lanterns added a sulfuric note to the moist atmosphere, as well as increased the temperature by several thousand degrees. The air, so heavy it coated her tongue with a slimy film, required a barometric reading in order to properly measure the bullet's velocity.

Callie persevered. She ignored the trickle, not really wanting to know whether it was sweat or drool from the moldy ceiling, and fixed the target in her sights, a hay bale covered by a sheet with a life-sized feminine figure sewn on. She'd marked the head and the heart with red X's. And if, in her mind's eye, she imagined a certain over-jolly nursemaid in its place, where was the harm?

29

One, two, three reports.

One in the head, two in the chest.

Callie squealed, did a little spin. Caught herself, then remembered she was alone. She kissed the butt of her revolver, a gift from Lady Odile de Volanges prior to her wedding voyage, before reloading. Callie scribbled down the test result and a note to send her another thank-you letter. She dug six bullets out of the hidden pocket in her bodice and filled the entire cartridge. Just as she considered whether to shoot them all into the same spot or try to land each at a different extremity, she felt it.

The stillness behind her sang, a soundless vibration that tracked the source of the trickle up her spine, spiking her nerve endings. Her entire body magnetized toward this presence, a true north as distant as the pole. Closing her eyes, she calmed the quiver in her arm before she raised it, refocused her senses on the target and not the so very welcome intruder.

Bang, bang, bang. On a whim, she'd shot blind. Even with wax plugs in her ears, Callie knew she'd shot true. One in the head and two in the heart.

She holstered her weapon, corking her giddiness. Considered forcing him to show himself. It was the game they played, who could sneak up on the other. Who could read the air, hear with their skin, see behind. She always won because she would never not know him. Her circadian rhythms had attuned themselves to his from the second they met. She did not believe in the paranormal; their connection was the closest she'd come. How her blood quickened, her pulse skipped. She'd made herself into the only person from whom he could not hide.

"Impressive," Han complimented once she'd popped out the wax.

"My skill, or the gun?"

"Both." Only then did he emerge beside her, contemplating the target like the latest Turner. "Save your canvases, if you don't mind."

"Whatever for?"

"An idea."

He rarely said more about his creations, even once complete. His theory of art, much like his theory of life, was that one could make of it what one would. On a case, he debated motive. Otherwise he embraced people's complexities. It was one of the things she adored about him.

"Have I been making a ruckus? Has Lord Darlinghouse complained again?"

A subtle smirk. His lordship, the only neighbor with whom they shared a wall, was half-deaf but forever moaning about strange sounds that robbed him of sleep. To be fair, the members of their household got about a great many peculiar things, most of which would have Lord Darlinghouse reporting them to the local constabulary, so he likely couldn't hear a thing.

"The occasional rattle disturbs Minnie, but you know how she is about the Wedgewood." Han's smirk deepened, which Callie considered her second win of the day. "I'm afraid it's Mrs. Pankhurst."

"Mother? Has she taken a turn?"

"Nothing so serious. Yet." For the first time since his entrance, he met her eyes. "She and Miss Kala are two hours late returning from their stroll."

Callie couldn't help herself. She laughed.

"Is that all?" She took a cautious step toward him, felt him tense. The dance that never stopped, around and around each other, never permitted so much as a touch. "One could be forgiven for thinking you simply longed for my company."

His censorious look annoyed her. "Regardless of what you think of Miss Kala, she never fails to be punctual."

"Please do continue to tell me what I think." She crossed her arms over her chest, a reminder to exercise restraint.

"You've made no secret of your disdain."

"I've never said a word against her."

"Aloud."

She cinched in her arms till she was practically cradling her shoulders. "Have you developed extra-sensory perceptions that allow you to know my mind? How extraordinary."

"Hardly. My technique is a simple one."

"Oh, there's a technique to it? Do tell."

"I look at your face."

He did so then, in that way that told her she was not a fool to hope. Or as much of a fool as she sometimes felt.

Callie sighed, a concession. "And I suppose you disapprove of my unspoken dislike?"

"Not that it remains unspoken." His brow stitched as he attempted to unravel the strands of the issue. "I ask only that you consider what kind of life Miss Kala led before joining us, and the change that's come over Mrs. Pankhurst."

"I do." Callie bowed her head, not that it did much to hide her scarlet cheeks. "I shall."

Han nodded. "Two hours."

"And Angus has not sent word in that time?"

"He's taken Jie and Ting on their Sunday outing."

"Of course. Hiero?"

"Constructing a hermitage with his bed linens."

"Really?"

His shrug spoke volumes.

"How should we proceed? Retrace their normal route? Enlist a few lighter boys? Summon Mr. Stoker?" Her hunter's instinct knew there were too many variables at play. "Wait them out?"

A screech from above decided for them. Aldridge met them at the kitchen door, hurried them into the parlor. They found Miss Kala crouched beside a small table, struggling for breath. Her intricate hair bun lurched to one side. Perspiration-slick tendrils lacquered the frame of her face. Her skirts had drawn a path of mud from the side entrance. Her red coat flapped off of one arm, a flag of war.

Callie's mother was nowhere to be seen.

"Get the girl some water," Callie instructed, staying Han with a sharp look.

"Oh, Miss Pankhurst!" Miss Kala bleated, then burst into sobs. Callie hoisted her onto the divan, then took the seat beside her. "What you must think of me..."

"You must calm yourself." Callie's hands hovered over her, unsure of where, or whether she should, offer comfort to the woman who had no doubt lost her mother.

"What Miss Pankhurst means is catch your breath," Han translated in a tone Callie had never heard before. She straightened, hands clasped in her lap to keep them occupied. "Here's the water."

Aldridge had had the good sense to bring a pitcher. Miss Kala drained two glasses, struggling to pour a third before she'd composed herself enough to speak.

"They took her."

Bile rose to Callie's throat. "'Took her'?"

By the looks on their faces, it had come out a roar. Miss Kala hugged a pillow to her chest; Han sprang to the edge of his seat. Callie opened her mouth to speak, but acid seared the root of her tongue.

"You mean Mrs. Pankhurst has been taken against her will?" Han confirmed in that soft tone that made Callie want to stab her ears with a hairpin.

"Against her will?" Miss Kala wiped her nose with her sleeve. "She don't know what her will is. That's why she needs... needs me." She blubbered. "Please don't put me out, Miss Pankhurst. This was my last chance..."

Callie dug her nails into her palm to keep from strangling her where she sat. Her every breath further stoked the fire, so she kept silent. She watched Han offer Miss Kala his handkerchief, almost cracked a bone in her hand when their fingers brushed.

"Aldridge," Callie interrupted before she'd said a word. "Please rouse Mr. Bash and inform him of..." Realizing the absurdity of her instruction—Aldridge having had his tongue cut out decades ago—she ended on a croak. Nevertheless the butler slipped away.

"Tell it from the start," Han prompted Miss Kala, giving her his full attention.

With an audible gulp, she took a final sip of water and set the glass aside.

"We walked to the park, as we always do. North, by Grosvenor Square, to stay well away from the Serpentine. Mrs. Pankhurst don't care for the swans. Speakers Corner was lively, so we stopped to listen. Lil—Mrs. Pankhurst likes that twaddle. Pretends, you know, she can follow. I don't know what they're on about half the time. Then we saw them. Or her, more like."

"Her?" Han encouraged. Callie read the suspicion in his eyes and forced herself to focus.

"The strange one, from the embankment. With all the lovely veg. The sisters...?"

"The Daughters of Eden," Han confirmed, then gave a tight frown.

Swallowing a yelp of panic, Callie asked, "You knew one of the speakers?"

"She'd taken a liking to Mrs. Pankhurst that day we went to see the duke prince and his new wife. She and her sisters saw Mrs. Pankhurst in the crowd today and called her over. We got to chatting—there's one girl who's very nice—and helped them hand out their pamphlets. Mrs. Pankhurst was enjoying herself, so I didn't see no harm in it. And..." She darted her red eyes from Callie to Han and back again, tears welling at the corner. "Sister Juliet—that's the weird one—she was gonna speak again later, and they had a picnic basket with sandwiches and cordial to share. So we sat with them awhile, and I thought..."

Callie felt as if the chair under her collapsed. "You left her."

"Only to fetch tea!" Fat rivulets cut drenched Miss Kala's cheeks, poured off her chin. "The spring wind… We were shivering. The stall was across a busy street. Lil would never have made it. They were so kind, and she was so easy with them. Smiling, chatting. I only thought to pop over and back. I blinked and…" She buried her face in the pillow, heaving with sobs.

Callie stood, escaped to the window. She felt as if a part of herself stayed on the divan, slumping into its velvety cushions. As if part of her were still underground, firing round after round into a pile of straw. Outside, in the square beyond, couples strolled, children frolicked despite the looming gray of an overcast day. If they saw the gaunt, ghostly woman in the window staring out at them, they paid her no mind.

Someone had stolen her mother.

If she were honest, there had been times, many times, in the throes of her madness, when Callie had wished her gone. When she'd been trapped in the filth of their apartment, too small to even reach the knob on the door, with no servants and no father and a howling banshee. Her Uncle Apollo had come for them.

She would not fail her mother now. She fought to recall the events of her mother's first encounter with the Daughters at the embankment. Even lacking the darker shades of Han's description, Callie's mind painted a detailed portrait of their intentions toward a woman of seeming wealth like her mother. How they could twist her devotion and her troubled mind into a donation or two, eventually persuading her to sign her fortune over to their cause.

They would feel the burn of the dragon they'd unleashed when stealing Lillian Pankhurst away.

She whirled around to find Han kneeling before Miss Kala, petting her on the shoulder. After whispering a string of curses so foul a seaman would blanch, she marched back to the divan and stood over them, lit with purpose.

"Everything, again. From the beginning. Spare no detail."

Chapter 3

$\mathcal{T}$im cursed his height—or rather his lack of it—as he rounded the corner to find yet another red stone wall obscuring the Daughters of Eden's compound from view. Only the dainty white petticoat gables that lined the chimney-stacked roof of the main building peeked over. He'd walked the perimeter for three blocks but had yet to find a gate. Not an immediate cause for alarm, given he had not been invited to the Daughters' Sunday service and directed himself based on an incomplete map.

The city's ravenous outward growth had not yet consumed the village of Shepherd's Bush. Though some streets had been cobbled and a train station provided a vital link to the city center, farms still spotted the landscape, some with no neighbors to speak of. That made it all the more curious the Daughters had barricaded themselves behind such towering battlements. Tim would count them lucky to cause such outrage as to be attacked by pitchfork-wielding villagers.

A turn around the final corner revealed a graveyard of black carriages parked around a cricket field, their drivers playing an impromptu match with a fencepost and a ball of twine. Tim crossed the road, hoisting himself halfway onto one of their abandoned seats to gain a better vantage. All the curtains were drawn in the main house's windows. The building itself was pretty, if commonplace: red brick, three story, with a conservatory spanning its entire first floor on the eastern side. He could see little of the fabled gardens, only a small orchard of trees around the conservatory and a vague impression of green at the rear. A long one-story building with a clock tower stretched beyond the orchard, this enclosed by a tall iron fence. The chapel, no doubt, and Tim's destination.

Pretending to emerge from one of the carriages, he straightened his hat and his posture. Affecting a slight limp that forced him to lean on his walking stick, he slowed his pace to a leisurely stroll. The pins that fitted one of Hiero's luxurious waistcoats to his more slender frame scratched with every step, but the discomfort kept Tim focused. He hadn't needed to borrow the other emblems of wealth he wore: the jade cufflinks, the gold filigree pocket watch, the side-buttoned spats. All were "necessities," in Hiero's estimation, during their far too numerous visits to Monsieur Henri's salon. Tim had to confess they had been useful on more than one occasion, such as his present mission.

A pair of women in pristine white uniforms, their hair in labyrinthine plaits bound into a winglike formation, guarded the chapel gates. Falling in behind a trio of elegant patrons who looked to be a mother and two daughters, Tim attempted to blend into their party, only to be stopped by one of the angelic women carrying a genuine olive branch.

"Who has come to heed the prophet's call?"

"Mr. Gregory Kipling." Tim accepted the branch she gave him, wanting to pet its glossy leaves.

"Welcome, pilgrim. Open your heart to Her wisdom and be a shepherd of Her good work."

"May She come to light our way." Tim had practiced the Daughters' greeting a hundred times the night before, but it still fell awkwardly from his tongue. The woman's kind smile did little to reassure him. He nodded his thanks, then hurried along the path to the chapel, forgetting his limp.

Tim stopped halfway to collect himself, wishing he'd picked a more comfortable guise. The mustache he'd grown itched like a bastard. His muscles fought unfamiliar movements. One of the pins had stabbed through his skin over his right shoulder blade, pricking with every gesture. For the briefest moment, he wished Hiero were there to finesse it all away. But then he remembered his goal—reinstatement—and berated himself for his weakness.

A child's life was at stake.

A row of cedars ensured the main house was obscured, though whether the Daughters wanted to keep others out or the girls under their care in was but one of the many questions Tim sought to answer. The institutional quality to the place undermined any efforts the Daughters had made to add cleanliness and character, though Tim imagined that appealed to some of their more zealous patrons. The women they took in shouldn't seem to be rewarded for their transgressions.

The sparse decor of the chapel underlined this message. Rows of humble wood pews divided by a center aisle led up to a stone altar with a side podium. A shrine to founder Rebecca Northcote—a portrait lit by candles, a withering bouquet of wildflowers, and copies of her most famous books chained to the wall for easy reading—adorned the opposing side. Instead of the stations of the cross, the room's perimeter told the story of Mother Rebecca in mementos and sketches. No vulgar collection plates for the Daughters; instead a few well-placed signs asked patrons to do all they could to "make way for Her return." A painting above the altar depicted this second coming in riotous colors.

Tim milled about, pretending to take interest in one of the sketches while surveying the sizeable crowd. He recognized several childless widows and rich spinsters of social renown. Whether they went on behalf of the adulterous fathers, brothers, and nephews who contributed to the Daughters' trade or out of their true devotion, Tim could not know. That the Daughters understood how to appeal to the highest in society to serve either the lowest, or their own coffers, was certain. Perhaps even something to be admired.

But to what lengths would they go to avoid upsetting their apple cart?

A murmur of intrigue rustled through the crowd. Tim looked to the front, expecting to see Sister Juliet Tattersale, the current prophet, take the stage, and found himself staring into a sea of faces turned toward the rear. He swung about to watch what he assumed would be a procession...

And sighed. Profoundly. He waited to catch the eye of his lover and sometimes nemesis, his Hiero, inexplicably dressed as a Roman Catholic priest. Tim knew in his bones Hiero would not fail to notice him, just as he knew the fearsome attraction that linked them had drawn him into his orbit, fiery sun to Tim's placid moon. That or Han had been tasked with following him.

The slips of gossip that slithered through the crowd in the wake of Hiero's entrance had more hiss than bite. The Daughters' religious beliefs skewed closer to the Roman Church than the Church of England, so Hiero's choice of costume did not cause as much controversy as that of his companion. Head bowed and face bare of makeup, Tim almost failed to recognize Callie. Eschewing her blonde wig and finery for her natural chin-length black hair and a long white-and-gold cloak, she had dressed to provoke. A simple wire crown of stars, little more extravagant than a string of daisies, encircled her head. Tim couldn't see them all, but he didn't doubt there were twelve, calling to mind the Woman of the Apocalypse from the Book of Revelation. By the increased volume of chatter in the chapel, the patrons hadn't missed this detail either.

What was Hiero playing at? He would not have gone to such lengths just to chastise Tim. Worry gnawed at his nerves. He couldn't decide what scenario would be worse: if they had taken a new case without him, or if their investigation interfered with his own. Regardless, any action on his part would have to wait on the ceremony's completion. That he had thus far escaped Hiero's notice was the situation's only blessing. At the chime of a bell, he settled into the most advantageous seat, with a view of the altar, the podium, and the wily Mr. Bash.

The procession he had looked for earlier began, with Daughters filing in from all corners, each bearing a basket of fruit, vegetables, or flowers. These were placed around the edges of the altar as tribute to the Messiah of the painting. The last of these gift-bearers carried an ornate box—the Northcote box, or so Tim had read, in which Mother Rebecca's end-of-the-world prophecies were sealed, to be opened when all the Bishops of England were assembled before the announcement of the Messiah's return, after forty days and forty nights spent in deep contemplation of Mother Rebecca's writings.

Tim had to credit her ambition in trying to bring the British clergy to heel. But such was the mystery, and likely the appeal, of Northcote's philosophies. She had the good sense to mingle in social reform with the apocalyptic fervor.

After setting the box in the middle of the altar, one of the Daughters opened the lid. *Not the real box, then, but a symbol,* Tim noted. A dove flew out, to the amazement of all. The bird circled above them three times before landing on the Daughter's outstretched arm. As they took their place with the other Daughters at the sides of the stage, Tim could almost hear Hiero's internal grousing about how the simplest forms of magic were the easiest way to sucker you in. He stole a gaze in Hiero's direction and chuckled at his frown.

A cornsilk-haired waif in a gold-and-cream confection of a dress wandered up the center aisle, caressing the heads and cheeks of everyone she passed. She clasped the hands of those who reached for her, her elfin features radiating warmth, wonderment, and the vacant innocence of the touched. Sister Juliet, no doubt, and, if Tim's instincts bore fruit, the reason for Hiero's presence today. He would have taken an instant dislike to such an obvious charlatan, and it would be all the more impossible to dissuade him from exposing her for the sake of Tim's case.

The one he couldn't tell Hiero anything about.

"And the Lord Jesus said," Sister Juliet proclaimed, standing before the altar with her arms outstretched, "'Remember therefore from whence thou art fallen, and repent, and do the first works. He that hath an ear, let him hear what the Spirit saith unto the churches; to him that overcometh will I give to eat of the Tree of Life, which is in the midst of the Paradise of God.' Revelations 2:5, 2:7."

She pressed her hands to her chest and bowed to the painting. Everyone, the Daughters, the parishioners, performed the same gesture. Casting a bewildered glance across the field of bent backs, Tim caught Hiero's notice. He kept his pious mien, but his dark eyes twinkled with mischief and, Tim hoped, some surprise. Tim permitted himself a smile, oddly reassured by Hiero's presence despite its complications. Then everyone rose, and he was again surrounded by strangers.

"To overcome." Sister Juliet moved to the front of the dais to face her audience. "That is our charge as daughters of Mother Eve, with whose original sin we are burdened. The first work of Adam and Eve, as instructed by the Lord God himself in the Book of Genesis, was to till the soil. The work of growing nourishment for our bodies does the work of nourishing our souls. That is how we overcome the sins we inherited from our great mother. And to those who overcome, the Lord Jesus Christ will give to eat of the Tree of Life and welcome them into the Paradise."

A titter of light applause broke out, which more experienced parishioners shushed. Sister Juliet waited them out with the look of a patient teacher.

"To our Holy Mother Rebecca, the promise of Paradise after death did not go far enough to repent for Mother Eve's sin. She wrote, 'As she at first plucked the fruit and brought the knowledge of the evil fruit, so at last she must bring the knowledge of the good fruit.' We must do the work of restoring the Paradise to Earth. Of planting a seed of virtue in every man, woman, and child. Of nurturing a garden of devout souls, ripe with the knowledge of the

Word of the Lord and of our glorious prophet Rebecca!"

A chorus of cheers rung out. Sister Juliet raised her arms as if to catch them.

"Our first work is Her redemption. With our every deed and action, we move closer to restoring Her garden, as Mother Rebecca foretold." The Daughters fetched the baskets of fruit off the altar and began distributing them among the parishioners. "Our garden is bountiful, and we invite you to share in it. But our real work as Daughters of Eden is done not in our fields, but in our nursery. In our midwifery. In redeeming the fallen and their innocent babes, in bringing them the knowledge of the good fruit.

"And through this work shall you all be redeemed and earn your place at Her side. She will remake of this Earth a paradise where we will be blithe as the angels!"

To ecstatic cheers and shouts of "Hallelujah!" Sister Juliet stole a ruddy apple from one of the other Daughters' baskets and chomped off a huge bite, inviting her congregation to do the same. Tim noticed many who took the fruit replaced it with a donation envelope. Some parishioners formed a line to speak to Sister Juliet. Just as Tim made to join them, a few of the Daughters rushed forth to usher them back to their seats. It seemed the return of Eve and the Garden of Eden to Earth weren't the Daughters' only ambitions.

A demure Daughter with coarse black hair entered, cradling an infant. By the sighs and "awws" of the crowd, Sister Juliet knew exactly how to play to her audience. Tim could only imagine how Hiero received this blatant heartstring-tugging. He felt his gorge rising at how cunningly they would use a child, especially given the reason his investigation had led him to their door.

"Look at this cherub!" Sister Juliet took the babe—a girl, by her pink bonnet—and cleaved her to her bosom. "A miracle the Lord gifted us through our Mother Eve. This little one will not know shame, or guilt, or be lured into temptation. She was born into our fold, and so we are charged with her soul's care." An older well-to-do couple were led to the side of the dais. Sister Juliet whispered a blessing on the infant's forehead, then waved them over. "And so we can lift ever more children out of the unfortunate circumstances of their birth, we call on the faithful to share our burden."

With a final kiss, she handed the girl over to her adoptive parents. "Mr. and Mrs. William Thornhill, will you raise this child in the light of Lord and teach her the ways of our Holy Mother?"

"Yes, oh, yes!" Mrs. Thornhill exclaimed, weeping as she embraced her daughter for the first time. Even Mr. Thornhill looked a bit misty eyed, clearing his throat and avoiding the crowd. More than a few handkerchiefs had been deployed around Tim; he repressed a sigh. Struggling to keep an open mind—and to protect his cover— he coughed into his gloves. He didn't doubt the infant would be loved by the Thornhills, but he couldn't fail to wonder if every child born under the Daughters' care was so blessed.

"But when will She be born back into the world? When will the time be ripe for Mother Eve's return?" Sister Juliet asked, seemingly of the heavens, or at least the ceiling. "The question has weighed on my sisters and me since we first heard Mother Rebecca's teachings. In her sixty-five prophetic tomes, she wrote of the many signs that will herald Her return. Unexpected visits from the faithful living abroad. A vision of the Woman Clothed in the Sun. The floods. The cleansing of the Dragon's fire. The sacrifice—"

An eerie whimpering echoed from the back of the chapel. A few heads turned, but Sister Juliet ignored the sound.

"Our beloved Sister Zanna examines each young mother brought to us and every babe born under our eaves for the prophetic marks. But even these signs cannot replace the feeling we each hold deep within ourselves."

The whimpering intensified, underscored by a music-boxlike tinkling that spiked the hairs on the back of Tim's neck. He watched for Sister Juliet's reaction, wondering if this was all part of the ceremony.

"Our Holy Mother described it as a euphoric sensation, being in the presence of the One. A joy that shoots out from the very heart of you."

A wild cackle scraped their ears. A screechy note was sung out. Sister Juliet reached out to her audience as if to grab back their attention. Some of the Daughters walked the perimeter of the room, searching for the culprit.

"'Even as you rejoice, a yearning will carve a hole out of you only She can fill. When you are near her, you will know true serenity. When apart, a feeling of purpose.'"

The tinkling grew more melodious, ethereal music ringing down from on high.

"And her purpose, and yours as her shepherd, is to—"

Behind, a thud. Tim caught a flicker of fury on Sister Juliet's face before turning in time to see Callie prone in the aisle, clutching her abdomen and muttering feverishly. Father Hiero raced to her side, crooning to her in Italian as he helped her to her feet. Callie fainted into his arms, still babbling nonsense, the crowd riveted. A shudder quaked through her, then another and another until Hiero couldn't hold her anymore. She slammed to her knees, crawling forward even as she thrust an arm toward the painting of the Messiah.

"Mother!" Even Tim startled at her scream. "Mother! She is my mother I am her mother she is my mother I am her mother..."

A posse of Daughters raced to silence her. Hiero, brandishing his robes like a cape, hissed them away with another burst of Italian. Tim bit his cheek to stifle a laugh.

Sister Juliet, perhaps recognizing when she'd been out-acted, bid them halt. She floated down the aisle to Callie, seizing her out-stretched hand and clamping it to her chest.

"Daughter, have you been called to us?"

Callie grabbed the sides of Sister Juliet's face and kissed her fiercely, first on the lips and then on the forehead, to audible gasps from the parishioners.

"Hear *me*, Daughter," Callie, lit with half-crazed elation, implored. "I am the hope and the light and the spirit manifest. I am the Holy Vessel and the Queen of Queens. I am stalked by the Dragon and crowned by the stars. The bounty of heaven lives in me, loves through me, aches for the world. Prepare! Prepare!"

Callie convulsed as she reached out to a recoiling Sister Juliet, the better to show off the beads of blood pearling at her wrists and neck. Audible gasps from the crowd and the Daughters gave the tension in the air an extra charge. With a mercenary swoon, Callie collapsed into Sister Juliet's arms as Hiero rushed forward.

"Sorry, I am so very sorry to disturb."

Sister Juliet, still reeling, looked a bit peaked herself. Two of the Daughters hurried to support her; she grabbed for them to steady her. "She is with child?"

Tim rolled his eyes when Hiero nodded. Of course that would be their meddlesome plan.

"We will speak later." Sister Juliet turned to her companion. "Let her take rest in the prayer room."

"Forgive me," Hiero objected, "but she is in my charge."

"Come with me," the demure Daughter invited, and all three disappeared through the back exit.

Tim stifled a growl of professional jealously and refocused on the task at hand. But Sister Juliet's concluding remarks fell on deaf ears, as everyone in the chapel, Daughters and parishioners alike, were abuzz with speculation. Only Tim understood not one, but two frauds had been committed, and a child's life hung in the balance.

Any hope of infiltrating the main house with their performance was lost as soon as they were escorted into the prayer room, little more than a storage area at the back of the chapel. Two Daughters eased

Callie atop a dusty chest. Hiero did not miss how they gawked at her stigmata stains before rushing out. Maintaining the pretense of her indisposition, Callie slumped back against the wall, arms splayed and head lolling, still muttering nonsense. The wire edges of her starry crown had pricked blood from her temples and brow. Hiero would have taken a moment to admire her commitment if he were not still immersed in his role.

He unclasped his cloak and blanketed her, tucking it around her belly to give the impression of a small bulge. He shoved up her left sleeve to reveal the large birthmark—quite natural, as it turned out— those so inclined might see as the shape of a tree. Hearing footsteps approach, he knelt in prayer before her.

The shy ledger-keeper from the embankment celebration found them thus. She inhaled to gather her strength in the doorway before pushing herself into the room. Hiero could only imagine what horrors in this woman's past had scared off her confidence. Having suffered and overcome his own, he took an instant liking to her.

"Here. Some water." Telling that the woman handed the glass to Hiero, not Callie. She flicked her watchful eyes once, twice, longer, to Callie's birthmark. She swallowed a smile. "I am Sister Nora Hawfinch, Sister Juliet's personal secretary. Do you think your… Does she require a doctor? We have a midwife…"

"Father Giacomo Coscarelli, late of the Vatican." Hiero bowed. "May I present Mrs. Caroline Sandringham." It had been some years since he'd used his Italian accent—The Gaiety's *Romeo & Juliet* burlesque, *Two Ignoble Houses Both Alike in Infamy*, had fallen from popularity after their Juliet, a dizzy lad named Leslie, impaled himself with the wrong prop dagger and died a week later, killed by an infected splinter. "Alas, there is no cure for her condition. She will be restored when the Mother wills it."

"The Mother, yes." A slight stammer gave away her interest. "And you have come seeking Sister Juliet's counsel?"

"I go where she leads." Hiero remained on his knees so as not to tower over her. "We were headed to mass at the English Martyrs when she announced that we must go west. She navigated the streets as if they were her own. When your sister began to speak, all became clear. More I cannot say." He cast a meaningful glance at Callie, going for a mix of awe and anxiousness. "But yes, we must see her."

"She's in great demand after services, as you might imagine." Sister Nora worried her bottom lip, considering. "Perhaps it would be wise to set an appointment since your companion Mrs. Sandringham is unwell. That way we'd all have time to prepare."

Meaning they wanted to verify his identity. Hiero almost laughed at the thought. He couldn't believe she would dismiss them after their dramatic interruption, which would prompt chatter among their parishioners and must have left a question in the Daughters' minds. But perhaps they had underestimated the amount of secrets the Daughters had to hide.

A lifetime of experience in convincing people to go against their instincts allowed Hiero to read her like an open book: zealous but protective, eager to please, but only if you'd earned her trust, and terrified of exposing those close to her to ruin. He nudged Callie's foot with his calf; her babbling intensified.

"The dragon is near… He covets my child… I must flee to the wilderness… Where are my angels?" Callie bleated.

"Hush, hush." Hiero patted her hand. "I am here. If this is not the place we seek, we will look elsewhere."

"She is with child?" Sister Nora asked, looking more surprised than Hiero would have expected given how many hints they had dropped.

Hiero nodded, casting a reverent gaze up at Callie. "She is the vessel."

Sister Nora glared at him, mouth open, her faith holding back her suspicions. A cacophony of curious chatter broke out in the chapel beyond, signaling the service's end and their patrons' interest in what became of "Mrs. Sandringham."

"Wait here a moment," Sister Nora instructed before speeding out the door.

And locking them in.

Hiero held in his shudder through sheer force of will—he hated tight spaces—and moved to the small round window. He unfurled a scarlet-red handkerchief from an inner pocket of his robes, signaling Han.

"What do you think you're doing?" Callie demanded as she stood, stretching her shoulders and neck. "We can't give up now we've got their attention."

Hiero fluttered the handkerchief in her direction. "Caution, not surrender. Han may be able to scale that wall, but your mother will require our assistance."

Callie huffed. "Not to mention the fuss she'll stir. She's never taken to him."

"She's not herself."

"She's the only version of herself I've ever known." Callie eased off her crown of stars. She dabbed a finger into a bloody spot at her temple, winced. "Blasted thing. Mad or sane, dear Mother never possessed the most sound judgment."

"She had the good sense to take refuge with Apollo when he offered."

"Desperation, like those ladies in there. The whole place reeks of it." She scoffed. "If you look to the skies to solve your problems, don't be surprised when someone pisses out a window."

Hiero wanted to laugh, but he knew it would only encourage her. So he laughed.

"The game the Daughters are playing is as old as their good book. And their saintliness is their slyest maneuver. A lady might have a reputation for being silly or stupid or naive, but a devout woman working on the poor's behalf is never questioned. Their ridiculous prophecies are for the widows and maiden aunts, but their virtuousness is how they evade scrutiny. And therefore..."

"Where they are vulnerable." Pensive, she massaged her scalp. "How should we proceed?"

"We must prove ourselves even more devout." He moved to the door, listened. "A lamb like Sister Nora will be easily swayed."

"But Sister Juliet is a wolf."

Hiero curled his fingers around the knob, counting back from twenty in his mind. He wanted out. Better, a glass of 1837 Château Haut-Brion Pessac-Léognan. Better, for his intrepid Kip to pound down the door, demanding an explanation for Hiero's theatrics, thereby finding himself, quite inadvertently, embroiled in the very affair he swore against. Of course, his presence in the chapel indicated he *was*, in some unknown way, embroiled, though perhaps in a different affair. Either way, Hiero felt cheated.

And still trapped in the oppressive prayer room. Hiero fought to steady his breaths, to convince himself of how much space, how much air, there was in the room.

"She will not permit you to leave," he argued, because why not? "She will separate us to see what you are made of."

"Iron and vinegar. Or so Han says."

Inhaling deeply, Hiero stepped back from the door. He turned, took her hands.

"These are not the amateurs I anticipated. We know only what they have shown us, not what lurks within the main house. If our aim is to retrieve your mother..."

"I'd do well not to require rescuing as well," she grumbled. "Yes, very well. So we retreat?"

"Not quite yet."

"Have a few more tricks up your sleeve?"

"I'm a marvel of prestidigitation."

A click of the knob was all the warning they had to resume their positions. Hiero belayed Callie from putting on her crown, taking a seat beside her on the chest and using his handkerchief to clean her wounds.

"Entranced or recovered?" she whispered as the lock clicked.

"Recovered but weak."

Callie folded in on herself, a tipsy smile curving her lips. Hiero approved of the choice—'exhausted but spiritually fulfilled by communion with Eve' struck exactly the right note. He folded his cloak to act as a pillow. By the time Sister Nora reentered, Hiero held the cup of water to Callie's lips, begging her to take another sip.

He didn't miss the look of wonderment that lit Sister Nora's features as she slipped back into the closet.

"How is she?"

Hiero sighed. "Her burden is also her bliss. Like the martyrs, she finds joy in her suffering."

"It is much the same for Sister Juliet."

"As are all touched by the Mother."

"All?"

"*Sí.* Your Mother Rebecca, her great torment at the end. A beautiful but imperfect vessel." At her shocked expression, Hiero added, "I knew her of old."

"You knew..."

"I fear it will be the same for Mrs. Sandringham. The Mother's power is fierce, and the time must be right. That is why we seek others out. Perhaps together..." Hiero assayed the same world-weary look that won his Macbeth such accolades. "Your Sister Juliet. Will she see us?"

Her lip quivered. A more obvious tell, Hiero couldn't have imagined. A lamb indeed.

"She's taken to her bed. The service, you see... She gives everything."

Hiero nodded sympathetically, waiting for the reversal.

"But if Mrs. Sandringham cares to stay, perhaps converse with her this evening, she is most welcome. Our nurse, Sister Zanna, can tend to her, and Sister Merry makes a much-fortifying broth. If you would care to return tomorrow, Father—"

"A Samaritan kindness, and most appreciated. But I have consecrated our rooms at the Albion. Certain rituals must be observed... Well, you know better than I. What time tomorrow would be convenient for me to call on Sister Juliet?"

Callie ground her heel into his foot. As well-versed in the language of torture as Hiero was, he couldn't decipher her message.

Flustered, Sister Nora stammered, "I'll have to consult her diary..."

"Very good. I will wait for your note."

He scooped Callie up to her feet so quickly she let out a loud yip. Startled, Sister Nora leapt up to bar their way, resulting in an awkward dance where neither party wanted to insult the other by admitting they were trying to escape or prevent them from leaving. Just as Sister Nora grabbed for Hiero's fallen cloak as an excuse to get hold of Callie, a solid figure blocked the door.

Han. Though relieved, a small part of Hiero had anticipated someone more Kip-like. Had the unexpected crossing of their paths not intrigued his stalwart detective even a teensy bit? Did his agnostic mind fail to see the hand of fate in such an odd coincidence?

"Padre?" Han offered an arm to receive Callie, whom he tucked tight against him.

Hiero issued strict instructions in Italian. Which Han did not speak, but neither, he wagered, did Sister Nora. Once Han and Callie were out of sight, he performed an elaborate bow—perhaps too elaborate for this particular character, but he missed his audience—and thanked her for her help.

"I'll send word as soon as I know," she confirmed, worrying her hands in the manner of the crueler half of Shakespeare's king-slaying couple.

Hiero, who did not believe in omens, but, like any actor, held his fair share of superstitions, shuddered through his escape.

Chapter 4

*A*fter well over an hour of waiting, the sleek black carriage rounded the far corner onto the street where Tim awaited them. Stuffing the pamphlet he'd been skimming into his inner jacket pocket, he jogged into its path, tipped his hat to Angus the driver, and vaulted onto the side step. Accustomed to this maneuver, Angus didn't even bother to slow the horses. Latching one-handed onto the upper rail, Tim pried open the door and swung himself inside before any of the passengers could utter an oath.

Which Miss Pankhurst did, belatedly, as Tim settled himself into the seat beside Han, who welcomed him with his customary nod. Miss Pankhurst frowned at Tim but appeared too exhausted to protest. Her theatrics had taken their toll on her skin by the livid scratch marks on her temples. Hiero, in his blanketlike cassock, dozed against the plush upholstered sideboard, cradling his favorite flask.

Tim's grand entrance had been intended to shock them. He'd meant to follow up with scathing disapproval of their dramatic baiting of the Daughters of Eden. But they looked so domestic, so cozy, so... defeated, he found he didn't have the heart.

"It appears our paths have converged, Mr. Stoker," Miss Pankhurst observed, lifting her hand to hide a yawn. "Unexpected but intriguing."

"As was your performance." Tim matched the strength of her

gaze, drawing on all his interrogative prowess. Hers was one of the shrewdest minds he'd ever encountered; if she ever turned to crime, she'd be a fearsome nemesis. "To what end, I wonder?"

"I should think our intentions obvious enough. Yours, however..."

"I'm afraid this isn't a case of quid pro quo."

"This isn't your case at all, given that you've recused yourself." The conversation had revived her sting, if not her energy. "Or have you finally screwed your courage to the sticking place and broke out on your own?"

Tim met her annoyance with patience. Stare never wavering from her clenched face, his silence refused to justify his actions. She bristled but looked to Han.

"Perhaps it is time Mr. Stoker be brought in," he suggested.

"We've only just begun," Miss Pankhurst countered.

"And you must bring your efforts to a swift end." Tim canted his torso toward them, a direct appeal. "The Daughters are dangerous. They are more than mere charlatans. Lives are at stake." A tense quiet overtook the carriage, punctuated only by Hiero's soft snores. "You must stop at once."

"Whose lives?" Miss Pankhurst demanded. "The girls they take in? The Daughters themselves?"

The urgency in her tone rattled Tim. "I cannot say more."

"Or you will not out of sheer obstinacy and a lack of honor!"

"Calliope," Han warned.

"How many cases must we work together, DI Stoker, before you trust that we will keep your secrets? Before you've gathered enough evidence of our talent and our discretion? Before you stop begging for scraps from the Yard?"

Tim sighed. "Miss Pankhurst, might I remind you that the terms of my involvement are dictated by my superintendent, and he has—"

"Oh, stuff your terms." A hint of a smile played on her lips when Tim recoiled. "Han saved you from being devoured by lions.

Hiero pleaded your case to your superiors after you rejected *and* investigated him. These are the actions of men, Mr. Stoker, honorable men. If you would distance yourself from the likes of us, then it must be a clean break."

Tim shut his eyes, exhaled deeply. Her words had hit their mark. He couldn't forget his dissatisfaction the past few months, the tedium of the cases and his annoyance with their methods. Sir Hugh dangled the key to his future success above him; Tim had only to take the leap and grasp it.

And yet Miss Pankhurst and the team had managed to rattle the Daughters with an ease beyond Tim's capabilities. To say nothing of the restrictions due to his gender. And they had both found their way to this case, a portent Tim couldn't ignore. Still, there was no question of betraying Sir Hugh, even to his associates.

"My word of honor as a detective prevents me from disclosing the details of my case. My client insisted upon this condition before explaining his predicament. This commitment is as vital to me as my allegiance to all of you. There is no knife to my throat. I keep his secrets as I keep yours, out of respect and gratitude for all you have done for me."

Miss Pankhurst blew out a forceful breath, deflated. Her beseeching eyes landed on Han, then on Tim, then flew out the window. She bit the corner of her lip, her jaw rigid and trembling all at once, fighting an expression Tim had never seen on her before: misery.

"They have my mother," she revealed, and Tim felt as if the ground had fallen out from under him.

With a violent snort, Hiero roused. After a flurry of blinking, he peered, bleary eyed, at each one of them in turn. His gaze grew fond when it landed on Tim, and he welcomed him with a smile.

"Ah! The prodigal... someone... returns." He dismissed the error with a wave of his hand. "Never was much for religion."

"And yet you've taken a turn toward the pious." Tim gestured toward his robes.

"You approve?"

"More than I care to."

That comment brought the twinkle back to his dark eyes. "Oh? Care to make a full confession?"

Tim fought the blush Hiero's leer prompted. He'd thought of little else in the few private moments allowed him since their last encounter. He appreciated how engrossing his case had become for that very reason, less so the fact their paths seemed intertwined to the point of being impossible to unravel.

"Perhaps later." Tim shifted his boot so it pressed into the curve of Hiero's foot. The heated look Hiero shot back at him almost made Tim forget his name. He turned back to Miss Pankhurst, refocused. "For now you must tell me everything."

Han cut short her growl of protest. "I believe we've made our feelings clear on the matter of quid pro quo. What of your vow to your client?"

Tim considered this, thinking out loud. "I will keep his name and the details of his predicament out of it. But there is some larger puzzle to map out here, some scheme that goes beyond a simple fraud, and we each have a piece. Whether this constitutes the whole remains to be seen. But what has been made plain to me is we must suss it out together if we are to have any hope of getting to the heart of what these Daughters are up to."

"Well reasoned," Han agreed.

"Huzzah!" Hiero bellowed, raising his flask.

"Callie." Tim hesitated over the name, the impropriety awkward on his tongue. But if they were to be allies—and if he were to make amends—they had to do so as equals and friends. "I leave the final word to you."

She frowned as she scrutinized him, perhaps unconvinced by his about-face. But then her relentlessness was one of the things he respected most about her.

"Welcome back, Tim."

Callie escaped to her bedroom as soon as they arrived at 23 Berkeley Square, stopping only long enough to ask Aldridge to have tea sent up. Though her costume was light compared to her regular dresses and she was unburdened by her usual wig, as she climbed the back stairs, she carried the leaden weight of the knowledge that her mother remained trapped with the Daughters. After learning the details of Hiero's first encounter with the Daughters and what they knew of her mother's capture during the carriage ride home, she'd become all the more incensed that this was allowed to happen.

The warning signs had been there for anyone to see. Indeed, if all the wealthy widows and maiden aunts among Sister Juliet's worshippers today were any indication, elderly, lonely women of means were the wellspring from which the Daughters sourced their donations. Her mother's near-infantile state of mind made her even more susceptible to their methods of persuasion. Han and Hiero recognized this and failed to take the proper precautions. To say nothing of that flibbertigibbet Miss Kala, whom Callie would use as further inspiration for her target practice.

Eager to throw off every vestige of her performance—spiritual as well as sartorial—she almost missed the couple huddled in intimate conversation on the landing between the third and fourth floors. Or, rather, Han craned over the diminutive Miss Kala, a willow tree shading his favorite swan. Callie's slow, quiet steps had masked her approach. She stood on the second floor landing, watching them through the gaps in the banister. The odd acoustics of the house muted their voices. Callie didn't dare move higher lest she draw attention to herself.

Miss Kala wept. She gripped Han's arms, pleading. For her job, for his support, Callie couldn't know. She resembled the heroine of a Gothic novel, with her wild sheaves of black hair and unkempt nightshirt. Her skin had lost all of its buttery sheen in the days since her charge's kidnapping, gone waxy and gray. Her despair infuriated Callie. Who was this woman to mourn the very person her neglect had lost? What gall to push her grief on them without lifting a finger to right her wrong!

Even though she wanted to spit in her face, Callie couldn't tear herself away. Even when Miss Kala pressed her hands into Han's chest and gazed up at him, beseeching. Even when Han folded her into his arms, rubbing her back. Even when the anger roiling in Callie's gut caught flame, scorching up her throat until she felt she could breathe fire.

She fled to her room, slamming every door in her wake. Wanting to topple the statues that lined the corridor. Wanting to pound her fists into the carpet until she exposed the wood. Until the whole house crumbled down around her.

Instead she grabbed a hatpin from her dressing table and stabbed it into her thigh. Once, twice, three times, picking at old scars. She found her reflection in the mirror, as boyish, pale, and angular as Miss Kala was curvy and sensuous.

A knock at the door saved her putting her fist through it.

Aldridge with the tea. Before bidding him enter, she covered her leg and speared the hatpin into one of the poppets Minnie had knit for her. A tongueless man with much to say, the warmth of Aldridge's smile was its own comfort. He made an elaborate show of pouring the tea, a ritual from when she was small. Callie remembered riding through the house on his back. How he would position himself behind Hiero when they played cards, his stealth gestures helping her cheat. How he stood by her when she had to shoot her favorite horse.

After serving her, he poured himself a cup and dragged over a chair. They drank in silence, sharing no more than a look until Callie found her smile.

Hiero took a long, satisfying sniff of his soup bowl, drinking in the spicy wafts of steam. He shut his eyes. His nostrils prickled with the smell of garlic, cumin, cayenne, and mint, massaging his senses with the scent of nostalgia. Their cook, the not-so-mini Minnie, knew how to sing to his heart. Through his stomach, of course, but neither of them would have cared for the normal route.

As Hiero took up his spoon, he glanced across at his Kip, slurping with gusto. He might have predicted Kip would be undaunted by spice, but it was, as always, good to know his instincts had been proven right. And wonderful to have Kip back where he belonged, in his seat at their table. He resembled something of a Gulliver amongst the Brobdingnags, flanked between Han and Angus—Hiero hadn't noticed how abnormally tall his household was until the advent of Kip and Miss Kala—but the comparison suited him. All was right with the world, in Hiero's estimation, so long as they adventured together.

Hiero relaxed into his seat, content to observe his makeshift family as they bantered and bickered. Angus flirting with Jie while she cleared the soup bowls, bouncing their daughter Ting on his knee. Minnie fussing over the roast Aldridge carried out. Shahida regaling Kip and Han with tales from a youth spent helping her parents run a dockside inn. Callie in a world of her own, brooding over some aspect of the case. The empty chair ever reserved for his dear, departed Apollo at the head of the table appeared less empty than usual, or perhaps it was simply that Hiero felt full.

When Kip caught his eye, an upraised brow questioning Hiero's quiet, he barely resisted the urge to reach across the table to take his hand. To pull him over to claim his seat at Hiero's side. To link arms, nudge shoulders, bend their heads together to whisper sly comments and witticisms. Why weren't these good people, this haven, enough for Kip? The home Hiero had schemed and scrounged and slain giants for, Kip regarded as a burden. Worse, a cage.

Hiero knew better than anyone how his eagle could soar. But even noble birds of prey needed a roost.

"*Sachertorte?*" Kip gasped when Minnie set her pièce de résistance in the middle of the table some time later.

How long, Hiero couldn't say. He'd pecked at his meal, preferring to watch Kip eat. That he lunged at every plate like a vulture over a fresh carcass gave Hiero yet another reason to fret over his current lodging situation. But something about their—rather magnificent, as it turned out—pudding had sparked more than Kip's appetite.

"A favorite?" Hiero queried.

Delicately, as one would a newborn babe, Kip cradled the plate proffered him. "My first taste of Vienna, the day we arrived." He forked off a piece and shut his eyes, savoring. And smiled. "The taste of the new."

Hiero was grateful when Han asked, "A holiday?"

Kip shook his head, swallowed hard. "My father's work. He'd gone ahead. Mother and I followed once he'd found rooms." Hiero didn't miss how Kip stuttered on "Mother," the memory of his parents as raw as the day they died. He never spoke of them; this was its own rare treasure. "Travel didn't agree with her, especially by sea. The Danube is a gentle river, but it turned her green. Once Father had settled her in our flat, we went exploring. With all the new places, new people, new languages, I spent most of the afternoon clinging to his trouser legs."

"Bold to transplant such a young family," Callie woke from her brooding to comment.

"We lived in Venice when I was an infant, but this was the first place that marked me." Kip scarfed down another bite as if it might disappear. "And what child wouldn't be marked by stall after stall of sweets. A garden of sweets! In every color and flavor I could imagine." Little Ting squealed with delight when presented with her own piece. Kip chuckled. "Precisely, young miss. I couldn't choose, so Father decided for me. The royal *pâtissier* had just that year given common bakers the recipe for his greatest confection, *Sachertorte*."

Kip broke off a large morsel and scooped out the apricot filling, smearing it across his tongue with the back of his fork. Hiero had never before been jealous of jam.

"Magnificent, Minnie," Kip declared when she finally joined them. "You've given me a… a touch of home." He blinked away a glimmer in his eyes, bowed his head.

Hiero wanted to shoot across the table and seize him. Make a thousand promises he couldn't keep. Banish the specters that would forever haunt his Kip's heart. Instead he cleared his throat.

"And us the secret to fattening you up. Another slice for Mr. Stoker, if you please."

Kip scowled in his direction but didn't refuse.

A rap on the door heralded a note from the concierge at the Albion, one of Han's spies who intercepted any correspondence they preferred be kept away from the house. Armed with coffee—spiked, in Hiero's case—and good-night kisses from Ting, they adjourned to the study. Kip had spent the hours before supper filling the chalkboard with facts and strategies. Hiero had taken a much-needed nap. But when he saw the results of Kip's labor, he felt a sudden surge of drowsiness.

"Now to the matter at hand," he announced to no one in particular. He sprawled out in his usual armchair with what he knew was an air of virile insouciance and fixed his eyes on the only thing in the room of any consequence. "What wood mouse perished in the name of that regrettable attempt at a mustache? What possessed you to commit such an atrocity against such a poor, defenseless creature, i.e. your upper lip?"

Kip blushed to his ears. Han and Callie succumbed to coughing fits.

"You disapprove?" The shy look Kip cast his way dissolved in the heat of Hiero's smile.

"I object. Strenuously. It's such a crime you should arrest yourself."

A quirk to the corner of his lips. "You may deploy your razor as you see fit once our plans for the morrow are set."

"Ha!" Hiero beamed. He did love it when Kip came out to play. "Well said."

Han cleared his throat. "The note."

"What note?"

"That you received just now."

"Ah, the note." To Hiero's surprise, it was still in his hand. Instead of his cup. He thrust it at Han. "Read it, will you?"

With an audible sigh, Han perused the contents.

"Sister Juliet's act of contrition?" Kip guessed.

"Quite. Shall I spare you?"

"No, let's have it."

"Mrs. Sandringham,

Forgive me. You alone can understand the terrible burden. When the Mother calls, we cannot fail to answer, though it cost us in body, mind, and self. She has whispered your name in my ear, and so I welcome you, Daughter. Your place is among us. Bless us with your presence tomorrow, alone, and together we will sing her name.

Yours faithfully,
Sister Juliet Tattersale"

Callie sighed. "Her commitment is admirable, in its own way."

"Hardly commitment if she believes it," Han countered.

Kip, to everyone's surprise, looked to Hiero. "Thoughts?"

Stunned by Kip's confidence in him, he collected himself. "Her first move is to cut out Mrs. Sandringham's most trusted advisor. Amateur. The instinct to create a connection is smart, but in a note? Misjudged."

"You think they mean Mrs. Sandringham harm?" Han asked.

"Undoubtedly. She's made the minimum effort to woo her. She smells a rival."

"Not entirely without merit," Kip remarked. All eyes turned to him. He shrugged. "You struck too soon. Being charlatans, they recognize charlatans."

Callie huffed, folding her arms under her breasts. "My performance convinced."

"Your performance *did* convince the zealous," Kip insisted. "But it was unwise to present yourself as a rival. Most of the Daughters are there for virtuous reasons. Your Sister Nora, for instance. But will she take your side against Juliet? Will any of them? No. I agree with Hiero's assessment. By insinuating you are also possessed by Mother Eve's spirit, you've endangered yourself."

Anger fired her. "We all endanger ourselves with every case. You took on a cage full of lions!"

"Not by choice."

"You would not put such restrictions on Han or Hiero. I am as capable as any of you."

"And so you are. And so are the Daughters capable as any of the villains we've encountered. This isn't a question of womanhood, but of risk."

"You will not prevent me from retrieving my mother!"

"I have no intention of doing so. But your original plan is forfeit. To surrender yourself to the Daughters without a guardian is folly."

"Hiero will accompany me."

"They already wish to cut him out. They won't hesitate to do so. As a man, they can and will insist he lodge elsewhere."

"You wish to prevent me from learning about your case. If I'm too close, I'll discover things that will reveal the identity of your client."

"That is unlikely, as I mean to do most of the discovering my-self. Though I may call upon you, if need be. But your first and only mission must be to retrieve your mother. Not to prove the Daughters frauds..." He turned to glare at Hiero. "... and not to reveal the contents of Rebecca Northcote's box."

Hiero's eyelids had, admittedly, drooped a bit during their quar-rel. They shot open now, to be confronted once again by Kip's upraised brow.

"What? *Moi?*" He tried and failed to project an air of innocence. "What possible interest could I have in a long-dead swindler's trinket-holder?" All three of them now stared at him with matching pointed looks. "Anyone searching for other than her false teeth and the deed to that house are in for a disappointment." Unwavering, their gazes sharpened such that Hiero felt pinpricks across his chest. "Oh, very well! The box will remain untouched." Each in turn nodded, withdrawing their attention. "Until such a time as dear Lillian is safe. After I make no promises."

Hiero resented their collective eye-roll.

"I may have a solution," Han said, "to the matter of Miss Pank-hurst infiltrating unaccompanied." Hiero did not miss how he appealed to Kip, not Callie. "A ladies' maid."

Callie's face turned the color of a ripe plum. "No."

"Explain," Kip forestalled her.

"The story we've concocted for Mrs. Sandringham is that she is a wealthy widow whose husband perished at sea and stranded her in Italy. She discovered herself her pregnant, but not by his efforts. Not by anyone's efforts, in fact. A religious woman, she turned to prayer in the gardens of her local convent, where she met Father Coscarelli. She decided to return to England when she heard of Mother Rebecca's prophecies from a trusted friend. Perfectly reasonable that a ladies' maid would continue on with a mistress of means who had always been kind to her."

"With her husband gone, yes." Kip tapped his piece of chalk on the desktop. "But anyone we send would be in just as much danger from the Daughters."

"Not if the woman in question—"

"No," Callie growled at Han. "Absolutely not."

"She is more than capable," Han countered. "She can defend herself. She's of likeable character. She'll go unnoticed by the Daughters from society backgrounds and ingratiate herself with those from poverty. And she will know how to get word to us the second trouble strikes."

"If you think her so skilled, why not send her in my stead?" Callie hissed.

"Forgive me, but of whom are we speaking?" Kip asked.

"Miss Kala," Hiero enlightened. "Much as it aggrieves me, I must second Han's proposal." He deflected the daggers Callie shot his way with a flick of his hand. "She will protect you with her life."

"She's the reason Mother was taken!" Callie fury flamed so hot she turned to the wall to smother it.

"For which she's desperate to make amends." Han moved to her side, reached for—but did not touch—her shoulder. "Let her help."

"No," Callie snarled into the wallpaper. Which was, Hiero observed, a fitting shade of crimson.

"Overruled." Kip's gentle voice reverberated with such authority that Hiero went weak in the knees. "If the Daughters welcome you into their fold at your appointment tomorrow, you will do so accompanied by Miss Kala. Otherwise I will proceed with my investigation and make every effort to liberate Mrs. Pankhurst in due course." Kip glanced at Hiero and Han for confirmation. "Gentlemen, are we agreed?"

"Call yourselves gentlemen if you like." Callie whirled around to confront Han. "You're no better than the men who set those women on the path to the Daughters."

Appearing bewildered, Han answered, "Pity you won't accord

Miss Kala the same confidence you seek from us."

"She has done nothing to deserve it."

"And you have everything to lose if you're discovered." Again he ghosted his hands along the edge of her arms. "No one on this team can do this alone. It's not a matter of belief in your abilities, but awareness of the situation's limitations."

"Mark that." Hiero twiddled a finger in Han's direction. "Wis-dom." He received a crude gesture in response.

Callie exhaled so forcefully Hiero was astonished she didn't blow Han halfway to Reading.

"Very well. If Miss Kala is amenable…" Hiero sensed she couldn't bring herself to complete the sentence.

The perfect opportunity to change the subject.

"And you, my fine ferret-lipped swain." He made bedroom eyes at Kip. "Will you be joining our party?"

"Not likely to be a better opportunity to gain access in an unof-ficial capacity," Han noted.

"And we are somewhat adept at providing the requisite distrac-tion." Hiero pulled out his handkerchief, twirled it about, and—poof!—made it disappear.

Kip chuckled with delight.

"Yes, why not invite the entire household?" Callie grumbled. "Han could pose as a conquistador seeking spiritual retreat, Angus as his bannerman, Jie as a harlot bearing the spawn of Satan, and Minnie as her midwife-cum-exorcist. Beware, you doting Daughters, the circus has come to town!"

She collapsed into the armchair opposite Hiero before stealing a sip of his coffee. All three men were now afflicted with Han's earlier bewilderment.

"Drat," she declared with a pensive expression. "I do see the reason of it. Tim, you must come. But how will we explain your presence?"

"By not explaining it." Hiero once again drew their hawkish stares. "Coincidence, my dears, is the conjurer's neatest trick."

Chapter 5

Callie shifted in her seat, wishing herself able to mask her restlessness as Hiero masked... well, everything. Except the depth of his attraction to Tim, who fidgeted beside him. Not from nerves, Callie thought, but due to Hiero's proximity. The comedy of mannerisms playing out before her—Hiero using the tilt of the carriage to lean closer, Tim angling to receive him before remembering himself; Hiero laying a hand beside Tim's thigh, Tim contorting in a casual manner to nudge it away—might have amused were she not so anxious.

A pair of magnets, they were, attracting or repelling by virtue of direction. Their aura, visible only to those closest to them, gave one the tingles. Callie almost envied them until she remembered how dangerous that aspect of their partnership was and how secret it must remain.

She attempted to settle back against the velvet cushions, closing her eyes while she communed with what Hiero called the core of her character. Anything to avoid the thought of Miss Kala riding up front with Han. How he endured her indefatigable stream of chatter, which underscored the rattle of the wheels on cobblestone, Callie didn't know.

The starch in her freshly laundered white robes prickled the hairs on her legs, arms, and neck. Callie had eschewed her crown of stars for a sky-blue cloak meant to evoke the other Mother of Us All, the one suspiciously unmentioned in all of Rebecca Northcote's prophecies. The cloak's silk sparked against the velvet cushions, jolting her whenever she moved. Only the cold steel of her MAS revolver, sewn into a hidden pocket in her knickers, gave her any peace.

Three hard knocks on the ceiling signaled their imminent arrival. Callie felt as if they pounded on her skull.

"No improvisation." Tim's warning forced her attention, though his message was for Hiero. "More than one life hangs in the balance."

The carriage slowed to a halt. With a pointed look at Hiero and a wink of encouragement for Callie, Tim slid out the door. His plan was to petition in person for an appointment, which they would interrupt, insisting he join them for their interview with Sister Juliet. Relieved her part in this was minimal, Callie concentrated on evoking just the right "troubled angel" expression, the one that had duped Sister Nora.

Callie counted out five minutes under her breath before the carriage lurched forward, only to stop again after rounding a corner. She listened to the muffled argument that erupted outside, ignored Hiero's glimmer of pride as he watched Tim through the door, waiting for his cue. Once Han had wrenched it open, Father Coscarelli sprung out, all Italian charm and magnanimity. The deal was struck before Callie emerged, feigning dazed contentment. Han pressed a supportive touch into the small of her back as he helped her out of the carriage. Her inner smile instantly became an inner frown when he passed her off to Miss Kala.

"How do you want to play this?" Miss Kala asked sotto voce. "Touched invalid or hysterical imp?"

"Concentrate yourself on not giving us away. I'll worry about my performance."

"That attitude'll do you no favors if we're to find your mum."

"We wouldn't be here if you hadn't lost her," Callie sniffed, "so follow my lead and try not to get us found out."

Miss Kala scoffed. "Yes, sir."

Stifling a twitch, she allowed Miss Kala to escort her through the gates and along the path into the main house.

A fleet of women in varying stages of pregnancy scrubbed, dusted, and polished the entrance hall. Daughters of Eden, distinguishable by their winged plaits, supervised the group, reciting a passage from Rebecca Northcote's teachings in eerie unison. Callie had memorized a few of her pamphlets in anticipation of their meeting, but didn't recognize this one. She felt the tension in Miss Kala's arm grow tighter and tighter the farther they delved into the house but did nothing to soothe her. If anything, Callie appreciated the pain.

"Welcome, Daughter! Welcome to Castleside!" Sister Juliet crowed from the landing of a wooden staircase in the small, square main hall. Sister Juliet bypassed Hiero and Tim to clasp hands with Callie and stare fiercely into her eyes. Callie had no trouble staring back, believing herself to be the equal, if not the better, of this formidable woman.

"Daughter." Callie infused her smile with maximum beatitude. "I have brought Her home."

"Oh, blessed day!" Sister Juliet's eyelids fluttered, though Callie saw no tears. "If only Mother Rebecca had lived to greet you herself."

"My dearest wish." Callie met and matched her fervent grip. She kept her face firmly in character, even when she felt Sister Juliet slip her thumb into her sleeve to trace the outline of her birthmark. "Though I feel I know her already and long to know more."

"Come, then." Sister Nora beckoned from behind. "Let us retire to a more private chamber." Callie didn't think she imagined the possessiveness of the hand she laid on Sister Juliet's shoulder as she steered her away. A glance at Hiero confirmed he had seen it too. "This is Father Coscarelli, Mrs. Sandringham's guardian and spiritual advisor, and this is…"

She did a little hop, as if noticing Miss Kala for the first time. "Shahida Kala."

"She keeps me." Callie patted Miss Kala's hand and beamed her a fond look. "I can't do without her."

Sister Juliet saved the awkward moment that followed. "Welcome to you both."

"And this is Mr. Kipling," Sister Nora continued, "who—"

"—wishes to donate to your most worthy cause." Tim pushed into Sister Juliet's personal space, forcing her to let go of Callie. "My wife and I have prayed for many years, but the Good Lord has denied us a share in his bounty. We turn now to the Mother's grace. We want to open our home to an orphan child."

Callie smelled both Daughters' ears burning at the mention of a donation *and* an adoption.

"The favor of a godly man is like manna from heaven," Sister Juliet complimented as Sister Nora herded them down a side corridor. "May I ask how you came to hear of us?"

"Lady Westlake sings your praises nightly. And Lady Cirencester has thrice pressed us to attend your Sunday sermon. My wife, as you may know, is her youngest sister."

By the radiance that overtook her face, Sister Juliet did know. Callie marveled at the deftness with which Tim dropped society names, and well-chosen ones at that. The Duke of Cirencester held so much power and influence no one would dare question him on whether "Mr. Kipling" was a relation, and everyone who knew anyone knew his youngest sister was barren. The lady in question was infamous for her quest to conceive, in her desperation poisoning herself with the latest elixirs and tonics and wearying her health with quack procedures. More significantly, her father had invested a sum in the five percents for her that yielded a thousand pounds a year.

Callie found her nauseating and avoided her company at all costs. Which was the general consensus, and why none of the

Daughters would question her absence. If anything, they would coddle Mr. Kipling all the more.

As evidenced by Sister Juliet linking arms with Tim and turning him back in the direction they had come. The smile she beamed at him could have melted the Thames in February. Tim blushed—an honest response, Callie thought—and gazed at her quizzically. Callie saw Hiero tense, but he stopped himself from intervening.

"Dear Nora, perhaps you should give our new guests a tour of the grounds while Mr. Kipling and I conduct our business." She extended her free hand toward Callie, who didn't move to meet her. "Then I can devote myself to you completely, Miss Sandringham."

"Mrs.," Callie corrected. "For I, like the Mother before me, gave myself faithfully to the Lord's sacrament when called upon."

"Mrs. Sandringham," Sister Juliet amended with a silken tongue. "Observe for yourself our good works. I am certain you will find a place here." Callie fought to keep her skepticism from her face. "Sister Nora will be your guide. I'll join you shortly."

With that, Sister Juliet steered Tim toward the front of the house, disappearing around a sharp bend. A long stunned silence ensued, during which Callie prepared for act two of their infiltration. She listened for one of Hiero's nonverbal cues instructing her on how to proceed, but none came.

"Well," Sister Nora sighed, not quite hiding her resignation. "Shall we begin where all things began?"

"In the garden?" Callie asked.

"Precisely."

Hiero had never been surrounded by so many women, let alone so many women with child. The effect was somewhat unnerving, as if he'd stepped into some sort of breeding factory. Which, he supposed, was not far from the truth. The few factory workers he'd known had the same pinched, determined expressions as the Daughters of Eden's charges, aware of the precariousness of their place in the world and desperate not to fall into further disgrace. A feeling he knew all too well.

From the moment he'd crossed through the gate, Hiero caged away the impulse to roust the loony Daughters and take their charges under his wing. To hold them not under the banner of heaven but under his proper management and care. Or, rather, the proper management and care of someone qualified. But Hiero had long ago reckoned with reality that he could not save every miserable soul in London, only the few fate and circumstance dropped into his lap. Such as one Timothy Kipling Stoker, whose state of being he was doing everything in his power not to think about. Better to channel his empathy into his performance, that of the virtuous shepherd.

As Sister Nora guided them deeper into the house, they passed an inordinate amount of closed rooms. The decor consisted of so many wooden crosses that Hiero would have been forgiven for thinking himself in a pauper's graveyard. A haunting silence reigned until they passed a short offshoot of the main corridor, at the end of which loomed a black door.

Bestial keens and wails roared from a woman within. The dull chant of communal prayer fought to drown her out. Hiero swallowed dryly, kept his gaze forward. The squeal of hinges; the clang of shackles; the crash of a projectile shattering on the wall. His scared rabbit heart thumped double time. A cry ripped through the door, up his spine, spiking the base of his skull—

"Exorcism?" Miss Kala asked, and suddenly he could breathe again.

"Birthing room," Sister Nora explained. "Not long now. Perhaps Mr. Kipling will be able to meet his new son or daughter this very day."

Hiero wondered what dear Mr. Kipling would think of him

rescuing mother and child from this damnable place. He might not be able to save them all, but he could play his part.

"But that is the end of a novitiate's journey, and I promised you the beginning." Sister Nora glanced over her shoulder, offering them a shy smile.

Not a natural deceiver, Hiero thought.

"What happens to 'em once the pea's out of the pod?" Miss Kala queried.

"Most have places to return to or prefer to continue on in service. When they first come to us, we encourage them to secure a letter of recommendation from their employers. Of course, that's not always possible. But those parishioners who cannot adopt often help our girls find a place."

"Anything to 'scape the workhouse."

"We'd keep them on, if that was their only option. But as you'll see, our girls leave here well-trained in most essential skills."

They segued from the tomblike corridor into a conservatory awash in springtime sun. A circle of women in the last stages of pregnancy knitted scarves, hats, jumpers, or hand-warmers in drab colors, their busy hands propped atop their bellies. Completed pieces were folded and dropped into baskets at their sides. The dizzying swing and sway of their rocking chairs forced Hiero to look away, out across the lawn, where another crew of women hung bed linens the size of ship sails to dry.

An aroma rich as any Parisian perfume lured Hiero around a bend, where a row of meat pies cooled on the sill of an open window. The clink and bustle of an active kitchen drew him closer. He poked his head around to watch a baker's dozen Daughters and novitiates prepare the evening meal. A peach-cheeked girl rolling out a ball of dough spotted him; he performed a quick sign of the cross over the pies, then scooted off to rejoin his party. He found them out on the lawn, heading toward a fieldstone fence so wide it blocked off the back half of the compound.

"You've certainly taken the dictum about idle hands to heart," he commented upon his return.

"As Mother Rebecca wrote, 'The sinner lit by new life shall be cleansed by godly deeds and industry.' Rehabilitation is the only way forward for the fallen. Our aim is to scrub every soul that comes into our care."

"Ol' Liz Gaskell had the same idea." At Callie's sharp look, Miss Kala squawked, "What? I read!"

"*Ruth* was a great inspiration to Mother Rebecca and continues to inspire us all," Sister Nora agreed. "There's a signed copy in her library."

"Ah!" Hiero felt a revelation coming on. "In her box."

Sister Nora let out a nervy laugh. "Oh, no, Father. The library is far too extensive to fit in her box. That contains only the most sacred, secret texts."

"Then you have seen these marvels with your own eyes?"

"Sister Juliet has." A wistful look overtook her sweet face. "Mother Rebecca is her aunt, you know. She was there at the very beginning, the day she sealed the box. It hasn't been opened since."

Hiero would wager every drop of his favorite tipple, past and future, that this was not the case. But prophecies, even the messianic drivel Rebecca Northcote peddled, couldn't be sold on air alone, and so somewhere there was a box full of nothing, or nonsense, waiting for his idle hands to crack the lid and expose it to the world. His fingers itched at the prospect.

Callie stopped, her wide-eyed gaze reaching into the beyond.

"A not-so-distant day, of greatest joy, will see all locks sprung and all secrets out." She clutched her stomach, fingers tented to emphasize her womb. "When She is come, when She is come, when She is come..."

Sister Nora had gone the color of turned cream. Never one to miss a dramatic moment, Hiero sped to Callie's side, taking her hand and gripping her by the back of the neck.

"Mother?"

Callie gasped, blinked. With a sheepish smile, she said, "Forgive me. I never know…"

"You are the vessel," Sister Nora confirmed, a bronze shine of color returning to her face. "As foretold. It is time you walked the Garden."

A simple but sturdy wooden gate joined the two sides of the high fieldstone fence. Four silver padlocks, removed by those who'd entered that morning, slotted into hooks on the stone.

"Better guarded than me mum's garters," Miss Kala quipped as she passed.

Hiero followed the three women through the threshold into a new Arcadia. At least five acres stretched out before them, as lush and verdant as a fairy land. A blossoming orchard gave way to rows of growing vegetables. Hiero recognized cabbages, cauliflower, beets, carrots, and asparagus, rails of beans and vines of tomatoes, and he'd never so much as picked a berry in his life. Bushes of those gemlike fruits clustered by the roadside wall near a craggy ledge decorated with long, flat boxes of sprouting herbs. A small barn and chicken coop, hinting at a concealed second exit, lined an enclosed yard where poultry, geese, and pigs frolicked. A shallow noxious-smelling pit Hiero identified as compost had him tongue-kissing his handkerchief.

As buzzy as the bees that swarmed the pair of hives, the Daughters and their charges pollinated every row and copse. They tended to the budding plants through their fragile first trimester. The stout Daughter from the embankment oversaw the whole production from a potting shed, giving out tools and advice to the muddy-aproned girls who sought her out.

But just as in most fairy tales, the bucolic setting hid signs of an encroaching darkness. A line of spiky rosebushes formed a natural barrier between the practical and ornamental gardens. A serpentine path slinked through overgrown thatches of wildflowers. Benches carved from lightning-struck trees scattered the landscape. A moatlike brook pooled at the base of a hillock, then disappeared into a small cave, its entrance choked with reeds.

At the far end, shrouded in fog on a clear day, stood a tree of uncommon magnificence. Even Hiero caught his breath at first sight of it. Its lowest level of branches stretched out like arms yearning for an embrace. *Or to snatch you up,* he thought. Tiers of glossy leaves billowed up to a regal peak. The broad, solid bulk of its trunk brought to mind past lovers; the tufts of grass that skirted between its roots invited a midafternoon snooze.

From his first glimpse of this enchanted place, Hiero understood why the Daughters thought it holy, and just what they might do to protect it. It was indeed a tiny Eden.

Sister Juliet's office proved surprisingly ornate compared to the rest of the house. Wallpaper sporting a tree-and-apple motif sent a too-obvious message, in Tim's opinion, but its cheerful green and cream colors brightened the room. An elaborate sitting area tucked her small writing desk into the far corner, facing the wall. Divans upholstered in lush fabrics and pillows galore invited her guests to unburden themselves. A portrait of Sister Juliet with Rebecca Northcote hung in pride of place, perpendicular to the window to get the best light.

A larger portrait of the founding Daughters dominated the longest wall. Tim moved to examine it, recognizing only Mother Rebecca. By their style of dress, Tim dated the painting to the late 1840s—a fact he'd be sure to mention to Hiero later, ever the apt pupil.

"Are any of these fine ladies still with you?" Tim asked.

"Only two." Sister Juliet pointed to two of the younger-looking ladies. "Sister Marie returned to her family in France when she became too frail to carry on. Sister Eunice still teaches knitting, although Sister Violet has taken over the ledgers and scheduling the deliveries."

"Deliveries?"

"To the workhouses. Wool coats, hats, mitts, scarves. We don't believe in confinement, Mr. Kipling. Even those furthest along can be productive. Toward the end, that's knitting, sewing, crochet. Whatever we can't use for ourselves is donated to the poor souls not fortunate enough to be so cozily sent out into the world."

"Are all the children born here adopted?"

A look so morose as to be comical came over her elfin features. She clasped her hands to her chest, over her heart.

"That was the dream when I plighted my troth to our Mother. My part of her great work." With a sigh, she gestured to a loveseat. "Do sit. Tea?"

"Thank you."

She pulled a long gold rope hidden by the curtains, then stationed herself on the loveseat at hand-holding distance. The tactic might have worked on a different man. As it was, Tim could only think of the five tricks to convincing someone of your sincerity Hiero had once taught him.

"We've each of us had our particular revelations. The Mother spoke to Aunt Rebecca to prepare for her return. I continue that work in her stead, but my call was to provide for the children of the fallen. I believe them innocents, Mr. Kipling, longing for a place and a purpose."

Tim nodded to encourage her. "How can it be otherwise?"

"My belief exactly. What ends with a child begins with a father and a mother. But it is the women who are shunned, sacked, shoved into filthy laying-in houses, or forced to make the decision that is no decision at all. I came to understand that to lift the children up, their mothers must also be lifted up. And together we can all work to welcome the Mother back to a new Eden."

Tim admired how deftly she had skipped him down an alternate path to the destination of her choosing. He wondered if she was even aware she hadn't answered his question.

"And you find good homes for each and every child?"

Sister Juliet slid her hands toward him, stopping just short of touching his knees.

"Would that every day someone of your associations and character called on us, Mr. Kipling. Too few of your situation seek to open their homes to an orphan."

"You keep the rest here?"

"As many as we are able. The need is so great." She looked to the heavens, as if the answers were etched into the patterns on the embossed ceiling. "For every fallen girl who takes one of our beds, we turn away twenty. The garden provides for we Daughters, and so does selling our overstock at market, but we donate everything else to those in greater need. Spreading Mother Rebecca's good word is a business unto itself. And a vital one since it draws in faithful men like you. Tonight we will all sleep easier knowing the next child born will be safe and loved."

A shock of guilt punched Tim in the gut. Unlike Mr. Gregory Kipling, distant relation of Lord Cirencester, this child was not a fabrication. A living, breathing, squalling babe might push into the world that very evening with the expectation of being welcomed by a caring family. Who was he to promise everything, then turn his back on a little baby?

But all children born had the same expectation. A walk down any street in London sobered one to how many were forgotten, neglected, abused, forced to work till their bones didn't grow right, destined to starve from the second they took to their mother's dried-up breast. Most orphan asylums turned away any child not lawfully begotten, which left fallen women with even fewer options.

Still, these Daughters promised much, but what did they actually deliver? The Winterbourne boy, more fortunate than most, had a father willing to pay for his comfort. But where was he now? What had Sister Juliet and her apostles done with him once he'd lost his silver spoon? To say nothing of Mrs. Pankhurst, whom the

Daughters were likely persuading to donate all her monies, jewels, and worldly goods as Tim and Sister Juliet conversed.

Tim woke from his musings to the realization the tea had arrived. He muttered out his number of lumps, adjusting his strategy. The sizeable donation, more than a month's salary, that Han had entrusted to him to bait her sat heavy in his inner pocket. A potent lure, but could he bring himself to give it over, even to secure himself a second interview? Could he stomach adding to the Daughters' wealth when it might cost a child?

After accepting a cup from Sister Juliet, he took a long sip of his tea. Tim wished some part, any part of this case held easy answers.

"Who's this you've brought us, Sister Nora?"

The stout Daughter rushed over to greet them, already reaching for Callie and Miss Kala. She clasped them both by the hands, forming an impromptu circle. Hiero made note of the Daughters' tactile natures, a maneuver most often deployed by swindlers. Especially effective among the British, who tended toward aloofness. A few maternal pinches and pats, and even the haughtiest man would surrender his wallet. Not that Hiero had any experience of that...

"In't you a pretty one," the Daughter cooed to Miss Kala. "All that lovely hair. You'll fit right in. And you!" Callie lurched forward as the Daughter tugged her in to, yes, pinch her cheek. "A princess! And, like one, needs fattening up. You'll eat your fill here, m'lady, I promise you."

"Sister Emerald is our head cook and tends the growing part of the Garden," Sister Nora explained.

"Oh, don't listen to her 'Sister' nonsense. Call me Merry."

Hiero didn't miss Sister Nora's pinched mouth as she made the introductions.

"This place is so familiar," Callie dreamily commented, wandering off to admire a dense square of cornstalks. "I feel Her in every leaf and branch budding on the vines..."

Sister Merry chuckled. "Well, Sister Juliet's got her prophecies and Sister Zanna her healing, but I say this is the Mother's true work. You don't get any closer to Eden than in tending Her garden."

"Where once She fell, She'll grow anew..." Callie caressed one of the long, waxy leaves.

"... and make a heaven on Earth." Sister Nora completed the Rebecca Northcote quote.

Sister Merry winked at them. "With a little help from Her most faithful."

Exasperated, Hiero sought to steer the conversation elsewhere. "Your commitment to service in the Mother's name is admirable. Tell me, are all your novitiates put to work?"

Sister Nora nodded. "Mother Rebecca held we are all equal before her eyes. Rich and poor, man and woman. Even those whose hearts are closed to her message will have a place in the garden when She returns."

"An afternoon scrubbing pans or mucking out the pigs usually does the trick," Sister Merry seconded.

"No strangers to hard work here." Miss Kala leaned in to Sister Merry, fast friends. "My mistress gets so bored with mistressing she'll shuck her skirt and clean the chimneys. She swoons over dusting to the point I've given up! Once I found her ironing shirts in the wee hours, and her husband not a week passed."

"Oh, the dear! Even while she's in the pudding club?"

Miss Kala opened her mouth to speak but slyly swallowed her reply. Stunned by the implications of this, the Daughters shared a look. Hiero could have applauded. For all her cheer and bluster, Miss Kala was a docksider through and through and knew how to sell a trick. As plainspoken interpreter of Callie's high theatrics, she may very well prove to be their secret weapon.

"Where has Mrs. Sandringham gone?" Hiero asked. The three

women gasped at Callie's disappearance.

Unworried since he'd seen her slip down a row of corn—probably for some peace and quiet—Hiero snuck into the potting shed and stole a few fortifying sips from the flask hidden in his robes. A glance around revealed nothing of note. Boxes of gardening tools and bags of seeds warred for space. Hiero rested his flask beside a padlocked chest on the nearest shelf, then quickly snatched it back when he spied the skull and crossbones painted on its lid.

The treacle-sweet smell of the enclosed space had him gagging. Awash with pride at his investigative skills, he scampered out... right into the chest of one of the giants Jack must have summoned down the Beanstalk. Or perhaps one of the Jills among the Daughters.

"'ullo, Father." The giant smiled, peering down at him through the clouds.

Himself a tall man, Hiero had met few outside the odd carnival act who dwarfed him. He wondered at the giant's presence here. Muscle? Guardian? Stud? Surely prim Sister Nora had something to say about such a powerful man living among them.

"Good day, my son. And who might you be?"

"Not your son." A look of bewilderment wrinkled his bushy brows. "My dad's dead."

That's when Hiero noticed the scar slashing across his forehead. He took a step back, poorly stifling a shiver. For the second time that day, a shadow passed over his grave. Or, rather, the grave of the man he'd buried long ago.

"Don't mind our Amos, Father," Sister Merry reassured him, hurrying to intervene. "Back to your saplings, Amos, and don't bother the padre no more." She shooed him off with a fond sigh. "My brother. Number thirteen of seventeen, and the devil's never let him forget it. He's had his troubles, but I'm keeping him on the righteous path."

"He lives here?"

"With me, yes, in the farmhouse. Tends the other side of the garden, well away from everyone." She kept her smile, but the light had gone from her eyes. "He'll be no bother to your Mrs. Sandring-ham."

Hiero didn't have to feign sympathy for this woman and the life she must have led before finding sanctuary here. A reminder to him that while the Daughters as a collective needed to be scorched, some members would need help rising from the ashes.

"Our Lord's mysteries are as infinite as our Mother's compassion."

"Amen." Her inner spark flickered back to life. "You'll be wanting to follow Amos through the roses. He knows the safest path. They've gone to pray at the Tree of Wisdom."

Hiero hardly needed to ask which tree this was, but, as he bowed in farewell, he considered whether he should join them or do a bit of snooping. They had yet to locate Lillian, for one, and—

A scream ripped through the air.

Tim scrounged the recesses of his brain for yet another way to ask what happened to the babies not placed with adoptive families. *If any truly are,* he reminded himself. Sister Juliet had expounded on how they chose the fallen women they took in (an "aura of purity" Tim suspected was the sheen of a hefty donation), how they evaluated each babe for signs of being the Messiah (the "pull of the Mother" within her and a splash of holy water), and listed off a string of patrons any politician would envy. The only thing she'd managed to convince Tim of was the true epidemic of London was highborn men raping their household staff. Hardly a revelation.

"Your wife," Sister Juliet prompted.

"Hmm?"

"She did not accompany you today."

"Ah, no. Forgive me. She did not." Time for some confabulation of his own. "I fear my Claire has become disheartened by the whole endeavor. This is not our first attempt at adoption. We sponsored a girl introduced to us through an acquaintance we thought trustworthy, only to have her disappear with the child—well, her child, to be fair—and her final allowance at the last moment. We've toured local orphan asylums, but these are..."

"Sordid places."

"Yes. And one never knows the provenance..."

She rested a hand on his shoulder. "Of course not."

"Claire has convinced herself she will be content to play aunt to our nieces and nephews. But I know her, and I know myself." Hiero had suggested that last line. Its effect on Sister Juliet boosted Tim's confidence. "When Lady Westlake took up our cause, it was the first time in months I'd allowed myself to hope."

"The Mother's work in motion."

"Amen to that."

Tim inhaled a shuddery breath, only half performance. "But hearing you speak, I feel moved to offer more. So many children in need. So many Claire and I could help beyond the one or two adoptions." He fixed her with his most ardent look, turning one of her cheats against her. "Tell me... where do you send the children now?"

He saw her stiffen, force her smile to widen.

"Mr. Kipling, I fear no answer will satisfy someone as devout as you."

"'The one who speaks the truth from their heart utters no slander,'" he quoted. "How can I be of service to these children if I do not know their circumstances?"

With a sigh, she twined her hands in her lap and shut her eyes. Tim had never had a suspect deflect by praying before. Part of him was tickled, excited to share the story with the team. After what felt like several eternities, Sister Juliet set her gaze on him, decided.

A shriek that could flay the skin from his face echoed through the house.

Chapter 6

*H*e lay in a nest of branches, under a blanket of petals and leaves. His shock of red hair stood out against the dark wood, a lick of flame that failed to spark the kindling. Cheeks sunk and limbs lank, neglect had stolen his cherubic plumpness. The cleft in his prominent chin had grown to a hollow. The tattered shift he'd been shrouded in looked no better than a piece of burlap, stained and coarse. Tim kept staring at his little blue lips, parted in a cry no one would ever hear.

Winter born. Gone by spring.

The Daughters encircled him from a respectable distance, praying and weeping. Hiero leaned against the trunk of the massive tree under which the babe had been laid to rest, cradled between two gnarled roots. His black eyes, whose twinkle Tim so often sought out for reassurance, were dull and vacant. Callie and Miss Kala held tight to each other, unable to mask their horror.

He'd barely begun work on his case, and still he'd taken too long. Though it was impossible to say without further investigation how long the boy had been dead, or whose child he was, Tim's heart knew this was Sir Hugh's son. Just as he knew he would avenge his murder with the fiery justice of the Archangel Michael, whoever he proved to be.

"Let me through!" One of the Daughters pushed through the novitiates gathered around the base of the small hill from which the tree sprouted. Her beaked nose and gray, wing-plaited hair gave her a falconlike quality. She flew up to join the other Daughters with, to Tim's surprise, a medical bag in tow.

She moved past the prayer circle, crouching before the body. Before Tim could intervene, Sister Juliet knelt beside her, barring her from opening her bag with a patient hand.

"Zanna, don't disturb him."

"He might be frozen from the cold. There might be a chance."

"He doesn't have a chill!" a stout woman barked. One of the others fell to her knees, sobbing. "And no one is to touch him. I'll have Amos fetch the constable."

"No," Sister Juliet announced in that ethereal way of hers. "He's with his Mother now. Let us sing him to his final rest and give him to the ground." The other Daughters murmured in agreement, save Sister Zanna.

"He needs to be examined," she insisted.

"He's beyond earthly cares." Sister Juliet stood on one of the roots to better be seen. "As the prophet said, 'A child lost to the world is one gained by heaven.' We've known our share of loss here. Whoever cared for this little one had it right when she brought him to the tree. Let him be buried, and so to his eternal rest."

His warrant card burning a hole in his pocket, Tim looked to Callie, who shrugged, and to Hiero, who shook his head. Unaccustomed to the shock of such an incident, their powers of deduction and persuasion had abandoned them. He thought of the boy, who'd been robbed of a better life by one of the wolves in holy white uniforms, and knew his mind.

"I'm afraid that won't be possible." All eyes turned to him as he lifted his warrant card for all to see. Tim heard Hiero's sigh of exasperation as he breached the Daughters' circle. "My name is Detective Inspector Timothy Stoker of Scotland Yard, and I declare this a crime scene."

Panicked chatter erupted among the Daughters, silenced with a whistle by the stout one. They retreated down the hill to give Tim the stage. Sister Juliet glared at him with unbridled fury.

"Serpent," she hissed.

"Save your harsh words for the one who did this," Tim chided.

Sister Nora hastened to intervene. "DI Stoker, what a blessing. One might almost see the Mother's hand in it. You being here just as..." She shut her mouth to steady her quavering voice, then continued. "May I ask why you've come to us now?"

"Investigating another matter. That's all I'm at liberty to say." He didn't miss the whispers, a ghostly chorus behind him. He gestured Sisters Nora and Juliet to the side for a more private interview. "I understand you are not eager to draw this kind of attention to yourselves. Neither am I inclined to see my case overlooked for this dark business. Therefore I propose a truce."

Sister Juliet scoffed. "As the prophet said, 'The righteousness of our cause shines brighter than all the world's sorrows.'"

"Need I remind you of the strange case of Margaret Waters? Given what I've seen so far of your practices, I wouldn't be so quick to flaunt your reputation."

Sister Nora gasped. "Our mission is to serve the women who find shelter among us *and* the babes born here."

"Which I'm certain my investigation will bear out," Tim reassured her. "If I'm given free rein to conduct it. In exchange, I swear the murderer or murderers alone will be brought to justice, and not one word will be spoken by me to my superiors or written in the press against your good works."

"M-murderer?" Sister Nora hugged her arms. "But surely..."

"Someone meant for this babe to be found, whether as a message or a warning," Tim said for all to hear, sending one of his own. He dropped his volume to add, "It serves our interests to keep this matter private. You would not, after all, wish for a child-murderer to walk free among you?"

This sobered them.

"No," Sister Nora confirmed. "Especially not now…" She flicked her eyes to Callie, who had joined the Daughters' new prayer circle.

"Then we are agreed?"

"For now." Sister Juliet invaded his space, her icy blue eyes spearing him through. "But beware, serpent. The Mother won't fall for your tricks a second time."

"I rather think she'll be too preoccupied with yours to bother." Tim met her intimidation with steel of his own. "No one leaves the premises until I've concluded preliminary interviews. And you'd best appoint me a chaperone. Being a serpent, I know all the tricks."

An all-too-familiar clearing of the throat set Tim's nerves on edge. Before he could decide how to react, Hiero insinuated himself into their group.

"Your pardon." He performed a little bow. "But I could not help but overhear your deliberations. If *Signore*…"

"Stoker," Tim grunted.

"If the inspector requires assistance in this matter, I would be most happy to oblige."

"Kind of you to offer, Father," Tim said through gritted teeth, "but I have my own man."

"I hope you aren't considering leaving these two alone with any of the girls." Sister Zanna rose from her crouching position by the body to object. "They've suffered the attentions of enough strange men, or have you forgotten our purpose here?"

"She's quite right, Father." Sister Juliet turned her frigid smile on Hiero. "Our novitiates have sought sanctuary here from the world of men. They will be intimidated enough being questioned by DI Stoker, let alone…"

"Under the seal of the confessional?" Hiero mirrored the gesture Sister Juliet had used when greeting Callie, but to such subtle effect Tim doubted she even noticed. "You forget, my child, that anything said to me in confidence cannot be repeated. And is immediately absolved, through the Mother's grace. I have not been living here among you, so I am not party to the politics the way one of your Daughters might be if she were to chaperone. Whatever secrets are revealed will be for our ears alone."

To Tim's surprise, Sister Nora hastened to agree.

"This may be the best course of action for the innocent," she counseled. "They will be on the premises—"

"Skulking about," Sister Zanna countered. "Wherever and whenever they choose."

"Their movements can be monitored."

"This is our sanctuary."

"And this is our time." Sister Nora's limpid brown eyes made their final appeal. "*She* is so near to us. We can't have her arrival sullied by suspicion, false accusations…"

"Or those who wish you harm," Hiero darkly added. Tim stifled a groan. "If there is one among you who has committed such an act… I cannot allow Miss Sandringham to remain here while danger lurks, hidden but on the hunt."

Spooked, Sister Juliet turned to Tim.

"You think someone wishes us harm? Has done this to…"

"I cannot say for certain," Tim replied, considering his words as he spoke them. "But know this. If there is a snake among you, it is no man. The body is too withered to have been a recent death. The good Father and I have been watched from the moment we entered the compound. The killer must be among you."

"From a woman this child was born," Hiero echoed, "and by a woman's hand he died."

Tim almost chuckled at the shiver that ran through them all. Few could resist the effects of Hiero's dramatic pronouncements; he certainly couldn't.

Sister Juliet shut her eyes, glided over to the base of the tree as if guided by a divine presence. She pressed her palms into the aged wood, bent her head. They waited, rapt, for her to emerge—all but

Callie, who looked to the sky, arms open wide.

"Very well," they said in eerie unison. "Cut this serpent out and squeeze the blood from its heart."

Hiero drew Callie and Shahida aside, away from Sister Nora's prying ears, while the Daughters closed ranks. Kip had instructed them to gather on the lawn and take roll, accounting for every one of the compound's residents in case someone had fled. By the tension in Kip's jaw and shoulders, Hiero saw he already felt the weight of his burden as sole investigator. Even one as indifferent to city crimes as he knew that normally a team would be assigned to a case involving so many suspects and such expansive grounds. But for reasons of his own—reasons Hiero would wheedle out of him by day's end—Kip had chosen not to consult his Yard colleagues. Hiero quietly vowed to support him in every way he could.

"You will not keep me out of this," Callie insisted, though her face remained contorted in a semblance of beatitude.

"Oh, we're up to our necks in it," Shahida scoffed, "and it reeks. Let's grab ol' Lil and be gone."

"As soon as we spot her, you're free to do just that." Callie fixed Hiero with her sternest glare. "I'm staying."

"As well you should," he agreed. "Don't spoil our dear Kip's fun, but this murderer won't be outed through interrogations. Where there's silence, there's conspiracy, and where there's conspiracy..."

"There's some unhappy snot willing to blab."

Hiero flinched at Shahida's blunt way with words, but he couldn't disagree. "Infiltrate. Insinuate. Gather information. Other *I* words." He couldn't resist a scapegrace grin at Callie's sigh of frustration. "You must do what we cannot: learn their deepest secrets."

"What they'll only share with their best gals."

"And those they'll take to the grave."

Callie nodded, mollified. "Find me afterward."

"In the infirmary. With Sister Zanna." Hiero gave their hands a squeeze before shooing them off. "A sharp pain in your side, I think, around... five o'clock?"

He heard Shahida cackle, "Is he always this crafty?" as he wandered back toward Kip.

A few of the Daughters waited for Callie and Shahida at the bottom of the hill, including their escort, Sister Nora. Hiero watched them flutter across the grass, a flock of doves in mourning formation. He found his flask again, took a bracing gulp. Offered it blindly to Kip, as yet unable to turn back in the direction of the body. Instead he contemplated this second Eden, once again spoiled by... well, that was the question. Hiero had known darkness, true darkness, in his time, but this monstrous act scrambled the order of things in his already scrambled mind.

A soft press to the small of his back startled him.

"If you'd prefer not to linger," Kip murmured, "I can manage this part alone."

Hiero took a final sip, then stowed his flask. "Not your first, I take it?"

"No. Nor the worst I've seen."

That sent Hiero's thoughts spiraling down deeper and danker wells of possibility. He struggled to keep his head above the surface. He'd never before considered what Kip might have witnessed in his line of work, or what it might have cost him.

Kip exhaled a long breath. "The killer, or whoever staged the body—I'm not convinced they are one and the same—thinks of the babe with a certain reverence—"

"Reverence!"

"Yes. The makeshift bed, the petals, the location... They wanted to pretty it up. To lay the babe to rest where it will be sheltered, its soul cared for. This was no sacrifice to an unconventional god."

"You think his death was unexpected?"

"It's possible." With a patient nudge, he guided Hiero back to the boy. With Kip at his side, he found the courage to confront the body anew. "There are signs of severe neglect. Starvation, unsanitary conditions. But given how our city treats its poor…"

"That in itself is not evidence of murder."

"No. But this scarring around his neck is." Hiero followed Kip's hand—a man's hand, large and thick—remembered how gentle it could be. Tried to ignore the direction in which it pointed. "A cloth or some kind of kerchief, cinched."

"To stop him wailing." Hiero shut his eyes, wished he could shut the information out of his brain.

"Normally consistent with an impulse killing. However…" Kip sighed. "What do you know of baby farming?"

"As little as possible. Aim to keep it that way."

"If only there were a way to test…" Kip scrutinized every detail of the scene, his green eyes shining with compassion. For the little one, for the shell-shocked Daughters earlier, for Hiero when he shied away. "Really, you don't have to stay. Take advantage of their distraction to find Mrs. Pankhurst and make a swift retreat. Having her near this would only compromise things further."

Though Hiero knew Kip only meant to excuse him from an upsetting situation, the suggestion stung.

"Might the babe's death be related to your original case?"

To his credit, Kip didn't lie. "I won't be certain until I can identify him, but… I suspect yes. It's too much of a coincidence."

"You were searching for this boy on someone's behalf?"

Kip huffed in annoyance. "You know I can't say."

"I know you would be rid of us." Hiero straightened his posture as he moved toward him, for the first time deploying the difference in their heights against him. "That you refuse to confide in us. What defies my own admittedly inferior deductive skills is why?"

"My client—"

Hiero waved away his excuses. "Do you really think us so incapable of keeping his secret?"

He saw the moment Kip's expression flipped from understanding to anger. "On the contrary. I am intimately acquainted with your ability to obfuscate and... and adorn yourself in an armor of half truths. Baring not a peek of skin." Hiero adjusted his collar, which had grown scratchy and hot. "But my client is not a man to be trifled with, and this, as you can well see, is no longer a trifling matter."

"How noble," Hiero quipped in his most mocking tone. "You mean to protect us by shooing us away."

"I mean to avenge this child's death, no matter who he is." His green eyes flashed with defiance. "Given that, in my dallying, I could not prevent it."

That statement salved over much of Hiero's irritation. Of course Kip would see this as his failure, not the work of a twisted mind. Hiero hadn't missed his Kip's tendency toward self-persecution. Why stick to flagellation when a hair shirt doubled your torment? He was surprised Kip hadn't contrived a way to pluck out his own fingernails.

"This babe's destiny was writ long before you took on the case."

Kip scoffed. "Finally found religion, have you?"

"Call it divine intuition." After a quick glance around to assure they were not observed, Hiero slid a hand around the nape of Kip's neck, kneading at the knot of tension that always coiled there. "Wait! The goddess sends another message. Oh, yes..." He was relieved when Kip met and matched his smirk. "You won't solve anything without our help."

"Oh? How so?"

"My dear Kip, how has one of your vast and deep intelligence missed the fact that we are the feather against which your heart is weighed? The jam to your clotted cream. The Albert to your Victoria. The Marlowe to your Shakespeare..."

"You're silky, tangy, and will die young?"

Hiero gave a lock of his hair a sharp tug. "We balance the scales."

"Ah." Kip considered this. "I don't see."

"You will."

Kip chuckled. "In any case, it's clear I won't be rid of you."

Hiero gazed down into his pale, freckled face, marveling once again at how someone so unremarkable could stir such wild emotion in him. The impulse to peel back his own layers—of clothing, of skin, of secrets upon secrets upon secrets—tugged hard at his heart. But would Kip still hold him in soft regard once exposed to Hiero's skittish, shriveled core? He was not the only one who had yet to prove himself.

"Perish the thought." Hiero remembered where they were, took a step back. "Now how do we go about our vengeance? Callie awaits our—or rather, your—deductions."

"Quite." Kip confronted the scene anew. He picked up a fallen branch still heavy with leaves, circled around the body. With a sweeping motion, he brushed some of the petal blanket off one side, careful not to disturb the ground beneath. He frowned when this revealed nothing but grass. "Tell me how he was discovered. Were you present?"

"Chatting with Sister Merry and her brother by the garden shed. The ladies had gone ahead with Sister Nora. I believe it was Miss Kala who first sounded the alarm."

Kip looked up at this. "They permit a man to reside on the property?"

"He's not..." Hiero wiggled his fingers to mask his shudder. He thought of Brother Amos's scar and felt the strange urge to cross himself. "He's known some hardship. He's no rooster in the henhouse."

Kip's brow crinkled. "It's unlike you to trust someone so readily."

"I would be more suspicious if there were anyone there to suspect."

"How do you mean?"

"I mean it's rather more complicated."

Kip inhaled a breath as if to query him further, then thought better of it. His incisive gaze bore into Hiero, waiting, watching. Learning him in a way that had never felt uncomfortable before.

"What have you found?" Hiero asked in a bald attempt to divert him.

To his surprise, Kip smiled. "This." He reached down to pluck something out of the debris surrounding the body.

A paper wing.

Hiero crouched beside Kip as he cupped it in his hands. Someone had taken great care in folding and decorating the little wing, on which was inscribed *B371DOE-M-01-10-74*. A metal clasp punctured one of the edges, around which looped a few threads of blue yarn. They found its match tied around the babe's wrist.

"Was he catalogued in some way?" Hiero wondered aloud.

Kip nodded. "A standard classification system. Baby number 371, Daughters of Eden, male, born January 10th, 1874."

"Not politic, I suppose, to paint the names of the child's parents for everyone to see."

"Or his origins were of no consequence." Kip tucked the wing into an inner pocket, then delicately slid the thread over the boy's tiny fist. Hiero once again had to look away. "In our interview I thrice pressed Sister Juliet on what becomes of the children no one cares to adopt. She evaded each time."

"You think they shuttle them off to local orphan asylums despite their claims?"

At Kip's long pause, Hiero's heart sank. "Perhaps." He patted Hiero on the leg, resumed his sweeping.

"You must be all a-tremble at the chance to rifle through Sister Juliet's ledgers," Hiero quipped in a vain attempt to reinvigorate himself.

"I rather think Sister Nora mans the books, don't you?"

"I trust your instincts as a renowned paper-sniffer. You know I have no affinity for organization."

"You forget," Kip teased as he cleared the last of the leaves and petals. "I've seen your closet."

"Yes, well, every collection of *objets d'art* needs a curator."

"Curator, artist, and muse, in one svelte package. Remarkable."

Hiero stood, stared down at the sylphlike babe, a caterpillar crushed in its chrysalis. While he appreciated Kip's efforts to cheer him, everything felt wrong about flirting over a corpse. He thought of Ting, his little bun-headed sprite, and how desperate a pregnant Jie had been when Han first happened upon her. What might have become of them and Angus if Hiero hadn't been so drunk with grief that Han went out to consult a healer friend in Limehouse and came back with the small family?

He saw them every day as he travelled around the city, children who had escaped a similar fate, only to be condemned to a life of extreme poverty. Women of lower means than the servants the Daughters sheltered, cast out by families who could barely scrape by, begging to stay out of the workhouse or selling themselves until they began to show. If they didn't throw themselves in the river. He blocked out their voices, their gaunt, pleading faces and wounded eyes, because he couldn't save everyone. Because he'd only just clawed his way out of the muck.

But this little one... Hiero would amplify his voice into a scream heard round the compound, if not London entire. He would do everything in his power to see he rested in peace.

"Perhaps we should give him a name."

Kip glanced up from his work. "A name?"

"Between us. When we discuss him, as we must. It won't do to refer to him as B371."

"No, I see," Kip said. Hiero wanted to shrink away from the

kindness that lit his face. "I only wonder if his parents might object."

"They are hardly present and accounted for."

"His mother has fled, true, but his father... Well, if he proves to be his father."

"And who's that now?"

Kip chuckled. "Still not telling, clever boy." He appeared to give the matter some thought. "How about... Little Bean? He rather looks like one."

"I suppose Ginger Curls would rather give the game away." Hiero tried to laugh, but it caught in his throat. "Forgive my ignorance, but what will become of him once..."

"A potent question." Kip surveyed the area as if the trees had ears. "I don't care to surrender him to the Daughters or see him buried here, in the place that wronged him. If this is indeed my client's child..."

"He'll want some say in where he sleeps."

"But where to keep him in the meantime? And can we sneak him out without upsetting the Daughters?"

"We must call upon a higher power." Hiero moved to the summit of the hill, let out a series of long, low whistles.

A few minutes later, Han dropped in over the edge of the closest wall.

Chapter 7

A kick to her ankle woke Callie with a start. The discordant screech of a hymn—the Daughters were no Viennese choir—helped smack her into the present. Head still dropped as if in deep reflection, she surreptitiously glanced around the Daughters' shrine. For hours they had been praying the murdered babe's soul up to heaven, watched over by an enormous unbecoming portrait of Rebecca Northcote and the lump of coal that was her fabled box. Callie had endured reading after reading from Mother Rebecca's inane prophecies, recitations of her twist-tongue prayers, and testimonials. Testimonials about the life of a baby! She'd chewed the inside of both her cheeks raw from boredom.

And all this while stuffed into a small front pew beside Miss Kala, whose curvy body proved to be a pillow-soft incubator and whose perfume reminded Callie of the floral soap Jie used on the bed linens. Little wonder she'd sailed off to dreamland.

The hymn ended with a sour note on the organ. Sister Juliet, who some of the Daughters cleaved to like pups at the teat, rose to speak once more. Callie knew she should take this opportunity to display some of her character's "powers," but the will to live had been drained out of her by the endless dirge of mourning. Better to devise some means of escape.

A glance at Miss Kala revealed her to be pert as a march hare. She listened, rapt, to Sister Juliet's every word, the smile that stretched her face so sickeningly infectious Callie repressed the urge to spit. With nowhere to stow a pocket watch, she couldn't guess at the time; sneaking a hand into Miss Kala's skirts would be, at best, misinterpreted. Too many pairs of eyes strayed in her direction, curious about the newcomer, for Callie to get away with sticking a finger down her throat. A bit of vomit always expedited things.

When they raised their voices in some bizarre chant, Callie used the moment to curse Tim for keeping her out of the investigation, curse Hiero for inventing this absurd part for her to play, curse Han for forcing his pet Miss Kala on her, and, most of all, curse herself for convincing them her infiltration of the Daughters was a good idea in the first place. Instead of hunting down their very first murderer, and of a child no less, she'd stuck her hand in a basket of asps too stupid to bite her.

Anger roiled in her stomach, which reminded her she had not eaten since breakfast. Hiero had taught her to harness whatever emotion she was feeling toward her performance, so she repeated this litany of curses over and over. Thought of these fiends who'd kidnapped her mother. Tim's look of relief as she left the crime scene. Han's hand on Miss Kala's arm. The women she met that day, forced into these circumstances by laws and the hypocrisy of men, shunned and maltreated and ostracized till they bore their bastards—

She lurched forward, coughing. Acid scorched her mouth. With a moan, she fell to her knees, retching. A dozen hands reached for her; Miss Kala barked them away. Callie cowered against her, surprised by the strength with which she was lifted, supported, the diminutive Miss Kala acting as a crutch all the way into a private examination room in the infirmary.

Sister Zanna ordered her to lie down, tea and a compress fetched. Dimmed the lights, then set off to gather a few supplies. The door latch clicked, locked. Callie didn't care about being imprisoned so long as she was, blessedly, alone. After a few deep breaths, she stretched, sat up.

And found Miss Kala beaming at her with something like glee from her post at the bottom of the cot.

"How'd you do it?" she marveled. "Hot to the touch, pale as a ghost. Made yourself sick!"

Callie shrugged. "I was bored."

"Ain't exactly nightingales, are they? Still and all, some of those prophet bits make you think."

"And while you were thinking, did you happen to spot my mother?"

"Problem, innit." Miss Kala nodded. "Ain't seen hide nor hair of Mrs. P since we got here. Not even when they were linin' up. I wonder where they stashed her."

A sudden chill prickled Callie's nerves. "If she's even here."

Miss Kala did her best impression of an owl. "Not here?"

"I didn't think of it before. You left her with the Daughters. But what proof do you have she went with them?"

"It has to be! I was only gone for..." She began to stammer, steeled herself. "For a minute. Just for a minute. Not like before."

It was as if time itself stopped. Sound muted into the vacuum of space. Light blurred and movement halted. There was only Callie and Miss Kala, frozen, staring, wide-eyed with realization.

"'Like before'?" Callie enunciated, fisting her hands into the sheets. Wishing there were surgical instruments within reach.

Miss Kala's entire demeanor changed. She straightened her posture, glared with keen ferocity. Here, finally, was the girl raised on the docks of East London. Street-savvy, vicious, spoiling for a fight. Callie ravenous for the first swipe of her claws.

"Aye, like before. You try being stuck in that attic for a month, see how it suits you. How you figured Lil would get any better, cooped up there like a pigeon lost a wing, I can't reckon. And me barely an afternoon a week off to wash my petticoats and grab a breath of air. So aye, I left her. With this lot, who—and you might think on this awhile—paid her more mind than you ever have."

Callie's outrage choked the words in her throat.

"She's a good egg, Lil. A little spotty, but that's no surprise. She's suffered, your mum, more than most. If I'd been chained to your dad, I might flitter off to fairy land myself. I give her all I've got. But I need something of me own. Surely you—with your growls and your airs and your investigating—can understand that?"

"What I understand," Callie seethed, "is my mother has been missing for over a week, and we're only just now leaning you haven't the faintest notion of where she's gone."

"I know I bunged it. But I'm here, and I'm trying to make it right." Her voice broke. Callie wanted to slap her. "Ever think the reason you're so scared is you don't know her to say where she's gone?"

"*You* lost her," Callie growled under her breath. "She trusted you, and you lost her."

"May have done, yeah." She raised her chin defiantly. "But we're here now, and I'll be damned if I go without checking every nook and cranny. By the by, heard some girls sayin' there's a cellar. Like they don't ever want to be sent down there."

Before Callie could reply, the door lock rattled. Miss Kala grabbed her hand, began to stroke it. Vibrating with the need to punch her in the face, Callie exhaled violently, then sank down onto the cot. Sister Zanna, armed with tea and medical kit, slipped into the room.

"How are we feeling?" She set the tray down with a plonk and promptly ignored it. Miss Kala took that as her cue to play mum. "Sister Constance, who runs the kitchens, sent along some oat cakes. Do try to get one down." She pressed the back of her hand to Callie's brow, nodded. "No fever. I suspect it's nothing more than a missed lunch and the madness of the day, but, if you don't mind, I'll check you over."

"She's passed her daily sickness," Miss Kala said. "Probably just a turn."

"I won't argue. But if you'll be staying, I'll need to see where we are." With a briskness Callie found oddly soothing, Sister Zanna grabbed her wrist to take her pulse. She betrayed only a flinch of hesitation while folding Callie's sleeve back, which uncovered her birthmark. But any gains her prophetic mole might have made with Sister Zanna were undone by smooth fingers searching for stigmata scars—and finding none. After a minute she set Callie's arm down with a pat. "Elevated, but there has been a good deal of excitement. How are your bowel movements?"

"Er, regular," Callie stammered.

"Good. Any frequent urination? Normal for a lady in your condition, depending how far along you are."

"No. And... four months."

Sister Zanna whistled. "That's some precision. Memorable night, was it?"

"Yes." Callie shone her eyes up at the ceiling, rubbed her stomach. "It was."

When her gaze drifted back down, Sister Zanna's hawk-eyed scrutiny confronted her. How such an observant woman had been recruited by Sister Juliet, she couldn't fathom.

"How silly of me!" she exclaimed. "Asking all these bold questions and forgetting to introduce myself. Zanna Lawless, midwife to the novitiates and healer of ills."

"This is Mrs. Rebecca Sandringham," Miss Kala interjected. Callie had to credit her improvisation of a given name, a stroke of genius. "And I'm Shahida Kala, her companion."

"*Mrs.* Sandringham? Little wonder you're so sure of your date of conception."

"Widowed some two years' past." After shoving a cup at Callie, Miss Kala returned to the tray. "How do you take your tea, Sister?"

"Black." She lunged forward to help Callie take a weak sip. "And my condolences on the loss of your husband."

Callie sank back against the pillows, finding it easy to fake exhaustion. This never-ending feint skinned years off your life.

"A storm off the coast of Italy. His boat capsized. All were lost. Our marriage… His family disapproved. Refused to forward his allowance. I took shelter at a local convent. Assisi. It was in their gardens I first heard Her call…" She bent her head forward for another sip. "I know the very hour, the very second it happened. A joy so hot it burned away my grief. And ever since, Her voice in my ear. A light within."

Sister Zanna still hadn't broken her stare. Lawless? More like relentless. Also unconvinced. Callie wondered anew what had brought her here.

"If you've come for sanctuary, you've found it. You don't need to be a saint to be welcomed among us, just in need."

Callie heard the hidden message: *Stop the pretence, and we'll still accept you.* Sister Zanna obviously believed it; she wondered how true it was.

"I go where She leads. Your readiness is all that matters now."

"*Our* readiness?"

"For Her return."

Sister Zanna ill-concealed her smirk. "Of course."

Her audience drifting and her energy waning, panic seizing Callie. She'd been prepared for everything but cynicism. She sensed Sister Zanna didn't just doubt her, but the Daughters' whole enterprise. Unless Callie could root out her motivation for helping the Daughters and exploit it, their entire mission was at risk.

She recalled one of Hiero's most cunning pieces of advice: When nothing else works, strike fear.

She lolled her head around in a wide circle, once, twice, thrice. Isolating the leg closest to Sister Zanna, she let it spasm and shake. A heady froth of high-pitched giggles escaped her, ending on a screech. Miss Kala dropped the plate she was holding. Both women jumped as it smashed. Callie had taught herself the old medium's trick of rolling her eyes white.

Sister Zanna grabbed for her shoulders, but Miss Kala got their first.

"Tell us," she whispered. "Tell us, Mother, what's to come?"

With a final wild laugh, Callie shot into a seated position and pointed an accusing finger at Sister Zanna.

"The lamb was slaughtered. He was no sacrifice. There is rot within you, down to the root, down to the very soil on which you stand. Rot, rot, rot..." Sister Zanna crossed her arms against her words, but Callie could see her left eye twitching. She'd hit a nerve. "Bury the lamb in your garden, but even he cannot cleanse you of sin. The sin is in your souls. The sin is in yourselves. More will suffer, but none will rise until the poison's out. Weed her out, weed her out, weed her out!"

Dead pale but defiant, Sister Zanna grabbed the plate of oat cakes and tossed it in her lap.

"Thank you for that, Mrs. Sandringham. I'll consider myself forewarned." She twisted her fingers to stop them trembling. "Take some rest and do try to eat something. That's all for today, but a word to the wise. I will eventually have to take a look down below."

With that, she sped out of the room, leaving Callie shocked to the core.

"Well." Miss Kala sighed, snatching up an oat cake and stuffing the entire thing in her mouth. "Ain't she a darling. Still, you must be chuffed about your stay of execution."

"My what?"

"She's gonna poke around your fanny." Miss Kala made a crude gesture by way of explanation. "And not in the nice way."

"Not if we get to our work." Or so Callie reassured herself. She regretted not consulting an experienced midwife before agreeing to their plan.

A gentle knock at the door saved her from her worries.

"How's the patient?" Hiero slunk into the room with his catlike grace, then curled himself up at the bottom of the cot. "Ooh, tea! All this piety has left me parched. Pour me a cup, will you, my dear?"

"Don't recall being kicked down to servant," Miss Kala grumbled. "But aye."

Callie heeled at his leg. "What news?"

Hiero considered this for a long as it took Miss Kala to serve him the tea. After a fortifying draught, he considered some more. A shot to his kneecap set him to rights.

"Brute," he huffed. "The details are too gruesome to recall, but suffice to say, the evidence is insufficient."

"What is the evidence?"

"Did you not hear me? I don't recall."

Callie felt a sudden surge of empathy for the murderer. "Was the boy killed at the tree, or elsewhere?"

"Hmm... couldn't say."

"What was the cause of death?"

"Oh! Yes, yes, this I... forgot."

"Does Tim suspect anyone in particular?"

"Tim who?"

She jabbed him in the thigh. "Next one aims higher. What instructions has your Kip given you to give to me?"

"Ah!" Hiero produced a slip of paper from his inner pocket. "Being a gentlemen of high intelligence, he had the foresight to write you a note."

Callie nabbed it before he even finished his sentence.

"Don't get down on yourself, Mr. Bash." Miss Kala chuckled. "At least you've got your looks."

Hiero nodded. "The greatest of my many gifts and the key to opening all sorts of locked things."

Callie gripped the edges of the paper tighter at her snort. "It says Tim and Han are conducting a search of the garden while the Daughters are preoccupied, but he fears they will not complete the task before nightfall." She peered over the top at Hiero, foot tensed and ready. "Why, pray tell, are you not with them if we're so undermanned?"

"Scrounging around in the dirt? You've answered your question."

"Do you mean to play any part in this investigation other than Chief Hand-Holder?"

"I resent the implication. I take great care to keep my palms supple and soft."

Her reservoir of patience dried to a drop, Callie returned to the note.

"Miss Kala, we are to undertake a search of the main house, particularly areas our gentlemen friends will be barred from. Mr. Stoker has made a list of items we should be on the lookout for. This dovetails well with our original ambitions. We'll begin this very night."

Hiero dropped his cup into the saucer with a loud clink before Miss Kala could reply.

"A word regarding that. Shahida, would you permit us some privacy?"

Miss Kala nodded, though appeared reluctant to divorce herself from the plate of cakes. "I'll just find out where we're kipping tonight, shall I?"

Hiero's sudden stillness unnerved Callie, as well as how he bowed his head. At once she saw the toll this particular adventure was taking on him, though she didn't quite understand why. The discovery of the boy's body had raised the stakes and disturbed them all, but Hiero had seemed off his game since they entered the compound.

"I know you will accuse me of playing papa, or worse," Hiero said, "and I know I'm your guardian in name only and rarely act it. But in light of today's events, I would ask you to reconsider our ruse."

With the last vapors of her goodwill, Callie attempted to decipher his meaning without huffing and puffing. "You mean abandon my mother?"

"No, no, of course not." He laid a hand on her ankle, whether as an appeal or to stave off any further abuse, she didn't know. "I mean that together, we claim the death of the boy has made us rethink our commitment to the Daughters. The Messiah cannot be born in a climate of death, et cetera, et cetera. We depart tonight and return tomorrow with Kip as our very own selves. With the freedom to investigate as we see fit."

Callie gaped at him. "Whatever for?"

Hiero stirred and stirred the dregs of his tea as if he might read his fortune there. Knowing him, he likely could.

"For your safekeeping." His hand flew up to halt her protests. "You are capable. That is not in doubt. But so are the women here, and they outnumber the pair of you by dozens. They have already disappeared your mother. I couldn't..." Callie wanted to recoil from the emotion in his eyes when he finally looked up at her. They never really spoke of what they meant to one another—just trusted, from the first. "They will not have you. The risk is too great, and there are other means. Safer means."

She inhaled deeply, reflecting. His words were as unexpected as they were sentimental. But he had never objected like this before and, for that reason alone, she gave them proper audience.

"We've made such progress. We have them almost convinced." Her recent conversation with Sister Zanna notwithstanding, but that would hardly strengthen her argument. "We'll never have the same kind of access as ourselves."

"I swore to him I would give you your freedom but intervene when necessary." Callie didn't wonder why her Uncle Apollo had been unable to resist Hiero's eyes when they turned so soft and melty. "I believe that time is now."

She let out a blustery sigh. "That's emotion speaking, not reason."

"A babe was murdered."

"Hundreds have left these halls unblemished."

"Have they? Are you certain? Kip says the boy's mother fled after his birth. What if she didn't?"

"Now you're being absurd. There's no evidence supporting that, and until we uncover some, I'm staying." She declared her decision before she made it, but it had the ring of truth. "To unearth secrets of this magnitude, it's vital to have a woman on the inside. We have two."

Hiero deflated before her eyes. "Very well."

Surprised by how readily he conceded the fight, she reached out a hand to him. He rose to set his cup on the tray, gather himself.

On impulse she asked, "What is it bothers you about this place? If they weren't possible kidnappers harboring a murderer, I'd almost admire their endeavors to lift up fallen women."

"Echoes," came his cryptic reply. Then, "Those who set out with the highest ideals often do the most damage."

Chapter 8

*A*rmed with a rake and an oversized pair of gloves, Tim was just about to tackle the compost pit—the most obvious site in which to dispose of vital evidence, alas—when the singing stopped. Han poked his head up from behind the rails of string beans, turned toward the main house. Tim whistled for Angus, who searched the corn rows and cursed.

They'd been racing the sun. Still not enough time, but with three men, a decent start. Twenty able souls would not have been enough to cover this kind of ground, so even if they had called in the local constabulary, there were still too many variables to contain. Dozens of suspects, five full acres, and three major buildings... Even the Yard would have been hard-pressed to canvass such an enormous space in the eight-hour post-discovery window. Half the officers required would have taken at least three to arrive.

If they would have bothered for an orphan child. For the legitimate newborn son of Colonel Sir Hugh Winterbourne, the entire Metropolitan Police Service and half the Royal Army would have descended upon the Daughters, truncheons and sabers at the ready. But all Little Bean had in his corner was Tim's wits and Hiero's savvy—effective weapons, to be sure, but hardly comparable to a knight's arsenal.

In the distance, white-robed women fluttered out the conservatory door and spread across the back lawn like daisies on the wind.

One bloom in particular wafted toward the garden gate at daunting speed.

"What now, Inspector?" Angus's Scottish burr gave the question a sinewy melodiousness.

"I wish I knew."

"They won't be pleased to discover us here uninvited," Han reminded him.

"Worse, I'm about to lock them out of their garden."

"That's nae gonna work. There's a man still here, a gardener."

"Blast." Tim sighed. "I thought he'd gone with the others."

"Not allowed to leave the garden, or so he says. Seems a bit off, but nae in a murderous way."

"I'll thank you to let us be the judge of that." Tim rubbed a hand over his face as he looked to the sky. The Daughters likely rushed here because they only had an hour or so of daylight left. Tim didn't know much about farming, but he imagined there were end-of-day chores to be done. And they hadn't turned up anything of note so far. As was his custom when at an impasse, he turned to Han. "Thoughts?"

"Aside from 'This is lunacy'?"

"Of the best and most noble sort."

"Someone's rubbing off on you." Han chuckled. "We pick our battles. What must be done before we decamp for the night?"

"Everything possible to prevent the destruction of evidence."

"But we dinnae ken who's doing the destroying," Angus said.

"True," Tim acknowledged. "But we can guess who might hasten to dispose of certain records that might lead to the killer's discovery."

"Or the uncovering of certain facts they don't wish exposed during the investigation," Han said. "The Daughters in question would have had to be seen during their prayer session."

"But once that's done..." Tim nodded, mostly to himself. "I must see their ledgers and accounts before they've a chance to alter them. The rest of the search will have to wait on the morning. I can't think they'll allow us to rifle through their trunks and cupboards through the night."

"Callie and Hiero will be here."

"And so will I, if only in a carriage outside the front gate."

"So will *we*," Han assured him.

"Good man." Tim smiled for the first time in hours. He often found himself paired with Han during their investigations and had come to enjoy their talks. He was also one of the rare people who knew when to be silent. "Angus, if you'd be so good as to go to a local inn and fetch us some supper? And borrow some blankets and supplies, if they're amenable. Then you can retire to Berkeley Square."

"With pleasure, Inspector."

Han grunted. "I suppose this means I've a rendezvous with the compost pit."

"And a pair of tickets to the rugby in the offering." Tim gave the rake a twirl before handing it over. "You can use the time to ponder which of your lady friends you'll invite."

"Devil take me. He's remade you in his image."

Tim barked a laugh while Han yanked on the gloves, which fit him perfectly. He grumbled all the way to the compost pit. Tim watched him go, only to be confronted by the united front of Sister Nora and Sister Merry when he turned toward the garden gate.

"Have you concluded your business, then, Inspector?" Sister Merry asked. "This weary garden needs her rest."

Before Tim could answer, Sister Nora exclaimed, "Who is that?!"

"My associate, DS Han." He chuckled inwardly at what Han would think when he learned he'd been appointed sergeant. "Time is against us, as you well know."

"He cannot—"

"He'll remain within the garden walls until the search is done or the sun is set. I believe your brother is also permitted to work within these confines, Sister…"

"Emerald Scaggs. Merry for short. And yes, but that's 'cause I'm with him."

"You can finish the necessary chores for tonight, but no one else is to enter until we do a final sweep in the morning. I'd ask you and your brother to keep to your residence. DS Han will secure the potting shed and the barn with a lock once he finishes with the compost."

Sister Merry snickered. "I don't envy him that."

"Nor do I." Tim winked. "Benefits of seniority."

"I'll get about my work, then, if you're done with me, Inspector."

"We'll chat tomorrow," Tim confirmed, waving her off. "And how fortuitous you've come to fetch me, as you're just the person I wanted to see."

Sister Nora couldn't mask her shudder. "Oh?"

"I'll wager it isn't Sister Juliet who keeps the accounts."

She shook her head.

"I'll need to see your records."

"B-but…" Sister Nora stammered. "But that's impossible!"

Tim held up a placating hand. "For the moment I have no need to view the amount of donations you receive or how you use them. If you cooperate now and help me identify this boy, I may never. But in order to avenge him, I must know his name. And if you intend to keep me from that information, I must ask myself why."

She inhaled a shaky breath, which did little to calm her. "Then you must ask Juliet's permission. I am but her clerk. She controls the estate and authorizes all transactions."

"Oh, I dare say you are far more to her than a mere clerk." Tim gave a little Hiero twist to his words and watched her eyes go wide. A suspicion confirmed and a question raised. "Take me to Sister Juliet."

"She's indisposed." Withering under Tim's scrutiny, she tugged at the frilly ends of her sleeve. "The shock of the day. Our Mother has called her to her bosom. She isn't to be disturbed in such a state."

Tim monitored her expression for any sign of deception. He knew Sister Nora could have interrupted Sister Juliet's suckle session if she deemed it necessary. The greater mystery was her devotion to Rebecca Northcote and her prophecies. Which, in his estimation, appeared genuine.

"Then if you would be so kind as to escort me to where your records are kept, I'll begin my search."

She opened her mouth to protest further but stopped herself.

"The sooner I have the information I seek, the sooner I'll take my leave for the night," Tim reminded her. "And with your help, the time will pass quickly."

She shook her head as if to scold herself, then spun on her heel. "Follow me."

They adjourned to a small office tucked beside Sister Juliet's. The room was made small by the wall-to-wall bookcases, stuffed ceiling to floor with ledgers, books, and boxes. A heavy door, with locks to match, complemented the vaultlike quality. All but the highest panes of the window had been boarded up with homemade shelves. Filmy dregs of sunlight reflected through as if they were on a ship built in a wine bottle. Tim was relieved when Sister Nora dragged an anchor-shaped stone into the entryway to keep them from being caught in.

He was even more relieved when she lit a lantern, depositing it on the desk shoved into the join between two bookcases. Tim perused some of the labels on the ledgers and boxes as she gave her desk a quick tidy. The boxes were organized by year—likely photographs. She and her predecessors had dedicated a notebook to each Daughter past and present. Records from Rebecca Northcote's time were closest to the door; she'd want more recent accounts at hand. Or hidden on the bottom shelves behind the desk.

"Quite the monastic atmosphere," Tim observed. "I suppose the

Mother approves."

"Cleanliness is next to godliness," came the tight, trite reply.

"Has Sister Juliet ever set foot in here?"

Sister Nora cleared her throat. "Whyever should she? There's a bell."

"Of course." Tim smirked, a deliberate provocation.

"'Each is called to serve, and shall serve how she may.' Juliet is as useless at sums as I am at preaching. I'm grateful my place here grants me work I would not find elsewhere."

Tim recoiled from the blade of her words, a pointed reminder many of the Daughters had sought sanctuary in coming here, not necessarily salvation. No business in the city would hire a woman like Sister Nora as a clerk—to their detriment, as she seemed more than capable.

"You're from the colonies?"

"Herefordshire born and bred. My father was a vicar. Fifth son of an earl."

"So you're continuing in the family tradition."

"After a fashion." Something in her eyes betrayed her. "Father also had no head for sums. Or schedules. Called me his hourglass. Said you could set the time to my prompts."

"And he permitted you to take over the vicarage accounts?"

"So he did," she said with a pinched smile. "Now what information do you require, Inspector? There's much to see to before evensong."

"The children born here. How do you keep record of them?"

"By mother's name." She knelt behind her desk—score one for Tim—to retrieve the 1873 ledger. She'd made the same logic leap Tim had, that the mother would have come to the Daughters the previous year. A peculiar way to track the progress of children, by always referring to the past, and a definite feint. No one as fastidious as Sister Nora made a child's provenance so impossible for others to find. She'd made her first mistake.

Instead of giving him the ledger, Sister Nora deposited it on the desktop and flipped open to September 1873. A more innocent time for them both, Tim mused.

"She's not likely to have come here earlier than that." She ran her fingers down a column marked *Issue*. "I imagine the legend is clear enough. *M* for a boy, *F* for a girl, and *WG* is—"

"With God."

"It seemed kindest."

"'Suffer little children, and forbid them not, to come unto me: for of such is the kingdom of heaven.' But I suppose your Mother Rebecca has her views on the subject."

"She would never deny a child the arms of God, Inspector. Our Mother's work, our work, is His work. And all our lost angels will return to us when She returns to her garden." She pressed her knuckles to her lips, fighting her grief. Whatever else might be said about her, she genuinely mourned the dead boy. "What will become of him? Will you permit him to receive the final sacrament?"

"In time." Tim hastened to change the subject. "Did you recognize him?"

"I did not. But I rarely spend time with the babes once they're born. Sister Zanna may be of use to you there."

"Not even those earmarked for adoption?"

Again she worried her sleeve. A tell, or just general nervousness? Her entire conversation had been painted in varying shades of truth.

"It's true some of the babes wean with us, but not for long. If we've a home ready, most newborns are there within a week."

"But the infant I saw last Sunday. She must have been at least eight months old."

"An exception. Most couples choose by mother, so the child is born to them. The Thornhills chose one of the babes we're paid to keep."

"By your wealthier clients?"

"For their servants, yes."

"Then you do farm some?"

Sister Nora grunted. "That word. Tainted by the foulest of the foul. How can it be a sin to care for the children of the fallen in their stead?"

"No sin I can see, unless you murder them whilst continuing to collect."

"We *succor* them," Sister Nora underlined, "until their mother can make more reliable arrangements."

"The rare father, you mean, who won't see his issue, even illegitimate, raised by wolves."

"A school or a reliable guardian," Sister Nora persisted. "Or when they are old enough to behave, in the household. Perhaps begin their training to one day go into service themselves."

Tim fought to stay on topic, disgusted with her naivety. "Was this boy among those you kept?"

"No." She clenched her shoulders as if preparing for an eventual blow. "We only have six places. No boys at present."

Tim could guess why. "Any threat to a legitimate heir is swiftly dispatched to the orphan asylum." She nodded. "Do you adopt them?"

"Impossible without the mother's permission."

Tim watched her mind work, sorting and tallying the facts as he'd presented them.

"Then how do you explain this boy? Three months of age, on your premises, when he should have been sent to the orphan asylum?"

"I cannot." For the first time, she stared at her hands, unable to match his stare. "Someone must have kept him back."

Tim let out a long breath. "Indeed. Now will you show me the correct ledger, the one that lists the children and their placements, that I may find him some peace?"

A bell rang before she could make her decision. A little gold cloche with angel wings, hung in pride of place above her desk, under a plaque in a romantic script: *Juliet.*

Tim could have thrown the desk over at the sound.

"Forgive me, Inspector, but you'll have to return tomorrow."

"Sister, I must impress upon you the urgency of my task. Someone among you—"

"The door will be locked." She blew out the lantern to end the conversation. "I am the only one with a key. Surely you cannot think—"

"I've come to no conclusions for or against anyone in this house. Yourself included."

"How disheartening." She heaved the anchor stone out instead of in, aiming for his foot. Tim jumped back. "I'll have further thoughts for you tomorrow."

"But—"

"Sister Juliet requires me." The door careened into its frame with a thud. She clanked on both locks. Their commitment to security would have impressed if it did not so impede his case. "And you, Inspector, must go."

She had the courtesy to escort him to the front gate. Tim would ponder over their encounter long into the night as he flipped through the tiny silver book he'd stolen off her desk.

Hiero stared at the pallet as if it might stand up and dance a jig. A cold, windowless corner of the farmhouse had been curtained off by a quilt hanging on a piece of rope suspended between the walls. A second more threadbare quilt lay folded on the bottom of the pallet, its mash of straw not even covered by a sheet. A few stalks poked out of the holes in the pillowcase. A hand-carved wooden cross dominated the back wall. If Hiero stretched his arms wide, they'd span the length of the cell-like space.

Hiero fought back the shudders, the surge of bile to his throat. Only the smell of stew bubbling on the fire kept him tethered to this place and time, the brush of the quilt against the back of his hand that was not the iron door to a cage. Imbibing a gallon of scotch might get him drunk enough to sleep here; he had only a few sips left in his flask, and the Daughters abstained. He would be haunted by the usual rogue's gallery of ghosts tonight—of that he was certain—but sleep would elude him.

Another reason, of many, to curse this place.

"Not as grand as you're used to, Father, but I hope you'll be comfortable." Sister Merry poked her head around the edge of the quilt.

Hiero drew in a deep breath. The show must go on.

"I have been spoiled by Mrs. Sandringham these past weeks of travel. My room at the rectory was as humble as this. If the Lord is with me, I feel quite at home." He gestured to the cross to divert her attention. "A magnificent piece. Your work?"

"Oh, no, that's Amos. The blow stole his wits, but not all his gifts."

Hiero dropped his voice to a whisper. "There was... an incident?"

"Clopped in the head by a spooked horse when he was a young'un," she said at full voice. "No shame in it—in't that right, Amos?" The giant himself grunted while refilling the firewood trough. "Ask your questions, Father. We've nothing to hide."

"You have perhaps mistaken me for the detective inspector."

Sister Merry chuckled. "Well smart of you to volunteer to help him. You'll have all the good goss tomorrow eve. I do hope you're aiming to share?"

"I am there for the girls, under the seal of the confessional," he reminded her.

"As what regards the crime. Not their other business." She winked.

"If it's stories you want, I have more than a few to tell."

His first glance around the modest farmhouse had told him all he needed to know about how he would be spending his evening. Unwilling to abandon Callie and Shahida but barred from sleeping in the main house, bunking down with Sister Merry and her brother was the only reasonable option, made all the more unreasonable by the fact that this meant being locked into a pitch-black garden where a child was recently murdered, his lover and his best friend preferring each other's company to rescuing Hiero from this oppressive tedium.

With nary a book or a pack of cards in sight, Hiero recognized the only form of entertainment would be what he could provide. And he was always happy to sing for his supper. At this point, it was a matter of survival.

"Oh, Father, we're simple folk," Sister Merry said. "I'll leave you to get settled while I set the table." Hiero drew in a sharp breath as she reached for the curtain. "Oh! Almost forgot." She brandished a book from her apron, *The Book of Eve* by Rebecca Northcote. "Something to pass the time."

"How kind." He tucked it under his arm with a fond pat, resisting the urge to toss it in the fire. Then she did sweep the curtain closed, and he bit his tongue to keep from crying out.

Hiero focused on the flame of the lone candle, listened for the crackle of the hearth. Ignored the sharp throb that stabbed the back of his eye, the boulder of ache that stretched his skull. The rabbit skip of his heart, the cockroach skittle of his nerves. Warmth and comfort only steps away. He could leave anytime he wanted to. He *could* leave. Even lost in the dark of the garden, he could scream for Kip or Han. They would hear him.

But would they come? Would Kip ignore the call of his client's demands if Hiero cried wolf? Or would this be counted as another bumble, another distraction, another little drama of Hiero's meant to divert Kip from his mission and compromise him yet again? The trouble with presenting oneself as a perpetual mystery was one's every action tended to be shrouded with disbelief.

He imagined his bedroom at Berkeley Square. The wardrobe so wide you could cozy up with a book. The oasis of his bed, overflowing with lush fabrics and soft blankets, with—when the wind blew south by southwest—a taut-muscled Kip to snug up with. Han's regal statues in place of that oppressive cross. All the paraphernalia he'd collected over the years: antiques and costumes and satin robes and *billets doux*. All the things that were his, that burst from his heart like showers of gold leaf and garnets. The life he had earned in ways dishonest and unimaginable.

Hiero snuffed the candle's flame with his fingers, enjoying the burn. Remembered Little Bean's shrunken body in its petal bed. There was work to be done and, for once, he was eager to prove up to the task.

"Do you require any help, Sister?" Hiero asked, grateful to have a reason to exit his cell.

"Nothing to be done but ladle up." She placed a basket of bread buns in the center of the two-person table set for three.

Dinner would be a very intimate affair, Hiero thought with a shiver. Sister Merry waved him over to one of the end chairs as Amos brought the stew pot over from the fire. Barehanded, Hiero noticed. His palms were thick with calluses that might easily have... But Kip said the boy had been strangled with a kerchief, which ruled out a man of Amos's strength. And that kind of impulse killing.

Hiero was so proud of himself for that deduction that he attempted to make another. For so long that the sudden clearing of Sister Merry's throat startled him. He found a pair of eyes staring at him and a trio of bowls cooling in the damp air. Hiero fingered the handle of his spoon, cowed by their scrutiny.

"What a rare treat, in't, Amos?" Sister Merry finally remarked. "To have a priest bless our meal."

"Ah!" Hiero was too practiced an actor to miss such a cue. "Forgive me. I find myself much preoccupied with the day's events."

"All the more reason to eat up. If you would, Father."

Hiero wrung his hands in his lap, unsure of which of the five poses of benediction to enact. He decided to steeple his fingers over his bowl, as it seemed the most humble. While he intoned one of the only liturgical speeches he knew, he felt a surge of gratitude toward Barnaby Douglas, playwright, papist, and drunkard, who had hornswoggled him into playing Thomas à Becket in *Canterbury Tale: A Fowl Murder is A-Foot*. The Skaggs' facial expressions when he was done perfectly mirrored those of the audience for its one and only performance. And some of them must have understood Latin.

"This looks splendid." Hiero basked in the savory scent of the broth.

And it was. The Skaggs made much of what little they had, and, with a vibrant garden just outside the door, it would take actual work to ruin such fresh produce. Their love for the land and her bounty sung from every slurp. Hiero found himself asking for seconds before he could get them talking. But as the stew and bread were replaced by tea and a lip-smackingly tart berry crumble, Hiero grew more curious about his amiable hosts.

"Thank you, both of you, for opening your home to me." Hiero toasted them with his teacup. "I confess I did not expect for Mrs. Sandringham and I to be so warmly welcomed among you."

"Sister Juliet's got the gift," Sister Merry said. "Sees right into your heart."

"Forgive my impertinence, but it seems you must have known this Mother Rebecca?"

She nodded. "I was one of her last novitiates. She ascended a year later."

"You have a child?"

"Oh, no." She chuckled. "Nothing like that. That work started with Sister Juliet. I remember the day she came to Rebecca, skinny as a goat except for her belly-full."

"Sister Juliet has a child?"

"Aye. Had, rather. Stillborn." She leaned in closer despite the fact they were alone, save for her brother. "Between you, me, and the wallpaper, it was her coming that ruined things for Rebecca's situation. No Messiah wants to be born in a house with a blood mark."

"She wasn't no Moses," Amos added, making Hiero jump.

"An' we in't in Egypt," Merry agreed.

"So you were passed over?" Hiero asked.

"Warned, more like. The sickness fell upon Rebecca soon as Juliet came. We all doubted, at first, that hers was the new way forward. For some, losing the child was sign of her wrongness. But as soon as she was able, Juliet was nursing her aunt and preaching her scripture. Didn't think we'd recover after Rebecca ascended with her own unborn babe. But Juliet..."

"Had the magic touch?"

Sister Merry threw him a stern look. "I witnessed it, the day the Mother first came to her. She lay hands on Rebecca, and she just... flew into her! Her spirit, silver and sparkling, before us all. Then it swooped over Juliet, hugging around her, two gold wings. And when she spoke, we heard the echo. Mother Eve, Mother Rebecca... three voices, one song. It was glorious."

Hiero was certainly impressed Sister Juliet had somehow convinced her followers they had witnessed astral projection. He feigned a beatific smile, shouted out to the heavens in praise. More Latin— suitably, a cry for help.

"And she hasn't led us astray," Sister Merry continued. "It was her who bought the extra lot to stretch the Garden, opened Sunday services to all. Invited the fallen women to find shelter with us. Redeemed us in the Mother's eyes. And now Mrs. Sandringham brings us her blessings."

"Are you surprised Sister Juliet herself is not the vessel?"

"How could she be? Her son died before he could be born. And she's said many times we are her second chance."

"Her redemption." Hiero nodded in understanding, admiring how deftly Sister Juliet had woven herself into the tapestry of their beliefs. "Thank you, Sister Merry. You have put my heart at ease. Ever since Mrs. Sandringham came to me, worry is my constant companion."

"You're home now, Father." She patted him on the hand. "And a better one you're not likely to find. Right, Amos?"

"Garden keeps us. Better than before."

Sister Merry sighed. "Hard to say how much he remembers."

"You came from… difficult circumstances?" Hiero asked.

"Farm life in Suffolk. It's a common enough tale. Dad kept busy tilling the land, Mum kept busy having babes. When the last one came, Dad fell sick. Older boys took over the farm, but were more interested in distilling the grain than selling it. Their love of liquor and a few rainy years spoiled too many crops. Mum minded some of the local children—raising 'em up was all she knew, and we girls could help. Staved off the inevitable for a few years, time enough for me to grow and get out. I took Amos with me as thanks to her. He was always my favorite. Wasn't you, sweet boy?"

"Aww, Merry."

"You were, at that. Came to London hoping to work in one of them rich houses, in the garden or the kitchen. Didn't know how rough it would be. Heard Mother Rebecca speak at a market, and I knew we'd found our place. She was kind to Amos and me. I said her tomatoes looked like they had the pox. She asked, 'Can you do better?' And here I am."

More echoes. The details differed, but the basic facts of their lives were the same. Born into a large, stifling family. A dream of escape, never to be realized. Hardship, then fate intervenes. And suddenly a way out. A way to be the person in those dreams, if you worked hard enough and made the right alliances.

"Mistress of a magnificent garden," Hiero said.

"It'll do." Sister Merry chuckled. "I'll be more at ease when the inspector catches the fiend who…" She shivered. "Such wrongness shouldn't live where goodness grows."

"In peace," Amos declared.

"What's that, sweet boy?"

"Rests in peace."

"Aye, but our garden isn't a graveyard, is it? It's no place for such a thing as that."

"Give him to the ground so he will rise up."

"You'll have to forgive him, Father. He's confusing scripture with what's happened."

"I think he has the right of it," Hiero said. "What better place for a little one than in the Mother's garden? I half think the killer had the same notion."

"Of course you're right, Father. I didn't think of it that way."

"If I may be bold… Where do you bury those, like Sister Juliet's son, who…"

"Ah, the unfortunate ones. Depends on their mother's wishes, but nowhere here. As Rebecca said, 'Our Garden is a source of abundance and renewal. It will nourish those who hunger; it will cleanse those who ache.' I'll have to pray many an hour to forgive the one who fouled it." She shook her head as if to clear it of such dark thoughts, then stood and gathered their plates. "Is there anything else you'll be wanting before I head out, Father?"

"You're going?"

"Aye, to Castleside." A glance over her shoulder caught his surprise. "Oh! You didn't think I'd be staying? It wouldn't be proper, even for a woman who wears her years. But don't you worry. Amos won't be any trouble, will you, sweet boy?"

Amos furrowed his bushy brows so deep Hiero could trace the outline of the hoof that had clopped him.

"But Merry, the creepers."

Hiero struggled not to gape at him. "Beg pardon?"

"At night. In the quiet. 'Cree, cree, cree!' They steal my sleep."

"Oh, don't start with that rubbish. You'll scare the father!" She cuffed him upside the head—not the punishment Hiero would have chosen, given his history.

"When clouds cover the moon. All night, all night. 'Cree, cree, cree!'"

"Owls," Sister Merry almost growled. "We've screech owls and other birds nesting in the eaves. He don't understand."

Hiero tried to laugh it off, but his chuckles rang hollow even to his ears. "Fear not, Master Amos, we'll brave the beasts, fake or fowl, together. I'll summon down St. Michael himself should someone threaten us."

Amos leaned over the table, locked eyes with him. "You'll see, when they come for you. You'll see. 'Creeeeeeeeee—'"

A loud bang sounded. Hiero white-knuckled the arms of his chair, fighting the urge to hide under the table. Sister Merry, ladle in hand, hammered the pot a second time. Amos curled into himself, whining at the top of his lungs.

"Forgive us, Father. He hasn't been himself since—"

"No need to explain. If you don't mind, I think I'll retire. I wish you both a peaceful night."

Hiero never thought he'd be so happy to draw the quilt curtain closed. He checked his candle supply, then retreated to the pallet—too hard, too short, too cold for comfort. As he huddled under the thin cover, he played an old game with himself, listing the ways this miserable situation was better than times in his past.

He wasn't wet. He wasn't hungry. He was alone. Straw was better than dirt or cobblestones. A candle was better than none. His clothes were thick and clean... but with no Kip to complain about them, Hiero knew it would be a long night indeed.

He almost looked forward to the creepers.

Chapter 9

Callie turned her hand mirror until it caught the moonlight. Curled up on the sill of their third-floor side-facing room, she peered into the dark street, searching for the outline of the carriage. She felt confident Tim and Han hid themselves on the side street and not on the cricket field across from the front gate. But given the height of the building and the lack of local tree cover, they had few other options. Unless Tim didn't care to conceal the fact of his surveillance from the Daughters, a strategy she doubted he'd embrace.

She huffed a long breath. Whorls of mist drifting off the cricket field thickened the blackness and diffused the scythe moon. The deflated-balloon wheeze of Miss Kala's snores warned her away from crawling back to bed. She pressed her face to the windowpane in a vain attempt at expanding her view. The chill of the glass soothed her brow but did little to reveal the carriage's whereabouts. If only she knew which direction to aim for…

A soft knock at the door startled her. Callie fumbled her way into lighting a candle, then, tossing on a robe, answered it. Sister Juliet, bruise eyed and spectral pale, hovered in the hallway beyond as if only half-tethered to their dimension. Sister Nora loomed in a doorway down the hall, her expression watchful, worried, expectant.

Sister Juliet glanced over Callie's shoulder into the moonlit bedroom.

"Have I disturbed you?"

"Not at all. It's a rare night my thoughts permit me to rest."

"I am much the same. I can't help but think of all the work there is to be done, even though sleep would better prepare me for it."

Callie smiled. "The burden and the privilege of serving the Mother."

"Amen." A second glance told Callie she expected to be let in. Callie eased the door open enough to reveal the slumbering Miss Kala. With a nod in her direction, she slipped into the hallway. "Are you comfortable? Do you want for anything? I heard you'd taken ill."

"To speak of one who doesn't sleep." Callie rubbed her belly. "Forgive me for interrupting your prayers. I fear the events of the day quite overwhelmed me."

Sister Juliet sighed. "We turn to prayer and reflection in such times, and yet they seem somehow inadequate." She seized Callie by the arms in that way of hers, as if unsure whether to coddle or to kiss. "I hope you didn't take it as an omen."

"I took it as it was. A tragedy." That, at least to Callie's mind, was the truth. "I have been called here by the one who rules me. For what reason I cannot yet say. But I do know this: I was meant to find that boy. I was meant to bear witness. And if I have been called here, then my purpose shall reveal itself in time. Perhaps it already has."

Sister Juliet slid her hands up to Callie's shoulders, almost cupping the base of her neck. She wondered if her intent was romantic or murderous. Or both, given the manic zeal that dewed Sister Juliet's eyes.

"What a blessing it is to behold you, an eye of calm amidst the storm."

Callie fluttered her lids, flashed her eyes white. "I fear thunder will roil and lightning crash before the break of a new day. Beware."

Sister Juliet shrank away from her. "Of what?"

"The serpent, the dragon, the One." Callie returned her clench with equal fervor. "Did you think he'd failed to notice the quality of your works? You are being tested, like all holy ones before you."

Sister Juliet recovered herself quickly. Only the clenched corners of her mouth hinted at any distress.

"Are you their harbinger?" she whispered, the caution in her tone unable to disguise the curiosity. "Is that why you have come?"

Callie didn't have to feign her outrage. "I heed only the Mother's call. She's rallying her angels, branding each one with her sacred mark." She yanked up her sleeve, played her trump card. For the prophet herself couldn't dismiss hard evidence, even in a private conversation.

"The Tree of Knowledge," Sister Juliet murmured, retreating into her touched naif routine. She stroked reverent fingers down Callie's exposed forearm. "Forgive me, Daughter. I am rightfully humbled. I should have known you from the first."

"Nonsense. You have proved nothing but an inspiration." Callie spread an extra layer of butter on this particular piece of bread. "I'm eager to learn, to grow under your guidance. And not just outward." She laughed, patting her stomach.

A flicker of something in Sister Juliet's face tempted her to push for more. Instead she tucked it away for later use.

"As I look forward to your company and counsel." Sister Juliet found her smile. "A true sister. The Mother's ways are mysterious indeed. But bed for now. You've given me much to reflect upon. For which I'm grateful and say welcome home, Daughter."

"I feel at home." Callie met her hands in a clasp. "Good night."

As she tiptoed back into her room, Callie heard the slow creak of the door closing behind her.

And the hard click of the lock being thrown.

Tim lifted the lid off the small pot of stew Angus had fetched from the inn. The savory aroma that wafted up had his stomach singing an aria of gurgles in anticipation. His hands shook as he broke off a piece of bread roll and dipped it into the rich gravy. It was lukewarm and not quite to Minnie's standard—dinners at Berkeley Square had reminded him how good food could be and spoiled him for every future meal, except perhaps dinner with the Queen. But ten minutes later he licked the last from his spoon, wishing there was more.

Han, so still in the seat beside him Tim might have mistaken him for one of his statues, poured him a mug of tea from a towel-shrouded pot. Also lukewarm, but Tim appreciated the effort. They clinked mugs, then settled in for the long night's surveillance. Han had fashioned a small blanket bed in the carriage's main cabin, but it was too early for one of them to retire. If sleep managed to lure either of them under that night. Though they had both seen far worse in their travels—or so Tim assumed of Han, of whose history he knew little—they would not soon forget the discovery of Little Bean.

Tim wriggled around in the tartan throw that mummified his legs and lower torso to dig Sister Nora's silver book out of his pocket. He considered daring a small lantern, angling the shutters away from the house, but thought better of it. As soon as the wind blew the clouds off the weak moon, he'd have enough light for a cursory examination. If not, he'd retreat to the inn for an hour. Or five.

"Your client." Han's sonorous voice startled Tim out of his thoughts. "What will you tell him?"

After dealing with Hiero's curlicues and quotation marks for so long, Tim had come to appreciate Han's forthrightness. This wasn't the first long night's surveillance they had passed in each other's company, and he had come to enjoy them.

"Hopefully that I'm making progress. Though I doubt that will be the end of it."

"You think the child his?"

"I'll need proof before I bring this to him, but... yes. The resemblance is strong."

"A rich man?"

"An important one. I fear his reaction."

"For yourself or for justice?"

"Both." Tim topped up their mugs to keep the nervous quiver out of his hands. "As undermanned as we are, this case won't be solved by half the Yard stomping the grounds, intimidating the Daughters. It requires our special touch."

Tim caught Han's curt nod out of the corner of his eye.

"I admire a man who can admit when he's wrong."

Tim took a long sip of the cooling tea. "Is that what I've done?"

"Not to all the injured parties, but I trust you will." Han let out a snorted cough, the closest he ever came to a laugh. "Hiero is particularly fond of groveling."

"I dare say Callie isn't much averse to it."

A grunt. "No."

"Is it wrong? To want to prove myself to my betters? To desire to serve this city as I was meant to?"

Han remained silent for so long Tim began to fear he'd offended him.

"How is what you are doing now any different from before? You said yourself no other team has a hope of bringing the boy's killer to justice. Why do you wish to return among the ranks of those who banished you? What would it prove? That you are worthy? You are." A hint of a smirk quirked one of his lips. "That is why Hiero fought for you to join *our* team."

Tim felt pinned into his seat by a lodestone at this revelation.

"He... he never shares anything with me."

Han sighed. "He wears the coat of the enigma too well. Wraps himself in it until there's nothing but silk and mist. But this freedom—to be mysterious—is hard won. So many have deceived and manipulated us. To be able to mirror them is our small victory."

"And I am glad of it. But I am not one of those men."

"Anyone can see that."

Tim scoffed. "Not everyone."

"If you think his liaison with Apollo Pankhurst was one of equals, you are mistaken." Han twisted the reins in his hands until the leather chafed. "Pankhurst gave him a long leash, but Hiero was still tethered to him."

"But Hiero loved him."

"He took the collar willingly. Out of love? Perhaps. Pankhurst courted him a long time before Hiero agreed to be his consort. Made him many promises, which grew more and more elaborate as the months wore on. One in particular Hiero couldn't refuse."

"His freedom?"

"When you've lived as we have, was it really a choice? Or the best of bad options?" Han exhaled a long breath. "I believe he came to love him. Pankhurst was a sweet man. And Hiero, or rather Horace Beastly, could have continued on without his patronage. But to rid himself of his past forever? Pankhurst was his only choice."

The stone sank farther into Tim's chest, choking him. "So I have no hope of ever knowing him completely."

"I cannot say. He's in constant metamorphosis." Han chuckled to himself, his fondness for his longtime friend writ bold across his face. "But you are the first lover he chose for himself. Think on that."

Tim hugged his arms around his middle, more for need of comfort than the cold. He suddenly felt as if he were in another country than Hiero, rather than across the garden wall. Perhaps they had always been two solitudes, sharing a border but not much else.

"Until this case came our way, he was all I could think on." He attempted to sort the matter, struggling to make Han's words and Hiero's actions match, a jigsaw of ideas Tim couldn't fit into a unified image. His ever-curious mind required more pieces to distract from his worry and his longing. Because while the detective side of him wanted to plug the holes in the puzzle, the human side fretted over his friends' well-being. And if he was honest, that Hiero would somehow find a way to further complicate things. "How did you come to know him?"

Another snort-cough. "Very deft maneuver. You must know I would never betray his confidence."

Tim did know, but a gamble was a gamble—it didn't always pay off.

"Ah, but is it a confidence if it's your own tale?" Tim affected his most innocent smile. "You must have one."

"As most do."

"And here we are, with hours of time to fill."

Han shook his head. "Very well. But you will hear nothing of Hiero."

"Why do you think I am any less intrigued by you?"

He had no answer for this. Instead Han reached into the basket the inn's cooks had made up for them, pulled out a bottle of cheap whiskey, and poured them both a teacupful.

"On a night such as this, I sometimes imagine I hear the knock of the boats that used to lull me to sleep. Though I've lived on this island for more than fifteen years, I still feel the rock of the waves. I was born on the water, lived on it, named for it. Tak Hai means 'To reach the ocean.' I am one of the Tanka boat people of Macau." He glanced over as if to check if Tim was bored. To his disappointment, he hung on every word. "My uncle was a fisherman, and Mae sold our wares at our market stall in the Inner Harbor. We lived together, Mae and me, on a green junker, M *Mermaid*—with a fish scale pattern on one side. My grandmother would always complain it was too colorful, but Mae... She loved to paint. If she could not be an artist, she would decorate her world. Her greatest wish was for me to travel where she could not, sail the oceans."

"And so you did."

Han exhaled a long breath. "Not by choice. I was a half-breed.

My father was a Portuguese sailor who was shipwrecked before I was born. Though there were many of us half-breeds around, we were never accepted by mainland society. Mae's dream was for me to roam far and wide, but I wanted her dream."

"To be a sculptor?"

"An artist, but yes. When I grew old enough, I saved to buy a stall of my own, for my paintings and sculptures. But the high-class patrons don't go to the market, let alone buy their art there. But navy captains do."

"They do love their portraits."

"One in particular gave me many commissions, enough that when he offered me passage to England on his vessel, with the promise to introduce me to all his Admiralty friends..."

"Your mae must have been beside herself."

Han sighed. "If not for her urging, I would not have gone. She wanted so much for me." A few telltale blinks encouraged Tim to look away from his face. "So I left her, left everyone... only to be press-ganged onto a slaver ship at the next port. The captain's keen eye for art was no match for his gambling debts, and the commander of the slaver needed someone strong and intimidating to keep his cargo in line. I fled as soon as we docked—being strong and intimidating means you can turn the tables on your captors—and made my way to Portsmouth, thinking I could find more naval patrons and eventually earn enough to return to Macau."

"But you remained."

A terse nod. "I wrote home as soon as I had settled in London. It was almost a year before I heard back that... there was no home to return to."

Tim resisted the impulse to reach out and squeeze his arm, afraid it would be refused.

"What happened?"

"The details don't matter. Or so I tell myself."

Tim attempted to comfort him with words. "The last thing she knew of you, you were following the dream she had for you. You continue to serve her memory through your art. That must be some consolation."

"I've made my peace. Like Hiero, like all of us at Berkeley Square, the life we live is our own. Servant to no master but the family we choose. Fate led me to this place, these people, a life I cannot regret." He looked up as if contemplating the moon, which had reemerged. "But perhaps your place is not with us. Perhaps that is why you are so unsettled."

"We were travelers. Four cities in fifteen years. I've never known a stable home."

"Except your fellows at the Yard."

"Even there..." Tim rubbed this knuckles along his jaw, feeling restless. "The crumbs of work I have to share don't attract many pigeons."

"So you befriend your cases." A final decisive snort-cough. "A lonely life."

"Not lately."

Han spared him a pointed glance, then turned back to the moon. "No."

Chapter 10

"*G*ood morning, Father."

Hiero ceased overstirring his tea at the sound of that familiar voice. Which he then remembered ought not to be so familiar to a priest late of Italy. With the control of a longtime performer, he schooled his face before looking up at his Kip. And so very Kip-like he was in his sensible gray-green suit, boring-patterned waistcoat, and mud-tramping boots, his will-o'-the-wisp mustache the only remnant of yesterday's disguise. Today DI Timothy Stoker reported for duty, rumpled and red eyed but revved with energy. Hiero could almost see sparks flying off of him.

He repressed the urge to kiss him, to sneak him into a forgotten corner and seize his mouth. How long had it been since they'd enjoyed a moment alone together? Days? Weeks? Too long. Lying on that torture device of a bed last night, becoming intimately acquainted with the beams across the ceiling when not chased out of sleep by nightmares, Hiero longed for Kip in a way he had never before wanted anyone: for comfort. The sag of the mattress that signaled his presence. The stretch of his arm across Hiero's back. His quick, breezy inhalations—the sound of his mind working, even in slumber. His firm chest to hug against when the creepers shrieked the walls down.

Hiero rose to greet his too-perceptive eyes, limned with concern.

"Are you quite well, Father?" Kip asked, struggling to keep his distance. A natural dissimulator his Kip was not. "It can be a challenge to quiet one's mind after such events as you witnessed yesterday."

"Someone of my vocation is well acquainted with suffering in all its forms, Mister, er…"

A curl to Kip's top lip. "Stoker. Detective Inspector."

"Ah, *si*. Forgive me." Hiero only then awoke to the bustle about him. Forced to break his fast alone in the conservatory due to the threat of his masculinity, he had not yet seen Callie or Miss Kala. Or much of anything save four cups of tea, two thick slabs of bread with butter and jam, and an ancient Daughter with eyes so fogged he wondered how she avoided the furniture. Though not blind, which she proved once she looked at him, her wrinkles spelled out *foreigner* in bold alarm. Strange since the novitiates came in most colors of the rainbow. "Where shall we begin?"

"The nursery and medical ward. It has been cleared this morning for our inspection"—Kip's pinched jaw told Hiero just what he thought of that—"and Sister Zanna has made herself available for interview."

Hiero raised an eyebrow. Kip shook his head. Though none of the Daughters were in the immediate vicinity, they were being watched.

"I am here to serve, Inspector. Lead on."

Kip reached out—to stall him, Hiero knew, but couldn't help wishing his outstretched hand had made contact, however brief.

"A moment." As if to taunt him, Kip stepped closer. Though his stance remained respectable, the frisson of energy that blurred the very air around him tickled Hiero's skin. "I wondered, Father, if you had observed anything of interest during your night here? I, as you may know, was banished from the compound."

"If I had known it was I who would be interrogated, Inspector, I would have been more vigilant." Hiero noticed Kip's eyes twitched in the effort not to roll them. He fought the sudden urge to lick his lids. "After my final visit with Mrs. Sandringham, I became the charge of Sister Merry and her brother Amos. We dined in their humble cottage, and then I retreated to my pallet to pray for the little one's immortal soul."

Kip pretended to take this in.

"How was their conversation?"

"Bountiful."

With a soft grunt of frustration, Kip whispered, "And what did you reap from this harvest?"

"Sister Juliet first joined the Daughters not to serve her aunt but because she required their particular services."

Hiero wished he could feel the smile that stretched Kip's lips, the toothy glint of a hunter who scented fresh prey.

"You'd make a fine sergeant, Father, with such observations."

"Pity I prefer to take the lead." He inwardly cheered Kip's blush.

Sister Zanna proved to be Hiero's least favorite kind of person: sensible, no-nonsense, and efficient, with the right opinions on everything and a brisk but aloof way about her. *Nonsense* being synonymous with *fun* in Hiero's mind, he tuned out her conversation as soon as they entered the nursery.

Five pudge-faced cherubs gurgled for his attention, each more adorable than the last. He drew signs of the cross on their foreheads as an excuse to pinch their cheeks. The Daughter on duty, taking pity on him, let him cradle the fussing one she held, little Felix, who couldn't have been more than a day old. With his tuft of black hair and wrinkled brow, he looked more wise man than newborn. The babe relaxed when Hiero hugged him to his chest, entertaining thoughts of spiriting him away.

Not even Mother Rebecca knew what would become of him otherwise.

Hiero noticed Kip had turned his back to him, a maneuver he often deployed when he could not suppress his instincts. Sister Zanna smiled at him over Kip's shoulder, her look soft—perhaps he had misjudged her. No other member of the Daughters of Eden, save for Sister Merry, displayed even the slightest warmth toward him. With a pang of remorse, Hiero eased Felix over to the duty Daughter and focused his attention on the conversation.

"These will wean for a fortnight with a wet nurse," Sister Zanna explained. "The novitiates are granted time to decide if they still want to follow their chosen course. Most do not waver—their circumstances being profoundly unjust and their choices limited—but some do find another way."

"Another way?" Kip inquired.

"The women placed with us either have a patron they cannot defy, a job they cannot afford to lose, or a little money of their own squared away. Those savvy enough to fall into the latter category sometimes secure passage to the colonies to begin again or other such arrangements."

"So not all babes born here are doomed to abandonment?" Hiero asked, affecting an air of relief.

Sister Zanna straightened her posture in what Hiero at first interpreted as defiance of their interview but came to understand was against her fellow Daughters. She nodded them into her small adjoining office, so devoid of character Hiero wondered if she ever spent any time there.

"They'd like you to think that, with their talk of adoption and the six they keep back," she grumbled as she kicked the door shut. She only then realized there weren't seats for two, let alone three, and hopped onto the edge of her desk. "I first came here for the 'fallen' women—though I despise that word with everything in me—and it's for the women I remain. The children they bear are currency, which is a kind of power, but one they are not permitted to wield. One that can be wrenched away at any moment. The knowledge I hold close to my heart is we provide them with care and compassion they could not find elsewhere. That in itself is a kind of holiness. And a very few of their babes land softly. But those who do not fall into circumstances no better than those born in the workhouse."

"Local orphan asylums?"

Hiero at first thought her eyes flickered to the door, but then traced their line to the cross over it.

"Yes. Most are consigned there."

Kip sharpened, a hound who'd finally scented fox. "The boy. Do you recall him?"

"I do not." She sighed. Hiero could feel the weight of it on her, how she'd scoured her memory, how she wished she could give them a yes. "But I can confirm he was not among those held back. That I would remember."

"So he was sent to an orphan asylum?"

"If he's one of ours."

Kip nodded. "There's the rub."

"Quite so. I don't envy your task, Inspector, but I wish you well. I've long suspected something is rotten in our garden. But to be confronted with such proof..." For a flicker of an instant, she let her wariness show. "I hope you cut it out at the root."

Though not a very pious question, Hiero felt compelled to ask, "Why do you stay?"

"How can I not? You of all people, Father, must understand. When you're called to do God's work, you cannot but answer."

"And bless you for it, child."

The stern cast to her face softened for the first time since Hiero made her acquaintance. He fought the urge to reach out to her but remembered this was Sister Juliet's tactic. He bowed his head instead.

Kip cleared his throat. "Have any of the mothers of these unfortunates ever had second thoughts? Returned, perhaps, once their circumstances had changed?"

"Not to my knowledge. But of course it's possible." Sister Zanna shifted in her seat. "We try to discourage attachments. But the primal bond can be difficult to sever."

Hiero didn't miss Kip's quiet sigh. Even fourteen years after the fact, he knew firsthand how traumatic losing a parent could be. He suppressed another pang of longing for a private moment with his Kip, a chance to cocoon themselves away from the hard realities of this case.

"The state of the boy…" For the first time, Sister Zanna appeared hesitant. "I want to reassure you, Inspector, he received no such treatment here."

Kip played coy. "How do you mean?"

"The malnourishment. I can only imagine what conclusions you must have drawn."

"It is not my practice to draw conclusions until I have all the facts, Sister."

"Of course. I only meant to—"

"Unless you have come to your own. Which I would encourage you to share." With no reply forthcoming, Kip prompted, "Whether a spoonful of Godfrey's Cordial ever finds its way into their milk, for instance."

"Absolutely not." She bristled. "Inspector, I seek only to preserve life. Even the most misguided among us… that is our only goal."

Kip raised a conciliatory hand. "So I've observed. But you must have made observations at the tree. What were they?"

She white knuckled the edges of the desk, firmed her jaw, resolved.

"He looked as if he had been farmed. They shrivel, like a grape. His blue lips…"

"You've seen such things before?"

"Before I joined the Daughters, I volunteered with the Society for the Prevention of Child Starvation and the Poor Young Mothers' Society." She remained clear eyed as she elaborated on her work with these organizations, much to Hiero's surprise. Not a woman easily rattled, which spoke volumes of her disquiet now. "By the time such cases were brought to us, there was little to be done. Milk by the spoonful, and most perished in their sleep."

Hiero recoiled. Was there no end to the horrors of the world?

But Kip only prompted her with a nod. "And it is your opinion no one among the Daughters of Eden might be taking matters into her own hands?"

"Secrets aplenty haunt these halls, Inspector. But none so dark."

Kip made to speak, but Hiero interrupted him. "And yet even the lightest shade of gray cannot shadow the hearts of the faithful if they are to be welcomed at the final judgment."

Tim kept a watchful eye on Hiero as the same elderly Daughter that had escorted him in that morning supervised his search of the remaining rooms on Castleside's main floor. Though he repeatedly attempted to overwhelm the Daughter with his usual flood of chatter, Tim noticed the deep undercurrent of upset that broke the flow of his conversation at telltale moments. At first Tim had thought the constrictions and sobriety of his chosen character frustrated Hiero. But their interview with Sister Zanna had confirmed that, for all his protests he had seen it all during the mysterious life he had led, the circumstances of this case struck Hiero to the core.

The why of it nagged at Tim, poking his resentment. He could shield Hiero from the worst if he but knew the details. But since these tragic events, and much of the man himself, were as closely guarded as Rebecca Northcote's box, Tim could only rely on his instincts as a detective and as a lover, the latter of which were lacking, if Hiero's trust in him was any indication. Thus the vicious circle of Tim's concern and Hiero's evasion played out through the morning.

Midafternoon found them stationed in the corridor outside Sister Nora's office, Tim staging something of a protest by insisting he would not move until the Daughters' bookkeeper made herself available for questioning. Busy as a flock of courier pigeons, a series of messengers flew back and forth between the office door and wherever Sister Nora cooped herself up until their escort, in a fit of exasperation, left to seek her out.

Alone for the first time in too long, Tim lured Hiero into a convenient alcove, all too aware of how time sped away from them, only to find his mouth stopped by needful lips, his body caught between cold stone and a craven form, arms clutched around him as if they might never let go. Hiero broke their kiss to bury his face in Tim's neck, sucking in breaths that did nothing to steady the wild pound of his heart.

Tim pressed both hands into the small of Hiero's back, widened his embrace in an attempt to envelop him. Tried to make up in comfort what he lacked in size.

"How are you faring?" Tim whispered.

Hiero only hugged in tighter. Tim opened himself to him, rendered speechless by the force of Hiero's need for affection. Then as swiftly as he had come on, Hiero retreated, pausing only to straighten Tim's shirt. And jacket. And collar. And sleeves. Wipe a bit of powder from his cheek. Correct the part in his hair with deft fingers. Tim halted him before he knelt to polish his boots.

"You need not be present for this interview, if you'd prefer—"

"Oh, Sister Nora has no intention of presenting herself." Hiero waved this off as if disappearing it in a puff of air. "The reel dance of Daughters we witnessed was a cunning bit of theater. But make no mistake, they will wait you out until the end times. Patience is a virtue, or so they maintain. I've never seen the point of it, myself."

As usual, Tim struggled to navigate the labyrinth of Hiero's thoughts. "But I spoke with her just yesterday."

"Amidst the chaos, yes. But now that order has been restored..." He shrugged this off with the last traces of his upset. "She is the keeper of the final gate. She will hold the door or fall on her sword, but she will not grant you passage to Sister Juliet. Unless..."

"We find a chink in her armor?"

"Wonderful use of metaphor, my dear. But no."

"Dig a tunnel under her?"

Hiero made a moue of distaste.

"Apply the right pressure?"

This earned him the wily smirk he missed.

"We must make war on this unholy house," Hiero said. "Arm ourselves with knowledge. With secrets."

"The time is out of joint here."

"Your second Shakespeare reference today," Hiero purred. "My, but you know how to woo a man."

When Hiero closed the distance between them anew, Tim caught his face, dove deep into the black pools of his eyes.

"What is it about this case that troubles you so?"

For the first time in Tim's memory, Hiero averted his gaze.

"Echoes." A soft growl escaped him. "Injustice. To seduce a grown adult with myths and ideals, more fool they. To cripple a child before the hour of its birth..."

Tim kissed him then, a hard, ardent clash of lips and teeth and high emotion. And in that moment Tim took up the mantle of Hiero's last guard. He would keep his final gate, hold the door, fall on his sword rather than see him heartbroken.

Even if he never learned a thing about the mystery behind the man.

From her perch on the windowsill, Callie watched Miss Kala pace back and forth, back and forth, her heels shredding small holes in the carpet at the foot of the bed. She longed, absurdly, for a cigarette, if only to have something to preoccupy her hands. With one clenched in her skirts, with the other she traced the outline of her MAS revolver against the inside of her thigh. Every time her annoyance threatened a rash action, she would count down the next minute backward. She could not lose her focus, especially with Miss Kala churning like the engine of a runaway locomotive.

What had Hiero always taught her? Find the advantage.

They had yet to be let out of their room. Various Daughters had visited throughout the morning and into the late afternoon with trays of food, pots of tea, holy texts for study, or quick examinations. Each time a phalanx of subordinates guarded the outer side of the door, charged with the keys; each time Miss Kala grew more desperate. Callie had talked her down by reminding her their absence would not go unnoticed. And while she was not well pleased to be spending a day enclosed instead of learning all she could about her captors, especially with a partner as unseasoned as Miss Kala, she clung to Hiero's other adage: never break character.

She too could wait them out. Callie kept the carriage outside in her periphery, a hand on her revolver, and her raptor's gaze fixed on the line of light under that door. Once a cold supper had been served, the sun had set, and the occasional twitter of conversation in the corridor beyond had quieted, she struck.

Miss Kala, curled at the foot of the bed and pulling feathers out of a threadbare pillow, leapt up at the first sign of movement.

"Have they come for us?"

Callie scoffed. "We aren't in any danger. What do you think the Daughters' plans are, to sacrifice us at the full moon?"

"Wouldn't put it past them, would I?"

"If they come fetch us with no explanation or clear destination, then we worry. For now..." She hoisted open her chest of clothes, rummaged around.

"Let me." Miss Kala shooed her off. "What you after?"

Callie shoved her away. "I'm perfectly capable."

"Forgive my doubts, but you've been sitting on your Lady Godiva all day, begging them to collar you."

"Put this on." Callie threw a pair of black trousers and a black tunic in her direction.

"You're joking."

"White doesn't lend itself to concealment."

Once she'd dressed, Callie applied a slick of pomade to her hair. Fortunately Hiero had as many slippers as he did smoking jackets. Miss Kala's pair dwarfed her tiny doll's feet, but Callie appreciated their snug silence against the cold floor. A hidden panel in the bottom of the chest gave up her snoop's wallet, which she tucked into the back of her trousers. Except for the pair of surgical instruments she used to defeat the lock.

"What!" Miss Kala exclaimed in a stage whisper. "All this time…"

"We need an advantage," Callie explained. "If they believe us content to obey them, they'll be less inclined…" She eased the door open an inch, peering into the corridor. "Empty." She shut it again, turning to confront Miss Kala with her sternest stare. "If you're to be a hindrance, I've no objection to exploring alone. We chance it either way. Here you might convince them I snuck off while you were asleep. Out there you risk as much as me. What do you say?"

"Wait." Miss Kala dug into the small section of the chest where she kept her spare uniforms and extricated a leather pouch she tied around her waist. Callie didn't miss the glint of her knife hilt as she tucked it under her tunic. "Ready. What's your plan?"

"Back stairs to the first floor. Map what parts we can. Find the cellar."

"Free Lil. Sound."

After bolstering the covers and extinguishing the bedroom lights, they crept into the black maw of the corridor. Perhaps to discourage such nocturnal excursions, not a lamp glowed or a twinkle of moonlight gleamed. A moan from the room they snuck past—Sister Juliet's, if she wasn't mistaken—forced them against the wall, hoping to meld into the gloom. Two voices, one keening, one cajoling, murmured within. Shahida muffled a giggle with her fist; Callie did not bother to quiet her huff of annoyance. She counted out a minute before moving to the stairwell.

Callie felt her way down with one hand on the banister and the other crushed by Miss Kala's surprisingly firm grip. The tunnels beneath 23 Berkeley Square had accustomed her to the soundless dark. If the occasional skitter or snore startled her, she breathed her way through it—slow, even draughts that steadied her heartbeat and her mind.

Measured as a barge through a canal, they navigated a series of locks: at the top and the bottom of the stairs, in and out of the kitchen—where they found a storage room but no access to the cellar—from the rear living quarters to the business end of the first floor. Miss Kala's only question involved the logic of locking the doors behind them, but Callie saw no other option. They would be discovered certain sure if they left anything askew. Standing in the shadows beyond Mother Rebecca's illuminated portrait in the main hall, the only light they'd encountered in their whole journey through Castleside's upperworld, Callie punched the wall. The burst of pain across her knuckles in no way quelled her mounting frustration.

While Miss Kala drew a quick map of their route in the dust on the wood paneling, Callie channeled, of all things, the clockwork logic of DI Tim Stoker.

"What have we learned?" she whispered.

Miss Kala stopped to consider this. "No one can sneak."

"How do you mean?"

"Locks, locks everywhere. How many sets of keys, do you think?"

Callie nodded, encouraged by this line of thought. "No sense in that kind of security if every Daughter has a set."

"I'd limit it to three, at most. And not every set the same."

"Restricting access, yes. But also distributing responsibility.

Easier to identify the one to blame."

"So... who do you reckon?"

"Sister Juliet," Callie suggested. "They pretend she needs to be contained, but she wields the most control. Sister Nora looks to be in charge of security."

Shahida snickered. "If that's what you like to call it."

"And perhaps Sister Zanna, with certain restrictions? I can't see her waking the other sisters if one of the novitiates goes into sudden labor."

"Her room's off the medical ward. Spied it yesterday."

"So perhaps only two. Or someone we've yet to meet." She huffed with dragonlike intensity. "Tim has the right of it. There are too many variables."

Miss Kala returned to her map. "Here's a thought. How do they get a message out?"

"They quite obviously don't."

"No one ever takes ill in the night? Needs a cup of water? Plays the two-finger pokey?" Her gesture confused rather than offended Callie. "They're jailed till dawn and nobody ever says a peep? Don't believe it."

Following her logic, Callie added, "They wouldn't disturb Sister Juliet from her prayers or Sister Nora from her myriad chores for such trivialities. Anyone tasked with such a job would need be awake all night..." For the first time in two days, Callie found her smile. "There's someone important, someone vital, to whom we haven't been introduced. A night owl."

"A night guardian, you mean."

"Yes. A Daughter free to roam the halls, bar whichever doors she sees fit, and alert whomever she pleases to whatever's going on. Or not."

A satisfied quiet hung between them as they pondered the possibilities. Until Miss Kala let out a groan and sank against the wall.

"We're going back," she griped.

"We've work to do." Callie leaned beside her. "We must find and befriend this night guardian. She may be the key to both our mysteries."

"You think she's keeping Lil?"

"Possibly. Or in league with the murderer. At the very least, someone who can be bought."

Miss Kala nodded. "Places like this are rife with secret economies. Only way to survive." She contemplated the cave mouth of the nearby corridor, shivered.

"You speak from experience?"

"My pops has got this idea I need to be tamed. Forgets that guests come to our inn just for my conversation, not his ales or mum's fish pie. Better to be lively and forget your troubles, no matter the circumstances, is my motto. Can't blame me for wanting a good time, to see something of the world, can you? Only took this post with Mr. Bash after his name was in the papers and remembering he's an old friend of Pop's. Figured I'd be in for some fun here. Wasn't wrong."

"Even... saddled with my mother as you are?"

"What, Lil? She's the best of you. We have some right old adventures... Too many of late—you're not wrong there—but she needs the distraction. Your dad done her a right turn." Miss Kala flicked her gaze in Callie's direction. "To you too, I reckon."

Callie balled her hand into a fist, letting her nails tear at her skin.

"We'd best inform Han of our discoveries before he storms the barricades." She broke away, diving into the darkness until it enveloped her. "Come."

"Where we going?"

"For a breath of fresh air."

They retraced their path to the conservatory. Relieved to wade into the murky fathoms of moonlight that grayed the windows and ghosted around the hanging plants, Callie weaved her way to the far edge of the back of the building. Miss Kala held a rocking chair still while she stood on the seat. From this vantage, she was just able to make out the road beyond the brick wall that lined the compound.

Sliding her hand mirror out of her belt, its refracted shine finally reached Han. Callie bit her tongue to keep from squealing at his response, the flame of his lantern bright with concern to her overactive mind. She lingered perhaps too long after conveying her message, wishing herself brave enough to say things that could never be said, even in code.

The crack of the chair beneath spooked them. They scurried back to their cell, quiet as dormice, before the night guardian could discover them.

Chapter 11

*H*iero exited the farmhouse in a sweep of robes as black as his mood. Another night of terror dreams had killed any sense of balance he felt after the previous day's investigations with Kip. He'd hoped that hearty meal with Merry, whose jollity and good sense lived up to her name, would have quieted the echoes of a hard-forgotten past that plagued him since this infernal case began. But the creepers—rodents or squirrels, he suspected—had been at their creepiest, wrenching him from whatever tortured sleep he'd fallen into.

He descended on the lush garden like a storm cloud, scowling at the novitiates elbow deep in mulch and glaring at the Daughters who watered the rows of fresh cress. He couldn't even muster a smile for Amos, who chattered nonsense at his chicken friends as he fed them. Irritation and fatigue and, worst of all, sobriety roiled in him such that the gate opened as if by its own accord. Hiero hissed at the Daughter who scurried past him, cowering like one of the creepers made real.

When he spied the crow of a Daughter on the conservatory steps, his keeper for the second day in a row, a blast of curses in a tongue Hiero had not spoken since his wee years burned up his throat. Only the last binds of his civility saved him from unleashing them. He had not felt so restless, so *provoked* by everything and everyone around him since...

A very dark time, indeed.

Slowing his progress across the lawn, he remembered his circumstances had improved; he had a professional standard to maintain; he had remade himself from nothing into a demigod of misrule. The wretched Daughters had imposed their self-mythology on him long enough. Time for a spot of mischief.

"Blessed morning to you." He folded his hands in prayer and performed a little bow. "Please inform Mrs. Sandringham I would care for an audience with her as soon as possible."

"I'm afraid, Father, she's communing with the Mother and cannot be disturbed."

"Then at her earliest convenience."

"I'll convey your message to her nurse."

When hell freezes over, Hiero noted she failed to add. "And our intrepid detective inspector? Where might he be found?"

She made a face as if she'd swallowed a sea urchin.

"DI Stoker sends his regrets. He's been called out with his man on an errand." A twitch of the old bird's beak told Hiero what she thought of Han.

Hiero clasped his hands behind his back to keep from worrying them. Little could have made his morning worse; Kip's client must have a special talent for soul crushing. But then Kip had again run off without scribbling Hiero so much as a coded note at a time when just a word from him would have made all the difference. Hiero wished he could chalk up Kip's repeated abandonment to trust in his abilities. Instead he felt like an afterthought.

Something had to be done.

With a melodramatic sigh, Hiero grabbed the dour Daughter by her arms à la Sister Juliet. She braced her shoulders and grit her teeth but did not recoil.

"Tell you true, that is the most glorious news. These many weeks of travel have robbed me of time to reflect, to sing the praises of our great Mother in my humble fashion. Please, Daughter, is there somewhere, anywhere, a quiet spot where I might read and pray?"

Wrong-footed by his fervor, she backed away. Hiero could see her mind working. She'd expected protest, not gratitude. She struggled to reformulate the little speech she'd been fed by her superiors, her jaw canted at an awkward angle. He pressed his advantage.

"Oh, but of course! What better place to be close to Her than in Her garden, under the very branches where the forbidden fruit hung. I will retreat there now, Daughter, and let you go about your day. Don't give me another thought."

He spun, flaring the sides of his robes so that they billowed out behind him as he returned to the garden. Hiero listened for her to catch up, to call him back, but, as expected, she was glad to be rid of him. He chanced a glance over his shoulder halfway to the gate—she'd disappeared. He diverged behind the rows of hanging linens, re-retracing his steps to the conservatory entrance. Not one of the rotund, rocking mothers-to-be looked up from their knitting as he slunk into the main house.

Black on black in a dimly lit corridor played to his advantage. Hiero slipped past the devil door that had unnerved him on their tour, still seething with wrongness, still compelling him to his doom. A far more propitious destination awaited: the box room. Or, rather, the shrine to Rebecca Northcote and her works.

Hiero had played in some of the most beautiful theaters in England, and these theaters had nothing on the shrine. Gold leaf etched the heavy wooden doors. A tree-motif silver podium sprouted out of the altar's floral carpet as if Mother Rebecca had grown it herself. Immaculate pews by the finest craftsmen canted toward the front. No paintings or statuary sullied the room. The unilateral focus was the box, a seamless rectangle of iron with no clear lock or hinge, lit in a chiaroscuro of colors from the stained-glass window behind. It depicted Mother Rebecca in the Garden, of course, the reborn Messiah swaddled in her arms.

It relieved Hiero to know someone in the Daughters had a flair for the dramatic. Sister Juliet's fugues convinced, but their improvisational nature meant they lacked staging. He wondered if she felt intimidated by such a room, obviously the work of her predecessor. He almost wished he could turn back time to witness Rebecca Northcote in her prime. On such a stage, with the full power of her persuasiveness, she must have brought down the house.

Revivified by this bit of skullduggery, Hiero raced over to the altar. Lifting his robes to skip up the few steps, he was finally alone with the box, Mother Rebecca's legacy of flummadiddle. He painstakingly circled the podium, scrutinizing every inch of the flawless surface. No notch or fissure to be found. He smoothed his hands over all five sides, then lifted it to examine the bottom. Nothing. A quick feel around the podium itself proved no more illuminating.

Two theories came to mind, both disappointing. The likeliest, this was not "the" box, but a facsimile. The doors, after all, had been left open. No one with any sense would leave their most priceless treasure out where any old light-fingered passerby—like himself—could pilfer it. The second, the box was solid iron. No mysterious contents, no apocalyptic revelations. A herring so red it had gone off. The ultimate fool's gold.

Hiero traced the dull edges of the box as he considered his options. Short of painting it chartreuse—improbable, given his lack of supplies—there was only one way to light the kind of fire that would bring the Daughters' cauldron to a frantic boil. Trouble was he would be the likeliest suspect.

Not that being a target had ever stopped him before.

"Irresistible, isn't it?"

Sister Juliet strolled down the center aisle, a well-worn Bible cradled to her breast. The white-gold wings of her hair and widened pupils of her eyes gave her an owlish look—and also conveyed more wisdom than she'd ever betrayed in Hiero's presence. But owls had claws and consumed their prey whole. Hiero's whiskers twitched at the thought.

"Temptation rarely comes in such humble form."

"Ah. You've caught on to the symbolism." She waited for him at the base of the altar. With a final pet to the podium, he descended.

"A thing most desired in its least desirable shape? Hard to mistake Mother Rebecca's intent."

Her weak smile lacked any mystery whatsoever.

"Acting on the instructions of our Great Mother, of course. Exiled from Her garden by temptation, she creates an even greater one to herald her return. The symmetry is... breathtaking."

"Some might call it vengeance."

"And what of it?" Sister Juliet scoffed. "To be denied the thing you love most, the place you grew and tended with your own hands. The only home you've ever known... Why not triumph over those who wronged you?"

Hiero pretended to give her arguments due consideration, not caring to debate a dogma he did not ascribe to.

"And so it shall be, when She is born again." He gestured to a nearby pew. "But you have been seeking Her solace, and here I've interrupted. Shall we pray together?"

"Perhaps, once all is said that need be." She climbed the steps to the box, pressed a kiss to its side. Hiero didn't miss how the maneuver evened their heights. "You must go from this place. Your path lies elsewhere."

It was so amateurish he almost laughed.

"I was appointed Mrs. Sandringham's guardian and spiritual adviser by Cardinal Ferretti himself. I have the seal of Rome."

"Rome!" She chuckled. "What precisely do you think we're about here, Father? We reject the doctrines of Rome, and Jerusalem before it. She comes to stake her claim in the rich earth of England, to grow Her garden out from our sacred isle. Why do you think She called Mrs. Sandringham to us? We are where she means to dig in her roots, to bear her child and see the Mother come anew. You are a shepherd and have played your part in bringing her to us. Now you must leave her to her sisters."

"If these are Mrs. Sandringham's wishes, let her express them to me herself. I do not obey false prophets."

Sister Juliet shook her head, smug. "At the first sign of challenge, you reveal yourself as the apostate you are."

Hiero did laugh then, at this silly, power-mongering woman, at her petty bid for control, at her delusional beliefs. And vowed to smite every single one.

"I am a man of God and a servant to the Mother. I carry Her in my heart. She knows it to be true. Keep me from my charge if you dare. Banish me, curse my name, strike me from this Earth. You cannot shake my faith." A burst of inspiration had him adding, "And if you mean to keep Mrs. Sandringham from me and both of us from ascending into the Mother's light, you will bear the consequences of your actions as She bore God's wrath."

Hiero flew up the stairs, his talons unfurled. On instinct Sister Juliet grabbed the box, hurled it at him. Hiero caught it deftly, smashed it to the ground. The impact didn't make a dent. A small, cruel smile twisted Sister Juliet's lips seconds before she started to scream.

"Be gone! Be gone, devil!"

Her shrieks brought the cavalry. They descended upon Hiero like a flock of murderous doves, smothering him in their feathers, deafening him with their caws. In their frenzy to be rid of him, they failed to notice the box tucked under his voluminous robes.

Tim folded the note over once, twice, three times and stuffed it deep into his pocket. That Sir Hugh required an update on his progress came as no surprise. They'd last spoken well over a week ago, although that report had a far more promising outlook. He scrawled a quick note saying he would meet him at the house in two nights' time, whispering a silent prayer as he did so to have concrete answers for him, not just news of the murdered child. Tim stared at the address long after he'd slipped it back into the same envelope. Unless the next forty-eight hours saw a hard reversal of their fortunes, he would have to recommend involving the Yard.

And somehow learn to embrace the totality of his failure.

With reluctance Tim surrendered it to one of Han's little spies, a fat-freckled youth who might have been his younger brother. Or self. He added a shilling, earned a smile. As the boy scampered off, Tim turned toward Han, who practiced his way of watching without looking while monitoring the movement around the orphan asylum. Or perhaps the gaol-like structure across the street captivated his interest. Ready for action, his stillness enervated Tim. He missed Hiero's busyness, though Han's solidity would probably prove more effective in this particular interview.

"Word from your client?" Han asked.

Tim nodded. "I'm late with my report."

"I don't envy you such a task."

"The trouble isn't the message; it's the mystery. Confirming the boy's identity would save a good deal of bother."

"Was there nothing of use in the silver book?"

"Other than inspirational quotes and a timetable of the Daughters' monthlies? No." Tim laughed to stave off despair.

Han flicked the ash edge of his cigarette into the small pile at his feet, offered Tim a draught. He refused.

"How do you think he'll take the news?"

"Impossible to say. We discussed the possibility at the outset, but the reality..." Tim shook his head. "He's a man alone in the world."

"Too old to start anew?"

"No. But old enough to consider his legacy."

Han scoffed. "Legacy: the white man's burden. Forever chasing windmills." He crushed the last of his cigarette with his boot, slipped another out of his case. "Do you fear any repercussions?"

Tim considered this as he scratched a match on his heel. "Only that a child's murderer goes free."

"To your brilliant career, I mean."

"Of course. But perhaps I should take my lesson from a certain gadabout of our acquaintance. Better to be your own man than to be a puppet on a string."

He felt more than saw Han's glance of approval.

"Confront your client with that in mind, and you won't go wrong. Direct him toward the conclusion you wish him to reach."

"There's too much dishonesty in that approach for my liking."

"You prefer he tells tales of your incompetence to your superiors?"

Tim let out a long, tortured breath. "He is my superior."

Han swore in his language. "Quayle?"

"Higher. Much higher."

Han sucked in half his cigarette, then blew out a bullet of smoke. "You do like a challenge."

Tim couldn't help a smirk. "That's where I thrive."

A whistle from Angus pricked his ears. At the approach of a horse-drawn wagon, Tim gestured for them to step into the carriage's shadow. He recognized the driver from Hiero's description: a giant in coveralls with an angry scar. Amos Scaggs hopped down to open the gate, then drove the wagon through. Squalling could be heard through the tarp that covered the back.

"No better than pigs to market," Han seethed, stomping out his second cigarette. "Shall we?"

"Most definitely."

They jogged across the road. The unlocked gate gave them no trouble, only adding to Tim's irritation at the lack of security and the disposable way they treated the children. Han hurried around a corner of the building to observe Amos in the act of giving over his wares while Tim knocked at the front door. He hoped this double assault would divide their attention long enough for him to sneak a look at their ledgers. Though given the ease with which they had infiltrated, he didn't expect much in the way of organization. Underfunded, understaffed, charity-dependent orphan asylums rarely had time to order their books.

A harried-looking woman with a bird's nest of brown hair and hawkish eyes answered. She stared him down until spooked by his warrant card. She performed a curtsy before ushering him to the office. Her colorful commentary so aggrandized the stark hallways, scuffed floors, and crumbling walls that Tim almost mistook himself as being on a tour of the Great Exhibition.

But there was no mistaking the sorry state of the classrooms they passed or the children in them. Little ones with littler hands struggled to learn trades like sewing and carpentry. Those who didn't misbehave out of boredom had the cowed, vacant gazes of the bullied. Surreptitious head scratching and disheveled uniforms told Tim all he needed to know about the sanitary conditions. And these, he reminded himself, were the lucky ones, not made to work at an age that didn't yet number in the double digits.

A crack bisected the door pane that announced *Michael Crook, Headmaster.* Mr. Crook stood, immaculate, behind a desk that teetered on spindly legs amidst walls papered by a tornado of lists and schedules. After shaking Tim's hand, he waved him toward a chair Tim feared would collapse under his weight. He lowered himself delicately, exhaling when the wobbling ceased.

"What can I do for you, DI Stoker?" Mr. Crook asked in an accent that defied his station. Youngest son of a philanthropic couple, Tim guessed. "I assure you, we've had no noise complaints in several months."

"Pleased to hear it, but I'm here on a separate matter. I require a list of the societies that bring unwanted children to you and, if one exists, a record of those children received over the past year."

Mr. Crook relaxed into his seat. Curiosity sparked in his eyes.

"Would you care for some tea?" He rang a small bell on his desk. "Millicent!"

The door swung open so fast she had to have been listening. "Hmm?"

"Tea for DI Stoker."

Tim, who hadn't given any indication of wanting tea or not, wondered if Crook meant to distance prying ears.

"There." Mr. Crook exhaled, confirming Tim's suspicions. "You may of course have any information you seek. Though I must, as a matter of form, ask if this institution or anyone in it has come under investigation?"

Tim stifled his instinct's answer: *Should they have?* "I cannot confirm or deny the details of an active investigation. As you well know. But if you have anything to report..."

A touch of derision spiked Mr. Crook's laugh. "If only. The crime we are most guilty of is boredom. Hence my interest."

"A natural one." Tim resisted the urge to cast about the office for clues. Instead he met and matched Mr. Crook's level gaze, waiting him out.

"The records, yes."

He capitulated, Tim suspected, to dig a chink out of Tim's stone wall. Mr. Crook fished out the key that hung around his neck, retrieved a ledger from a locked drawer. Slapping it on his desk, he invited Tim to peer over his shoulder as he flipped back the pages to the beginning of the year. He conceded a little ground by canting the book in Tim's direction but otherwise was determined to follow his every move.

Mr. Crook explained the neat columns' legend. "Date of intake. Name, if any. Sex. Age, if known, or approximate. Parentage, whether alive or deceased. More detail in their individual files. Provenance, the very thing you're looking for. We do get a few 'donations'—babes in baskets left at the gates, for instance. These are left blank."

Tim skimmed the rows until he came to January 1874, noting multiple entries for DOE under Provenance. And found himself grateful for Mr. Crook's honesty. Until he saw just how many baby boys they had received in the period under consideration.

"Do you list physical attributes in their personal files?"

"If possible. Most newborns aren't very distinctive."

"Do you employ a classification system? Are the children tagged?"

For the first time since Tim's arrival, Mr. Crook inched away. "I beg your pardon?"

"Babes, as you say, look somewhat alike."

"Ah, I see. Perhaps the ladies in the nursery do employ such a method. But individual files are by name, whether given or assigned." Mr. Crook fingered a well-worn page edge, an automatic gesture.

Tim snatched his pencil, ticking off each possible match.

"Then we must go there."

"Go where?"

"To the nursery."

"Whatever for?"

"To account." Tim tapped the butt of the pencil on the desktop. "I'll need to review these individual files."

"Forgive my confusion, Inspector. To account for what?"

Tim bookmarked the ledger with a stray slip of paper, snapped it shut, and tucked it under his arm before Mr. Crook could vanish it.

"For each of the children listed here. And you'd best pray your nurses are as thorough as you say. The consequences will be dire if there is but one missing boy."

Mr. Crook stood. "There is not."

Tim very much hoped he was wrong.

Chapter 12

Callie stared into the dregs of her morning tea, wishing she could divine her future, if only for entertainment's sake. Had Hiero been there, he would by now have half convinced Miss Kala of her right to the Norwegian throne via a series of misadventures involving a shipwreck, a fleet of sea turtles, and a monogrammed handkerchief. What Callie made up for in mechanical ingenuity, she lacked in imagination. Her characters were studies, not improvisations. Perhaps why she had not been able to coerce their way out of their infernal room.

Without a genuine book to read or much knitting ability, the hours inched by with the speed of a frozen river. Come nightfall they'd infiltrate the house anew. They'd plotted out their new strategy in the wee hours after their return, giddy on their success at evading discovery. The feeling did not survive the dawn; Miss Kala snoozed in her chair while Callie inherited her restlessness. With so much to be done and their advantage secured, wasting daylight seemed the ultimate crime. Though whoever designed the floral motif on the yellow wallpaper deserved to be imprisoned in their place.

As if in answer to her impatience's call, the door lock rattled. Callie kicked Miss Kala awake, spilling her cold tea down her front. Murderous eyes grew wide when she heard the door. Miss Kala yanked off her spoiled apron and sat on it seconds before Sister

Nora marched into the room.

"With me." She gestured for them to stand.

"The Mother's blessings to you, Daughter," Miss Kala huffed. They'd straightened in their chairs, but neither had obeyed her order. "How you faring out there?"

"That is of no consequence. Sister Zanna requires you."

"Whatever for?" Callie committed to her innocent act, excited by the prospect of going somewhere, anywhere.

"An examination. You're long overdue."

Callie swallowed her gasp but couldn't force down her fear. Here was the only test she might not be able to pass. And she'd be taking it in minutes.

Sister Nora clapped her hands, but they failed to rise. She sighed. "You'll follow me."

"Might she not be convinced to accommodate us here?" Callie almost choked on the words, but she knew her decision to be the right one. Another Hiero adage: keep control of your environment. Any chance she had of convincing Sister Zanna she was with child hinged on remaining in their room.

Sister Nora shot her a petulant stare, wanting, Callie recognized, to refuse. But some internal scolding—in Sister Juliet's voice, no doubt—prompted a curt nod.

"Very well. I'll have her assemble all her equipment"—Callie could hear the eye-roll in her tone—"and tonics and files and bring them here. Is there anything else you require?"

Hands clasped in her lap in such a way as to emphasize her "burgeoning" belly, Callie met her scowl with a sunny smile. "Not for myself. Miss Kala?"

"Chamber pots ain't gonna empty themselves."

Callie didn't think the dark stain on Sister Nora's cheeks was a blush.

"Of course."

After she'd called one of the novitiates in to tend to that chore, which she supervised, Sister Nora locked them back in with an exuberant clank.

"What the bloody hell were you thinking?" Miss Kala demanded in a harsh whisper once Sister Nora's footsteps retreated down the hall. "Air! We could be breathing slightly less stale air!"

Callie worried her hands as she searched the room for some form—any form—of inspiration. But the same vomit-yellow wallpaper glared back at her, unrepentant.

"That she won't bother with more than a medical bag and whatever hocus pocus the Daughters employ. If she can't perform a full examination, she might..."

Miss Kala blinked, twice. "Might?"

"Conclude that all is well."

"How would she come around to that idea?"

"In the normal fashion."

"The normal..." A smirk twisted Miss Kala's lips in a way that had Callie shrinking in her seat. "You've not got the first notion about midwives, have you?"

Callie scoffed weakly. "They help usher babes into the world. What else is there to know?"

"What she's about to do to you, for a start."

"She's to examine me to determine my general health and whether I'm with child."

"'Cept you're not."

"Yes, I am aware. Hence the problem." Callie gripped her arms so tight she tore into her sleeve. "If she's separated from her instruments, she won't be able to perform a proper test. She might retreat to an older method, which I could more easily pass."

"Instruments? Test? Pass? Rubbish. Ain't no science to this, miss." Miss Kala bit her lip, Callie suspected, to keep from laughing. "What comes of being raised by gentlemen, I tell you."

Callie glared at her. "If you mean to scold, you can begin with my absent mother."

"Fair deal," Miss Kala conceded. "Not likely she'd have known enough to tell you."

"Tell me *what?*"

The click of the lock silenced them. Callie mashed her tongue with her teeth, desperate to scream. Everything they had learned, everything they might have learned, dashed by a deception too far. She wanted to hurl herself out the window.

Two Daughters in nurse aprons carried in two long metal posts with weighted bases, which they planted on either side of the bed. They strung a sheet width-ways across, curtaining off the pillows and most of the top. Two elephant-trunk sleeves jutted out of the lower middle of the sheet, flanking an oval-shaped retractable flap...

She pressed her fist to her mouth, catching the shriek in time. Gulping back shuddery breaths, Callie grabbed a bread knife and stabbed it into her palm.

Two warm hands enveloped hers. Miss Kala knelt before her, her gaze consoling, her round face soft, calm. Once the Daughters disappeared, she eased the knife out of Callie's grasp.

"You weren't joking about..." Callie couldn't bring herself to say it.

"No." Miss Kala sighed. "I'm not sure how this happens. I just heard it does. I got lucky in my auntie is a wise woman." As she spoke, she dabbed a napkin on Callie's cut. "Are you still a maid?"

"The household is unconventional, but we're not improper."

"Course. Just that makes it a bit tougher to explain. There's a part of you, deep inside, that holds the baby in while it's growing. And when you're knapped, it gets darker. If Sister Zanna's a midwife, that's what she'll be looking for."

"And this happens every time?"

Miss Kala shrugged. "Can't say, really."

Callie's breaths quickened, eyes prickled. Fear would solve nothing, would give the game away, but this... She never could have prepared for this. She needed a miracle.

"I... I don't want..." She couldn't even look in the direction of the bed.

"Don't I know it." Miss Kala's chuckles somehow helped her to breathe. "No question, if you're a maid. But don't worry. I'll sort you."

"What? How?"

And then the blasted door swung open.

"Blessed morning to all."

Sister Zanna flew in with two Daughters on her heels. She dropped her black bag and a file folder into a chair and moved to examine their work on the curtain. One of the pair wheeled a half table that extended over the bottom edge of the bed into place, then set about lining medical instruments up along its surface. The size and suggestiveness of these gave Callie heart palpitations. Miss Kala shoved a teacup into her shaking hands—also to cover up her still-bleeding wound—and stood.

"Mightn't there be somewhere more private for milady to disrobe?"

"Has she dressed for the day?" Sister Zanna looked to them and sighed. "I warned Sister Nora, but... well. Not everyone cares to speak of such things."

"As I only know too well."

"Ah." Sister Zanna appeared to have received some unspoken message from Miss Kala. Unable to decipher it and irritated at her disadvantage, Callie returned her focus to the wallpaper. "We'll start slowly then. Shall we?"

Callie pretended to be in one of her altered states as Miss Kala led her over to the bed. She slumped onto the bottom edge, ever conscious of the curtain behind her. When Sister Zanna ordered all of the shutters opened, she shrank back from the light that exploded into the room. Even the weather was against her, with London experiencing an abnormally sunny day. All the better to shine a light on her most intimate parts, expose her for a fraud while these kidnappers luxuriated in the shade of their garden. The injustice of it made her want to spit.

Particularly at Sister Zanna, who snapped her fingers to wake Callie from her feigned reverie.

"Mrs. Sandringham, hello. I wonder if I could learn more of your history?" She began by taking Callie's pulse, cool, firm fingers on the soft of her wrist. "Has a doctor examined you since the miracle occurred?"

"In Assisi."

"And he counseled...?"

"Rest. Not to overtax myself."

"And how thorough was this examination?"

Digging deep within herself, Callie located the spirit of her character and smiled.

"He needed no intrusions or impropriety to heed the Mother's call. He believed."

Sister Zanna pressed her tongue-tip pressed to her teeth, but she saved herself from tisking.

"I wager he has not lost as we have lost. Mother Rebecca's child perished with her. We want to assure ourselves that this time the way is clear for Her return."

"What shall be is as She wills it." Callie fisted the sheet on her far side to keep from lunging at her. "I am at your disposal."

Sister Zanna nodded. "May I begin?"

The gentleness of her touch surprised Callie. Sister Zanna concentrated on her abdomen, feeling around for devil knew what and pressing in at certain spots. Her face remained impassive throughout, not a hint of intrigue or disapproval coloring her features. Every so often she paused to scribble a note into Callie's file. Another snap of her fingers sent the other Daughters out of the room, and she rose as if to follow them.

Callie didn't dare hope her ordeal was over.

"Combination or chemise and drawers?" Sister Zanna asked

Miss Kala.

"Drawers."

"Good." She turned back to Callie. "You need only remove those, along with any underskirts. If your corset is tight, you might care to loosen it. Lay back and fit your legs through the sleeves. I promise it will be quick."

"I'll sit with her," Miss Kala said.

"Yes, do." Sister Zanna stared at Callie for a long moment, as if daring her to refuse. "I'll fetch a lantern. Be ready when I return."

Callie didn't hear her leave, couldn't hear anything at all over the clamor of her inner wails. She woke up when Miss Kala hitched up her skirt and yanked down her petticoat. She then thrust her buttocks at Callie, who nearly reached for her revolver.

"Corset laces, if you please."

"I don't understand."

"No time. Just do it."

Callie plucked the knot loose and pulled open the corset's binds. She gaped as Miss Kala fussed with the crotch seam of her drawers, then disappeared behind the curtain.

"Well, come on!"

By the time Callie rounded behind one of the metal poles, Miss Kala had slotted her legs in the elephant trunks and her maidenhead straddled the flap. Or so Callie assumed since she'd covered herself with her skirt.

"What... You can't..."

"Hush yourself and get back here. She's supposed to think it's you."

"But..." Choked by a mixture of anxiousness and gratitude, Callie crawled onto the bed. And didn't hesitate to take Miss Kala's hand.

"Now, now, don't fret. Not my first time in this position, let me tell you."

"What if she looks back here?"

"Haven't the foggiest. You're the actress. Get ready to improvise."

Callie squeezed her hand harder as Sister Zanna entered the room. Her lantern illuminated a shadowplay of action on the other side of the curtain, with more detail than Callie cared for. Callie held her breath as the seconds ticked by.

"Ready?" Sister Zanna asked after an eternity.

She glanced at Miss Kala, then replied, "Aye."

Sister Zanna peeled the flap open, but no part of her could be seen through the hole. Miss Kala let out a long, slow breath, spared Callie a smile. Though a part of her remained horrified by this intrusive process, Callie had to admit she also wanted to sneak around to the other side and peer over Sister Zanna's shoulder. When else would she have a chance to observe firsthand the workings of the female anatomy? Then her brain supplied the answer Hiero would likely give, and she scowled.

"There. All done."

The flap closed. Callie heard a pen scritch as Sister Zanna completed her notes. Miss Kala wriggled out of the elephant trunks, and they hurried to switch places on the bed, muffling their nervous giggles. Belatedly Callie shimmied out of her petticoat and messed her skirt. She affected a serene look as Miss Kala slung the curtain back to receive their verdict.

Sister Zanna, for her part, beamed. "All is as it should be. Nearer to five months along, I'd say, Mrs. Sandringham. Or should I call you the new Mother Rebecca? Time will tell."

Callie concentrated on hiding her relief so totally it wasn't till Sister Zanna was gone and the lock clanked back in place that the truth occurred to her. And she remembered the scene in the back staircase at Berkeley Square: Miss Kala despairing, Han consoling...

She whipped her head around to confront Miss Kala but found her anger smote by the sight of her tears.

"Please don't tell Mr. Bash. Not until we find Lil."

"I won't," Callie said, stunned by her words. "Of course I won't."

She staggered off the bed and over to the street-side window, her mind aflame. As she pressed her throbbing brow to the pane, Callie wished for the cool of evening, for the cover of night, for a means of escape. Not just from the Daughters' clutches, but from herself. From a body that longed for Han's steadying presence seconds after learning he could never be hers. From a brain too scorched by betrayal to reason their way out, a heart that kindled empathy for the woman who had acted on desires Callie couldn't admit to having.

She flexed her fist open and closed, wanting to hurl something, to punch through the window. Instead she shoved a finger in her mouth and chomped down on a knuckle. She glared at the wallpaper, the floral pattern resembling more and more the links of a chain. Yellow, the color of apathy. If only.

Once the fires within burned through her last reserves of contempt, she cast about for something, anything to occupy her time till nightfall. And spied a slip of paper on the chair. Callie lunged. To no avail—nothing but a few numbers and some bland observations about weight and coloring. Until lightning struck.

"Her files."

"What?" Miss Kala blew her nose loudly.

"Sister Zanna keeps private medical files on all of the novitiates. She evaluates everyone who enters here."

Miss Kala gasped. "She'd have one on Lil."

"We'll find out tonight."

No sooner had Tim hopped off the omnibus at his usual stop than a pair of apple-cheeked girls accosted him. Fortunately he recognized them as the twin daughters and principal message-bearers of his new landlady, Mrs. Fitzgibbons.

"Mr. Stoker! Mr. Stoker!" they chirped in unison. They tended to ignore the fact he was a detective unless reporting a petty crime.

"Maisie, Molly," he greeted in proper order. Not even their mother matched his success at telling them apart, much to their delight (and occasional disappointment). "What's this clamor?"

"A gentleman's come calling for you," Maisie breathlessly explained.

"He's caused ever so much fuss," Molly elaborated.

Tim stilled. Unless a new client solicited his help—and none had ever done so here at his lodgings, preferring the luxury of Berkeley Square—Sir Hugh's impatience had gotten the better of his reason.

"Has he now?" Tim offered them his arms out of courtliness but also to control their pace. He searched for signs of a carriage as they strolled down the block.

"Insisted on being let into your rooms," Molly continued, no doubt parroting her mother.

"Turned up his nose at the parlor," Maisie said.

"That's just as well." Tim stopped them again, his mind scrambling to prepare as he added, "Girls, those who come to visit me do so for very private, very sensitive reasons. Often when someone or something precious to them has been lost. So you must not think less of them if they don't want a chat and a cuppa."

The two of them bowed their heads, looking so serious Tim couldn't help but chuckle. With a skip to his step, he led them on. They found their smiles.

"Is that why he wouldn't take tea?" Maisie asked.

"Most likely. Though perhaps he didn't want any."

"And he brought in so many baskets?" Molly queried.

"He... what?"

"Mummy was quite beside herself," Maisie, all of eight years, observed. "He asked so many questions her face grew hot."

"Like when she used to help Simon with his maths," Molly said.

Tim paused a third time, reevaluating.

"Questions, you say? Of what sort?"

"About everything!" Maisie stretched her arm wide to encompass the world. "The furniture and the blankets and the lights."

"What we eat. How often you eat with us."

"How many apartments are let. Who lives in 'em."

"And about the walls." Molly shook her head, still dismayed. "How thick they are. What's on the other side."

This prompted Tim to quicken his step, such that the girls had trouble keeping up.

An overgenerous reward from a previous client had permitted him to move from a clean but cramped lodging house in Pimlico to a larger, more respectable apartment in Kensington. As one of the first tenants to lease in the refurbished building, his comfort and contentment was of particular interest to the widowed Mrs. Fitzgibbons who, Tim soon realized, saw in him a potential second husband. That even someone as oblivious to the attentions of the fairer sex as Tim recognized her intentions spoke of how overzealous they were. Work, and a key to the back-alley exit, served him well.

Mrs. Fitzgibbons waited for him in a chair by the front door, hands clasped over her sternum and arms tucked under her bosom for emphasis. No sooner had he released the girls than she launched herself at him.

"Oh, DI Stoker, forgive me, forgive me! I told the gentleman you weren't in, to leave his card, but he was so insistent!"

Tim patted her shoulder as he eased her back.

"Don't trouble yourself, Mrs. Fitz. The gentleman is a client of mine. We have much business to discuss."

"I hope no threat oppresses you, DI Stoker? Should I send word to your colleagues at the Yard, just in case?"

Tim forced a smile onto his lips, wishing he had misjudged her character.

"Nothing of the kind, I assure you."

"It's just he inquired so thoroughly after the security of the apartment."

"A precaution only. He does not care for his business to be overheard." He leaned in, pretending to take her into his confidence. "Foreign Office, you see. A matter of international secrecy."

"Goodness! I had no idea you were involved in affairs at such a high level, DI Stoker."

"I will no longer be, if word gets out about his visit." Tim gave her shoulder a squeeze, gazing deep into her eyes. "I hope I can rely on your discretion?"

"You have my word." She tilted her chin upwards, inching toward him.

"And my gratitude, Mrs. Fitz."

With that he raced for the stairs, taking them two at a time as he climbed to the third floor. Tim left his brain no room to speculate as to the whys of Hiero's visit, too eager to be reunited with him after another frustrating day. After matching every one of the thirty-eight listings in Mr. Crook's ledger to a living child, Tim had been forced to conclude Little Bean had never been delivered to the orphan asylum. Unless Han's spies uncovered another orphanage the Daughters donated to—unlikely given how many babes they put into Mr. Crook's charge—Little Bean had been kept somewhere on their compound. Which meant Tim must go back to pounding on brick walls for information.

With Han volunteering to act sentry outside the Daughters' compound that night, Tim had retired to his apartment to strategize and reconsider his options. Not that he expected to accomplish much of either now—somewhat of a relief, given the day's frustrations.

Tim exorcised himself of his case-related thoughts as he paused to adjust his clothes and smooth his hair. Wisps of smoke with the unmistakable aroma of Hiero's cigarettes snuck through the cracks in the door. Just as he did whenever he visited Hiero's dressing room at The Gaiety, Tim shut his eyes and listened, letting his ambitions for the evening play out against the blacks of his lids. Whatever transpired always bettered Tim's peepshow imaginings, Hiero more inventive and inimitable than the limits of his mind.

Tim couldn't keep himself from grinning as he swung in. Dimmed lamps lined a short corridor, the end of which bloomed with candlelight. As he shut and locked the door behind him, Tim felt something akin to Mrs. Fitzgibbons's earlier swoon. He shed his overcoat, hanging it beside a fur-trimmed cape whose provenance stoked his excitement. He petted the collar, reveling in the feel of it against his bare skin. A quick adjustment to relieve the pinch in his tightening trousers, and he entered the parlor...

... to find its spartan atmosphere transformed. A fire blazed in the small hearth, enhanced by the closed curtains, smothering all but a brilliantine line of sunset between them. Swathed in a sateen throw and adorned with a small feast, Tim barely recognized his table. A sultan's boudoir's worth of fabrics draped over every piece of furniture, and a plush carpet textured the floor. Peacock's-tail pillows turned his favorite armchair into a throne. A crystal decanter of garnet-red wine and two slinky glasses rested like the crown jewels atop a tray on his desk.

And slouched across the far seat of his divan, a sleeping beauty.

Hiero, debonair in a red velvet smoking jacket, paisley cravat, and black silk trousers, curled around a gold-and-green brocaded throw probably meant as a cover. His cigarette, now naught but ash, had burned a hole in the cloth. His squinting face betrayed an intense concentration; his staccato, panting breaths warned Tim off waking him. But even in the throes of a dream, his wild handsomeness affected Tim. If he'd had any artistic talent, he would have sketched Hiero then and there: languid yet vulnerable, enthralled but untamable. A rare lapse in a life spent on guard against such intrusions. Tim took the compliment.

And wondered what to do. He didn't care to disturb Hiero but considered he might be more comfortable on Tim's bed. Tim admitted to himself how he longed to see him there, snug under his mother's favorite quilt. How many nights had he fantasized about Hiero stealing into his bedchamber, stripping in the moonlight before blanketing Tim with his long, sinuous body?

He leaned on the far edge of the divan as he shed his jacket and boots, letting the scenario play out in his mind's eye. Let his fingers wander across the top of the wooden frame, tangle in the sin-black waves of Hiero's hair. Tim felt Hiero's tension ease as he petted his proud head. His shoulders drooped and his breaths evened when Tim slipped his hand down to caress the rich brown skin at his neck. Hiero's arms sagged and the throw flopped to the floor. Tim approached slowly, cautiously, sliding in to replace the cloth before easing Hiero against him.

He floundered under the crush of his weight, too much for him to lift.

A soft moan purred in his ear. Arms still heavy with sleep anchored around him, pulling him down against the cushions. Hiero clung to him as if adrift on a roiling sea, shivering even in the parlor's balmy climes. Tim hugged him close, kissed his perspiring brow.

"They've come for me," Hiero mumbled.

"Who's that?"

"The creepers."

Tim feared he'd taken fever. When he reached up to feel his brow, Hiero clasped his hand. With a sharp intake of breath, his head flew up. The fight rushed out of him when he saw Tim, who wasn't sure if he was entirely awake.

"You came." Hiero sighed, rubbed their cheeks together.

"I rather hope so. It's my apartment."

"Your..." He turned to take in the room. "So it is."

"One might even come to the conclusion you were waiting for me."

Hiero burrowed against him, tucking his head into the crook of Tim's neck. Not a disagreeable position.

"I was, yes." A weak chuckle. "Surprise."

"And a happy one at that." Tim stroked a warming touch up and down the length of his back. "Are you quite well, my lovely one?"

"Tired," Hiero said in as straightforward a manner as Tim had ever known of him. Which led him to suspect something was deeply wrong. "I've slept poorly these past nights."

"Then take your ease awhile longer. I've some notes to compile, then I'll have a wash. Clean off some of the day's disappointments." Tim nudged him forward, all he could manage. "Come, you'll be more comfortable on the bed."

"Mmm..." He'd already begun to drift off.

Tim wrenched the two of them upright, which sent the right signals to the semiconscious part of Hiero's brain. He let himself be tugged to his feet, staggering the few paces into the bed chamber before collapsing onto the mattress. Tim folded the two ends of the quilt around him. Fortunately it was wide enough to almost double-wrap Hiero at the top. Tim pressed a soft, lingering kiss to his lips, a promise to be fulfilled at a later hour.

He watched over Hiero for some time after, struggling to silence the noise of questions that deafened the normal workings of his mind. Answerless questions asked of an enigma, no better, Tim knew, than screaming into the void.

Chapter 13

$\mathcal{H}$iero drifted awake to the clink of a spoon against the side of a bowl. Kip reclined against the baseboard of the narrow, creaky bed in which Hiero had been entombed. The cover that shrouded him was thin and starchy, its stained edges sign of being well-loved. Under the nose-itching scent of laundering soap lingered a fresher, earthier smell. Not quite that of Kip's skin or sweat, but in the same family.

And then Hiero understood why. He suddenly felt no rush to rise or escape from the cocoon of near warmth the quilt provided. Even if it ended midcalf, his slippered feet jammed between the bottom edge of the mattress and the wooden board. Through a curtain of hair, he watched Kip scarf down what was likely his second, perhaps third, bowl of pudding, a berry trifle Minnie had seasoned with orange liqueur instead of sherry. Swathed in a familiar teal-green robe and nothing else, his taut-muscled limbs splayed and his damp hair mussed, he looked every inch the gentleman of leisure. If that leisure involved gymnastic bouts of sex.

"I'd wondered where that had got to." Hiero wriggled onto his back into a pose he hoped looked inviting. It did, if Kip's answering leer was any indication.

"If you'd wanted to keep it, you shouldn't have insisted I wear it."

"At Berkeley Square, not on walkabout."

"Then you shouldn't have bought me a second one."

Hiero scoffed. "Sticky-fingered imp."

"Overgenerous clotheshorse."

"Do try to barb your insults, my dear. Otherwise I might get the idea you're actually fond of me."

"I confess I am rather partial to your presence. Especially in my bed." Kip scooped up the last bit of trifle, then set the bowl aside. "To what do I owe the honor of this visit?"

"It has been brought to my attention by a certain injured party that I've never ventured here before."

"Ah." With a soft chuckle that in no way masked his delight, Kip shifted to his knees and slid off the robe. Much as Hiero suspected, he wore not a stitch beneath. "And dare I ask what you think of the place?"

"A temple."

"Really?"

"No." After Hiero raked his gaze down Kip's lean, powerful frame and back again, two things became apparent. First, he'd developed an unnatural obsession with freckles, and second, Kip had spent a portion of Hiero's sleep time preparing himself. His semihard cock glistened as it thickened. A sparse trail of coppery hair dusted his navel and grew dense as it swirled around the base of his shaft, lacquered to his skin by a coat of oil, leaving Hiero to imagine how far back and how deep the coating went. "Your magnificent self, however…"

"Flattery. Hmm. A diversionary tactic?"

"Does your attention feel diverted?"

"Not at the moment." Kip unwrapped the cloying cover from Hiero, then prowled up the length of him, hovering just above his chest. "One thing in particular is stealing my focus." He spread himself atop Hiero until he felt the press of every decadent inch of him. Hiero stroked his hands down the broad sweep of Kip's back, purred as he curled them around his meaty buttocks. His answering erection prodded Kip's thigh, which flexed in welcome. "Are you recovered from your earlier fatigue?"

"Bushy tailed as a spring hare."

"Are you hungry? Would you prefer to eat?"

"Ravenous." He pinched a tight buttock. "And no. I've a well-established preference for fucking."

"Little wonder we get along so famously." Kip carded his fingers through the waves of Hiero's hair, an almost bashful smile playing on his lips. His moss-green eyes contemplated Hiero's face, devoid of the searching quality that normally tinged his gaze. "I'm glad you've come. I've wanted for you."

Hiero fought the hitch in his breath when he admitted, "So have I."

"Good."

The heat of his kiss came as something of a relief after that shiver of sentimentality. From the first brush of his lips to the full sweep of his tongue, Kip methodically unraveled him, paying Hiero the kind of lavish attention so few of his former lovers had. Pinned to the mattress by his compact but powerful body, Hiero was at the mercy of Kip's talented mouth. Even his wisp of a mustache tantalized him when it tickled his top lip.

Lured deeper and deeper into passion by every clutch and caress, Hiero almost forgot to breathe under the onslaught of Kip's sensuous lips. He gasped when Kip broke off to scrape his teeth down Hiero's neck, only to mourn his absence and whimper him back, not ready to quit his long, luscious kisses. If only every day could end with Kip so wanton and willing, every night bear witness to scenes of sensual debauchery. Hiero felt drunk on Kip already, his head spinning and his limbs honey slow, the hot pulse of his loins set to a lazy rhythm.

The second time Kip eased away, Hiero chased after him, catching and worrying his bottom lip between his teeth. He drank deep of Kip's chuckles but hissed when Kip pinched a nipple through the cloth of his shirt with a pair of nimble fingers. A flick and a twist set him cursing. When Kip began to rock his hips in time with the twirl of fingertip around Hiero's nub, his eager cock met and matched the grind of Kip's shaft.

Eyes gone devil dark, Kip increased the pound and pinch until Hiero let out a growling moan. He dropped a kiss to Hiero's tormented nipple, dragged it down the length of his chest until he hovered—panting, smirking, rapacious—over his sheathed erection. Kip rubbed his flushed cheek up and down the side of the prominent bulge, nipped the head through the silk.

"May I?"

Hiero, too breathless to speak, nodded his assent.

With the last of his strength, he hoisted himself onto his elbows for a better view of Kip easing his cock and balls out of the flap in his bed trousers. Hiero spread his legs that Kip might settle between them, moaned as he clamped a firm grip around his base. Reached for his gingery head to guide him down, not that he needed any encouragement. Kip's mischievous expression before he licked the length of Hiero's cock made him quiver with anticipation.

Hiero let his lids slide to half-mast, dulling his other senses so every lap of Kip's tongue, every suck of his singular mouth, wrung double the pleasure from him. Kip's masterful technique had stunned Hiero in their first encounters until he understood just how many had come before. That Kip now gave of himself in this way to Hiero, and Hiero alone, intensified his enjoyment. He took perverse satisfaction in imagining Kip with his forebears, on his knees in an alley, in a carriage, in a box at the theater, being schooled in the ways of the flesh by a dozen faceless masters. But Kip couldn't ignore Hiero, couldn't turn away from him. He kept coming back, desiring him, drawn to him by forces beyond their earthly plain, the only otherworldly power Hiero believed in. The greatest of all aphrodisiacs.

Hiero cried out as Kip deep-throated him, digging his nails into the nape of Kip's neck as he rode the riptides of sensation. A hard throb in his bollocks warned of his imminent end. Hiero keened, bucked, only for his lover to strand him on the precipice. With a manic grin, Kip gave the head of Hiero's prick a final, consoling peck, then lunged. Slamming Hiero back into the mattress and straddling his hips, Kip hung over Hiero until his fever cooled.

"Fiend," Hiero panted even as the hard stop ignited a firestorm of pleasure within him.

"Are you denying me a chance to join in the festivities?"

"I heard no objection when you were smiling around my prick." He gazed up into Kip's giddy, luminous face and forgave him everything. "Kiss me."

"Not yet."

"Rascal."

"You've no idea."

"Show me."

He lifted his hips and, with painstaking deliberation, lowered himself onto Hiero's shaft. Kip breathed out a blissful sigh, head and back arched as he sank down to the root. Hiero could have spent hours admiring him: the flush that rosied his skin, the damp tendrils of copper hair that framed his face, the jut of his thick cock. How completely he gave himself over to the rut—this thinker, obsessed with motives and minutiae, fucked with rare abandon. And this most beautiful part of himself, this emulsion of his inhibitions, he saved for Hiero alone.

With brutal slowness, Kip raised and lowered himself so Hiero felt every inch of penetration. He grabbed for a knee, a calf, cursing the fact they communed on such a cherished quilt. Kip caught his hand, crushed it, a tether that only amplified their indelible connection. Thoroughbred thighs set a pounding rhythm, but the true spark was in Kip's expression. Hiero watched as arousal turned carnal, as pleasure became passion and ecstasy evolved into rapture. Hiero felt both one with his body and apart from himself, transformed into the implement that broke and remade Kip from within.

"Harder," Kip urged, shifting his hips in search of the perfect angle. "Please, Hiero, make me feel it."

"Anything for you," Hiero panted. "Everything for you."

With a deft maneuver, he flipped Kip onto his back. Kip's brawny thighs hugged his sides as he found Kip's sensate center.

"More," Kip hissed, lifting to mingle their heavy breaths, couple their hot mouths. "Everything."

Hiero hammered into him, chasing their bliss. Wild howls of joy staggered with moans licked Hiero's ears and tickled his spine and stirred an answering pulse in his groin. Kip's ebullient eyes, the phosphorus green of a sea anemone, locked with his as ecstasy overtook him.

Hiero burst with unexpected violence; marrow-deep pleasure infused his bones; stars singed his eyes. He sought shelter in the familiar slope of Kip's neck as his body shook and his senses celebrated, Kip's dizzy chuckles vibrating his cheek in the wake of his own completion. They stayed tangled up in each other until the air chilled, then quickly resumed their embrace once under the covers.

Even held snug against Kip's chest, Hiero struggled to sleep. Kip dropped off after an extended kiss that almost reignited them, but Hiero, despite the languor of afterglow, couldn't quite rest.

Never one for self-reflection, he instead reconsidered his location. They were, he would admit only to himself, suitable apartments. Adequate for a man of Kip's social standing and tendency to be consumed by his work. Not cozy, but not without character. Kip wasn't the type to splash his personality across his walls. He showed himself in details: the tidiness, except for that one overflowing bookshelf; the shrinelike alcove stuffed with family portraits; the minuscule wardrobe of same-y suits, with the two Hiero had bought him in front of the others, in place of pride. His kindness toward his landlady despite her being so painfully besotted with him. His extra truncheon on a hook by the door, prepared to confront whatever dangers might threaten.

The makings of a comfortable life. One Hiero would never be a part of. One he saw no reason to lure Kip away from, no matter how loudly an inner voice protested that Kip belonged at Berkeley Square.

Hiero had always been kept. First by villains, then by Erskine, then Apollo. He'd expected, once he came into his own, to be the one doing the keeping. It was the only way he knew how to be intimate with someone. But from the first, Kip had resisted. Anyone could see he was his own man. Coming to this place, visiting the Yard, following Kip about as he led their investigations, it became increasingly clear to Hiero he hadn't the first clue how to be with someone so independent. How to share, not captain, a life. That one day Kip would tire of him and sail off on his own adventures.

With a heavy heart, he shut his eyes, welcoming the darkness. But sleep proved as elusive as peace of mind.

Hiero emerged from the black fugue of his thoughts sometime later to find a gentle hand petting his head. He shifted so Kip's warming touch might find his shoulders and the nape of his neck, but that only encouraged Kip to thread his fingers through Hiero's hair. Like Solomon before him, Hiero knew a good deal of his strength and seductive power lay in his locks, which he kept unfashionably long for just that reason. He also knew Kip favored these types of caresses because he did not wish to stray to parts of Hiero's body he'd been warned away from.

Though grateful for this show of respect, he suddenly rued having imposed such restrictions on Kip. He longed for Kip to unleash himself on his person, to give over to his artful lovemaking. But Rebecca Northcote, like Pandora before her, understood the consequences of such revelations, the lure of an unopened box. That certain secrets held more power in being hinted at than revealed.

"What's troubling you, my lovely?" Kip redoubled his efforts to stroke Hiero into a submissive puddle. "No evasions or digressions. I've seen the flicker of something like fear shadow your face too often of late."

Hiero cursed in seven languages under his breath. "I'm not afraid. For myself."

"Say the word, and we'll escape Calliope and Miss Kala from Castleside."

"Not for them. Or Lillian. Or anyone at all."

Kip huffed out a very unconvinced sigh.

"The past is the past," Hiero insisted.

"Unless something in your past has bearing on your present situation." Kip stroked a persuasive set of knuckles down Hiero's cheek. He swallowed back his instinctive purr. "It's not my intention to mine your history for nuggets of insight. And I'm well-versed in your reasons for secrecy. But I see you suffering, and it maddens me that I can do nothing to alleviate it." He dropped a crown of kisses to Hiero's brow, each one more tender than the last. "Sometimes I wonder which of us is the greater fool."

Hiero stilled. "How so?"

"Myself, for caring for someone who will forever remain elusive, or yourself, who dallies with a lover who will never cease his questions. And inferences."

"'Inferences'?"

"One of the consequences of bedding a detective." Kip slid his hand down to massage Hiero's neck. Then lower, under his collar, to the ridge of scar tissue that prevented him from feeling anything at all. On his back, at any rate. He tensed, fighting the urge to rip away, to flee into the night. "We intuit patterns. If we've observed a certain behavior before, seeing it again in someone new will trigger our instincts. We can't help but notice everything. Especially in those who seek to hide."

"How long have you known?"

"I know nothing. I've suspected. Not the details of your story, but the outline." He withdrew his hand and resumed his caresses, drawing Hiero into an embrace so strong, so heartfelt, he wanted to claw his way out. "A familiar one to anyone with our inclinations."

With the fortitude of a man who had reinvented himself after countless hardships, Hiero held fast to his resolve.

"Has it never occurred, Detective Inspector, that I *am* the man I was always meant to be? That there's no great mystery? This history of mine was an act of becoming. I may have had other names. I may have lived other lives. But I have always been Hieronymus Bash."

Kip fell silent. He continued to run those consoling fingers over every approved area of Hiero's upper body, letting their fevers cool. Every brush of his hand repeated what Kip left unsaid: his devotion, his affection, his care. Why couldn't Hiero give in? What possible harm did he think would come to him if he shared a small part of himself with his lover? But everything in him screamed against it.

"My dear, dear Hieronymus. I don't want you to be anything other than the man I adore. But the past will out. I cannot protect you if I don't know where you're vulnerable."

"Protect me?" Hiero scoffed, but not even he believed this show of disdain. "Are you in the business of chasing specters?"

"The effects of this case appear quite real. And there's no telling what the newspapers or a motivated enemy might dredge up."

"And you would defend me?"

"With everything in me."

If he'd been looking Kip in the face, Hiero wouldn't have been able to trust himself after such a declaration. As it was, he bit the edge of his tongue bloody keeping himself in check. He dug deep into his arsenal of dismissiveness and flippancy for just the right weapon. Then he remembered: when in doubt, mock.

"But what would your hallowed superiors think of such a maneuver? Wouldn't you be duty bound to turn me in? What of your indefatigable sense of honor?"

"You are a good man. Is there no honor in defending a good man?"

Another volley deflected. Would he never draw blood? Hiero

attempted to appeal to Kip's innate sense of justice.

"You would not judge me so softly if you knew what I'd done."

Kip had the gall to laugh. "Ah, yes. Playing the part of the scoundrel yet again. Tell me, without revealing any incriminating details, have you ever... plotted against the crown?"

"Only Her Majesty's dressmakers."

"Committed a treasonous act?"

"Every second Wednesday."

"Forced yourself on someone?"

"Certainly not." Hiero shuddered. "I go only where invited, especially in matters of the flesh."

"Hurt or maimed a child?"

"My dear Kip, what do you take me for?"

"Have you... killed a man?"

"A thousand with my eyes." Hiero sighed, wishing he could somehow convey to Kip the complex circumstances of his origins... without reveling anything about those origins.

"I preferred to use my fists."

Hiero's racing thoughts stopped cold at that declaration. He flipped around to confront Kip, who wore a self-satisfied smirk. Hiero might have slapped him had he not been so curious.

"You mean all this time I've been the one bedding a murderer?"

"Surprise." Kip chuckled but didn't hesitate to explain. "My first year as a constable, the Yard was on the hunt for an arsonist. Chap had a bad habit of setting fire to the houses of royal mistresses."

"A radical firebug?"

"Something of the kind. They received information that he would strike in my division. They enlisted the entire station house. Being the newest, I was assigned a partner and positioned on the route he was least likely to escape from. Which, of course, he proceeded to take once the deed was done. He gave us quite the chase, all the way to the river. He tried to jump the rail. We caught him in time, dragged him off, but he gave us a fight. He had the strength of desperation—we struggled with him for what seemed an eternity. Finally I got a solid punch in. He spun, tripped, and cracked his skull on the guard rail. Stone dead by the time he hit the ground."

"Were you reprimanded?"

"Worse. Promoted." Kip nodded at Hiero's look of distaste. "It brought me to the attention of Sir Hugh Winterbourne, then a mere superintendent—"

"—now the commissioner. A useful friend to have."

Kip nodded. "Saved me from ruin twice now. In this affair and our business last autumn." His eyes turned inward. "I owe him not just my career, but my freedom. And there's only one person in this world I would defy him for."

Hiero inhaled a shaky breath, heart in his throat. He met Kip's tender, inquisitive gaze when it shined his way, let his giving arms hug him close. Accepted his Kip's confession.

But still could not find the words to make his own.

"I should away." He gentled a kiss to Kip's lips before he could protest. "Before the walls grow ears."

"If you must."

Hiero tried and failed to ignore the sadness in Kip's tone. He almost choked on the shame that filled him. He busied himself with rising, righting his clothes.

"Best we'd not give Mrs. Fitzgibbons further cause for resentment."

"Quite so." Linking their arms in a streak of possessiveness Hiero might earlier have appreciated, Kip escorted him to the door. "Still, I hope she won't deter you from a repeat engagement."

"Never." Hiero felt Kip's sigh of relief, despised himself all the more.

"Then we'll rendezvous at the compound once I've consulted with my client."

"Goodness. You've been summoned?"

"Yes. Still with nothing to show."

"Tell him..." Hiero thought better of his initial, more flippant counsel. "... to have faith. Rome wasn't built in a day and all that."

A trace of a smile twisted his lips. "I'll omit the fact the advice came from you, a godless thespian."

"Prudent."

Hiero lingered in the entranceway, desperate to be away but unable to bring himself to depart. Kip, melancholy but patient, stood fast beside him.

"Kip, I..."

"Good night," Kip hushed him, pulling him down for a farewell kiss.

He held the door as Hiero segued into the corridor. The click of the lock echoed through him, beckoning him back inside. But he could only move forward, out into a bleak and sleepless night.

Chapter 14

Callie suppressed a shudder as she peeked through a seam in the infirmary window's blind. The few visible beds were occupied by convalescing novitiates, their mountain range of bellies snow-capped by blue-tinted sheets in the eerie cast of the moonlight. Some slept with funereal stillness. Some stared at the gray void of the ceiling, eyes skull-like in shadow.

No candle or attendant that Callie could see through her sliver of perspective. No door leading to an office either. Only an audience to their nighttime skulking. Unless they'd all been sedated, any one of the novitiates could sound the alarm when she and Miss Kala infiltrated Sister Zanna's office. Presuming they could find it.

She crouched back down, crawled over to the next window. Same room, different perspective. Sister Zanna had a full house. Callie wondered if she locked them in; she didn't see any restraints. Silent as statues, no aches, no moans of discomfort. Not a single one clutching breasts swollen with milk. Some unknown influence scared them into compliance, of this she was certain. As outraged as she was, her mission was elsewhere.

A cry split the air. Callie turned in time to see a light dawn in the next window. No blind shuttered it. She crept under its sill, then eased her head up into the lower far corner until one eye peered inside. Six cots, at least one occupied, if the ear-shredding wails were anything to go by. One of the Daughters hurried to scoop the little one up and carried the babe over to a rocking chair, behind which loomed a door with a name plate that read, *Midwife*.

Then a second babe tested the power of its newborn lungs. Callie also wanted to scream.

With extra care, she made her way back to the outskirts of the conservatory, where Miss Kala hid amongst the shrubbery. Only once they were concealed did she let out a sigh.

"It's blocked," Callie whispered. "The only way in is through the infirmary and the nursery."

"Where the babes are sleeping?"

"Not sleeping, rather. And they've a nurse."

"Blimey. That's bad luck."

"I'm afraid we must abort the mission."

"Can't see why. More than one way to get in there."

Callie couldn't plot her way past a room full of crying babies. But then Miss Kala's wiles had proven their worth. "What are you thinking?"

"Of a diversion." She gestured toward a stick and patch of fresh soil. "Draw it for me."

As Callie dug a rough sketch of the layout, she set her mind to enumerating obstacles, ever the devil's advocate. She wouldn't act unless their success was guaranteed.

"Was the window bolted?" Miss Kala asked.

"Unlocked. But it'll rattle and rail, as ours does."

She bit her lip, considering. "Might work to our advantage to wake the babes. If there's a ruckus outside, they'll be expecting their cries."

"We must have time to search." Callie examined her crude drawing. "If their nurse is called away, one of the novitiates might steal the chance to see their child."

"And you think she'd lag on us?"

"I can hardly say what she'd do. They appeared drugged or... lifeless."

"Even the Daughters aren't crazy enough to kill new mothers." A spark fired her eyes. "But we might be."

"What?"

"A wolf in the henhouse. That would rile them up. Have the nurse racing to be rid of it and calm them down. Wouldn't be able to go for help until she did."

"Interesting. But what would do it? A rock through the window?"

Miss Kala shook her head. "Think high drama, Mr. Bash style."

"Pity he's not here." Callie felt a pang in her chest as she spoke the words. She'd missed Hiero's unbalancing influence these past few days. She never realized how serious the business of chaos-making could be. "A flaming rock?"

"Near babes? Bit too murderous."

"That's the flaw," Callie sighed. "Anything dangerous risks the children, and anything not is too tame."

"Quick to surrender, aren't you?"

"I will admit to not being terribly adept at improvisation. A trick like this would normally take at least an afternoon to plan."

Miss Kala shrugged. "Tomorrow's another day."

"Which gives the murderer another reprieve from discovery. Not to mention another day in which my mother remains lost, and we remain trapped here." Callie poked her head above the shrubbery line, scrutinized their surroundings. "We must act now."

"What about the tallywag in your thatched cottage?"

"I beg your pardon?"

"You know," Miss Kala appeared to snicker, "the ploughshare in your Miss Laycock."

"Are you speaking in tongues?"

"The trouser serpent in your fruitful vine."

"Speak plain," Callie groused. "I don't care to be mocked."

"Your pistol," Miss Kala whispered, pointing at Callie's trouser leg, where the outline of the MAS revolver was indeed visible.

Callie cursed under her breath.

"I thought we'd agreed no one would come to any harm."

"No one should, unless you're a naff shot."

Shooting her a withering look, Callie explained, "Glass won't stop the trajectory of a bullet. Even should I aim at the ceiling, it might hit someone above or ricochet. And Standish is my last resort."

Miss Kala cackled. "Standish? You named your pistol Standish?"

"Shh! You'll give the game away before we can have any fun." Callie wished she could snuff the flush that reddened her cheeks. "And he's a revolver, if you must know."

"Of intimate acquaintance, are you?"

She blushed so fiercely her skin steamed. "Perhaps if you focused your mind on the task at hand and not the gutter, we'd both be in far less trouble." She glared at Miss Kala's abdomen to underscore her point.

Which only made her laugh harder.

"I breathe trouble, or so my pops always says." Miss Kala wiped her eyes with her sleeve.

"Then turn yourself to mischief *not* at my expense. Or do you require discipline for inspiration to strike?"

She chuckled into her arm, pretending to cough. "Figured you for one of that persuasion."

"Is there a dictionary in which I can reference these allusions of yours?"

"No one's ever bothered setting them to paper. Too busy practicing, ain't they?"

Callie let out a long sigh. "I surrender." She waved a hand in the direction of the infirmary. "Problem. Solve it."

Tempering her grin, Miss Kala glanced about, muttering, "A wolf, a wolf, my kingdom for a wolf..."

Inspiration struck just as Callie opened her mouth to complain.

"Not just a wolf..." She nudged Miss Kala's arm, directing her attention to the garden wall across the lawn. "A henhouse."

Callie relished the thought of recounting the tale to Hiero later as she watched Miss Kala sneak into the chicken coop. After defeating the gate locks with ease, they'd scurried down the garden path, grateful for the silvery moonwash on the pebbles. The untamed half of the garden loomed like a black maw in the distance. The closer they got, the more Callie envisioned being swallowed up by some invisible predator. She normally didn't entertain such cut-rate fears, but something unnatural queered the air beyond the brook. She heard the rustle of leaves on a windless night, smelt the undercurrent of death beneath all this fecundity. Had another victim been buried under the tree? If so, the poor soul would have to wait till light of day.

Miss Kala emerged with a burly rooster, his beak clamped in her fist.

"Should we chance taking another?" Callie asked.

"Grab a hen if you'd like. It's your barmy plan." Miss Kala wrestled the bird as she slipped through the fence. "But I wouldn't want to risk her getting hurt. This one'll kick up enough of a fuss for five, I reckon."

"They won't want to harm him. He's too valuable," Callie reassured her.

"Likely not, but accidents happen." Another shrug. "It's a sound plan and the least dangerous of the lot."

"Then let's away."

They hurried to retrace their steps along the shimmering path. Once through the gate, Miss Kala hugged the wall while Callie fiddled with the locks. Not wanting to risk a sprint across the lawn, they detoured down the width of the garden to the outer wall, then followed it until they could cross to the conservatory without being seen. The light in the nursery had been extinguished, but Callie knew that had no bearing on whether the nurse was still about. Any sane person would kip in the rocking chair between disturbances, but then the Daughters had their peculiar ways.

She caught up to Miss Kala at the shrubs. For long minutes they listened, checking for any reason they should not proceed. Callie pet the rooster's fiery plumage, marveling at the thunderous beat of its heart. A yellow eye stabbed out through Miss Kala's brown fingers. Not afraid; furious. He would do.

"Ready?" Callie asked.

"For this brand of madness? Always."

Callie crawled on her hands and knees over to the infirmary window, a sizeable rock in hand. A glance back assured Miss Kala waddled behind her, twitching as their feathered friend clawed at her arms. Once they were in place, Callie leaned back, aimed, and smashed the rock through the glass.

They heard its thump on the wood floor. No one stirred; no one shrieked. Miss Kala popped up, tossed the rooster in. A flap of wings, the click of its talons on the glass.

Silence.

"Damn." Callie pressed a knuckle to her brow.

"Drugged, I wager." Miss Kala dodged a piece of falling glass. "The nurse hasn't come neither. Do we shuffle on?"

"I can't see—"

An eardrum-gashing crow threatened to wake the dead.

"That'll do it," Miss Kala said as the screaming started.

The hard slam of a door heralded a blaze of light from above. Callie had a leg through the nursery window when the chorus of babes began wailing their little hearts out. They rammed their way into Sister Zanna's office, Miss Kala monitoring the scene outside through a crack in the door while Callie bludgeoned the lock on the lone filing cabinet with the butt of her revolver. It fell, clanking on the toe of her slipper; she bit back a groan. She ripped open the first drawer... only to find it empty.

"Blast."

Three more drawers, nothing of consequence. She turned to the desk. Her file bisected a pile of what had to be current patients, likely those yelping and screeching in the next room. Not a scrap of paper on the children or anyone else.

"Hurry. The others have arrived."

"Have they caught him?" Callie searched every speck of the pristine office, hands quaking with desperation.

"Can't see through walls, can I? The novices have quieted."

"And the babes?"

"You gone deaf or something?" Miss Kala seized her arm. "Come on, or they'll catch us!"

Callie stilled, all five senses alight, nerves brimming with energy. In defiance of defeat.

"Perhaps they should."

Miss Kala grunted in disbelief. "You have gone barmy. Should have scarpered when I had the chance."

"Go now, if you want. It might be your only chance."

"And face Mr. Han when I return without you? I'll take my chances with these lunatics."

Callie covered the hand on her arm, squeezed it.

"You have more important things to consider. Go. If I don't signal by morning next, tell them to come for me."

The sound of cooing from the nursery frozen them to the spot.

"Tell them yourself. We're cooked."

The door flew open. Sister Nora stood in the frame, a glower contorting her heart-shaped face. A heavy ring of keys tinkled at the waist of her skirts.

The house on Dodger's Way had little enough to recommend it at night. By day the sunlight that filtered through the gray cloud cover exposed its drab, crumbling exterior. The tattered mulch of the lawn, the chipped brickwork, and the listing cant of the front steps all conspired to warn off any respectable callers. They would, however, attract a criminal element, which made Tim wonder why Sir Hugh kept the house in such a state. But then perhaps it had been better cared for when the late Mrs. Winterbourne was alive.

As he waited for the candle, Tim struggled to direct his scattered thoughts toward his current objective. But they returned again and again to Hiero. He did not think he imagined the feeling in his black-star eyes at the height of their passion. A feeling that—for Tim, but he believed for Hiero too—transcended the physical. Of understanding. Of belonging.

His fingers itched as he remembered how Hiero stiffened when Tim touched his scar, and then later, when he all but fled from Tim's bed. Every time they talked anything of substance, Hiero's resolve turned to sand and slipped from Tim's grasp. Was there never to be more between them than insinuation? Was he following a trail of crumbs that led not to a woodland cottage, but off a hidden cliff?

Tim had been overjoyed to see Hiero there in his apartment, among his things. Thought their evening the beginning of a new stage in their strange relationship. After their bed play, he'd wanted to make a gesture. To paint for Hiero a portrait of the man he knew. A kind man. A giving man. To share with him some of Tim's complexities. Perhaps he had revealed too much? Perhaps he wasn't the only one enchanted by mystery?

Curled up on the divan that still smelled of leather and strong coffee, of Hiero's maddening musk, Tim had fretted over his next move in this tangled dance of theirs. His ambition did not lie in learning all the steps, only to be led by his cunning paramour. Tim would have to grow more adept at reading his signals. He must make a study of his silences. He simply had to convince Hiero he did not lack devotion. And pray it was enough to bridge the chasm between them.

None of which prepared him for the very serious meeting to

which Tim had been summoned. When that disembodied hand slid the candle into the window, Tim straightened his posture and shook off his romantic preoccupations, prepared to play harbinger of doom. He inwardly enumerated his points of argument as he entered the house and retraced his steps to the vacant parlor.

Vacant except for the same two chairs, the bottle of Scotch and tumblers on the small table, and Sir Hugh by the hearth, his stern look tempered by the glow of the firelight. That he'd lit a fire to warm up the room spoke of its state of decrepitude. Despite the gothic atmosphere, this was no assignation. Tim marched forward and stood at attention until acknowledged, ready to make his report. Dispiriting as it was.

"Good day to you, Sir Hugh."

"DI Stoker." Sir Hugh gazed into the flames as if willing them to dispel the black cloud that hung around him. "What news of your investigation? What have you learned about these Daughters of Eden?"

"That they've piss-poor organizational skills and a talent for obfuscation." Tim had hoped that would earn him a chuckle, but Sir Hugh looked as somber as the grave. "Hardly a surprise given they are a charity. Impossible to accuse them of doing away with something there's no record of."

"'Doing away'?"

Finally Sir Hugh glanced his way. And Tim discovered he would have preferred to remain ignored. His eloquent brown eyes betrayed the depths of his worry. Underscored by a blur of purple and maroon, their whites boiled pink by insomnia—or worse, anguish— they bore into Tim with an intensity well beyond the necessities of command.

Confronted by those eyes, Tim almost couldn't get the words out. Didn't want to be the cause of their widening or their welling. His news would drown the last glimmer of light in them, and for that, he was dearly sorry. But duty, as ever, called.

"There's been a turn of events."

Sir Hugh regarded him for a pregnant moment. Then, shaking back into himself, he strode over to the small table and poured them a glass. Once fortified with a long draught of the Scotch, he sat. A horse ready to bolt.

"Make your report."

Tim cleared his throat, took the seat opposite.

"Secrecy is the Daughters' trade. The prophecies of their founder and spiritual leader, the protection of the fallen women they harbor, the discretion with which they barter with their benefactors. At first I learned everything I could about them, and then I sought to infiltrate them. I posed as a wealthy patron seeking to adopt from them. This disguise proved effective at first. I gained access to their current leader, Juliet Tattersale, in the hopes of learning what becomes of the babes born to them. They pretend most are adopted out, but in fact they are remanded to the local orphan asylum, whose records I've obtained. I mean to match them to the Daughters', but securing these has become a five-act farce. They keep records of the mothers, but not their children, you see."

"But that's absurd."

"And, I'm certain, a falsehood. I've seen several of the babes in their keeping. They each wear a coded tag." A half truth, but Tim wanted to ground Sir Hugh before he shocked him. He unfolded the paper wing from a handkerchief in his pocket, carefully displayed it for the commissioner. "But the ledger linking this code to their birth mother—and any potential benefactor—I've yet to uncover."

A tender expression softened Sir Hugh's face as he examined the tiny wing.

"With good reason, though it creates a challenge for us. I'm almost relieved it requires such effort to prove any association."

"If nothing else, your identity is well-protected."

"Quite." Sir Hugh settled back in his chair, not entirely relaxed, but less rigid. Tim knew his next words would change that. "Your disguise. You said it proved effective at first. What changed?"

"The aim of my investigation." Tim sucked in a deep breath, forced himself to meet the commissioner's stare. "During my interview with Juliet Tattersale, an incident occurred. A body was discovered half-buried under a tree in their garden. A babe." Tim watched as Sir Hugh fought to maintain his composure. "A boy."

"My... my son?"

A nervous twitch seized the left side of his face; Sir Hugh forced it still.

"As yet there is no evidence indicating it is your child," Tim explained. "I have found no way of connecting the boy to any parent, mother or father. He may not even be the issue of one of the fallen women the Daughters keep. He wore a tag—this tag—but that could be a feint. My objective now is to identify him and, by doing so, discover a motive for his murder."

Sir Hugh's head, which had dropped, pricked up at that. "Murder?"

"The boy had been strangled."

Sir Hugh shut his eyes, his chest rising and falling with locomotive force.

"Was there...?"

Tim could barely get his mouth to form the words, knowing the images they would conjure.

"Starvation? Yes. We searched for evidence of baby farming but have found none. Given that some of the mothers choose to keep their children with them or house them elsewhere, it could be a form of vengeance or accusation from someone who had been in their care. Or rejected by them and forced into desperate circumstances. Until I identify the boy, I cannot discount any possibility."

By this time Sir Hugh had diverted his eyes back into the fire, white-knuckling his fists around the arms of his chair. He struggled to still the tremble in his bottom lip. Sorrow and fury appeared to war within him, and both against the instincts of a career officer.

"Where is he?"

Tim stammered, surprised. "He is safe."

"*Where?*"

"I was forced to reveal myself to the Daughters in order to secure the scene and perform an examination. We removed him to a secure location."

"Damn you, Stoker, where?!" Sir Hugh seemed as startled as Tim by his outburst. He downed the last of his scotch, slammed the tumbler on the table. "Swear to me he is not with…"

"Sir Hugh, I have not broken my vow to you."

A scoff. "You put a murdered child in *his* keeping?"

"There is a cold room at his townhouse. I could not bring the body to the Yard without alerting suspicion. I could not trust the Daughters not to disappear the body."

"You could have brought him here!"

"No, I could not." Tim fixed his gaze on the empty space above the mantle, counted back from fifty. Prayed that was time enough for Sir Hugh's reason to return. "The task before me is not impossible, but it is large. A five-acre compound. A four-story house. Thirty active members of the Daughters of Eden at my best guess, to say nothing of the women in their care. I required the help of trusted allies. I have not spoken your name. They do not know my true purpose. Only that we chase a child murderer—a cause that needed no further explanation to enlist them."

Silence fell. Sir Hugh had sunken so far inward Tim couldn't tell if he had heard a word or was even aware anyone else remained in the room. Tim waited out his inner machinations, anxious, fidgety. No matter what Sir Hugh decreed, Tim could not abandon this case. For all his confusion, he knew only they—the team he'd finally learned to value—had a chance at solving it.

"Take me to him."

Sir Hugh's words were so unexpected Tim almost asked him to repeat himself.

"Sir, that would be—"

"Unwise? How well I know it."

Tim corralled every rational argument he could think of to dissuade him, abandoned each one in turn the minute they entered his mind. It would have been easier to fight off a snake with a spoon.

"Sir Hugh," Tim implored, "you know as well as I there are evils in this world that, once seen, cannot be unseen. As officers of the law, we think ourselves immune. But we are not. When it comes to those closest to us, we are not."

Sir Hugh drew in a long, shaky breath, then stood, resolute.

"I will see him, Stoker. Take me to him, or this is the end of our association. All of our associations."

Chapter 15

*H*iero observed Han observing the box with well-honed
nonchalance. His vision swayed to and fro—the combination of sleeplessness and day drinking making him tipsier than
usual—such that Han appeared to waltz around the desk in his
study. He swished the amber liquid in his glass in counterpoint to his
dancing friend, giggled. A thirsty sip, and finally the weight of his
heart began to lessen, buoyed by the half bottle he'd consumed since
the lunch he hadn't had.

Upon his return in the wee hours of the morning, he'd ordered a
bath. Hiero disliked inconveniencing his staff, but he was desperate
to scrub off every last speck of that place, every trace of Father
Coscarelli. Aldridge, always such a gentle soul, washed his hair and
buffed his nails. Held the mirror as Hiero trimmed and curled his
mustache. Worked the useless but rich-smelling salve into the
grooves of his back. All the while Hiero wished a thicker, softer set
of hands could soothe him back into himself. But he'd foregone that
privilege in the name of... what? Pride? Vanity? Fear of betrayal?

The memory of Kip's wounded eyes pressed hard upon his chest.
He poured himself another glass.

"He'll have your hide for this," Han declared, concluding his
examination by thumping the lid of the box. Or what Hiero assumed
was the lid of the seamless hunk of metal.

"Hardly the first time."

"That you've been had, or that he's had you?"

Hiero scowled, fingers itching for a cigarette with ash to flick in his face. But his case had been too far away earlier, and he too unsteady to fetch it.

"Don't be vulgar. Or, rather, do be vulgar, but about your business."

"Your well-being isn't my business? Then what have I been doing, following you around for the past thirteen years?"

"Haven't the foggiest. But as I've no complaints, do continue."

That almost earned him a smile.

"He'll be twice as tetchy when he sees the state of you."

Hiero set down his drink, attempted to stand, escape. Failed.

"I fear we won't be seeing much of dear Kip once this affair is ended."

Han looked like he wanted to chuck Mother Rebecca's box at Hiero's head. Hiero, for once, would welcome the pain.

"What have you done now?"

Hiero scoffed. "A panther doesn't change its stripes, no matter who comes stalking down the veldt."

"A panther doesn't have stripes."

"Precisely."

"Or spots."

"No matter."

"They live in the mountains or the jungle."

"Don't be a pedant."

"They're not social creatures. They don't crave an audience. Or someone, a special someone, to call their own. Perhaps even to keep them."

Hiero exhaled a blustery breath that threatened to turn into a raspberry. He lowered his gaze into his glass, wanting to lob it at the wall. Knowing he would miss and take out some objet d'art.

"He thinks I'm a good man."

Silence. Then a laugh. "He's a better judge of character than I would credit."

Han, standing over him, stole away his bottle and glass. After ringing for coffee, he resumed his scrutiny of the box, leaving Hiero to marinate in his missteps. Which he did for some time until a tall, ornamented carriage out the window caught his eye. It rolled to a halt before the front steps, but no one emerged.

"Who's that?"

Though not sober by any means, the coffee had stilled some of his wobblier aspects. Han joined him in peeking around the edge of the curtain.

"I can't place the coat of arms," Han said. "It's none of the noble houses."

"And no politician would dare be seen at our door. Curious."

"Should we prepare?"

"For whom? The Mother's return? The female messiah? We've said our prayers and lit our candles and sent our wards to be conscripted." Which gave him an idea. "You don't think Sister Juliet has sicced a benefactor on us?"

Before Han could reply, the driver hopped down to open the carriage door. His very own Kip emerged, face sallow and brow furrowed, followed by an exceedingly handsome man Hiero sought to murder with his eyes. A stunning Byronic beauty Kip somehow had the gall to escort up the front steps. The knock at the door set his teeth on edge.

"Handle them," Hiero ordered, sauntering over to the drinks tray at the far end of his study.

"I've never known you to be a coward. Or a fool."

Stung, he deflected. "You clearly haven't been paying attention."

"Clearly."

He felt Han wait until they heard voices in the entranceway, then slip out into the corridor. Perusing all the shiny bottles of jewel-toned liquids, Hiero considered which one to drown himself in. But the distant twitter of Kip's voice, a sunrise bird who wouldn't let him laze about till noon, pecked at his ear, interrupting his poison selection. Kip had come to him despite their contretemps the night before, for reasons Hiero couldn't believe to be anything other than the case. So who was his companion, and why had they turned up on Hiero's doorstep?

There was only one way to find out: eavesdrop.

After a fortifying sip of his neglected coffee, Hiero listened for the fade of their voices down the corridor. He poked his head out in time to see them disappear down the back stairs, Han behind them. What they wanted in the kitchens remained to be discovered. Assuring himself Aldridge had returned to his duties, Hiero toed off his shoes, then slunk after them.

He made himself small, which was to say the height of an average-sized man, as he crept down the back stairs. When the kitchen hall became visible, he lowered himself to hands and knees on the step and peered into the room. Not a soul was in sight, not even Minnie supervising the loaves of baking bread. Hiero inhaled deep of the cozy scent, considered stretching out for a nap like his feline forebears.

A loud crack reminded him of his mission. Where had they got to? And what business could Kip and a strange man possibly have in his basement? The point of snooping, of course, was to uncover things, so Hiero padded down the last of the steps into the vast, empty kitchen. Two rows of mini meat pies cooled on a rack. His lunch-skipping stomach gave a lurch. Stealing a dishcloth and one of the pies—venison with mushrooms and ale, unspeakably delicious— he surveyed all the adjoining doors he never paid any mind. All closed.

Brushing a few crumbs off his lapel, he discovered the shadowed entrance to a small corridor at the far end of the hall, hidden behind the washtub. Hiero stuffed the last of the pie in his mouth. If the Daughters craved knowledge of the truly divine, they should learn the recipe to Minnie's crust. He licked the corners of his lips as he tiptoed past the tub.

And froze. Not due to the misty wafts of air pouring out of the cold room, but realization. Of the reason for Kip's visit and the stranger's possible identity. Of the fact that no one had bothered to mention Little Bean's body was being stored beside the carcasses from last month's hunt, or what sort of scene he would be intruding upon. The venison pie threatened to reappear, but he measured his breaths until the feeling passed.

Then he heard the strangled gasp the stranger tried and failed to swallow, and he couldn't keep away. Sneaking past the half-open door, Hiero pressed against the outside of the frame and craned his head around. An awkward vantage, but one from which he could disappear with ease. The man—and thankfully, the butcher's block that served as an examination table—were beyond his view, but Kip wasn't. He hovered near his companion. His formal stance and controlled mien indicated it was the only sort of comfort the man would accept. Hiero read concern, trepidation, caution, and also intimidation in his expression.

One out of four wouldn't do.

"He is mine," the stranger declared, every syllable underscored by ache despite his dispassionate tone. "The picture of his mother."

"With the greatest respect for your instinct, sir, I fear we must have proof." This from Kip, and Hiero saw how much it took from him to counter the man's opinion. "If there are others, if there's a pattern, those responsible must be brought to justice."

"Justice," the man sneered, and Hiero had to agree. "All my life I've fought to uphold the laws of this land, of morality, and look..." Hiero saw Kip reach, and quickly withdraw, a consoling hand. "Look what I've done to my only boy."

Hiero blinked rapidly, caught unawares by sympathy. Kip had the good sense to remain silent. Long minutes stretched by. Hiero could imagine all too well what was transpiring in the room beyond, so much so he almost wanted to gouge out his eyes. He considered leaving but couldn't risk disturbing them.

"In your honest opinion, DI Stoker," the man asked, his voice raspier and harder than before, "can you resolve this matter to everyone's satisfaction? Do I need to involve the Yard?"

"Sir, your reputation—"

"Is done." The man wrestled with a shuddery breath. "As am I. I will resign my office as soon as I watch whomever's responsible for this hang."

"That would be a great pity. And a victory for the villain that's done this."

"They took advantage of what I set in motion. I could have kept them both. I could have married her. My pride wanted this. My hunger for status and reputation. This villain will pay for their crimes, but so must I. I ask again, are you confident you can bring me this fiend?"

"I can, sir, and I will."

"Good." Hiero sighed in relief, but the man continued in a growl. "Because if you fail me in this, if you let my son be buried unavenged... we'll both be done. Do I make myself clear, DI Stoker?"

"As crystal, sir."

The rustling of a sheet warned Hiero of their imminent exit. He sank back into the dark at the far end of the corridor, held his breath as the two men escaped the room. The grieving stranger strode toward the kitchen without a second look. Kip turned to lock the door... and saw him. An eye-roll preceded a staying hand before he pursued his companion out.

Hiero counted to twenty before making his retreat. He slipped past a stern-looking Minnie counting pies, dashing up the stairs in time to watch the front door close behind them.

Or so Hiero thought. He reentered the study to find Han and Kip frowning over the box, the latter grumbling under his breath. Hiero slowly started to back out of the room when his shoes betrayed him. By his tumbling over them.

A snickering Han helped him back to his feet. Once standing, Hiero was confronted by Kip's tormented expression as various factions within him warred for dominance. Annoyance, as was its wont, won out. Hiero rushed to take charge of the moment.

"Your client, I presume?"

"An easy deduction, given your attempt at spycraft. You might have asked for an introduction."

"Would I have been given one, I wonder?"

Kip let out a heavy sigh, not bothering to answer. He indicated the box.

"Why am I only learning of this now?"

Hiero's gaze strayed over to the drinks tray. Han shoved his now-cold cup of coffee into his hands. Hiero feigned a sip, set it on the desk.

"Shall I ring for more?"

"Once you've answered my question."

Hiero shrugged. "It was hardly the moment—"

"To alert me to the fact your cover is blown, you've stolen a potentially priceless item from the subjects of our investigation, and they at this moment might be plotting against you while your ward, her mother, and her nurse are trapped on their compound, you mean? You thought that cause for a seduction, did you?"

Hiero fought against the urge to cower, Kip's face aflame with a force of anger he'd never seen before.

"I-I hadn't slept."

"So fatigue dulled your wits. I see. And after?"

"We needed rest. To forget awhile."

"Do not pretend to speak on my behalf when only one of us was in possession of all the facts. As ever." Kip hissed a breath, fighting to rein in his temper. "The man who just left... My client. I know you understand the profundity of his loss. I know of your echoes, and your exhaustion, and the existence of things you will not speak of. But I must do everything in my power to prevent what happened to his boy from happening to anyone else. And if you impede me in any way…"

He didn't want to say the words. But Hiero heard them all the same, and they cut him to the quick.

"I understand."

Kip stared at him, still furious, still at war within until whatever he saw in Hiero's face satisfied him.

"I pray so." He turned back to the box, unable to mask his curiosity despite his lingering irritation. "Genuine or imposter?"

"Impossible to say," Han replied with a supportive glance Hiero's way. "If the contents are genuine, then they are fools to chance their exposure. If they prove unmemorable, then it could be a fake meant to ward off thieves."

"Or Mother Rebecca's secrets might not be so priceless after all," Hiero noted, forcing himself back into the moment.

"Either way," Han concluded, "there's no way of knowing until we open the box."

"They've gone to an awful lot of bother making an impenetrable nothing if it proves to be an imposter," Kip said. "I wager there's something to be found within. Whether that's worth any value…"

"One man's treasure is another man's tripe." Hiero clapped his hands, joining them by the box. "Such is the way of the world. The present mystery—"

"—is how to open it." Kip lifted it, gave it a shake. "It does feel rather solid."

"The world's most enigmatic paper weight."

Kip replaced the box with a dull thud. "What do you make of it, Han?"

Hiero forgot his troubles when he spotted the glint in his old friend's eye. Acquaintances often mistook Han's calm and quietude for reserve. In truth, he'd learned to share himself only with those who bothered to look deeper. And those who mined deep enough uncovered a trove of intelligence and a wealth of personality, and even a slight flair for the dramatic.

Han straightened to his fullest height, pressing the tips of his fingers to the far edge of the box's lid. After shutting his eyes, he hummed a low note. With painstaking slowness, he smoothed his fingertips along the length of the lid. He repeated the gesture along all four sides. Hiero struggled not to laugh, remembering the technique from their days with Erskine. How the audience would crane forward just as Kip did now, so focused they ignored the real trick being prepared all the while.

Han had known the solution from the first.

"Here." Han gestured for Kip's hand to replace his in the center of opposite sides of the box. "Hiero, come." He guided Hiero's hands to the lower edge of the front and back panels. "Gentlemen, lift very, very gently. Do not let your fingers stray from their spots." They did so. Han slotted his hands to the right of the top and bottom sides. "And now... push!"

With their communal effort, bars broke out of the seamless sides of the box. The rectangular shape morphed into something jagged and menacing. Hiero resisted the urge to toss it into more capable hands as Han pried out a bar, which he jammed into one of the other spaces. A flick of his wrist, a turn of the screw, and a lid within the lid popped open to reveal...

"DI Stoker," Han asked, "would you care to do the honors?"

Kip's rapt features betrayed not a trace of his earlier aggravation as he reached into the box. Hiero shivered, thought of those mythic faces carved into walls, inviting you to test your mettle by sticking a hand in the god's mouth and risk it being bit off.

"How very Mother Rebecca to insist we penetrate her most sacred orifice in order to find her treasure." His audience ignored him, too concentrated on their discovery for double entendres. Hiero sighed as Kip pulled a sheaf of papers from the box. "Now what have we here? Gunpowder plot or plodding dissertation?"

"Revelation, more like." Kip flashed them the title of the unfinished treatise. "As in Book of." He flipped through the pages. "With chapters on the Final Preparations, the Seven Signs, the Lord's Judgment, the Advent of the Messiah, the Mother's Return, and the Opening of the Garden. We've happened upon Rebecca's apocrypha."

"Nothing else?" Han asked.

"Just this." Kip dug back in and pulled out a scroll, which he unfurled across the desktop.

They pored over a map entitled *Eve's Tomb*. An apple marked her gravesite, with a nest of tunnels snaking out from there, color coded red and green. These connected to three other areas, one with a castle symbol, one with a gate, and one simply marked with an X. No legend, not even a compass point, hinted at the real-life location. At least not to Hiero's underwhelmed eyes.

"A subterranean labyrinth," Han said. "But to what end? The Daughters hardly need to sneak around their compound."

"Agreed." Kip laid books around the edges of the map to mimic the walls of the compound. "I can see the use of the cellar at Castleside—here—perhaps to store their most valuable or prized possessions, but the rest… Why not simply travel aboveground? The perimeter walls conceal everything from the street."

"Perhaps they are remnants from an earlier time. A papist enclave in the Jacobean era?"

"Quite possibly. And for our purposes, another avenue of investigation." Kip pulled out a ruler from Jove knew where—Hiero didn't recall purchasing any sort of geometric equipment—and began to measure different lengths on the map. "Supposing Eve's Tomb is indeed under the tree…"

"… this could be how the boy's body appeared without anyone noticing," Han finished.

"Or where others are being kept." Kip slammed his fist on the desktop, a very un-Kip-like demonstration. Hiero fought the instinct to lay hands on him, knowing they wouldn't be welcome. "I need unrestricted access to the Daughters' ledgers. There *must* be some way to account for any babes who have gone missing besides Little Bean."

"This opens a new avenue of investigation," Han reminded him. "Who had access to the tunnels and the opportunity to use them on the day the body was found?"

"About which I'm certain the Daughters will be just as forthcoming." Kip tapped an impatient tattoo on one of the books as he scrutinized the map. "But yes, we'll have to connive a way of searching them."

Hiero shrunk away from the desk, the thought of spending hours underground quickening his heartbeat and cinching his breath. He grabbed for the coffee Aldridge had ghosted into the room a few minutes earlier, scalding his tongue on his first sip. Still, he continued to pour the hot liquid down his throat.

"This here." Kip pointed to the area represented by the gate symbol. "Beneath the farmhouse, do you think? That's near the side gate."

Hiero barely stopped himself from choking with a violent cough, spitting coffee all over his fist. A tunnel beneath the farmhouse gave new meaning to the skitters and squeaks that had plagued him in the night. His days of bedding down with vermin of animal and human persuasion were well behind him.

"The barn. Less intrusive." Han bent over to follow Kip's measurements. "Your theory is we could access the tunnels without disturbing the Daughters?"

"A last resort, but yes. I'd like to take another crack at Sister Nora—"

Angus's much louder interruption caught their attention.

"Mr. Han, sir. One of your lads came calling, stationed at DI Stoker's lodgings."

He handed the note to Kip, who all but ripped it open. Hiero would never tire of watching the play of intrigue and amazement across his face in such moments.

"Another of Sister Juliet's missives," Kip announced. "'Dear Serpent. We've discovered the bad seeds you planted among us.'" He frowned as he read the rest. "She proposes an exchange. The box for Calliope and Miss Kala."

Han tore the note from his grasp. After reading it for himself, he crumpled up the note in his fist and launched it at the chalkboard. "We must go to them at once."

Kip nodded. "Angus, if you would be so good as to ready the carriage."

He was already halfway out the door.

Hiero couldn't believe his was the voice of reason. "You're charging into a trap of their making without accounting for... accountable things."

"And well I know it." Kip retrieved the balled-up note, smoothed it into legibility. "But if we're to press the Daughters to the breaking point, we must remove any leverage they have against us. Otherwise we're at their mercy."

Han, his upset sharpened into piercing resolve, rejoined their group.

"Callie's insights into the Daughters' ways would be more valuable *before* we answer their summons."

Kip sighed. "I concur. But their part in our gambit has somehow failed, and we must assure no harm comes to them. Besides, I do not think the Daughters bold enough to act against an officer of the law, no matter who counts among their benefactors."

Hiero snorted. "You mean to wager your safety against their respect for higher offices? The pantheon is the only authority they acknowledge. You're not even a demigod."

"They spotted your false prophetess with ease and turned her against us, so I hardly think you're in a place to judge."

"I thought you knew better than to feed yourself to the lions."

"The only martyr here is your sense of self-preservation."

"Control yourselves!" Han barked. "This isn't the time for a lovers' spat."

"Correct," Kip acknowledged. "It's time for action." He turned back to the desk, cutting Hiero out. "We'll need a copy of the map and the box restored. The most likely location for the exchange is Sister Juliet's office. Han, might you manage to infiltrate Sister Nora's vault and search her files whilst I have them preoccupied?"

He nodded. "We'll devise some means of distraction along the way."

"Have Angus at the front, ready for a swift getaway. I might remain to continue my inquiries, so as soon as Calliope and Miss Kala and, if we are lucky, Mrs. Pankhurst emerge, spirit them away."

Hiero cleared his throat. "And what of myself? You know of my allergy to omnibuses."

A chill silence fell.

"I will confront them alone." Kip foisted his bitter green gaze on Hiero. Still angry, then, and worse, disappointed. "There will be no negotiation if I return with the very scoundrel who stole their sacred texts. And given how the discomfiting echoes of being at Castleside affect you... it would be best if you held the fort. One never knows who might come calling."

At Hiero's weak nod, they set about their preparations with diligence and determination. He strayed over to the far side of the study, his absence unremarked upon. He clutched his coffee cup with both hands, blocking out the siren call of the drinks tray like Odysseus lashed to the mast.

Hiero stood beneath Apollo's portrait, admiring *his* benefactor's kind eyes and silvery mane. They had loved one another as befit their stations and something more beyond that. Rewriting their history in light of his relationship with Kip was of no interest to Hiero, but he had become aware of its limitations. Of his limitations. Of the challenge caring for Kip presented—to want more for himself, to be more for others.

He waited until they departed until emptiness shrouded the room. Then he drank the last of his coffee and set out on a late-afternoon call.

Callie woke to a living nightmare. With no light to focus on and no sound to sharpen her, she slogged through the slurry of consciousness until something stuck. Distant whimpering, the thread on which her mind could tug before it unraveled. With lugubrious purpose, she dragged herself out of the pit of medicated slumber.

The treacle stench of laudanum assaulted her first, spilled on her shirt as they'd fought to drug her. A mouthful of rust as a fat metal bar suppressed her tongue, violating her ability to speak. Her filmy, woozy eyes searched for light but couldn't see beyond the edges of the iron bars that crushed her head and cheeks, caging her face. Her heart too sluggish to pound, her lungs too pacified to pant, Callie drifted in the fathomless dark, unable to think beyond her fear.

Unable to scream.

The whimpering howled into a wail. Finally the clouds parted. A flurry of blinks and she made out several figures in the gaslit room. Some sat, some lay on scratchy straw mattresses. She reached to feel for her own, startled at the bite of a shackle into her wrist. Unlike the others, she'd been chained to the floor on both sides for her lock-picking sins.

Callie craned her neck around, found Miss Kala beside her in similar straits. Her head rocked from side to side, possibly an unconscious motion. Callie prayed the drug had no ill effects on the babe she carried. She doubted the Daughters would dole out any punishment that threatened the potential future messiah, but then, she also hadn't expected to be chained and gagged when she surrendered to them.

Scold's bridles encased their heads and silenced their tongues, robbing them of the ability to protest. But not of sound. In this damp, sulfurous underworld where the most rebellious novitiates were enclosed, they were permitted the company of their terror. Callie and Miss Kala had, at long last, found the cellar.

Her throat tightened, spasmed. Pinpricks of pain swarmed her eyes. Wheezing in frantic breaths, Callie chomped down on the bit, desperate to stave off the tide of emotion, of despair. She hadn't wept when word came her father had died, or when they were thrown out of their draughty little cottage in Portsmouth. Not when she broke her leg as a girl, or when one of her early governesses beat her for speaking out of turn. Not even on the day they laid her sweet uncle, her savior, in the ground.

But the wailing stabbed at something within her, hidden deep but tender. On and on it went, crying for them all. For why had these women been locked down here? Because they had questioned the delusional Daughters? Because they had succumbed to the temptations no man similarly inclined had ever been punished for? Because no matter where they went or what they did, they could never escape the strictures of their sex. Because they were owned.

Tears streamed down Callie's face, pooling in the grooves of the metal bars. She coughed around the bit till it choked her. A surge of bile scorched her throat, but she swallowed it back, scared it would drown her. She let out a sob to suck in a vital breath—then she couldn't stop. She lent her voice, her sorrow to the wailing woman until her throat had been scraped raw and her eyes squinted from swelling.

Numbed by defeat, Callie stared at the root-gnarled ceiling and attempted to steady her breaths. The woman wailed on, her grief indefatigable.

Annoyance poked at the back of Callie's mind. Why couldn't she give them a respite? Didn't she know her agony would go unanswered? That the more she pleaded, the more the Daughters would deny her? Unless…

Callie stilled, attuned all her senses to the woman's voice. Shame filled her as she realized how familiar the timber was, how similar the tenor to one that had haunted the corridors of Berkeley Square for the better part of a decade. So familiar, so provoking, Callie had long ago learned to tune it out. Until Miss Kala had come and killed it with kindness.

Mother, Callie cried, but only inside herself. Brittle relief suffused her, cracking at the thought of how torturous the past days must have been for her mother, trapped there in the slithering dark with her ghosts and demons. And now her daughter-rescuer just as trapped, just as helpless, just as foolish in thinking she could outwit the maniacal Sister Juliet and her alluring prophecies. *It was as you've always said, Mother. My head was held so high I tripped over my shoes.*

A second voice entered the fray, fought to be heard above the wailing. Lush and lilting, singing a tune Callie couldn't quite place. A lullaby.

The wailing gradually tempered. Instead her mother harmonized her voice to the song. Callie hardly needed to look over to know it was Miss Kala who comforted her charge, as she had every night since her arrival. Though the guilt of being unable to help her mother in the most basic of ways cut deep, she nevertheless sang along with them.

Some of the other women joined in, forming a choir of resilience that pricked Callie's eyes anew. The Daughters may have shackled her body and stolen her words, but they could not cow her spirit. As Callie gave herself over to the rush of their music, she began to devise a plan.

Chapter 16

Sister Nora met them at the gates to the compound. The twin pearls of her eyes glared at them from behind a mask of iron filigree. Tim could just discern the outline of her heart-shaped face beyond the dense metal mesh of the gate door, her white uniform disappearing the rest of her body at the neck. This floating-head effect ratcheted his already taut-strung nerves all the tighter. He pressed his arm to his side to remind himself of the presence of his truncheon, hidden in the inseam of his coat. Tim couldn't imagine any scenario that would prompt him to strike a woman, but if he'd learnt anything in his seven months with the Berkeley Square team, it was to be prepared for anything.

If only the Daughters themselves weren't still such unknown quantities. Tim felt the pinch of his limited resources as he searched the unrelenting stare locked with his for a sign of... what? Humanity? Hesitation? He'd curried no favor with Sister Nora from the start, and now that he'd been identified as an enemy to the cause, her bashful discipline had turned into righteous rage. Another unintended consequence of Hiero's little disappearing act—the box's theft had radicalized her.

"Good day to you, Daughter."

She blinked, unmoved. "Do you have it?"

Not even a foot in the door, Tim thought as he raised the black rectangle into view.

"And its contents?"

"Intact." Tim assayed a baleful chuckle. "We haven't been able to open it."

He got the distinct impression she'd raised a disbelieving eyebrow.

"Go to the visitors' chapel." She disappeared from view.

Tim cursed under his breath, waited until the brick wall hid him before consulting Han, who lurked there.

"Can it still be done?" Tim asked.

"Perhaps under cover of night. In the light of day, even in such gloomy climes…" Han shook his head. "I'd chance it if there was a window."

"Blocked." They'd planned to relieve Sister Nora of her set of keys with the old trip-and-pick routine on the way to Sister Juliet's office. The change of venue concerned Tim for more reasons than one, but he'd admit to being a little relieved. His touch was not nearly as light-fingered as that of Han or Hiero. "There's nothing for it. We'll have to return to fight another day."

"You won't meet with them?"

"Certainly I will. Though I fear they have no intention of surrendering Callie or Miss Kala."

A pinch to the center of his chest reminded him of Hiero's warning from the other day about the Daughters' infinite reserve of patience. And of Hiero himself, who, now Tim's anger had cooled, he wished had accompanied them. They could, if nothing else, have used his gift of persuasion.

"So we're left with an impossible choice." Han pressed the flat of his knuckles against the brick as a concession to his need to punch something. "If I sneak onto the compound to search for them, I leave you at risk. If I accompany you, we lose our only chance to rescue them."

Tim chuckled mirthlessly. "I am quite capable of handling myself, I assure you."

"We're blind to their numbers. Enough of them could overwhelm you."

"I'm as proud as any man, but I'm not above fleeing."

Han scoffed, dragged his knuckles down the wall. "He'll never forgive me if any harm comes to you."

"Then perhaps he should have thought twice before abandoning his charges and running riot over our plans."

Han sighed in what Tim pretended was reluctant agreement.

"Find them. That's an order."

Han nodded, clapping him on the back in solidarity before jogging off around to the far side of the compound. Tim whistled Angus over, apprising him of their changed plans and conferring him the box for safekeeping. He'd wait to see what stakes the Daughters raised before betting the only chip he had. He watched as Angus shifted the carriage into getaway position. His ever-busy mind assessed and recalculated the dangers to them all. The unknown variables burrowed under his skin, an itch he could never find to scratch.

The Daughters had been quick to connect him to Hiero. Had Callie or Miss Kala been tortured into a confession? Or had they somehow given themselves away by Hiero insisting they be allowed to investigate together? Another black mark on his not altogether spotty record. An unexplored aspect of the case was Sister Juliet's societal ties. She'd obtained Tim's home address from somewhere. Could that source also have shown her the recent headlines trumpeting Hiero's string of successes, which listed Tim as an associate? Could something as trivial as their growing renown cost Callie or Miss Kala her life?

Tim shoved those black thoughts out of his head, straightened his posture, and strode toward the chapel doors, determined to wrestle this investigation into submission no matter how monstrous it had grown.

In stark contrast to his first visit, with its inviting candle glow and trio of welcoming women, the empty chapel rung with the anticipatory silence of a pebble down a well. Tim's footfalls echoed as he walked down the center aisle toward the abstract of the Messiah. As a backdrop to Sister Juliet's preaching, the warm tones of the painting divinified her withy stature and water-sprite looks. Absent the otherworldly beams of sunlight from well-placed windows and the golden flicker of candle flames, its umbers and vermilions conjured a different image, more Dante's inferno than paradise lost. Only by suffering the fires of hell was Eve reborn into heavenly light.

A deep sense of foreboding sank into Tim's gut as the rear door cracked open.

Inch by inch
Bit by bit
Work your way
Out of it

The childhood poem had looped itself through Callie's mind for so many hours she'd knit herself a mental scarf. Or perhaps a shield. Not that a woolen shield would prove useful as anything other than a tea cozy. Though in point of fact, anything woolen would have improved upon the thin white uniform the Daughters favored, a linen shroud that little withstood the dirty, frigid damp of being entombed in their cellar. They had found time to throw it over Callie's shirt and trousers while she was unconscious, though whether for propriety's sake or to safeguard against the other girls harboring such revolutionary thoughts, she could not say.

Regardless, it complicated the task of retrieving her MAS revolver, bound around her left calf. The fingertips of her left hand, if she pulled the shackle toward her body, just dusted the uniform's fabric. And so she had been working, inch by inch, bit by bit, to drag her skirt up high enough to bend her leg back against her chest. A stupid twist of luck had prompted the Daughters to forget to cuff her ankles. If Callie could worm her way down far enough, she'd be able to reach her left leg with her right hand and unleash her revolver. Then came the chancy work of firing at the chain that restrained her opposite wrist. Likely as not to lose her a finger or two, but what was an escape plan without risk?

Once the singing had faded out, a tranquil hush had fallen over their cell. The distressed had been soothed, but the quiet spiked Callie's blood. Though she normally treasured time to herself, this enforced solitude, this loneliness amidst a voiceless crowd, fired her rage. She'd quaked with too much unspent energy to succeed at any of her initial plans.

An attempt to communicate with Miss Kala via Morse code had resulted in a lot of indecipherable grunting. She'd tried to swing herself upright by wriggling her feet beneath her buttocks. That gave her pins and needles and a wrenched ankle. In a fit of needing to *do something*, she'd kicked wildly at her opposite wrist, never making contact. For five crazed minutes, she'd sought to break the rusty bridle apart by slamming her head against the back wall. That brilliant maneuver won her a blistering headache and possibly a cracked tooth.

So the revolver. Fingers numbed with cold barely registered the drag of the fabric. She lifted her head every so often to measure her progress, the weight of the scold's bridle too much to maintain. The hem had just slunk above her knees. Callie considered making a fist to restore some sensation to her fingers, but there was no predicting when one of the Daughters might check on them and dash all of her efforts. Or worse, spot the abnormal bulge around her calf.

Fighting through her shivers, Callie resumed the meditative breathing Han had taught her. Wove the threads of her addled mind into a knot of purpose. Imagined what it would be like to palm her revolver—the bite of the steel, the click of the safety, the resistance of the trigger until...

A nightmarish figure craned over her, claws out. Callie shrieked.

Until she recognized the inky whorls of hair spilling out between the bars of the bridle. Miss Kala blew out a breath that would have shushed her, were it not for the metal tong suppressing her tongue. She petted Callie's shoulder with bloody hands—blast, she'd somehow squeezed them out. It took Callie far too long to guess that she gestured for a hairpin. The relief that had flooded into her as soon as she recognized Miss Kala froze anew. The all-seeing Daughters had predicted they'd attempt just such an escape and loosed the pins from their hair.

Desperation choked her. Miss Kala's hand signals grew frantic; the cage that imprisoned her head rattled around as she searched the room. With a commanding grunt, Callie seized her attention. Hissing a curse into the metal bit, she lifted her left leg. She couldn't tell if Miss Kala's squeak was of relief or intimidation as she grabbed for Callie's revolver.

Callie wished she could call upon the Mother's grace as Miss Kala tore the gun free.

Hiero mashed the last of his cigarette under his boot as he considered the ivy-strewn garden gate. Like the front entrance, it spanned the entire gap in the perimeter wall, with not a fissure of space to peek through. No outer lock marred its uniform surface. Given his former acolytes were stationed around the compound and might at that very moment be reporting his presence to Han, there wasn't a second to waste.

However. He had misremembered the height and lack of footholds. And possibly his climbing abilities. He'd also never seen the gate from this side. His infiltration plan had seemed so clever and easy in the comfort of his study. On-site, Hiero became aware of its limitations. As well as his own.

Undaunted, he took a running leap at the door... only to crash into it and thump hard on the ground.

Sobering. After assessing the damage to his posterior, Hiero lurched back up to his feet. He confronted the gate anew. The seamless posts fanned in and out of an inner panel. Attempting to squeeze the toe of his shoe on the thin bottom edge, Hiero tested the balance with a little hop...

... and bashed his face into the door as he fell. Pressing the back of his fingers to his throbbing cheek, Hiero scowled at the latch-less gate, the frail filaments of ivy, his lack of foresight in not mentioning the box to Kip, at the preposterousness of the entire situation and his state of exile. His efforts had rattled the door such that any Daughters behind would be forgiven for expecting an angry mob of villagers. Hiero recalled the comforts—and open bar—of the local inn. He had walked—walked!—from the train station, which was surely a credit in his favor.

With a shudder and a click, the gate creaked open. Amos Scaggs poked his head out, scanning the area until he saw Hiero. He cradled a tiny piglet in his hands, which he fed from a bottle of milk. Hiero steepled his hands as if in prayer and shined him his most beatific smile.

"'Ullo, Father. Where's your dress?"

"Hmm? Oh, you mean my cassock." Hiero wondered if he should dizzy him with a labyrinthine explanation or tell him a simple lie. Remembering Amos's particular view of the world, he chose the latter. "It's in the wash."

"Merry says the creepers scared you away."

Hiero didn't care to admit how close he was to the truth.

"They did. But since they only come at night, I can be here during the day."

"They scare me. I want to leave at night."

"Then perhaps tonight you can come with me to the inn."

"They have nice pies." He pitched his voice to a loud whisper. "Better than Merry makes, but don't say."

"It's my job to keep secrets."

"Right!" Amos laughed with such force his breath billowed Hiero's hair. He stopped abruptly, shot Hiero a quizzical look. "What you doing out there? Come in."

Hiero hastened through the door into an empty garden. Not even the farm animals had been let out of their roost or barn. Even with the primordial stench of the compost heap befouling his senses, Hiero couldn't help but be struck anew by its lush beauty. A dark sort of magic had cursed the place, but if they could break the spell... well, there was nothing but bounty here.

"Where is everyone?" Hiero asked, veering toward the main path until he realized Amos had not followed. He turned back in time to see how he worked the door lock mechanism, not such a simple feat when holding a small pig.

"Penny tins."

Hiero blinked, filtering his words through his internal translator. Nothing. "Would that be ha'pennies or full pennies?"

This inspired a look of frustration that broke Hiero's heart a little. In Amos Scaggs he saw a road anyone might have travelled with the wrong kind of luck.

"Sister Juliet says they been bad and got to tell the Lord what they done wrong."

"Ah, penitence. So everyone is... what, confined to their rooms?"

"I don't go in the big house."

"No, and quite right. It wouldn't be proper."

"That's what Merry says."

"Very smart, she is." Hiero searched for a tact that would get him the information he needed. "And, of course, you tend the garden."

"I'm guarding the door." Amos said this with such pride Hiero felt his throat tighten. "'Gainst the serpent. He's coming for us."

"So he is, sweet boy." Hiero spun around to catch Sister Merry descending the farmhouse steps. She paused at the woodpile, gripped the handle of the axe dug into a tree stump. "We won't be having no trouble today, Father. You'd best go back from where you've come. Not Italy, is my guess."

"No." Hiero found conceding certain truths always helped when a deception was discovered. If they thought you were finally being honest, they were more likely to believe the new lies you spun. "No holy man either, as you might have guessed."

"I wondered when you forgot to say grace."

"Not one of my finer moments." He inhaled a shaky breath, calling up the humility that had enthralled audiences during his interpretation of Oedipus. "I apologize. When Mrs. Sandringham and I embarked upon this mission of ours, I never thought I would have to lie to such kind people. You opened your home to me, and I abused your trust. Please forgive me."

Her stare proved so incisive Hiero felt as if she'd scraped off a layer of skin.

"And you've come for one last favor, have you? Do you think me born yesterday, Mr...?"

"Sandringham." Amos, at least, had the grace to gasp. The piglet snorted, indifferent. "Rebecca's husband." Hiero paused to allow her to digest this news, collecting his thoughts as well. It wasn't the first time his talent for improvisation had raced ahead of his ability to reason. "Very much alive. I know it sounds madness, but we didn't think you'd believe her to be the vessel if I was still... well, around."

"You still claim she's the vessel?"

"With everything I am. With every ounce of my faith." Hiero marched up to her as if daring her to take arms against him. "I was on a pilgrimage when the great Mother visited her. At the shrine I had a vision. Like Joseph before me, She welcomed me into her light. But instead of Jerusalem, she directed us to London. To you. To Her garden." He opened his arms as if to embrace his surroundings, biting into his tongue to wet his eyes. "Neither of us expected what happened at that first service. How the Mother would speak through her now that she was finally with you. We meant only to observe you. Hence my disguise." He squinted out a single tear. "We should have confessed at our first interview. That was my mistake. It all happened so quickly…"

Hiero bowed his head, inwardly counting down the seconds until, as predicted, callused hands grasped his.

"It's the way of the faithful, innit? To trust without question." He didn't miss the note of worry still quavering her voice. "But whyever did you take the box?"

"Leverage." Hiero planted another seed of truth. "It's the Mother's will that I be with Rebecca, to love and support her till She reigns over Her garden anew. Sister Juliet refused to hear my message, banished me from the compound. I had to find some way to be with Rebecca again." Hiero met her gaze full force with his most desperate, pleading expression. "That's why I've come. I see now we've disturbed you here. I only want to reunite with my wife, and we will be gone from this place forever. Can you help me?"

Her eyes—weary, wise, and wistful—scrutinized every pore of his face. Hiero fought the impulse to squeeze her hands tighter. Instead he opened to her in every way he knew how, giving over to his sadness at injuring Kip, his regret of his actions, his determination to contribute to saving his friends.

"Come with me." Sister Merry turned back toward the main path, expecting him to follow.

Hiero made his own leap of faith.

A phalanx of Daughters led by Sister Nora preceded Sister Juliet into the room. They fanned out around the perimeter of the chapel's small stage. Sister Nora fashioned herself into a human shield locked in at Sister Juliet's side. Tim recognized Sister Zanna at the far end, shifting from one leg to the other—the only one out of step in their otherwise military precision. Sister Juliet, her angelic face framed by a gossamer cloak that floated around her like a fairy crown, crossed the room to bow before the portrait of Rebecca Northcote. She lit a candle on the small altar beneath the prophet and whispered a silent prayer. Sister Nora stood guard at her side, bowing her head but not closing her eyes.

It was high theater, and the why of it niggled at Tim as he waited to be acknowledged. He possessed something the Daughters wanted, true, but they had proposed a fair trade. In coming here, Tim had agreed to their terms. So why the display? Was Sister Juliet incapable of acting without an audience, or was this her way of remaining accountable to her troops? Either way, Tim's hopes sunk under the weight of his disadvantage. He'd never been one to strut and fret his hour upon the stage, especially not against an experienced player such as Sister Juliet.

Still, a detective had his ruses.

"I fail to count Mrs. Sandringham and Miss Kala among you. I must insist you present them at once, on penalty of a kidnapping charge."

A few of the Daughters' eyes went wide, but Sister Juliet giggled into her hand. She shifted on her small pew but did not rise, did not flick her gaze away from the portrait.

"Are you a devout man, DI Stoker?"

"I believe but do not ascribe to a particular faith."

"Come, then. Let us pray together."

Tim considered refusing but could see no harm in it. He knelt beside her at a proper distance, twining his hands in lieu of the traditional pose. He kept alert as Sister Juliet nattered off some composition of Rebecca Northcote's. Any troubles or desires he might confide to a higher power would not be made, even silently, in the presence of these watchful women.

"And may your light see fit to return to us that which we, in our negligence, lost, and stamp out the serpent amongst us," Sister Juliet concluded.

"I pray you mean the murderer. You do recall the babe found dead on your grounds?"

"Rest his soul."

A scratch across his left trouser leg delayed Tim rising. After ripping himself away from the bench, he discovered a patch of upholstery had been worn away by the bed of upturned nails beneath. Some bizarre form of penance from Mother Rebecca's time, no doubt. A scattering of lilylike flowers, which he at first mistook for decoration, were speared on the nails. Their phallic spadices jutted up like heads on spikes. The nails had clawed deep enough to draw blood—a slash bisected his shin—but not to deter him from his mission.

Tim paced the front of the stage, appealing to the crowd.

"You call me serpent, but I have only ever sought this child's killer. A villain who you continue to harbor and have taken no action against."

"You presume much if you think any of us know who committed such a black deed."

"I suspect. I do not presume." Tim stilled to address them all. An itch roped its way around his calf, prickly as a weed. "And I say fie to your terms. You will not have the box until I conclude my investigation. Now fetch Mrs. Sandringham and Miss Kala, or I assure you, there will be consequences."

"Of that I have no doubt." Sister Juliet's sphinxlike smile warned of further mischief.

Sister Nora burst forth, unable to hold her tongue a second longer.

"How did you come to be in possession of the box if you are not in league with the priest?"

"Father Coscarelli sought me out after he'd been banished. He claims you are keeping Mrs. Sandringham against her will."

"She came to us," Sister Juliet reminded him. "Called to us in our language. Bears the Mother's mark. If she wishes to be parted from us, she has only to leave."

"Present her, then," Tim insisted. He struggled not to twitch, the irritation coiling around his thigh spiky as a briar. "Let her speak for herself."

"That is not our way," Sister Nora interjected. "The prophet speaks for us."

"You seem to be doing a fine job as interpreter." Tim cleared his throat once, then twice, a sudden thickness afflicting him. "Or is that as the prophet wills it?"

"Who are you to come here and accuse us of such horrible things!"

"An officer of Scotland Yard, answerable to a higher court than you, Miss." Sweat broke out on Tim's neck and brow despite the toothsome chill of the air. The skin of his throat ballooned.

"Blasphemy!" another Daughter shouted.

The others chimed in, a choir of vitriol silenced by a wave of Sister Juliet's hand. The diminutive dame appeared ready for her soliloquy; Tim thought he might revisit his lunch.

"You may care to wonder, DI Stoker, how we obtained your address."

"I did find it curious you didn't send for me at the Yard," he rasped, the edges of his vision twinkling as if Sister Juliet wore a halo.

Despite his angelic imaginings, an enigmatic, vaguely mocking smile twisted her lips. Sister Juliet glanced over at Sister Nora, then up at the heavens as if sharing in a cosmic joke.

"We did."

Tim struggled for calm, though his halting breaths and sluggish heartbeat betrayed him. The fiery itch twisted around his legs to the point of numbness.

"And?" was all he could croak out.

"We have it on your superintendent's authority you are no longer on their duty roster."

"Correct." Tim fought for control as the room started to spin. "Due to my recent successes, I've been appointed as special consultant to a higher office. Much higher." He took some satisfaction in the fine skein of tension that brittled her features as Sister Juliet began to understand him. Completely. "A gentleman and military man of your acquaintance, I believe."

Sister Juliet blanched.

"What is it?" Sister Nora grabbed her by the arm.

The muscles of Tim's wounded leg knotted convulsively. The world swam; he grabbed for a pew to steady himself. The skin around his throat seared, cinching his airway. He thought of the handkerchief that had stolen Little Bean's breath as his squeezed off. His inebriated heart pumped an erratic pulse. Tim clutched his chest, collapsed to his knees.

"Now you lower yourself," Sister Juliet seethed amidst the Daughters' panicked chatter. "Now you beg."

"What have you done?!" Sister Zanna broke the line to catch Tim as he swooned. She slapped his cheeks to revive him some, then ripped off his cravat. "In Her name, what have you done to him?"

"What the Mother couldn't." Sister Juliet turned to her hellfire Eve and threw open her arms. "Strangled the serpent."

The Daughters' ecstatic cheers echoed in Tim's ears as he sank into the darkness.

Chapter 17

$\mathcal{I}$n the end, Callie hadn't lost any fingers, but it was a close thing.

Hands slippery and shaking, Miss Kala had briefly attempted to aim the revolver before beating at the chains that held Callie's wrists instead. Old and rusty, they snapped after a few judicious hits. The other women, roused as much by this glimmer of hope as by their activity, called for their attention—until Miss Kala shushed them with a sharp clap. She pointed to the ceiling, and they fell silent.

The cuffs rattled as Callie rolled feeling back into her wrists. She braced herself before rising into a seated position, the weight of the bridle skewing her balance. She felt every second ticking past, even without a clock, but knew it would serve no one if they rushed. Though it was difficult to tell just how long they'd been locked in, the ache in her bladder and the squeal of her stomach suggested it was approaching noon. She noticed Miss Kala disappear into the shadows and prayed the sounds of her relieving herself didn't inspire them all to similar action.

Four other beds were occupied. Callie didn't dare check which one berthed her mother for fear of being overwhelmed. They'd already risked summoning the Daughters down with the gunshot. Callie needed a tool, preferably one she could hide in her skirts should they be discovered. She searched the room but saw little of use. Shattering the gas lamp would poison them all. The straw in

229

their mattresses was too brittle. Wooden crosses embedded in the walls were the only decoration. They were barefoot, hair loose, no jewelry or...

Callie leapt to her feet. A wave of dizziness forced her to steady herself against a nearby wall. The bridle cinched her head so tight she felt every beat of her pulse, every whinge of her aching head. She pushed through, waving Miss Kala over as Callie hiked up her skirt. The poor woman's wrists looked like one of the Demon Cats of Scavo had sharpened their fangs on them. Callie ripped off a strip of her uniform and wove it around as a bandage.

Miss Kala caught her by the hand, squeezed. Callie didn't look up, knowing she would be undone by the earnestness in her eyes. She eased out of the clutch with a soft tap to Miss Kala's knuckles. Gesturing to her corset, Callie tore the fabric away until the spine was revealed. Soon they worked to pry out one of the bones, their grunts of effort blighted by the infernal bit. Callie grew so aggravated she might have chomped it off had the bone not chosen that very moment to dislodge. A few scrapes against one of the chain links to sharpen it, a few clicks of the padlock that held Miss Kala's bridle in place, and she gasped in her first breath of iron-free air.

Callie spat once she'd been freed, her tongue bruised and her gums prickling in the bit's wake. She rallied as Miss Kala unlatched her cuffs, but, to her shame, a few sobs escaped. After they readied themselves for the next stage of their breakout, oddly silent despite hours of quietude.

"I'd give my left tit for a cup of water," Miss Kala eventually quipped.

Neither Callie nor the other women stifled their giggles.

"You certainly spent a riverful."

Miss Kala slapped Callie's arm as she doubled over with laughter. The stresses of confinement had left them shaken and, apparently, easily amused. Feeling on the verge of hysteria herself, Callie focused on mapping the room. She spotted the bottom rungs of a staircase beyond the one exit and, to the right, the black of a corridor that led who knew where.

Better the devil they knew, then.

"We'll have to chance returning to the surface." Callie indicated the way out. "Did they drug you as well?"

A giddy laugh. "No. Some of us know to pick our battles."

"Do sober yourself, Miss Kala. We're only fighting for our lives."

"You'd think after all we've suffered, you'd care to call me Shahida."

"Very well, *Shahida*." Callie tested the name on her tongue. "Are we under the main house? Is this the fabled cellar?"

"That it is." She grinned from ear to ear. "Calliope."

Callie marveled at her Hiero-esque ability to poke fun while imprisoned by torture-loving fanatics. Then she remembered her mother.

They found her in the darkest corner, cowering against the wall despite arm and leg shackles. Her thrashing had all but shred the back of her dirt-streaked uniform. Packs of straw poked out of the threadbare mattress, scratching her skin. Her soot-black hair had been chopped into a patchy, severe cut, as if someone had taken shears to her plaits. Swallowing back the roar that pounced up her throat, Callie shucked out of her uniform and tossed it at Shahida, instructing her to tear off more strips.

Her mother shivered through a nightmare. Callie laid a hand on her shoulder. Lillian snapped around, hissed, then wailed in recognition... of Shahida. Reached out to her with skeletal hands.

Callie fumed as Shahida gentled Lillian. She exhaled until she earned enough calm to unlock the shackles and the bridle, but she could not keep her gaze from straying to her mother's jellied muscles and emaciated frame and the vile patch where she'd repeatedly soiled herself. As Shahida—wise, infuriating Shahida, who had disappeared the revolver into the folds of her uniform—hushed Lillian with her favorite lullaby, to keep herself sane, Callie dreamed up scenarios in which she revenged herself on the Daughters.

She would set their world on fire before she permitted them to do this to another person.

Once freed, Lillian crawled into Shahida's arms, mewling.

"Mama, it's me." Callie petted her coarse hair like when she was a girl, but her mother only curled further into her shell.

"She's not herself," Shahida whispered.

"No." Callie sighed against the rising tide of emotion. She preoccupied herself with bandaging her mother's ankles to keep from screaming. "Did you notice an inside lock on the door upstairs?"

"I think so. She used a key."

"Then let's get moving." With a final pet to her mother's head, she rose to her feet. "I'll scout. Can she walk, do you think?"

Shahida shook her head. "We'll have to carry her between us."

"Be ready when I return." Callie hovered above them, sick at heart but somehow transfixed by the sight of them hugged together. "I'll need my revolver."

"You'll have it. Don't think we're getting out of here any other way."

Callie sighed, then slipped away. The pools of gaslight from below only encompassed the first few steps. The cunning Daughters knew better than to light the way to the exit, so she felt her way up the staircase in ever-deepening darkness. Another trial her mother would have to endure because she'd trusted some kind-seeming women. Because of her love of gardening! As she pressed her cheek to the door to listen for sounds of life beyond, Callie enumerated all the ways she would ruin Sister Juliet. Her revenge would be total and epic. With the skill of her mentor, she'd seduce away everything the woman held dear, starting with Sister Nora.

With her fingertips she traced the surface of the right-hand side, searching for the lock. After testing her makeshift pick, Callie crawled back down again. Shahida had managed to get Lillian to her feet, though her shivering hadn't stopped. She'd wrapped the remains of the petticoat around Lillian—perhaps they could pass her off as the Messiah reborn if any of the Daughters came upon them. She looked so wild and frail Callie rushed toward her... only to be stopped cold by the fear in her eyes.

"Don't fret, Mama. We'll have you back home and under a doctor's care in a tiff." Callie slowly moved to her left side, slinked an arm around her waist. To her relief, Lillian collapsed her weight against her. "Careful now."

"What do you think you're doing?" Shahida demanded.

Callie shot her a glare. "Making an escape. Or would you prefer to remain imprisoned by addle-minded zealots?"

"I'd *prefer* not to abandon these three ladies behind us to wallow in their own piss and scream themselves dumb."

On cue, the women began to shriek and whine. Callie shushed them with a raspy whistle.

"The Daughters could return at any moment. We have to go while we still can."

"And leave them to suffer our boldness? I think not."

"We're half-starved. My mother has been tortured. We don't even know if we'll make it past the door." When Shahida made to protest, Callie spoke over her. "We'll come back for them. For them all, when we're strong enough."

"And here's me half-convinced you have a heart."

Shahida shoved Lillian onto Callie, sat on the floor. She had no choice but to ease her mother down, the weight and the wriggling too much to bear whilst defending her perspective.

"We don't know where their loyalties lie. They might give us up."

Shahida scoffed, pointed at the prone figures of the women.

"What do you think got them sent down here? Too much eye-lash-batting Sister Juliet's way? Memorizing every word Mother Rebecca ever shat out her holy mouth?"

"It would be akin to stealing."

"Only if you're of the opinion the Daughters own their babes, which I know you're not."

"We don't have anywhere to put them!"

"Right. Only a stonking big house with a staff that keeps more secrets than my shifty Uncle Rory."

"Cease your bickering at once and set them free," Lillian, to the astonishment of all, commanded. "Really, Calliope. Your uncle would be ashamed."

Callie wanted to whoop—out of joy, out of relief—but instead pecked her on the cheek.

"Yes, Mama." She hastened to obey. One of the few moments in her life where Callie was proud to play the role of dutiful daughter.

In the midst of finishing the last set of cuffs, they heard the door rattle. As they scrambled back into the shadows, a shaft of light streaked across the floor.

They'd run out of time.

The breeze that susurrated through a crack in the conservatory window, making pillow tassels dance and billowing the diaphanous curtains, was the only thing that stirred as Hiero and Sister Merry entered Castleside. Rocking chairs bobbed back and forth for a phantom knitting circle. Not a clank or sizzle emanated from the kitchen. The infirmary door creaked open to reveal upturned beds, a floor splattered with glass shards, and a crashed-in window, but no patients. The normally busy corridor stretched, wide and empty, toward an unimpeded view of the front entrance.

The oppressive quiet filled Hiero with dread. The women who populated these halls and the precious cargo they carried could be in their rooms or collected in one of the two chapels. Or perhaps they lay butchered in a mass grave under the Tree of Wisdom because a goat whispered a prophecy into Sister Juliet's ear. The trouble with fanatics was you could never be sure who or what they might choose to believe. The whims of a preacher became their call to arms.

Hiero felt the absence of life keenly. The echo of their footfalls on the wood floor sounded like gongs. *Hear it not, Duncan, for it is a knell, summoning thee to heaven or to hell.* How fortunate there was a Shakespeare quote for every occasion, even being led to your death.

Sister Merry's determined bustle did somewhat temper his suspicions. Too practical to deceive, too humble to fool, he doubted she believed one third of his tale of woe—perhaps only the Mr. Sandringham part—but her goodness ran deep enough she would give him a second chance out of her sense of justice. She threw a wary glance over her shoulder every so often, not to assure herself he followed, but to reassure herself helping him was the right decision. Her tell was how she fiddled with the heavy ring of keys at her belt, pressing their ridged edges into the pad of her thumb as if she could tell them apart that way. Would she lead him to Callie and Shahida, or some other purgatory?

Hiero couldn't conceive of such a salt of the earth breaking her promise to him. He tended toward a jaundiced view of people's characters and motivations, but they didn't come more authentic than Sister Merry. From her back-country bark to her withering gaze, it was a miracle she hadn't sussed him out the day they first met. Or perhaps she had, and this was the cause of her hesitation.

This assessment of her character—undertaken, it had to be said, to stave off his sense of foreboding—preoccupied Hiero such that he failed to notice the change in the air until they'd rounded a corner.

It began with a pinch between his shoulder blades, then spread out like the veins in a dragonfly's wings across his back and arms. His pulse fluttered, nervous and tittering. He couldn't catch his breath. The air buzzed as they approached the short side corridor, grew blurry and thick as they turned left. And Hiero remembered.

The hell door.

Hiero shrank back, anchoring a palm to the wall to keep from fleeing. Hissing voices slithered out the slits in the door frame, coiled around his chest, and squeezed. Sweat broke out on his temples and brow as Hiero fought for air, for control, for clarity of purpose. His eyelids twitched, each blink flicking from the present black door to its twin in his mind. Every step closer flared a memory: the weight of the chains on his arms and legs, the burn of the metal around his wrists, the compression of the straps around his chest, the crack of the whip and the sear of the forge iron. The days without end of staring at the same four blank walls.

The shame he had molted to become the man he was today. A man who would not be daunted by a door.

"Is my Rebecca within?" Hiero asked, choking down his breaths.

"She and her servant." Sister Merry made a show of checking their surroundings for interlopers. "You'd best not run back through the garden. I can't say how long the coast will be clear, if you catch my meaning."

"Where has everyone gone?"

"Don't dally over things that don't concern you. Especially if you care to escape."

Hiero noticed she hesitated before slipping the key in the lock.

"My only regret is leaving your good company. I cannot thank you enough for all you have done for my wife and me."

"Don't need thanks for doing what's right."

A soft snick indicated she'd turned the lock.

"Amen to that."

She glanced at him, vigilant, assessing, then eased open the door. A wave of rancid air nearly suffocated him, flashed him back to another time, another dungeon, the same reek of human waste. Hiero cowered back, but Sister Merry shoved him into the dank maw of the cellar, slamming the door behind.

Or so Hiero thought as he tumbled into the blackness. He landed hard on his shoulder, scrabbled for purchase as he banged and thumped his way down a steep flight of steps. He crashed headfirst into the hard earth, legs akimbo until gravity brought them down with a crunch. The dull pound in his head grew to a deafening hammer. Sparks erupted in the red mist behind his eyes. He could not move. He could not think. A permafrost bite sank into his bones, paralyzing him where he lay. Amidst the wretched, the mad, the depraved. Walls smeared with feces, shackles rusted with blood. And the screams. The incessant soul-withering screams, night and day, muddling time and place and sanity until everything you knew...

Something kicked his leg. His not-broken leg, although Hiero couldn't vouch for the other bones in his body. A series of smacks to the cheek slapped him into the present. He cracked open an eye to see, among other indignities, Callie craning over him, looking cross. Also oddly disheveled.

"Is this your idea of a rescue attempt?" she demanded at wince-inducing volume.

"'Idea' is too solid a word. Rescue notion, perhaps?"

"He'll live," came her diagnosis before she grabbed his arm and attempted to tug him to his feet. An attempt his injured, shuddering body resisted, much to his relief.

"Don't jostle him about like that," Shahida objected, adding to Hiero's relief. "He's just gone arse over teakettle down a flight of stairs."

"If he'd broken anything, his howling would have brought the Daughters down by now."

"That'd be one way to get them to open the door." Shahida guided him into a seated position. "How about some howling, Mr. Bash? I've heard you're one for the opera."

"Theater. And no."

The pun he was about to make died on his lips when Hiero finally opened his eyes. In an instant he took in the mattresses, the shackles, the tomblike room, the ghost-eyed women, the scold's bridles...

When he came back to himself, he'd crawled halfway up the stairs, screaming, "Out! Let me out!"

Callie hugged him from behind, eased him back down into the abyss. He shucked her off as soon as they hit firm ground, planting himself on the bottom step, from which he could see a thin line of light under the door. Hiero tucked his hands under his arms, an involuntary gesture learned in a place he forced his mind away from, though everything here reminded him of the years he'd wasted there. Callie disappeared—he knew not where, would not look—then returned with a bedraggled figure who hummed a lullaby to herself.

"Lillian." Despite their circumstances, Hiero flashed a smile as she sat down beside him. "At last."

"What a dreadful state you've kept the place in, Hieronymus," she huffed, curling around his arm like a cat left out in the rain. He drew her against him, comforted even by her unpredictable presence. At least they'd managed to solve one mystery, though it had led them to ruin.

"I couldn't agree more."

"Have you brought tea?"

"No, but now that you mention it, I could do with a cup." He shot a quizzical look Callie's way. "Shall we retire from here?"

"Only if you promise to sing me to sleep."

"Of course, dear Lillian. Once we're home, you'll have anything you desire." He still could not bring himself to glance about, so he was glad when Callie knelt in front of him. "Have you devised a way out?"

"I have. Through the door."

"Innovative. How do you mean to open it?"

She proudly displayed a long white stick that had been whittled into a pick at the end.

"Girl after my own heart," Hiero complimented.

"You'd think you never taught me anything, to hear you."

"Lesson learned." Hiero continued as if oblivious to the three pregnant women Shahida gathered around them. "Though if you think about it, in a roundabout way, I have come to your rescue."

He pretended not to notice her sigh.

"What sort of trouble awaits us upstairs?"

"Not a creature was stirring. Not even a Kip." At her dubious expression, he elaborated. "In high conference with the Daughters, and the rest confined to their rooms."

"Who let you in?"

"Sister Merry, traitoress. Escorted me from the garden, to which she most likely returned."

Callie nodded. "Then we haven't a moment to lose." She rose to her feet with a decisive hop. "Shahida, prepare them to move, swift and silent. At my signal we walk in pairs to the front door. Don't stop. Don't look back. You'll lead while Hiero, Mama, and I will bring up the rear."

Callie patted him on the shoulder before she scaled the steps. Feeling more centered, Hiero cast his eyes away from the small chamber to the shadowy passage that appeared to lead deeper underground. Toward the garden, if the map was accurate. He shivered, grateful this hadn't proved their only means of escape.

At the click of the lock above, he readied himself for flight, only to panic anew at Callie's whispered "Hide!" Lillian yanked him into a dingy corner before Hiero knew what he was about. The door above creaked open, a hulking figure filling the frame...

Who let out a familiar snort-cough.

"Here you are, then," Han greeted.

Hiero didn't miss Callie's soft whimper of relief.

"We found Mama," she informed him.

"As I knew you would. Hurry now. I think their business is concluding."

Shahida led the women up the stairs in pairs, as planned. Callie zipped back down to grab her mother from Hiero. He almost tripped over himself in his haste to reach the stability of the main floor. Once in the corridor, he staggered into Han as he had all those years ago, the tether of his supportive arm just as strong and comforting.

"Where is he?"

"In the side chapel. Come—"

"Alone?"

"We must away. We'll rendezvous afterward, compare notes." Han urged him toward the main hall in the women's wake.

"But if the Daughters discover us gone after he's struck a bargain..."

"If they meant to do an exchange, Callie and Miss Kala would already be with them." To Hiero's aghast expression, Han answered, "He knew the risks. We have to fly."

"No."

"We have what we came for."

Just as Hiero snarled a reply, a side door burst open. Han pulled him into an alcove moments before a group of Daughters carried in a weak, wheezing, half-conscious Kip, Sister Zanna leading the charge. A line of blood flowed across the floor from a wound at his calf, through which his lank feet dragged.

"Faster!" Sister Zanna cried. "We're losing time!"

Only once they disappeared into the infirmary did Hiero realize he'd battered himself against Han's bulkier frame. He wrestled with his longtime friend, but Han doubled him in strength and determination.

"Let... me... go!"

"You heard her. Whatever it is, he can't be moved."

"Kip!" Hiero bellowed.

"Shut your fool mouth, or we'll draw their attention." He seized Hiero by the shoulders and shook him. "Would you have us all captured?!"

"I'm not leaving him in a nest of asps!"

He stomped on Han's foot, forgetting his steel-toed boot. Han clapped a hand over his mouth to smother the resulting howl. Taking cruel advantage of Hiero's agony, Han threw him on his shoulder and raced for the front door. He battered his fists on Han's back and kicked at his stomach as they made for the gate, only to be shoved into an overpopulated carriage. Han hung from the frame, half-in, half-out the open door as they sped away. It took everything in Hiero not to push him into the street.

"Stop this instant! Let me go to him!"

"To what? Watch him die?" Han shouted over him.

"What's happened?" Callie asked.

Hiero coughed over a bleat of upset, his anger waning. The buck and sway of the carriage turned his stomach. He leaned over, hands to his knees.

"At least I'd be with him."

"If they let you near him. If they didn't target you as well. Which would be a mercy. Do you want to go back to that cellar?"

The very thought stole the breath from Hiero's throat.

"We get these women to safety. We rest, we regroup. We share information, and we plan an attack. That's the only thing that will save him."

"Don't sacrifice yourself to an impossible situation," Callie seconded. "From what I've observed of Sister Zanna, she will do everything in her power to preserve his life."

"What life remains to be preserved."

Hiero buried his face in his hands, succumbing to his weakness, if not to his grief.

Chapter 18

Callie hugged her arms around the bedpost, pressing her cheek to the ridged wood as she watched Shahida tuck the coverlet around a babbling Lillian. The doctor, just gone, had given her something to help her sleep; Callie wondered at the dosage. But then it wouldn't be the first time her mother had defied the odds.

Shahida sat with Lillian, petting her hand with rhythmic strokes. Callie hugged the post tighter, feeling an intruder but determined to do right by her mother in what little way she could. Her illness had was an invisible wall between them. Only now Callie wondered if the wall had been there at all. If it was a barrier of her making, meant to insulate her from her family's troubles. A barrier she still didn't know how to breach.

She knew something of her mother's suffering at the hands of her father, both when he was at home and Lillian's longing for him when he was at sea, but these were a child's mythic, impressionistic notions of the war between godlike parents. Her mother had never spoken, and she had never asked, about the reality. Her girlish cares had consumed her. Everything was forbidden when her father was alive, then, once her Uncle Apollo inherited them, everything became available to her. To seek adventure instead of scorn was forgivable at eight. It was less admirable a quality come eighteen.

When she felt her eyelids drooping, Callie relinquished the bedpost and slipped out of the bedroom. Not wanting to disturb

Shahida's efforts, she eased the door shut behind her. She eyed the poky-cushioned chesterfield with mild contempt, a small step above her straw mattress in the Daughters' cellar. Her mother had always had questionable taste in furniture; "Comfort tempts complacency" was one of her fondest dictums. Perhaps they could collaborate in renovating the attic sitting room? Shahida had made a good start with the greenery by the window, a miniature garden for Lillian to putter around in on rainy days. Perhaps in creating a space for herself here, she and Mama could find common ground.

The very idea of descending the stairs daunted her. Callie wanted her bed, her room, her familiar things. Strange she would want to be enclosed after her ordeal, but such was the nesting nature of instinct. She couldn't afford more than a couple hours' rest, if that, given the echo of Hiero's brooding from three floors below. But now that the doctor had finished his examinations, and Minnie and Jie had settled the three refugees in the guest wing, Callie could finally, blessedly, shed the tattered vestiges of her white uniform and cozy under her sheets.

If she could cross the sitting room without toppling over.

"How is she?"

Han's titanic frame engulfed the entranceway to the attic apartment. A gentle giant, Callie once would have had no qualms about pushing past him. Now she couldn't bring herself to meet his eyes.

"Recovering. It pains me to say, but I think Mama's itinerant relationship with reality helped her cope."

"I hope that is so, for her sake."

Callie nodded, continued to stare at the floor, considered flinging herself out the window.

"How is he faring?"

"As expected. I very nearly tied him to a chair."

"Do you think..."

"I have no earthly notion."

"If we'd all of us attacked..." She let out a heavy, quavering sigh.

"He wouldn't have abandoned us."

"No. But he would have insisted we get the others to safety before seeing to him, and that was not possible."

Callie laughed mirthlessly. "He's right, you know. We're the furthest thing from a team."

"We're still becoming."

"Becoming what?"

"That remains to be seen."

Callie did look at him then—tall, dashing, deferent Han—and wanted to scratch out her eyes. How could such a man go about the world unseen when he was the only one she ever looked to? How was it that in the course of a fortnight, she had lost everything she had ever loved?

The door opened and shut behind her, Shahida's presence like a bucket of ice water poured over her head. Callie turned to welcome her… friend. Yes, her friend. Whom she would rally behind. Shoving her greener impulses aside, she latched on to her arm.

"You should rest. I've written to Mama's old nursemaid. She's agreed to return for a day or two, that you might recover."

"Food first, then rest. I could murder a curry. Where's your own mum when you need her, eh?"

"Would you like me to send for her?" Han asked.

"No, no. I might pop round to visit them tomorrow, if you can spare me. We have… things to discuss."

Feeling as if a swam of wasps were trapped under her dress, Callie stifled a shudder and glared at Han, who affected his usual impassive expression, as if no one had spoken at all. Callie cleared her throat. He didn't flinch. Wishing the phantom wasps would put her out of her misery, she gave Shahida's arm a squeeze.

"Why not put it off a few days, that Han might accompany you," she suggested.

Shahida frowned. "Mr. Han's been more than passing kind through this ordeal, but it's time I take responsibility for my decisions."

Outraged, Callie demanded, "And what of his responsibility?" She whirled around to confront Han. "What of *your* responsibility? Are you really going to let this stand?"

He raised a quizzical brow. "Miss Kala's made her choice. Far be it for me to question it."

"No, but you are content to leave her to it!" Exhaustion helped Callie give over to her upset. "You make her no show of support, no offer... I thought you were a man of honor! You're no better than the half-hour gentlemen who give over their get to the Daughters' care." She turned back to Shahida, wrapped a protective arm around her. "I will go with you, whenever you like. Though I hope you know you will always have a place here."

To her astonishment, Shahida giggled. So fervently and so manically that for a time she could not speak. Callie fought the urge to recoil from her, glad when she doubled over, giving her an excuse.

"Oh, my dear heart." Shahida pressed her fist to her mouth but still could not stop laughing. "Han, she thinks you've tupped me."

Callie heard his strangled sound but could not bring herself to look his way. Lest he see her flaming cheeks.

"But I thought..."

"No, no. Of course not. Do you think me daft?" Shahida inhaled deeply, sobering. "Seems I haven't been quite honest with you. Reason enough for me to be gone. The day your mum was taken... not the first time I'd left her with the Daughters on market day. I had a fella. The clerk what used to do the books at my parents' inn. Thought the world of him, didn't I? But we seen nothing of each other since my pops sent me here. Sundays were our only chance on account of his job.

"Well, he's cut me now. I was late getting back that day because I just couldn't believe..." She sniffled into her sleeve. "Oldest story in the book, I know. All those girls the Daughters take in are proof of that. I went to Mr. Han to see if anything could be done. Deep down, I knew my beau wouldn't keep me if I had the babe. I thought Mr. Han would know someone safe."

"I expect he does." Callie, to her surprise, hugged her fiercely. "And if that is your desire, I will take you myself. But I will also have you know your place is here, with us, regardless. I don't care to be without my only lady friend now I've finally found one." Both would later blame it on the fatigue, but they found themselves sobbing into each other's shoulders. "And should you choose to add to our household, Hiero would be over the moon."

"I second that," Han confirmed.

Rubbing her eyes with her palms, Callie found the wherewithal to glance at Han, who wore an expression of indulgent bemusement. She resolved to beg his forgiveness in private after she'd had a decent sleep and regained sway over her emotions. Not that he would begrudge her anything, she knew. And so admired him for it.

Admired him for so many things, really. And as Shahida tugged her back into her consoling embrace, Callie let relief overwhelm her.

Hiero stirred his tiny spoon around and around his cup of coffee, the clink-scrape of the motion soothing. As a very young child, he would squirm between the gigantic pillows in the cushioned area at the back of his parents' coffeehouse and fall asleep to the sound of the patrons sugaring their beverages. Back before his world went topsy-turvy, before he earned his coat of many scars. Back when he answered to a name whose utterance was a curse to him now. Even if he could turn back time, Hiero wouldn't want to be that innocent boy again, dreaming of a life he could never have.

Even his hardships were hard-won.

Or so he attempted to persuade himself as he watched yet another cigarette burn down to ash. Straddling a chair at the table in his vacuous kitchen—unable to settle in his study, site of Kip's triumphs—Hiero retraced the events of the past few days over and over, trying to pinpoint where it all went wrong. Every speck of his being screamed at him to return to the Daughters' compound, to storm the barricades and rescue his Kip in a spate of derring do. Or, rather, the deftest sleight of hand he had ever accomplished. But even he knew better than to embark upon quite so quixotic a mission. For once he would listen to the logic of his confrères. If only he could convince his heart to do the same.

As the grandfather clock on the floor above struck one, heavy, familiar footsteps descended the stairs. Han, with a fish fresh from who-knew-what midnight market slung over his shoulder, nodded in Hiero's direction before setting to work. On so many nights, under so many different sets of circumstances, Hiero had watched him perform the same ritual of gutting, deboning, and slicing. Of lighting the stove—sometimes a campfire, sometimes a sheet of metal set over hot coals—and setting a pot of water to boil. The scent of fresh herbs roused Hiero's senses as Han built his stock. Hiero could have recited the steps if asked. Han's motions echoed those of the grandmother who taught him and the great-great-grandmother who taught her, the living dance of his ancestry.

All the while Hiero stirred his coffee and cursed his father's name and fought the tears that pricked the back of his eyes.

By the time the spices from Han's secret pantry misted the kitchen air, the family had collected around the table, bowls and spoons at the ready. Aldridge, the house sommelier, poured out a dry white wine. Minnie helped Ting slice up a loaf of almost-stale bread while Angus and Jie, moony and disheveled, cheered their approval. Callie, sharp as a guillotine's blade, waited for the right moment to strike up the conversation they should have had hours earlier. But then Han, with what little flourish he permitted himself, deposited the pot of fish stew on the table, and no one dared speak a word till the slurping was done.

Though Hiero dismissed them once they'd cleared the bowls, only Angus and Jie carried a fitful Ting off to bed. Minnie, ever the night owl, moved to the counter to make the week's bread, and Aldridge settled into his hearthside rocking chair with a stack of newspapers in case he was needed. Han set a crystalline bottle of Chinese *baijiu*—a grain liquor similar to vodka—on the table and distributed three shot glasses. Though tempted, Hiero turned his over. Callie threw back a quick shot, tapping her glass for another. Han obliged her with a smirk Hiero had not observed for some time, reminding him of the small successes of their last mission.

Not that he would forgive the losses.

"A question to begin." Callie wiped her mouth with the back of her hand, relishing her release from captivity. "What is the goal of our present course of action? To rescue Tim or to unmask the murderer? Or both?"

"Are you suggesting we allow Little Bean's death to go una-venged?" Han asked.

She let out a blustery breath. "A life is at stake. One of our own. We've blown our chance with the Daughters. If our only objective is to retrieve Tim, then I believe we may do so without impediment. To attempt more is to risk his life."

"He may already be dead. If we focus only on him, we might be wasting our last opportunity to find answers."

Hiero stared determinedly at his coffee cup, unable to debate what was unquestionable to his mind.

"We agreed to help Tim in order to retrieve Mama," Callie reminded them. "She is safe; he is not."

"And justice is thrown to the wolves?" Han sighed. "You would not be so cavalier if you had met the boy's grieving father."

This tempered her.

"Likely not." She tapped the tabletop at the speed of her thoughts. "I propose we pool our evidence to see if a suspect emerges. If one does, we make our plan. If not, we resolve to liberate

Tim and, once his health is restored, support him in any action he might take. Agreed?"

"Very well," Han answered.

Hiero gazed into the umber swells at the bottom of his cup, wishing for a few leaves to read. The random distribution of sodden flecks seemed more reliable than his judgment where Kip was concerned.

"There is madness to your method." He lifted his head, rallied. His Kip required him, and he would not fail him again. "I approve."

"Good." She clapped her hands together. "Han, you're in Tim's confidence. What deductions has he made?"

"Our search of the compound and his interviews yielded little in the way of evidence," Han said. "We cannot connect the little coded wings found on the body to a classification system used by either the Daughters or the orphan asylum. All babes sent to Mr. Crook at the asylum over the past six months have been accounted for. Amos Scaggs is responsible for delivering them there. He transports them in the back of a wagon. I myself searched Sister Juliet and Sister Nora's offices—albeit not as thoroughly as I would have liked—but could find no document listing the names of the parents of the children born under the Daughters' care. However, Tim is confident such a document exists, and it will resolve the question of Little Bean's paternity."

"There is also the map," Callie noted.

"Our untapped resource, yes." Han spread their copy of the map across the table. "Our theory is Little Bean was being held in one of the underground chambers, either under the farmhouse or under the tree. The cellar is too public."

"I saw no trace of children being kept there whilst I was captive."

"That fits with Tim's theory that there is one killer. Otherwise it's a conspiracy of silence, and they are all guilty."

"An attractive prospect, but no. Their reactions on the day the murder was discovered were too genuine."

"All but one," Hiero noted. "An exception that disproves the rule."

Han nodded. "The tunnels need to be explored. There is also the question of who knows they exist and who has access."

"With no easy answers." Callie scrutinized the map, tracing out different routes and muttering to herself. "The night guardian."

Hiero and Han shared a look at this pronouncement.

"How now?" Hiero queried.

"Shahida and I were hardly idle despite our imprisonment. We snuck about under cover of darkness, trying to find Mama. The Daughters and the novitiates are locked in their rooms from evensong to sunrise, making communication and mischief impossible. We posited that a night guardian walks the halls, providing whatever care is required and escorting anyone in need of emergency help around the building."

"Terrible yet fascinating," Han commented.

"As with most things related to the Daughters." Callie shrugged. "We eliminated Sister Juliet immediately as a candidate due to her numerous daylight duties."

Hiero scoffed. "And pretentions."

"Precisely. She doesn't cater to anyone, let alone at night. Sister Zanna examined me in my room and was let in by Sister Nora, so she doesn't have free access to the house. Odd since she delivers the babes, but there you are. Also, she seems..."

"Honest," Hiero said.

Callie chuckled. "You've taught me to presume otherwise, but..."

"Some exceptions *are* truly exceptional." His shoulders sagged. "Kip, for one."

She reached across the table, hand open. Hiero shook his head.

"We can forget this," Callie insisted. "Go for him right now."

Hiero shut his eyes, listened to the slow drum of his pulse in his ears. He wasn't the sort to be tested this way. Fortitude, morality, these were not his minions. Only one man had ever challenged him to do better. The one he trusted to guide his decisions now.

"Continue."

Callie returned her attention to the map.

"Shahida and I observed Sister Nora with a heavy set of keys. She also discovered us during one of our nightly escapades, which is how we found ourselves in the cellar. Though she is currently our favorite for the night guardian, one might suppose she is even more occupied during the day than Sister Juliet with the administration of the Daughters' affairs. Of course, we have no proof she attends to those affairs in the daytime. She may very well be a night owl."

"She's a nervous sort," Hiero said. "They often cannot sleep."

"She's also one of the newer Daughters," Han remarked. "If this is a case of baby farming, I don't think such activities would have gone unnoticed forever. Tim also theorized the person who buried Little Bean at the tree may not be the murderer, but someone who wanted to expose another's crimes without appearing disloyal."

"A better fit in terms of her character." Callie hummed as she worked this theory through all its permutations. "So despite her freedom of access to the entire compound unobserved and the time in which to commit the crime, the night guardian may not be the killer after all. Rather, she may have seen something suspicious and wished to bring it to light without the responsibility of making a direct accusation. All of which fits Sister Nora's sense of order and servitude."

"And Sister Juliet's agenda." Hiero clinked his fingernails along the rim of his cup. "She has the history—lost her son in childbirth. Perhaps this twisted something within her. Also, despite her protests, I am certain she knows who Little Bean belongs to and will not say."

"I concur," Han said. "Keys or no keys, she is the prophetess. She goes where she pleases, when she pleases."

"But not unobserved," Callie argued. "They worship her. No one would fail to notice her."

"Ah, but would they finger her?" Hiero inquired. "Speaking, not coincidentally, of Sister Nora. Who unquestionably would, given the right invitation."

"Stop speaking in riddles."

"She has been touched, you might say, by Sister Juliet's spirit." Hiero couldn't help waggling his eyebrows. "And wouldn't mind if her body followed suit."

Callie spared him a dubious look. "So your theory is Sister Nora exposed Sister Juliet's crime because of her infatuation?"

"Or as a warning," Han said. "'Stop this now, or next time I'll expose you.'" He leaned in as he warmed to his argument. "One of the main stumbling blocks to our investigation, right from the start, has been too many people had the means to commit the crime. Every one of the Daughters and all the women in their care can be seen as having motive since their business involves the birthing of babes conceived out of wedlock. A case could be made against any one of them. If someone wanted to send the murderer a message, the staging of the body in a public location with easy access could not have made it clearer. If the person who buried the boy under the tree is not the killer, then they wanted Little Bean to be found with no consequences to the one who strangled him."

"I'm convinced," Callie declared. "And thoroughly discouraged. By that argument it could be anyone, and we are no closer to the truth."

A hush fell over them as they each contemplated the Sisyphean task before them.

"Tim would bring clarity to all of this," Han noted. "Perhaps we should fetch him."

Hiero's heart sank. Though he could not rid his mind of his final image of Kip, beet faced and wheezing, he had promised to leave no stone unturned. And he was trying to be a better man, to earn back Kip's regard. As if his moss-green eyes encouraged him from afar, Hiero cleared his throat.

"Sister Merry also has a set of keys."

Callie's head bobbed up. "I know little of her. Is she a possibility?"

"As murderer or revelator?" Han asked.

"Either. Both."

"There's also her brother Amos. Could he have hurt a babe by accident while transporting them to the orphan asylum?"

Callie clicked her tongue. "Would a man of his size kill by strangulation? And there were signs of neglect."

"Perhaps he forgot one of the babes in the wagon."

Hiero shuddered, wishing he could un-hear that comment.

"Amos is a gentle soul, frightened by creepers in the night."

He suddenly found himself the focus of two sharp stares.

"Creepers?" Han inquired.

"Mice and other vermin in the walls of the farmhouse," Hiero explained. "'Cree, cree, cree.' The noise was incessant."

"You heard them yourself?" Callie asked.

"For two interminable nights, yes."

"And Sister Merry made no mention of them?"

"She dismissed Amos's complaint as foolishness, but I assure you, they were quite real. Though she does not sleep in the farmhouse, so perhaps she thinks them fantasy. Little wonder she stays away, with the place so infested."

They continued to stare at him until Hiero confronted them with a scowl.

"Sister Merry is the night guardian," Han concluded aloud, possibly for Hiero's benefit since Callie nodded in vigorous agreement.

"And I fear it is more vital than ever we explore the chamber beneath the farmhouse," Callie said, a tremble in her voice belied her decisiveness. "Though it haunts me to think of what we might discover there."

Han's gaze reached across the table where his hand dared not.

"Leave it to me."

Affronted, Callie scoffed. "Not for all the secrets in Lord Blackwood's trove."

"Elated for you both." Hiero smirked. "Now can we get about rescuing my Kip?"

Callie poured herself a final shot of *baijiu*.

"There was never any question Tim would be retrieved. And since your aversion to underground spaces is well established, you're tasked with creating a diversion that will permit us to sneak down into the tunnels. I trust such an undertaking is within your capabilities?"

Hiero found his smile. "One might say I was born to it."

"One might unless they knew about the circumstances of your birth." Callie chuckled to herself, visibly pleased to have caught Hiero out on his self-mythology.

"The side gate is our most logical entry point." Han pointed it out on the map, eager to turn the conversation back to their investigation. "How did you manage it this afternoon?"

"More luck than logic, alas," Hiero replied. "Amos Scaggs was put on guard. Not one of my more complex feats of persuasion."

"You didn't fare as well with Sister Merry," Callie reminded him. To Han, she said, "We should be prepared to encounter them."

"With Amos confined to the garden, I'd say it's an inevitability." Han sighed. "I'd prefer to do this without incapacitating anyone. Might your diversion draw him out?"

Hiero considered this, steepling his fingers under his chin. Visions of glorious chaos erupted within his nimble fire-starter mind. He allowed their smoke to dissipate before responding, reveling in their rapt attention.

"There may be a way," he began, "but I don't think you'll care for it. Indeed, I know of a particular someone who will be deeply, perhaps unforgivably cross."

Callie gasped. "By Jove, you don't mean—"

"Yes." Even Hiero couldn't believe he was about to utter these next words. "Call in the Yard."

They let the scene play out in their imaginations. Then, as one, hissed.

"He'll break with you," Han warned.

Hiero nodded. "So long as he's alive."

"No." Callie slammed her fist on the table. "This risks all the women in the Daughters' care. If the peelers don't imprison them, they'll force them out on the street. We cannot endanger them for the sake of one life."

"I'll see they are provided for," Hiero insisted.

"With what means? We have a full house with only three!"

Aldridge, by the hearth, knocked on the arm of his chair.

"Perhaps I overstated my earlier aversion to incapacitation," Han quipped. "We will deal with Amos, and Sister Merry if need be. Of greater concern is how you'll infiltrate without ending up in the infirmary beside Tim. The Daughters have proven they are willing to use any means necessary to protect themselves."

The knocking intensified; Hiero shushed him.

"The box."

"Useless. Or perhaps a fake after all." Callie looked surprised by their inquisitive glances. "It would have worked for Tim if it had any value."

Aldridge planted his fist in the middle of the table, startling them all. He leaned over to scribble something on one of the blank edges of the map. *Client.*

"A capital notion," Hiero complimented, already scheming. "If, of course, we knew who he was."

He chose to ignore Aldridge's exasperated expression, which spoke more volumes than any tongue could have uttered. Aldridge slapped one of his newspapers down on the table, planting a finger under a word in the headline.

Winterbourne.

Chapter 19

The sting of a cold compress on his brow lured Tim back into himself. He concentrated on following the drip trails down his burning cheeks and throbbing temples, the chill water pooling at the back of his scalp. The frigid bites to his eyelids soothed their ache, their edges puffy, as if stuffed with cotton. His entire face and most of his torso felt taxidermized, the skin unnaturally raw and distended. Except whomever had scraped out his insides had forgotten his brain and mulched his lungs.

The air was made of glass. Pinprick particles lacerated his windpipe with every inhalation. Tim panicked through his first few conscious breaths until a hand pressed to his chest.

"Slowly, slowly," Sister Zanna whispered.

Fighting down his shock and his questions, Tim measured out his breathing, counting his inhales and exhales until the blaze in his throat died down to a scorch. When Sister Zanna curled her fingers around his wrist, Tim searched for the beat of his heart. Steady but sluggish for someone with senses at full alarm. He distanced himself from the memories that threatened to rush in, concentrated on the cool of the cloth, the soft of the bed, the brush of Sister Zanna's hand over his hair. Despite being in enemy territory, sleep was likely the best remedy for...

A sharp scent woke him the second time. Candlelight. Breeze from an open window. A dirt feeling on his chest—no, a poultice:

peppermint and lavender and paregoric. His eyes scratched and his breath wheezed and his leg sizzled with itch, but his face had settled back into itself. Tim tested the muscles, the firmness of the skin. Dared to look about the still, sombrous room.

Sister Nora knelt by his bedside, praying.

"Water," Tim rasped.

"Oh, thank you, Mother." Sister Nora lifted her head to the skies before summoning help in a harsh whisper.

While a Daughter he didn't recognize helped him drink, Tim realized he probably shouldn't consume anything from the very people who had poisoned him. Not that he could have crawled out of bed, let alone escaped their clutches, given the itchy scabs on his shins. Sister Zanna floated out of the shadows. Tim had never seen her smile, and she did not now. She took his pulse again, this time at his neck, and tested his brow for fever.

"Do you think you could manage some broth?" she asked. "The water is refreshing, but something hot would soothe your throat."

Tim nodded, curiosity warring with exhaustion.

"I know the lure of sleep is strong." Sister Zanna petted his head in a manner Tim was ashamed to admit he found comforting. The last time he'd been laid up was at Berkeley Square. He tried not to wonder if he would ever see the place again. "But you could do with some nourishment to help you heal."

"What happened?" Tim did not expect the truth but hoped she would at least be honest about his prognosis. "Why am I here?"

Sister Zanna glanced at Sister Nora, who worried her hands in the way of the guilty since the first actor to play Lady Macbeth took the stage...

Hiero.

Where was Hiero? Why hadn't they come for him? Were Callie and Miss Kala safe? Had they surrendered the box? Tim groaned through a wave of nausea, his stomach bilious and empty. The broth would temper his indigestion, less so his upset. He longed with irrational fervor for the brush of Hiero's silk robes against his cheek, the caress of his magnificent hands. He knew his illness heightened his emotions, but he was too vulnerable to care. He let tears well in his eyes, his breaths quicken… and found himself anchored on both sides by firm yet giving grips.

"Steady now," Sister Zanna commanded, as she must have done to hundreds of women in far worse straits than Tim. "Keep your breaths long and slow. There is still constriction in your lungs, and you burned your throat when you purged. Do not excite yourself. The agent that caused this reaction has worked its way through your system, but its effects will linger. Some for a few days, some perhaps for a few weeks."

Tim took the time to let his whirlpool feelings still before asking, "Agent?"

Again a hard look Sister Nora's way.

"If you care to receive her," Sister Zanna explained, "Nora has been waiting for a word."

Tim struggled to focus on the nuances playing out before him, his body heavy and his mind overtaxed. But he had been anticipating a crack in the Daughters' wall of secrecy, and he could not help but peer through it. Even if Sister Nora's evidence went with him to his grave, he had to hear it.

A fit of coughing startled him. Thick, suffocating barks that spun the room until they forced his jaw open to receive a rush of water. Sister Zanna held his head so he could better inhale the poultice fumes, tapping out the rhythm against his temple that his breaths should follow.

"His people must be summoned," Sister Zanna insisted.

Sister Nora tightened her bone-breaking grip on his hand but shook her head.

"She will never agree."

"Then we must defy her! With everything that's happened, how can you—"

"If they come, we lose *everything*." Sister Nora sniffled. "The Mother demands I make my confession, but I will not jeopardize Her coming by bringing the rule of men down upon us."

"Do not fret," Tim husked, fighting for calm himself. "I am listening."

The moment upon her, Sister Nora lost her nerve. Shame sagged her sweet face; her jaw bobbed up and down as if it had forgotten how to form words. A grunt from Sister Zanna spurred her. She fixed her stare on the cross above the bed, and she relinquished his hand to twine hers as if in prayer.

"It was I who..." Her bottom lip trembled. "I only thought to make you ill. Or rather less ill than you are now. Just a bit of lords-and-ladies to make you itch. To keep you away."

"Impossible to know it would bring on a fit," Sister Zanna elaborated. "Normal reaction is a rash and a prickly tongue. Yours was particularly severe. A foolish act, but the intent was *not* to——"

"No. No!" Sister Nora fought to temper her breathing. "Ever since you came, we've been under constant attack! First with the discovery of that poor little boy, then your endless inquiries and insinuations, then that bedeviled priest and his charlatan wife who stole Mother Rebecca's box..."

Tim's train of thought hitched on that word, *wife*, and stowed it away for later consideration. He almost started another coughing fit out of pure astonishment at how her mind twisted the facts. He wondered how influenced by Sister Juliet's opinions her recitation was.

"You must see, Inspector, something had to be done," she finished.

"I imagine what DI Stoker believes should have been done was permit him to conclude his investigation in peace," Sister Zanna remarked.

Tim nodded.

"I see that now," Sister Nora admitted, sinking into herself. "I see… a great many things more clearly than before. Juliet has a way of making the smallest thing seem hugely important. The mere idea grows so enormous it overwhelms your thoughts, blocking out…"

"Your reason?"

"I only ever wanted to serve Her." Sister Nora bowed her head over her clasped hands.

Tim waited. He may have been indisposed, but it would take more than poisoning to distract his instincts.

"I will suffer any consequences you see fit and will be of no further impediment to your investigation."

"*And,*" Sister Zanna nudged.

"And." Sister Nora extracted a small locked diary from the pocket of her apron. "I believe this is what you have been searching for." She snuck the book under his pillow. "She wears the key on a chain around her neck. I cannot—"

"I forgive you."

The relief that brightened her face alleviated some of Tim's agony, if only for a brief moment. Then the broth arrived, and the shelter of sleep beckoned. A fog descended over his deductive mind, giving sway to practicality until his body mended.

The publican at the Wheatsheaf pub in Goldhawk Road cast a leery eye Hiero's way when he unlocked the door to the dawn traveler. The red-rose aura of the sky, a war banner if ever there was one, reflected in his shiny bald pate as he bowed in deference to Hiero's generous donation. He knew what he asked of this man—to rise mere hours after he lay down his head—and, worse, that it might be in service of a fool's errand. Prepared to spend every cent in his billfold and then some to save his Kip, Hiero thanked the man in both official languages of such transactions: verbal and monetary.

Hiero strolled into the empty pub, searching for the perfect spot from which to enact his ambush. The mahogany panels and columns framing the dark-teal walls assured the atmosphere remained austere even on a sunny morning. Rows of booths flanked a tight cluster of wooden tables, leaving little space between. To assure no patron left unliquored, the edge of the bar skirted the doors, with only a slip of burgundy carpet between. Hiero selected a booth midway on the windowed side—small rectangles of stained glass that skirted the ceiling—so he wouldn't be spotted from the outside. After ordering tea, toast, and a boiled egg, he hung Kip's overcoat and hat on the hook at the join of two booths. Hiero checked that, when seated, his head didn't poke over the join, then settled into the seat with his back to the door.

Patience is bitter but its fruit is sweet, he reminded himself as he count-ed the passing seconds. With nothing to preoccupy him but his carousel of thoughts spinning round and round on an endless loop to nowhere, he began to itch for company. He could not tempt the publican into conversation lest his visitor discover his identity and be scared off. He had forgotten his trusty pack of playing cards in his rush to depart. Not that there was anyone about to trick or tantalize or tell a fortune. For the first time since his last night at the Gaiety, Hiero was alone with himself. If there'd been a mirror, he'd have pulled a Gloucester and plucked out his eyes.

Three hours, seven cups of tea, four pieces of toast, and two eggs later, he heard the door crack open. Footsteps padded in, hesitated—scanning the pub, most like—then marched toward his booth. They paused again before a dashing figure swooped into view, only to freeze midturn.

"Bash," Sir Hugh hissed. "I might have known."

"For a military man, I did expect a greater effort toward punctu-ality," Hiero declared by way of introduction. Since he didn't need one. "Three hours to corral yourself into a response to a perfectly straightforward early hours summons? What would your old captain say?"

"He'd likely demand to know how you forged DI Stoker's handwriting."

"Really? How pedestrian."

He gestured to the seat opposite and snapped his fingers for a fresh pot of tea. Winterbourne stalled, shifting his weight from one foot to another as if he might bolt. Hiero, who'd been avoiding a full eye rake for fear of not measuring up, took him in. A wan complexion and a hollow stare somewhat wilted his lush Byronic beauty. Though his clothes were immaculate, his fingernails had been torn to nubs, and his slick, sculpted hair betrayed an overabundance of pomade. From under the assault of his cologne rose the fumes of indulgence. He was, quite possibly, still drunk.

This above all endeared him to Hiero. They were united in grief.

"Do sit," Hiero said. "I went to an awful lot of bother to lure you here. The least you could do is hear me out."

"You presume much." He tapped his foot. "Where is DI Stoker?"

"The very matter of our conversation. If you accept to have it. Sit? I've sent for tea."

"And I gave strict instructions, which appear to have been disregarded."

"Your little codicil meant to keep the details of DI Stoker's investigation quiet, you mean? I rather think it moot since you presented yourself at my home in full view of my staff, undisguised."

Winterbourne huffed but sat.

"Emotion," he growled. "If only we could cut it out like the tumor it is."

"'Put out the light, and then put out the light'?" Hiero queried. "Goodness. I see you've reached the third stage of bleak."

"Have you ever lost a child, Mr. Bash?"

"A childhood, perhaps. Not lost so much as thieved. Which is, by sheer coincidence, adjacent to the matter we are here to discuss."

"And why, after you've connived your way to this audience, should I pay anything you have to say any mind?"

"Because I've come to speak of revenge."

Which was how, sometime later, Hiero found himself at the gate to Daughters' compound, seconded by the commissioner of the Police of the Metropolis.

The unlocked gate.

Hiero swung the gate just wide enough for them to slip through, then eased it closed behind him. Though Winterbourne rushed up the walk to rap on the front door, Hiero had a cautious glance around before joining him. Everything looked much the same as the previous day, and someone could simply have neglected their duty, but given how disciplined the Daughters were... could this be a sign of munity?

They waited for long minutes after a succession of knocks, Winterbourne gusting out breaths like a dog straining his leash. Hiero struggled to harness his brash impulses, to stop himself from abandoning Winterbourne on the doorstep and sneaking around to smash in a conservatory window. While that would prove a mighty distraction, masking Callie and Han's maneuvers, it might also cost Kip his life. Though most of his plans tended to go pear-shaped, never were the stakes so high. Trouble was Hiero couldn't think his way around the puzzle to save his life, let along Kip's. His Plan A was the only letter in his alphabet.

"Where are they?" Winterbourne practically frothed at the mouth.

"Hiding the silver?"

"Do not tell me you have brought me here without doing the least bit of reconnaissance."

"Might I remind you it was your dallying dilly dicked up to the point of requiring our assistance."

"I hired DI Stoker, not your menagerie. A fact I freely admit was a gross miscalculation." He grabbed the knocker and gave it a quick, vicious pound. Little wonder his lady friend fled both him and their child. "Soon to be rectified, if the residents of this nunnery haven't already shuffled him off this mortal coil."

Hiero took some heart in this most obvious of Shakespeare quotes. Perhaps Winterbourne wasn't such a beast after all.

"None of the Daughters' dark deeds would have been uncovered if not for DI Stoker's efforts."

"If only he'd unearthed some evidence to convict them with."

He lifted his fist to pound again when the door creaked open. A lone brown eye peered through the crack, then shot wide. A spooked Sister Nora wordlessly bade them enter, curtseying with a deference that surprised Hiero. And had him wondering if this was the first time Winterbourne had visited Castleside, as he claimed. Given how quick she was to recognize him, Sister Nora was either as well versed in their clientele as Sister Juliet, or she'd had cause to escort him to her office before.

They hadn't traveled ten paces before Sister Juliet herself appeared at the end of the long corridor, a queen awaiting her audience. Winterbourne instinctively slowed his stride, giving weight to his every step. If he was half the soldier everyone claimed, he'd be assessing the terrain, noting the house's weak points and any lurking dangers. Hiero had warned him not to accept any food or drink and recommended not removing their gloves. Still, the charge in the atmosphere sparked Hiero's nerves. He fought not to twitch at every skitter and rustle in the so-called holy house. The rattle of chains seemed to echo around him the closer he moved to the viper in chief.

Though they towered over her, Sister Juliet vibrated with command, a pious Napoleon poised to conquer their kingdoms. Hiero noted she'd wisely evolved from her air of touched innocence to a steely pacifism. As with all career dissimulators, she was smart enough to know no one could win if she kept changing the rules.

"Sir Hugh," she greeted, her ice-blue eyes placid as a frozen lake. "To what do we owe the honor of your visit?"

"You know very well the reason I've come," Winterbourne snarled. "The only question that remains is what you're going to do about it."

Never bring a hammer when a chisel will do, Hiero thought, cursing Winterbourne's blunt nature. He rushed to save what little artifice remained in this gambit of his, stepping in front of the commissioner.

"Permit me to interpret." Hiero raised his hands to shush her. "I've apprised Sir Hugh of the recent death amongst your... offspring, and he requires a full and thorough explanation."

"Forgive my ignorance of the ways of the law." Perhaps she hadn't abandoned the wide-eyed innocent routine entirely. "But has DI Stoker not availed you of the results of his investigation?"

A telling gamble, to divide and conquer. Hiero moved aside to let Winterbourne answer. This he had prepared him for.

"He has, and they've proven most unsatisfactory. Much like my dealings with you."

"Your dealings?" Sister Juliet feigned astonishment.

Her first mistake. Hiero stole a glance at Winterbourne, whose wan countenance had warmed into the red of stoked embers.

"Let us adjourn to your office," he seethed through gritted teeth, "where we may discuss the matter fully."

"As you wish," she agreed, gracious as ever. "But if you mean to parrot the vile accusations of this thief and charlatan, I'll insist on the presence of a witness." She shot Sister Nora a meaningful look. Which, Hiero noted, inspired panic in her formerly faithful servant. "Interrogate us if you must, but I will not speak a word until what is ours is returned to us."

On cue, Winterbourne turned on Hiero.

"What does she mean? What have you stolen?"

"Her box." Hiero couldn't help the upward curl of his lip. "Or rather, the fabled one belonging to Rebecca Northcote."

"The first brick in a mighty foundation." Sister Juliet reached out to grasp Winterbourne by the forearms in her influential way. "Our most sacred relic, pilfered by this heathen whilst pretending to be a priest."

Hiero fixed his stare on Sister Juliet. "Little more than her prophetess' mad ravings and a useless map."

She whipped her head round, squinting at him with cold fury. Hiero gave a little wave to mask his grin.

"If that's the case." Winterbourne yanked his arms out of her grip. "I'll require your full testimony. On this *and* the other affair."

"Of course." To her credit, she rallied seamlessly. "I'm happy to provide you with any and all answers you seek. So long as that man is not party to our conversation."

Winterbourne gave curt nod. "Report to Constable Brooks back at the carriage. And while you wait, consider whether you might return the box to its rightful owners posthaste."

"With gratitude, Sir Hugh."

"Nora, see that he obeys," Sister Juliet ordered, "then join us."

After coiling her arms around his, Sister Juliet led Winterbourne to her lair. Sister Nora watched them go, her heart so transparent it was reflected in the shape of her face.

"Better, as they say, to have loved and lost," Hiero counseled.

She bowed her head but couldn't hide her upset.

"I've lost nothing but my moral compass. So everything." She gestured toward the infirmary and, by consequence, the hell door. "This way."

"Forgive me if I don't care to be reentombed in your cellar."

"Retire to the carriage if you must. But I dare say DI Stoker will be disappointed." At his reaction, she dared a smile. "It's him you've come for, is it not?"

"My dear girl." Hiero choked back his relief, hoping upon hope it was not premature as he followed her. "Let me be the first to say heartache becomes you."

Chapter 20

*A*stride a branch in a tall tree across the road from the Daughters' garden, Callie found herself riveted by the red dawn. Against such a fiery canvass, Castleside resembled an embattled fortress in the highlands, the flames of the surrounding villagers' torches roasting it alive. Flooded with crimson rivers of light, the garden stretched out—lush but empty—as though already slain. Only the Tree of Wisdom, whose leaf-laden boughs undulated in the breeze, remained animated.

The unlucky oak Callie perched in had just missed receiving the gift of the Daughters' green thumbs. Solid but husklike, with shards of peeling bark and anemic leaves, the tree and its beyond-the-wall siblings proved there was some overseeing magic guiding the Daughters' hands, at least where gardening was concerned.

Callie stretched out on her stomach, crossing her bent legs at the ankles and tapping her toes against the trunk of the craggy old oak. Decked in her Archie the Pageboy guise, she relished the scratch of the bark through her shirt, the snug of her breast binder, and the tickle of the ends of her slicked-back hair against her earlobes. Jie had sent her damaged corset for restructuring; she hoped it was beyond repair. She snickered as she imagined her dressmaker's reaction to the ripped and deboned corset. Callie prayed it caused a scandal.

A low whistle from below snapped her back to attention. She

braced herself as a carriage roared past, but the sturdy tree muted the reverberations.

"Sir Hugh, do you think?" she stage-whispered down to Han, who emerged from his surveillance spot in the nearby brush.

He nodded. "I spotted Hiero's handkerchief around one of the spokes. How does it look?"

"No one about. But let me…"

She straddled the branch, gripping two strong-looking offshoots in order to gather one foot, then the other, beneath her. After shifting her weight toward the trunk, she stood, testing the bough's support with a quick stomp. Skirting her fingers along higher branches to help balance, Callie walked out as far as she dared— which proved to be too far for Han's liking. Or so she interpreted his grumbling.

"Anything of note?" he asked.

Her slight change in perspective opened up another world. Specifically two busy figures stuffing boxes and bags into a delivery wagon.

"Quite possibly." She fell to her knees, swung around the branch, let her legs dangle a moment before dropping down to the road. She wished an artist had captured the expression on Han's face, a flicker of awe and delight she would linger upon when alone. "Prepare yourself. The wagon is coming out."

Callie threw on her coat and cap, fetched her revolver from the satchel they had stowed in the brush. Han patted each of his hidden pockets, checking for his knives, his horse whip, extra oil and matches, and of course their copy of the map. A small lantern hung from each of their belts in case they got separated. She wished they were better prepared, with bassinettes and blankets, and a rack to painstakingly stretch out a confession from the murderous fiend in question, but needs must. Part of her burned to bring this particular villain to justice. Part of her hoped they would find nothing.

"Who is it?"

"Sister Merry and Amos, with quite a bounty in tow."

"A bounty of...?"

Callie shrugged. "They could be going to market. Or the orphan asylum."

"Or fleeing."

"A situation they may or may not be the cause of."

"What's our approach?"

Before she could answer, the gate swung open. and the horse trotted out, driverless. Well trained, it stopped when the wagon had cleared the gate. Callie let Han take the lead lest she be recognized. They walked around the far side to block any escape attempts. While Han poked his head over the back of the wagon to see what it contained, Callie snuck over and unlatched the horse. They couldn't chance losing any suspects.

A scream brought her running back to Han to find Sister Merry near doubled over with laughter.

"Oh, you gave me a fright!" She pressed a steadying hand to her chest. "Amos..." She turned back to find no one in the yard behind her. "Amos! Where have you gone, sweet boy?"

"We mean you no harm," Han reassured her. "We are associates of DI Stoker's." He produced a set of forged credentials that would have convinced the Queen. "Come to follow up on some evidence."

"But the inspector..."

"Is indisposed. We know." Han waited a pregnant beat before adding, "Our superior is with him now."

Sister Merry's look of surprise could not have been faked. She darted her stare back and forth between them, both hands now clasped to her breast.

"As the Mother wills it. I'm sure Sister Juliet has everything well in hand." She flicked her eyes to the back of the wagon, their faces, the road to London. She cleared her throat. "Will you be needing any help with your inquiries?"

"Perhaps." Han played up his enigmatic nature to full effect. "If you could begin by telling us where you're going?"

She let out a blustery sigh. "Back to Suffolk, as the crow flies. No point in deceiving you. Leaving the garden's like leaving one of my own, if I had 'un, but..." She threw up her hands. "If life's taught me anything, it's take care of yours. It were different when Rebecca guided us, but that time's over." She bustled back into the yard, calling for her brother. "Where's that boy gone?"

"Told him your plan, did you?" Callie asked in her best Cockney basso profundo.

"It's the critters. He don't want to leave 'em." They followed her over to the barn, which proved empty except for the animals. "Only ones here ever paid him any mind."

"The other Daughters see him as a threat?"

"They'd never say as much, but we've been through this before. When the law can't find someone to blame, they look to the easiest."

"He's had troubles with the law in the past, your brother?" Han asked, moving closer to emphasize the difference in their heights.

Sister Merry glared up at him, undaunted. "He has never hurt another living soul. I swear it on the Mother's grace."

Callie believed she believed it, but that was no answer.

"Mayhap you could help us since you've been delayed."

Sister Merry firmed her chin. "What do you need?"

"Directions." Han unfurled the map from one of his hidden pockets. "To the cellar beneath the farmhouse."

"The what now?" Her surprise appeared just as genuine as before, but Callie edged toward unconvinced. "Oh, the grain room. Nothing down there but bags of feed."

"No bother for us to examine it, then," she countered.

"'Examine,' eh?" Sister Merry straightened her posture, crossing her arms beneath her breasts. Finally the matron emerged from her jolly, accommodating persona. "What's it worth to you?"

Callie and Han shared a look, then he asked, "What's your price?"

"I should think that be obvious: liberty."

"Not in the habit of letting suspects escape." Callie scoffed. "Boss wouldn't approve."

"Suspects, is it?" Sister Merry scowled. "Aye, you're like all the rest. All the dippy little princesses Juliet invites into our ranks with an eye to Papa's billfold. But the ones used to real work—the scullery maids and cress sellers and beggars and tarts—they never get to ascend, do they? Just shuck them and send them back to the hell they come from. And us, stuck with their get." She growled under her breath. "What reason have Amos or me to interfere with the likes of them? We come from dirt, and to dirt we return. Who are you to stand in our way?"

Han raised a pacifying hand. "If you fear we mean to scapegoat your brother…"

"Not you. Them." She glared toward Castleside but softened to a wistful look as she took in the garden. "I grew this patch from the roots, I did. It weren't nothing but a tree and a fallow field before I came. Haven't known a day's rest since I was spat into this world." She shook her head. "If he's the cause, you'll not take him from me. I've seen enough in my long years of life. I'll not see him hang."

They waited out her anguish, wondering if she'd just made her brother's confession. Callie cursed herself for using her Archie guise, wishing she could call upon her sisterly compassion without sounding a false note. In the end Han closed in on her, the solidity of his poise and size reassuring her as it had Callie so many times.

"Show us the grain room."

She nodded, chin still jutted up in defiance.

A frantic knock at the door woke Tim. Sister Zanna leapt from the chair by his bedside to answer. Tim lifted his eyelids to a slit to observe them. A Daughter he recognized as the nursery attendant, looking spectral with her white skin on white uniform and round, spooked black eyes, whispered a message into Sister Zanna's ear. They sped off. Neglecting to shut the door, but, after craning his head over the side of the bed, Tim saw the infirmary beyond was empty.

Though he still felt as if a rhinoceros had charged into his sternum, its savage horn tearing up his throat and crushing his windpipe, his alertness was improved after so much sleep. His fever had broken in the dawn hours. Weak from the stress of the case and the arduous poisoning, three bowls of porridge and fruit that morning had done their work restoring some of his strength. Enough to ease himself into a seated position, waiting for the world to still and his breaths to even before peeling back the sheets. He slipped his still-raw legs over the edge, testing them on the cold wood floor. His clothes lay folded atop the medical cabinet across the room. Conscious of the seconds ticking away and the wheeze in his breaths, Tim inched his way down to the bottom of the bed before daring to stand.

The screech of panicked voices in a nearby room nudged him on. He planted two hands on the lower board, then hoisted himself up. Ten breaths to steady, ten to recover. Every speck of him longed to kiss the floor except the small part that contemplated a leg amputation. He reached out for the cabinet. Too far. Shuffling his feet one by one until his anchor arm fully extended, he tried again. Too far. Frustration quickened his breaths; he wanted to dive back in the bed, pull the covers over his head, and not emerge for a decade.

Instead Tim lunged. He slammed his forearms on the edge of the cabinet, shouted into his clamped teeth and lips. Fell onto the window in the cabinet front, scrambling to stay upright, but didn't break the glass. Just as he grabbed for his clothes, his knees gave way. Fortunately he brought his suit down with him.

Tim rested his cheek on the frigid floor, counted out his breaths to slow them. The clack of heels running to and fro suggested Sister

Zanna's imminent return. Not bothering to shed his shift, though it reeked of the poultice, Tim wriggled his trousers over his rash-swollen leg, yanked on but did not fasten his waistcoat, and threw his jacket over his arm before discovering he hadn't the foggiest idea of where they'd stowed his boots.

And the diary Sister Nora had confided in him was still tucked under his pillow.

Summoning up the last spark of his strength, Tim shifted to all fours. What this cost him in air gained him in mobility. And perspective—he found his boots on the far side under the bedframe. He retrieved the diary, stowing it in the inner pocket of his jacket while taking a short rest. He collapsed his head and most of his torso on the mattress, sleep and lack of air tempting him back into oblivion. Perhaps if he just closed his eyes for a moment...

"Fetching as I find you in that position, my dear, even I know now is not the time."

Tim heard a soft click as the door shut. Tender fingers brushed through his hair, tested his brow. Tim accepted defeat. He'd fallen back to sleep. This must, after all, be a dream.

Dream Hiero crouched down and wove cosseting arms around him, pressing soft kisses to his temple as Tim reclined against him. With a gentle nudge of warning, he helped Tim sit up on the bed. Tim slumped into Dream Hiero's chest, flirting with exhaustion.

"My brave boy. What have they done to you?"

"A fit brought on by failed lords-and-ladies poisoning," he rasped, his voice still taxed by his damaged throat. Dream Hiero cupped one of his silken hands around Tim's neck, rubbing his thumb in circles around his Adam's apple, as if this could soothe the inner lining.

"'Failed'? Which lords and ladies?"

"An accidental success." A fit of coughs overtook him until Dream Hiero grabbed him a cup of water. "With a flower called lords-and-ladies. A kind of dark lily I'd never encountered before.

She only intended to give me a rash."

"Well, she's done the trick twice over. Perhaps not such an accident." Dream Hiero cinched his hold on Tim. "Sister Nora."

"How did you know?"

"Scoundrel's intuition."

Tim attempted a laugh, ended up coughing. "I'm still cross with you."

"How I know it," he chuckled. "And by now you have even more reason to be."

Tim sank deeper into his embrace, suspecting Dream Hiero was entirely too real, however ill-prepared Tim felt to deal with the consequences of his rescue. To test this theory, he gazed up into Hiero's dark-star eyes, twinkling down at him with the glint of a trickster god.

"Then it's as I feared." Tim hated himself a little when their lights went out. "You shouldn't have come for me."

"Unlike some, it's my profession to invent preposterous schemes to spare the lives of those I'm devoted to."

"And it's mine to fall on my sword for brave souls like Callie, Shahida, and Lillian. You should be with them."

Hiero grunted. "I'm exactly where I'm needed most." At Tim's huff of frustration, he added, "And so are they. Lillian recovering, Shahida nursing, and Callie on the hunt with Han."

Tim hoped his wheezing inhalation covered his shock. The slamming of a nearby door startled them both.

"What's going on out there?"

"Pandemonium. Nothing to trouble yourself with."

"What's happened?"

"What hasn't?"

"Hiero." Tim cleared his throat, a poor attempt at persuading him. "Tell me."

"No." A rare glower from Hiero stopped Tim's protest. "We are leaving this house of horrors with our lives intact. Let the damned

Daughters eat their young. You *will* survive this case."

Tim wished he could argue. But with the ladies safe... His heart felt five times too big for his chest, choking any objection. Hiero, whom he'd all but banished from the case, had saved them all.

Yet there was the small matter of his duty.

"Help me with my jacket, will you?"

Hiero was too shrewd a duelist to overreact to Tim's feint. And perhaps even he understood there was no way they could tread the boards of Castleside without involving themselves in the drama being played out. He hurried to tuck and tidy Tim's clothes into the bare minimum of propriety, pocketing his cravat instead of tying it so as not to constrict his ailing throat.

The rattle of the doorknob startled them apart. Hiero firmed his hold around Tim and tugged him to his feet just as Sister Zanna clattered into the room.

"And just where do you think you're going?" she demanded.

"Away from this hell," Hiero declared in a tone and of a temper Tim had never seen in him before.

"Are you quite mad? He needs another week of rest."

"Better odds than if he remains."

"Sister Zanna's not one of them," Tim insisted. "She saved my life."

"Or primed you to be sacrificed during one of their rituals."

Tim chuckled through the ache in his throat.

Sister Zanna was unamused. "Would have happily let him suffocate if I'd known he was in league with a thief like you. I may not know Mother Rebecca's every chapter and verse by heart, but I won't see her life's work sold for profit."

Hiero scoffed. "I'll deliver you your little box in a dreary gray bow so long as DI Stoker departs from here posthaste. With me."

She stared him down. "If you care for his life, you will not subject him to a journey he may not survive."

"I care for a great many things, least of which is your opinion.

Especially when it leads to entrapment."

Tim sighed. "Hiero, let's be gone—"

"A babe is missing." Sister Zanna clenched her jaw, possibly against saying more than she should, possibly against screaming. "There should be five in the nursery. We hid them when you came yesterday but returned them this morning, and…" Her breath heaved as if she, not Tim, had a scorched windpipe. "One is gone. Felix is gone."

A swoon of upset dizzied Tim. He used Hiero to straighten, to fight against it. He ignored Hiero's near-silent grumbling exhalation. It might have been a ploy to keep him, but Tim doubted Sister Zanna would parrot such a tall tale. Unless he had misjudged her from the start—a not-unprecedented turn of events if she was the baby snatcher.

"How long?"

"He was given to his wet nurse sometime in the night. The babes were upset not to have slept in their cots this morn and caused a lot of fuss, so Sister Bernadette didn't notice he hadn't been returned till now."

"Who is his wet nurse?"

"Sister Joan. But she's…" Sister Zanna inhaled a shaky breath. "She's just taken her vows. I suspect to stay with her child. Her daughter is among those being weaned. Why take another when—"

"—she could take her own. I see." Tim bowed his head and closed his eyes to think, wanting his bed, wanting his health, wanting this fiend to stop endangering little children until he could recover enough to catch them.

"Our friends are near," Hiero whispered to him. "Let's away from here and let them see to this."

Another untimely interruption gave Tim no choice but to act.

"Sister!" a voice screeched from the door to the infirmary. "You must come! She's gone mad! You must come now!"

At Tim's nod, Sister Zanna raced ahead. With a pointed growl,

Hiero helped him lurch after her.

They broke through the heavy doors of the shrine. Chaos reigned. The rows of pews had toppled forward, their scaled backs like molted husks of snakeskin. Something swishy had gored the floral carpet with mud. The podium had crashed into the base of the stained-glass window; a lightning bolt crack streaked up its center. A dozen Daughters prostrated themselves before the altar, praying and keening for salvation. Hiero wondered if their Almighty had finally sniffed the charnel scent of treachery on the wind.

Until he saw Sister Juliet in full, vengeful conflagration, chanting to the heavens and threatening to dash the candelabra she held over the carpet. Around her glistened a circle of oily liquid and, much to Hiero's dismay, tangles of gossamer hair. Sister Juliet had given herself a drastic chop, her cornsilk hair now more like a bushel of straw, her pale brow stained with a cross of ash.

Winterbourne slumped over the front row of the left bank of pews, a candlestick the likely cause of the head wound Sister Zanna tended. Sister Nora, meanwhile, begged Sister Juliet down from a safe distance outside the circle. Fervent chanting drowned out her desperate cries.

Kip's whimper brought Hiero back to the moment.

"We must stop this." Kip gestured to his throat. For a moment Hiero thought he had lost his voice. "She wears a key on a chain around her neck. I'll distract her whilst you retrieve it."

"I rather thought to leave them to it while dear little Felix is in the wind."

"There may still be women trapped here. We cannot let them burn."

Hiero clicked his tongue. Kip's righteousness, though rousing, proved damned inconvenient at times.

"Only once you're safely stowed with Angus. I'll not leave you here to be trampled or torched."

"I'll be fine." Kip gazed at him with eloquent eyes. "Work your magic."

Hiero sighed. How could he resist such a plea?

"Very well. But like the greatest illusionists, I'll do better without a hobbled assistant."

With more physical effort than he had expended in a good long while, Hiero righted one of the backmost pews and dropped Kip in it, ignoring his colorful protests. He fished Kip's cravat out of his pocket, securing his wrist to the arm of the pew with one hand whilst dabbing the sweat from Kip's brow with the other. A wink and a smile, and Hiero was off.

Catching Sister Zanna's eye, he waved her and an ailing Winterbourne over to care for Kip should everything go pear-shaped. Or prickly pear-shaped, given his history with Sister Juliet.

Hiero considered how best to approach the situation. When that failed, he straightened his shoulders, flared out the tails of his jacket, and strutted up the center aisle toward the main stage. He may no longer be the Gaiety's star player, but his luster hadn't dimmed a single spark.

"... and the world will know Her wrath!" Sister Juliet thrust up her candelabra like a fiery banner. "Daughters, we must cleanse our hearts and our bodies of all their earthly ills. As Mother Rebecca prophesied, 'The end will come easy to those who have labored in the Garden. Those of sweat-stained brows and soiled hands will be bathed pure by Her light.' It is time to wash ourselves in fire. Give ourselves to the Mother of Us All that She might rise anew!"

A loud clearing of the throat got her attention. Even in her fervor, Sister Juliet couldn't swallow her smile at seeing Hiero, the Beast to her beauty, the omega to her alpha, the snake in her... He shuddered as that last image took an unlikely turn. She could tend her own lawn.

"You see!" Sister Juliet bellowed to her devout. "'In the final hours, the Serpent will rise, and you shall know him by his black and wicked tongue. Cut it out, lest you succumb as I have succumbed. Cut it out, and claim my victory!'"

If Sister Juliet had intended this as a battle cry, the effect on the Daughters was far from revolutionary. Those who didn't stare at her dumbfounded cowered from Hiero as he walked, step by measured step, toward the altar. He challenged her smile with a smirk of his own, left eyebrow canted in a perfect, pointed arch.

"Be gone, Serpent! Be gone from us forever!"

"Happy to oblige once you're feeling a touch less murderous," Hiero said. "Too much of Sister Merry's special cider, or is it a full moon?"

"You mock and you sneer." Sister Juliet's rabid grimace rather reminded Hiero of black pots and kettles. "But you will never know the Mother's light, even as it cinders you."

"As the French say, *je ne regrette rien*." Hiero murmured his excuses as he breached the wall of Daughters. "Yourself?"

"Stop this instant!" Sister Juliet lowered the candelabra until it skirted the carpet—and, more dangerously, her skirts.

"Juliet, no!" Sister Nora ran up onto the altar. "Just give him what he wants, and he will go."

Juliet barked a laugh. "Such men never have enough! Of our souls, of our treasures, of our skin... Already the Serpent has taken our most sacred prophecies, and still his desire's not slaked!"

"Quite a turn from burning me alive. Unexpected." Hiero continued his march to the center of the altar.

"Final warning," Sister Juliet snarled, thrusting the candelabra directly at Hiero. "She will have Her revenge."

With a deft sleight of hand, he plucked the weapon from her grasp and snuck it to Sister Nora before she could blink.

"I do hope so," Hiero smiled. "That would be something to

see."

With an ear-splitting cry, Sister Juliet lunged at him. She rammed her angel-blonde head into his chest and pounded his sides with her fists. The effect was something akin to a Pomeranian battering a rakishly stylish Rottweiler. Hiero chuckled, patted her on the back.

Sister Nora, having extinguished the open flame, wrenched her into her arms. Sister Juliet wrestled against her, stomping and screeching.

"A valiant effort, but for naught," Hiero declared, dangling the key he'd pilfered from around her neck before tucking it into his inner pocket. "Now if you're done impeding the course of justice, we've an investigation to salvage." He coughed. "I mean conclude."

"Nora, dearest Nora," Sister Juliet blubbered as she collapsed against her. "How have you strayed so far from the path? Allied yourself with this… this…"

Too late Hiero glimpsed a flash of the fury that still lit Sister Juliet's eyes. Under pretense of gathering her into an embrace, she catapulted Sister Nora into Hiero and grabbed for the candelabra. Scaling the podium as they toppled to the ground, Sister Juliet smashed through the stained-glass window, a rain of dagger shards masking her escape.

Hiero turned to the back to the shrine before chasing after her to find no trace of Kip.

Chapter 21

Tim stole a few seconds of quiet as Sir Hugh perused the map, grateful for the wall that supported him and the cup of lukewarm tea Sister Zanna had retrieved from Sister Juliet's office. Sir Hugh vouched for it not containing any toxins, agents, or otherwise harmful matter, and so far, Tim had not felt any ill-effects. Except, of course, for the total humiliation of having succumbed to such a ruse, and having his client discover him the worse for wear. Oh, and being *tied to a chair* by his supposed partner. The fact that Sir Hugh had been involved in this escape plot at all he chose not to focus on, for that way lay further madness.

"Your theory, Stoker, is we may uncover evidence of the crime, and perhaps more, in one of these three underground chambers?"

"It is." Tim repressed the desire to hurry him. They stood kitty-corner from the infirmary at the intersection of the main hall with the small corridor that led to the cellar. Into which Tim would have already disappeared, if not for want of a lantern. "But might I remind you time is of the essence. Another babe has gone missing."

"A fact that, along with your current state, that carnival we just witnessed, and Bash's involvement, does not work in your favor."

Tim couldn't spare the breath to curse Hiero for involving Sir Hugh. Instead he appealed to his sense of honor.

"Sir, let me end this."

"Oh, it is over." He sighed. "Or would be if I had the manpower available. As it is, I fear you must count this as a loss."

"But, sir, the child."

"*My* boy, Stoker. You were tasked with reuniting me with my son."

"Someone's son will die tonight if we do not make haste! A boy named Felix is with the killer as we speak!" Tim regretted his shout as soon as it finished echoing, drawing Sister Zanna out of the infirmary with, thank the fates, several lanterns.

The doors to the shrine clanged open, cutting off Sir Hugh's angry reply. A few weary Daughters trudged out, with Hiero and Sister Nora hot-footing it behind them. Hiero's normal twinkle was overcast by a stormy look, equal parts annoyance and relief, when he discovered them in the hall. Tim canted his head toward Sir Hugh and shot Hiero a look in return.

Tim attempted a more even tone with his superior. "Sir, if you care to retire to the nearest division house, we will join our associates on the hunt."

But Sir Hugh had yet to pull his attention away from the map.

"Your associates are where?"

"At the farmhouse," Hiero explained, pushing into their circle. "Or perhaps they've concluded their search. We really must rendezvous with them to know."

"So they may be at the tree, or here... Where is this?"

"The question of the hour."

Sister Nora took a hesitant step forward. "May I see?"

While Sir Hugh relinquished a corner of the map to her, Tim mouthed, "The key?" to Hiero.

"Patience" was his maddening reply.

"The potting shed," she concluded, pointing to the fourth un-known chamber. "Must be."

"And why are some of the paths red and some green?" Sir Hugh asked.

"That I could not say."

"Our theory is they are impassable," Tim said, losing the fight against exasperation.

Sir Hugh dismissed this with a curt gesture. "If your associates are at the farmhouse, then it is clear we must investigate the chambers beneath the potting shed and the tree."

"We should break into teams," Tim suggested, "one underground and one over."

Hiero wiggled a hand. "A small point of contention. Sister Juliet has fled."

"Fled!" Sir Hugh growled. "You failed to secure her?"

"Rather I *succeeded* in preventing her from burning the house down."

"What you've both succeeded in is making a hash of this entire investigation," Sir Hugh proclaimed, his face simmering with choler. "Hear me now. I will chase down this madwoman myself. The pair of you are done. Stoker, you will retire to the infirmary. Mr. Bash, summon the Yard. Miss Hawfinch—"

"I *will* see this through!" Tim objected, raising his raspy voice to... a louder rasp. "Even if it kills me. Sir Hugh, you awarded me this case for a reason. Let me prove you right. Let me finish it."

"By the look of you," Sister Zanna interjected, "it very well may be your last."

"Then so be it." Tim ignored Hiero's imploring eyes. "I am a man of honor and a capable officer of the Metropolitan Police. I *will* solve this case."

Sir Hugh foisted his assessing stare upon him for so long Tim almost began to despair.

"Very well." He surrendered the map. "I will proceed overground; you may investigate under. We will rendezvous at the tree in thirty minutes' time."

"Agreed," Tim wheezed.

With a final nod, Sir Hugh set out with Sisters Nora and Zanna in close pursuit. Tim tested out the walking stick someone had fetched him but found he still needed support. Or perhaps he simply wanted to stay close to Hiero during their trip through the underworld.

Especially when Tim spared him a glance and discovered he'd gone gray.

"Have a coin handy for the ferryman?" Tim quipped, hoping to revivify his mood. "Otherwise we'll have to swim."

Hiero stared down the small corridor at the cellar door as if it had grown fangs and saw fit to devour them. He flinched away when Tim reached out for him. Then, realizing who beckoned, gave him his arm, only to tuck him in so close there was a question of who supported whom.

"What is it?"

"I... I cannot."

Hiero bowed his head, which didn't hide his shame from Tim's lower vantage. Tim hugged him, fighting the urge to stroke his cheek.

"Rejoin the others." Tim tried to appear more solid, to coax Hiero off so he didn't have to abandon his part of the mission, though even he didn't relish braving the tunnels alone. "Given what transpired before, I'm doubtful Sir Hugh will be able to handle the Daughters. He'll require a man of your particular skills."

That jolted Hiero back into himself.

"The madness is spreading if you think I'll abandon you to the dark." He shuddered. "The endless, writhing dark..."

Tim pressed a hand to his chest before he lost him to his private horrors.

"We must investigate that chamber. The murderer has used the chaos to cover their foul deeds and make their escape. They may be stealing the babe away through the tunnels as we speak." He eased Hiero's lantern out of his grasp. "Go to the farmhouse to see if Callie and Han have made progress before joining me at the potting shed. Find a weapon and, whatever you do, don't allow anyone to leave the compound." With a final squeeze, he pulled away from Hiero.

Only to find himself stalled by a crushing grip on his shoulder.

"You are in no state to confront a killer."

"And I'll not risk your sanity by dragging you into hell." Tim shifted Hiero's hand off his shoulder before continuing to hobble toward the cellar door.

"Kip…"

"There's no time! We may already be too late."

He almost cried out when Hiero latched a strong, if trembling, arm around him anew. The slinky surety of the man at his side saved him that indignity.

"Then we'd best make haste." As Hiero snatched the lantern back, Tim felt him gird himself for the trial ahead. "Though I rather think it's not *my* sanity that's in question, Detective Daring."

Tim hoped he was the right man to see him through.

A slanted door tacked to the back of the farmhouse proved to Callie they had been right in enlisting Sister Merry's guidance. Even an experienced investigator might not have noticed the slip of space between the chimney and the woodpile, almost an optical illusion from the open side of the house, with the far side hedged in by vegetable marrows. She doubted many of the Daughters knew of its existence beyond Sister Juliet and a couple of the older sisters.

Sealed by intricate swaths of cobwebs and swollen to cracking by damp, the portal looked like a relic from another time, as weathered and insect ridden as Mother Rebecca in her grave. After lighting his lantern, Han set a match to the filaments that snared the door handle, but they proved too wet to burn away. Sister Merry snorted, shooed him away. The door peeled off with a thunderous crack. She threw a few logs down to prop it open, then dove into the dark.

Han and Callie hastened to follow her down a rickety flight of stairs. Even sure-footed Han gripped the guardrail when it wobbled under their weight. Callie wondered how Amos Scaggs managed while carrying sacks of feed until she spotted a plank propped against the wall. Either the garden's magic enhanced the industriousness of its spiders, or the Daughters took great care to keep these chambers a secret, because the feed stores had been added to, and recently. Or perhaps Sister Merry was too accustomed to notice the fresh muddy bootprints that descended the stairs alongside them.

"How did you come to discover these tunnels?"

Sister Merry's laugh had a sinister quality that raised the hairs on Callie's neck.

"Papist ancestor of Rebecca's, or so she claimed. Built them for their rituals like the early Romans. My thinking is she had a rogue uncle—a smuggler or highwayman."

Han nodded. "Who used them to store his ill-gotten gains."

"Rumor has it there were a pair of them." Sister Merry snickered. "Once was a second house behind the tree, sharing the park with Castleside. Split their booty up between the four spaces, so no matter who was invaded, they could always escape to the other."

Callie chuckled. "A creditable plan."

The chamber proved to be as ordinary as described, half the size of the cellar under the main house and glutted with sacks of feed. Callie worked her way through the burlap maze, checking every corner and crevice, but knew in her heart only one type of farming took place here. She tested the bags to be certain they contained grain and spotted a few holes in those crammed against the walls. Perhaps the creepers were of the four-legged variety after all.

"Some of the founding Daughters talked of booby traps and pirates and the like," Sister Merry continued. "You know how girls like to gossip. You should've heard the tales we spun!"

"But Sister Juliet had some of the tunnels blocked when she took charge?" Callie guessed, remembering the red lines on the map.

Three black maws, offshoots that led to other chambers, spat their foul breath into the grain room. Consulting the map as she stood in the center, Callie marked the one to the main house on her left, the one to the tree to her right, and the one that led to an unknown location—linked with a red line—in front of her. She wound her way toward it, lantern raised high.

"No use for them, was there?"

"And costly to maintain, no doubt," Han observed.

"Wasn't a garden till Rebecca took charge," Sister Merry said. "You've got to let things take root if they're to grow. And once they do..."

"Woe betide those who try to stop them." Callie peered down the forbidden tunnel, the air hazy with dust and her view obstructed by gnarls of roots. A fecund scent of rich but sooty soil overwhelmed her senses at first.

But then, lurking in its depths, came the smell of rot. Normal, perhaps: she had never been underneath a garden before. But unsettling all the same. A sense of wrongness prickled over her skin. She moved in a couple of paces, hoping to see around a bend in the passage. Or a portion that had caved in—impossible to tell. Just as she reached her lantern around the curve, she caught it on her tongue. A sweet treacle stench. Laudanum.

"Han," Callie called, then heard a hard *thwack!*

He'd recovered, hand to his head, crouched down by the plank that had fallen by his feet by the time she'd spun around. He pointed to the tunnel that led to the tree, down which Sister Merry had fled.

They had no choice but to follow her.

Hiero kept his eyes shut until he heard the hiss of the igniting gas lamps. He inhaled a deep, shaky breath, counted out an exhalation, preparing to give the greatest performance of his life. That of a man who could explore a subterranean labyrinth without losing what was left of his mind. Even in his frail state, Kip vibrated with excitement—an adventurer to the core. Hiero had to coax his skittish mind into thinking against the will of his instinct, which had long ago chosen "flight" as its preferred response to danger.

"Into the belly of the beast," he murmured as they began their descent.

Unsurprisingly the stench had not improved. With lantern in hand and his other arm anchored around Kip, he could not even press a handkerchief to his mouth and nose. He gagged against the reek of human waste, wondering if he should recreate his tumble down the stairs, as that seemed to have inured him before. Instead he concentrated on each step so as not to upset the balance of lantern, lover, and light-headedness. Also to stop him screaming.

"What... what the devil?" Kip rasped, gaping at the Daughters' small dungeon.

Hiero didn't dare glance in that direction. He'd committed the piss-soaked pallets and scold's bridles to memory on his first visit.

"No time," he reminded Kip, veering him toward the entrance to the tunnels. The seething dark beyond the glow of the gaslights.

"They hold the novitiates there?" Kip asked.

"Only if they've been naughty."

"Whilst they're with child? That's..."

"Monstrous? Reprehensible? Deviant? Revolting? I can go on."

"I thought if we found the bad seed, the other Daughters might have a chance. Most of the work they do here is admirable, if one forgets the mad prophecies. But this..." Hiero felt him shiver. "Rotten to the core."

"And yet I wonder who might flourish if given the chance to emerge from the shadows."

The ones surrounding them only darkened as they traversed the last pools of gaslight. Hiero paused them at the edge of the black, grateful Kip appeared to require some rest. The moisture and foulness in the air belabored his breathing, and he grew paler every passing minute. Hiero knew better than to force him to retreat, but the fear of Kip fainting—or worse—almost overwhelmed his other causes for panic.

They'd come to a crossroads, two distinct tunnels veering off from the cellar. With trembling hands, Kip unfurled the map.

"Left," he instructed but made no move. He bowed his head, fighting exhaustion. "Not too late to turn back."

"I'll not let you murder yourself just yet."

"Martyr, you mean?"

"Even you, my dear Kip, would be denied sainthood for such obstinate dedication to duty."

"That and being a sodomite."

A sharp laugh ripped from Hiero's throat, scoring its delicate flesh. He'd admire Kip for attempting to lighten the mood if it didn't render them mute.

They pressed on. The passage's low ceiling forced Hiero to crouch, his insides wailing at the further constriction. His overstimulated nerves buzzed and blared like a child fed too much sugar. The scuttles and skitters of creatures lurking just beyond the light became the wailing moans of long-lost specters. The deeper they went, the tighter the fit until Hiero felt straightjacketed by something so welcome as Kip's hold.

He chased his breath but couldn't catch it, felt the world tilt though he could barely see. Reached out to steady himself, but his fingers sank into a crumbling wall. Spills of soil rained down from the root nest of the ceiling, smearing their faces and suffocating them with dust. They would be buried there, buried alive, food for the crops that let the Daughters lure others into their...

He collapsed, dropping Kip and the lantern.

"*Baba*," he mewled. "Baba..."

"Here." The tang of whiskey-laced metal parted Hiero's lips. "Drink."

Hiero moaned. Only a few blessed sips but enough to make him a believer. He emptied the flask.

"'No friendly drop to help me after?'" Kip asked, stowing it back in Hiero's inner pocket.

"Perhaps not the time to quote one of the tragedies." Hiero counted two long breaths, then cursed himself. "Kip. I can't go on."

"Nearly there." Kip sagged against him, his consciousness slipping. What a pair they made. "Too far along not to see it through."

"But what awaits us?"

"Whatever it is, we'll face it boldly. As you have done these past days, even when…" Kip exhaled a shaky breath, teetering on the edge of despair himself. "When I lost faith in you." Hiero clutched the clammy hand Kip sought to twine with his. "But I see you now, how brave you are. I see your heart."

Hiero lifted Kip's hand to his lips, too overcome to speak. A weak tug at his waistcoat urged Hiero back to his knees, if not his feet just yet.

"Come along now," Kip urged. "We've dragons to slay."

They staggered up to a standing position. The tunnel broadened as they approached a fathomless gray in the distance. Only when they were a few paces away did Hiero realize this was due to a thin gauze of light strewn through the boards of what must be the floor of the potting shed. A charcoal outline of a chamber could be traced around the gauze, with the hollow of another tunnel leading farther into the maze.

He heaved a sigh of relief, only to choke on a syrupy-sweet smell in the air. A coughing fit overtook Kip, who did what Hiero could not and nabbed his handkerchief as a face cover.

"And to think I'd been rather partial to treacle tarts," Hiero groused.

Kip stilled. "Laudanum. Must have dropped the bottle."

"Odd to think they'd store it with the gardening tools. Though I do recall the very same smell on my first visit."

"Your first..." He stared at Hiero. "You've been here before?"

"Mmm. Our first day."

"And you smelled treacle?"

"This cloying sweetness, yes." He watched a five-act tragedy play out in seconds on Kip's face. "Why?"

Kip pinched the bridge of his nose, fingers trembling with more than fatigue.

"Can you remain here a moment?"

"Alone?" Even Hiero heard the quaver in his voice.

Kip nodded. "You've suffered enough in accompanying me. Let me spare you this."

"But who will spare you?"

"That ship's long sailed." Kip hobbled off a few paces. "Remain here until I call for you."

Hiero fumbled for his flask as Kip merged into the gray light, clutching it with both hands to center himself.

The instant Kip disappeared, quicksand darkness swallowed him, filling his nose and mouth and throat, choking off his whimpers. A belt of constriction crushed his lungs. The hissing voices crawled up his neck and around his ears, tiny, shiver-inducing centipedes. Hiero cowered into the corner, his mind conjuring a metal door with an iron-barred window in the blackness.

Never again, never again, never again...

"Hiero," a broken voice beckoned, and he raced toward it. Kip caught him before he could blaze past him into the chamber. "No!"

Hiero froze. A patch of straw inside a wicker basket. A threadbare blanket tossed aside. A scrap of burlap. He could—but would not—imagine the rest.

And wee Felix still nowhere to be found.

"You have your evidence."

"Of little worth without a name to charge it to."

Rustling from above drew their attention. Scuttling footsteps, manic muttering. Bottles clinking, clattering—someone searching.

"Blast!" Kip whispered. He indicated a ladder which, when positioned right, led up to a small hatch. Hiero helped him dock it into place against metal widgets on the ceiling and in the floor. "Can you see who it is?"

Hiero nodded. Repressing his eagerness to be aboveground, he crept up the rungs as quickly as he could, then peered through a wide seam in two of the floorboards. In time to lock on to Sister Juliet's wild eyes as she knelt to unlock the hatch.

"Serpent." Her giggles had the sharpness of a shriek. "Here to tempt me, are you? With what, I wonder? Given you're the one slithering in the muck."

Hiero's gaze did not waver as he considered the forty-five ways this could go wrong for them. And the one way he might reach her.

"A taste of the forbidden, perhaps? A certain box you've been seeking." He saw her hesitate, rushed on. "A reminder that I am the only one aware of its location."

"And by yours, its contents are spoiled!" Sister Juliet dropped the lock, leapt to her feet. She threw open the lid of the poison box, gathered up several bottles. "Ruined, all of it ruined, a second Eden rotted to the core..."

"One bad apple, the bunch, et cetera." Hiero baited another hook, praying it would catch her out. "You have no care to prevent the murder of one of your charges? The butchering of an innocent babe?"

"If it is Her will that another sacrifice be made in Her garden," Sister Juliet declared, lifting the poisons to the heavens as if to sanctify them, "then so be it."

With a vengeful cry, she cracked open the bottles and poured their corrosive contents all over the floor.

Hiero dove at Kip, lifting him off his feet as he ran from the poison rain. Shoved him against a tunnel wall and covered him with his body as his senses registered the striking of a match.

He pressed a final, fevered kiss to his lips as the world exploded.

Chapter 22

Callie could have been forgiven for thinking herself in Wonderland while chasing down a white-tailed Sister Merry rabbiting through tunnels two sizes too small. As she stumbled over the jutting rocks and hidden potholes, she mused that this Wonderland could use a bit more wonder and fewer mad hunts through cramped passages. Self-annoyance and frustration at letting Sister Merry dupe them churned within as they raced to the heart of the garden.

For where else could Amos Scaggs be but the Tree of Wisdom? And where else could the finale of this wild drama of theirs play out?

A whiff of the earlier treacle scent stopped her cold. She heard Han skid in behind her. She sniffed the air, peered around a bend in time to see her white rabbit disappear around a sharp right turn. Callie consulted the map as she climbed forward over a pile of rocks. When they came to the fork in the tunnel, she again paused.

A rustling farther down the left passage pricked her ears. She shined the lantern in that direction but saw only another bend in the tunnel.

"Later." Han gripped her shoulders from behind but didn't steer her. "We've got to catch her before she meddles."

The treacle scent curdled, stinking of hot lead and lye, scratching her nose.

"Something's not right."

"No time to dither."

A flash of green-yellow light saw Han slam her to the ground. Callie shoved her face into his sleeve as the suffocating fumes of a chemical fire clogged the tunnel. Han pressed a handkerchief into her hand, pointing to their escape route. Callie crawled out from under him, a small part of her cursing their circumstances before a howl of agony seized their attentions.

"Are you hurt?"

"No. Are you?"

"Someone's down there."

A loud grunt followed by a string of curses in a language she recognized only too well echoed out of the smoke.

"Go!" Han nudged her in Sister Merry's direction. "Catch her up. I'll help them."

"No. They might be injured."

"I'll see to them." He tapped her revolver through the fabric of her trousers. "End this."

Torn, Callie hung about until two figures lurched into view at the bend in the tunnel. Two staggering, coughing figures— impossible to say who propped up whom—but both alive.

"Go!" Han barked.

She scrambled to her feet, jogging until she passed into a wave of less-toxic air, then broke out into a run. She grappled up an incline in the path until she spotted a circle of sunlight. Callie blew out her lantern as she reached the base of the hole, tucking it behind a stump that acted as a step into the garden. At first glance upward, a ring of foliage greeted her. She waited for her eyes to adjust before peering up over the edge.

She bit back a gasp. Under the heavy boughs of the Tree of Wisdom, Amos Scaggs cowered away from his furious sister while cradling a babe in his arms. A ring of flowers and leaves that matched the staging of the other boy's body decorated the grass.

Callie popped out of the hole, revolver aimed and ready.

"Stop!" she bellowed, charging toward them.

Amos yelped and swayed such that Callie feared he would drop the babe. Which, by its squeals, proved blessedly alive. She prayed luck would continue to shine upon her as she closed in on the pair, halting just far enough to keep them in her sights.

Sister Merry stared at the barrel of her revolver. She raised up placating hands, one for Callie and one for her brother.

"Now don't be doing anything rash..."

Callie only had time for Amos. "Put the babe down."

He trembled like a bird caught in a briar. "Merry..."

"In that patch over there, then step away." Callie flicked her gun. "Now."

"He needs his Mother."

"If you'll only let me explain," Sister Merry insisted.

"Now. Put him down *now*."

"Only She can shelter him!" Amos cried. "Only She can spare him!"

"He don't understand," Sister Merry pleaded. "You're scaring him."

"Nothing will happen to you or your sister," Callie reassured Amos. "We'll talk it all through. Just walk over to that patch and lay him down."

Amos cradled the babe closer to his chest, its shrill wails muffled by his shirt.

"She can see! She will know!"

The revolver's blast startled even Callie. She didn't remember taking aim. She didn't remember pulling the trigger. Only the report and the instinctive twitch of her hand.

The bullet smoked as it lodged in the bark of the tree but didn't ignite.

"Down. Now."

Amos scrambled to do her bidding, cooing to the frightened babe as he lay him in the grass. By the time he walked back to join his sister and she held them back with her newly cocked revolver,

Callie had resolved her mind as to the exact nature of the scene playing out before her.

But she had to be sure.

Tim slouched on the stump at the tunnel's exit, face raised to the sky. He gulped down breath after breath of clean air, the wheeze in his chest reignited by the noxious smoke of the explosion. He clutched the flask of water a well-prepared Han had given him, took a measured draught. His body quaked in half-relief, half-unspent adrenaline. Though an aura of exhaustion twinkled on the periphery of his vision, it would be some time before he could truly rest. They had a case to solve.

He basked in the—probably imagined—heat of the sunlight on his face, careful to avert his eyes from the sight of Hiero slipping on Han's jacket. The blast's aftermath flickered through his mind: Hiero lit by a halo of fire; rolling him against the wall to snuff it out; Han's hulking shadow in the distance as they dragged each other through the endless, fume-dark tunnel. The blaze had given Hiero an impromptu haircut, the singed ends somehow suiting him.

But his back had suffered the worst of it, scorched right through to his skin. Or what some vile bastard had left him of skin, scarred and striped into a thick layer the flames barely burned. Tim hadn't let his stare linger, but he recognized a whipping when he saw it. He fought now to give Hiero the privacy he deserved, to stopgap his questions and focus on the voices shouting above.

But then Hiero was there before him, clothes and handsomeness righted, hand extended toward him. Prepared to give more when he had already given everything. Shepherded the case to its completion. Saved Tim's life. So Tim did what any reasonable person would do upon reuniting with their lover after a brush with death.

He kissed the life out of him.

Like something out of a folktale, the fervent press of Hiero's lips revived something in Tim. It was as if Tim could taste his ache and worry, his senses engulfed by the rich scent of Hiero's relief. They kissed and caressed with fatalistic ardor until Tim broke from him to replenish the breath he'd stolen. And wished, in that moment, the world would fall away.

Then Tim heard the healthy, ear-splitting squalls of a babe very much alive and, with Hiero's help, heaved himself out of the hole.

"What have you done, sweet boy? What have you done?" Sister Merry wailed, crouched in a pietà with Amos in a too-familiar circle of leaves and blooms.

Tim also clocked Callie and her revolver. They'd all heard the gunshot, but Amos didn't appear to have been wounded.

"He didn't need it, Merry," Amos pleaded. "Her blessing. He wanted to be good. He wanted to be good!"

"Hush now," she cooed, petting his head. Spotting Tim amidst the bushes covering the hole, her face crumbled. "DI Stoker, please! He didn't know what he was doing. He doesn't know his own mind."

Tim could only cough in response, deciding to let the scene play out a bit longer. No one in it seemed aware of the chaos in the distance: the potting shed engulfed in flames, a small group wrestling Sister Juliet to the ground, Daughters flying across the lawn to save their garden.

"Everything in hand?" he asked Callie, whose aim and intent never wavered.

"Well in hand, sir."

A curse and a clatter behind him heralded Hiero's entry. He sauntered over to a nearby patch of grass, where little Felix still fussed. Tim couldn't help but smile as Hiero scooped him up, quieting him with coos and cuddles to be envious of. Han appeared beside Tim, offering his support. Aching too much to be ashamed,

Tim allowed himself to be escorted over to the tree. He settled into a spot on a slight incline above the others, giving him the feeling of a king attending a bizarre performance by travelling players. Ever the Gertrude to his Claudius, Hiero soon joined him, the now-slumbering babe cradled against him.

"'Hold, as 'twere, the mirror up to nature, to show virtue her own feature, scorn her own image, and the very age and body of the time his form and pressure,'" Hiero whispered.

"Quite." After another drink of water, Tim turned his attention back to the scene before him. "Make your report."

"I found them like this, forced them to surrender the babe." Tim listened closely to Callie's emphasis, trying to discern her thoughts from the words she underlined. "The gent gave me a bit of trouble but did it willingly enough once I fired a shot. At the tree, sir."

Tim nodded. "And what do you have to say for yourselves?"

"Inspector, sir, he's not right." Sister Merry released her brother long enough to make a direct appeal. Despite her firmed mouth and adamant posture, Tim knew she was begging. "He got Mother Rebecca's message mixed up in his head. Let me take him away from here. I swear to you, we won't go near anywhere with little 'uns. Just back to the farm, to the soil. He won't bother a soul."

Tim didn't respond, letting her believe such a fantasy was possible a few moments longer. Cruel, perhaps, but he needed the truth.

"And you, Amos? Tell me what you were doing here." As soon as Tim saw Amos flicker his eyes toward his sister, he gestured for Han to separate them. "Not to her. To me."

Amos worried his hands as he sat before him but looked Tim in the eye.

"He doesn't fear you," Hiero murmured.

"Nor the consequences of his actions," Tim agreed.

"That boy is in the Mother's light." He pointed to the babe, his features softening. "And She will protect him."

"Protect him from what?"

Amos shook his head. "He in't done nothing wrong. He's just a little 'un."

"Why did you bring him here?"

"So She would know. She would know what was being done." A sob wracked through him. "I'm sorry, Merry! I didn't mean it. I didn't..."

"Sweet boy." Sister Merry blinked away tears. "Inspector, please. Let me take him away."

"They are packed and ready," Han pointedly remarked. "Their wagon's at the side gate."

Tim sighed, wishing he could spare someone to go search it. "You meant to flee?"

"To go back from where we came," Sister Merry corrected. "Away from all this. To the land."

"You would abandon your garden?"

"My garden is burning." She turned her gaze to the blaze on the other side of the stream, tears spilling over. "Nothing here for us now."

He considered them, Merry and Amos, as he worked through a theory of the crime. He glanced at Callie, raised an eyebrow. She made her convictions clear. He looked to Han, who seconded them. He turned to Hiero.

"Care to take the stage?"

He snorted. "So ill-prepared? Never." Hiero cast his black-pearl eyes upon him, glowing with a mixture of pride and affection. "The audience is waiting, my dear."

Before he could begin, a ruckus at the base of the hill distracted them all. Sir Hugh charged toward them, dragging a smirking, manacled Sister Juliet with him. Sister Nora and Sister Zanna chased after them, their white uniforms and weary faces streaked with soot. They came to an abrupt halt on seeing Hiero and Tim, bedraggled but alive.

"Stoker!" Sir Hugh fell speechless at the state of them.

"Ah, Sir Hugh," Hiero greeted in his most obsequious tone. "How good of you to join us. And at the opportune moment, no less."

"What in blazes is going on here?"

"Rather a poor choice of words, given the state of the garden."

"Go back to your nest, Serpent, that She may smite all and everything of yours," Sister Juliet seethed, much to Hiero's delight. Or so Tim interpreted his snickers.

"You're done here, Stoker," Sir Hugh announced. "I'm summoning the Yard."

"That's rather fortunate," Hiero again intervened, "since he's about to solve the case."

Angry chatter broke out, everyone vying for their protest to be heard. Han's sharp whistle silenced—and slightly deafened—them.

"Is that so?" Sir Hugh asked, unable to conceal his eagerness.

"Mostly, though I'd offer a slight correction," Tim responded. "*We* believe we have identified the culprit." Tim spared a grateful glance to Callie, Han, and Hiero. "My team and I, that is. I'll endeavor to explain." Tim wriggled up so he sat taller against the trunk of the Tree of Wisdom, wishing he had the strength to stand. "From the first it was clear this is a case where motive reigned supreme. Yet that aspect proved the most difficult to determine. Can any sane individual understand what might prompt one to kill a child? Is anyone who commits a crime such as this in possession of their sanity? No. And so we, as investigators, ventured into the mouth of madness."

"But surely some had more means or opportunity than others," Sir Hugh interrupted.

"The location of the body and its staging did give us pause," Tim explained. "A question we considered was whether the killer was the one who buried the body. We think it unlikely. This brought up the question of collusion. Did the killer act alone? Or was someone helping or covering up for them? Why would someone do this? Was this part of a larger plot to farm babies plucked from those sent to the orphan asylum? If so, at what point in the process were the babes taken, and where were they kept? It was a case of endless complexities but few conclusions."

"I saw firsthand all the suspects had enough access to commit the crime," Callie elaborated, dropping her Archie guise and accent. Only Sister Nora gasped. "We theorized a night guardian with access to all the rooms in Castleside could have stolen the babes. But our adventures proved anyone with enough determination who could pick a lock could have managed the feat at night."

"Sister Nora and Sister Merry both have a complete set of keys," Han continued. "No one would have questioned Sister Juliet or Sister Zanna roaming the halls at night. Amos drove the children to the orphan asylum. All but he could have doctored the records. But as we've established the killer had an accomplice…"

A throng of rapt eyes looked to Hiero. He grinned, and looked to Tim.

"Proceed."

Tim chuckle-coughed. "Once we'd determined all of the principal suspects had means and opportunity, the question of motive became paramount. It may seem like a fool's errand to attempt to fathom the unfathomable—and certainly there can never be a satisfying explanation as to why someone might commit this horrible crime—but there may be enough dark method at work for us to narrow the suspects.

"Sister Zanna, unless I'm an exceptionally poor judge of character, I eliminated first. She has dedicated her life to birthing and saving children. If she cared to be rid of them, the logical method would be to dispatch them in the aftermath of their mother's labor. No one would question her verdict as a midwife. It would also prove complicated for her to snatch the babes on their way to the orphan asylum, and she has the least amount of freedom of movement on the compound.

"Sister Nora, the newest and greenest of the Daughters of Eden, might come under suspicion for just that reason. But she is the most purely devout among you and a staunch promoter of the faith. Though she obstructed our investigation, she, of all, would never do anything to compromise the work being done here. Although I sense she suspected a certain person of the murder all along and has been fighting to protect her."

"A noble pursuit," Hiero commented, "if misguided."

Tim downed the last of the water, hoping his voice held.

"When we learned of the way in which Sister Juliet came to be the shepherdess of this flock, I thought the case resolved. There was a dark logic to it: devastated over the loss of her child, she decrees the Daughters must begin helping fallen women, providing her with an endless supply of unwanted babes on which she could take out her anger. The plot was cunning and allowed Sister Juliet to play the part she adored: that of the benevolent, half-touched philanthropist."

Sister Juliet's stare could have cut glass. Gone was the wilding prophetess longing for redemption through Eve's blessing. In her stead, a diminutive woman with clever, lucid eyes pinned Tim to the trunk at his back. He shrunk back despite himself. Rarely had he borne witness to such hatred as inked her soul.

"But she commits her crimes in the light of day," Hiero said, breaking her hold on Tim. "Not skulking about in the shadows. She craves an audience."

"Like recognizes like, Serpent," Sister Juliet said through gritted teeth.

Hiero's answering smirk had a mercenary quality. "Precisely."

"Exonerated on one count," Sir Hugh warned. "But there are many more hanging over her."

Tim turned his attention to the center of their makeshift circus ring. Amos sat cross-legged, pulling off the petals of the flowers he'd brought to decorate the babe's grave. Sister Merry stood resolute beside him, a protective hand on his shoulder. Tim wished Han had managed to keep them separated, but he supposed whatever transpired was inevitable. Some situations were bound by the rules of a higher plain.

"And then there were two," he husked with the last shreds of his voice. "Amos, why did you bury the boy here?"

"He was crying."

"In the night?"

"Cree-cree-cree. He was hurting."

Hiero gasped. "The creepers!"

Tim touched his arm to hush him. "So you brought him here to stop him hurting?"

"Not the first. He died too quickly. But the others."

Tim shuddered. It was one thing to suspect, another to hear the proof. "You buried the others here as well?"

"Inspector, have mercy!" Sister Merry wailed. "He don't understand. He don't know what he's done."

Tim lifted a hand to quiet her. "But you put the others in the ground. Why not this one?"

Amos shifted away from his sister, cowering by Han's legs.

"It wasn't right, Merry. Them little 'uns was suffering. It wasn't right to give 'em the blessing."

"The blessing? You mean the laudanum?"

"Aye. Babes need milk. Need to grow. Not..." He violently shook his head. "It wasn't right!"

"You've done well, Amos. Thank you." Tim focused his attention on Sister Merry, who stood fast against his scrutiny with a stern, closed visage. "'Though this be madness, yet there is method in 't.' Shakespeare understood villainous ways better than most. To commit a crime of this nature is the height of lunacy, but there is reason embedded in its execution. A gentle soul such as Amos could not have planned and carried out such an elaborate deception. Not alone. And, in my opinion, not at all."

A chorus of gasps from the other Daughters. Sister Merry lunged at Amos, screaming and cursing, arm raised to deliver a battering blow. Amos, cowering, scrabbled behind Han.

A shot rang out, exploding the grass between them. Everyone froze.

Callie strode forward until her revolver was aimed point-blank at Sister Merry's head. Han hurried Amos away over to Sister Nora, who welcomed him into a consoling hug. Both wept, the day's misery-making revelations too heavy to bear.

"You would beat the brother who's kept your secret all this time?" Callie hissed at Merry. "Depended on you for everything. No family, no place, no home without you. And who would believe him if he tried to tell? He was your original victim, powerless, trapped in a hell he couldn't escape. But he found a way."

Sister Merry turned and spit in her face. Callie pressed the barrel of the gun between her eyes until a grunt from Han forced her slight retreat.

"I never asked for this!" Sister Merry cried. "Not him, millstone round my neck. Not our new mission, straying from our Holy Mother's wishes. Our Rebecca never would have approved! Not the endless wailing of the needy whelps we kept who killed Dad and ruined Mum. Kept me from the fields, doomed to watch my brothers let them wilt. Kept me from the land I loved. But always a greedy mouth to steal the milk from my cup. Always one, two, three squalling brats to bounce on my hips till I couldn't barely stand. Their crying ringing through my head day and night till I forgot my own name!

"I thought here, finally, I'd find some peace, but then she"—she stabbed a finger at Sister Juliet—"stole it all away! More hungry mouths, more caterwauling, mums and babes both! The gall of her to say Mother Eve wanted this… this…" Her voice cracked. "And now my garden is burning! All Rebecca's good work. All my pains and aches, my raw hands, my crabby knees, my knotty back… None of those little demons was ever going to replace Her! None of them's anything but food for worms!"

"Enough!" Sir Hugh bellowed, his handsome face contorted into the most anguished expression Tim had ever seen. "Get her from my sight."

Sister Merry had the gall to scoff. "I won't answer to a man who sells his mistress and child for sainthood. Wouldn't be a scourge of infants if your ilk cared for their own." She knelt down in the middle of the petal wreath, gazed up into the tree's billowing boughs. "There's only one who can judge me now." She steepled her hands in prayer. "Bless me, Mother!"

Only when she threw her head back did Tim spot the tiny bottle clasped between her palms. He let out a shout. Callie dropped her gun and raced forward, but the deed was done. Sister Merry's face swelled a violent red. Spasms wracked her as she choked, slumped to the ground.

"No, Merry! No!" Amos wrestled away from Sister Nora, fell down at her side.

"Sweet boy," Sister Merry wheezed, then sank into the grass.

The sound of Amos's wails echoed across the garden. Tim heard only the giggles of the all the babes she had wronged, their souls finally at peace.

Chapter 23

*H*iero stared down into the solemn little face of Felix, the babe he cradled. Short-lashed, boat-shaped eyes fluttered as he slept, oblivious to all but the heat that coddled him. His life was only a few days old and already tumultuous—kidnapping, attempted murder, almost buried alive. Hiero kept waiting for someone claim him, but the few Daughters busied themselves with caring for their patients. In the corridor beyond, the chatter of officers could be heard attempting to interview and reassure dozens of expectant mothers while dodging their questions, along with Callie enumerating, at top volume to Winterbourne, all the reasons why the Daughters should be permitted to continue on despite Sister Juliet's arrest.

Though his instinct was to spirit them all away once the Yard took the lead, Hiero knew Kip was not well enough to travel even the few short hours to Berkeley Square. After allowing Sister Zanna to redo the recovery work his obstinacy and—it had to be said—tenaciousness wrecked, Kip had given over to slumber. Hiero, not about to leave his side while they were still in enemy territory, had snuck a rocking chair into the quiet corner where Kip rested, hoping no one inquired about his back.

Despite the nose hair-withering stench of the poultice coating Kip's chest, Hiero felt his eyelids drooping as he rocked, the warmth of the babe in his arms and his empty brandy glass conspiring against him. To say nothing of his exhaustion. When a hand landed on his shoulder, he barely even startled. A familiar ruddy face peered over him.

"All's well, Mr. Bash?" Angus asked, grinning down at the babe. "And who's this, then?"

"The Daughters have named him Felix, though it doesn't suit."

"Handsome fellow, he is." Hiero didn't mistake the wistfulness in his eyes. "I've refitted the back of the carriage, as Mr. Han suggested. Soon as DI Stoker feels up to it, of course."

"I fear it will be some time yet before our business is concluded. Care to sit?"

Angus hesitated, eyes only for the boy. "Reminds me of our wee Ting, he does." He nudged a finger into one of the little hands. "Is the mother not about?"

"Returned to her post, it seems." Hiero sighed. "Like so many of us, he's alone in the world."

"He's not spoken for? A looker like him?"

Hiero watched the emotions play across Angus's broad-jawed face, letting him come to his own conclusions. When none were forthcoming, he pressed the issue.

"And will we be hearing some happy news from you and Jie soon?"

Angus, ever good-natured, chuckled. "You know very well that after the last time..." He blew out a breath. "A few hours longer, you say? Long enough for me to ride home and back?"

"If you care to make the journey twice."

He shrugged. "Was gonnae have to with DI Stoker in a bad way. Won't be two ticks."

Hiero couldn't help but smile as he raced off. He dropped a kiss to the babe's brow, welcoming him to the family. A strained chuckle from the cot drew his attention.

"You can't save them all," Kip rasped, his voice a shadow of its former self.

"How well I know it. But this charming one we did save." His gaze met Kip's moss-green eyes, red rimmed and squinted with fatigue but ever bright. "And before you object, I have plans for the mothers as well."

"Sister Zanna?"

"Yes. If this haunted place can be rehabilitated. If not, elsewhere."

"Good. Their work should continue. Minus the zealotry and torture."

"Precisely my thinking. Or rather her thinking, bankrolled by a consortium of patrons Callie and I will marshal." Hiero snickered to himself. "I rather think Winterbourne will be in for a hefty donation."

"I fear you may be disappointed on that account."

"I can be very persuasive. I've even been known to draw blood from the boulder-minded yobs at the Yard."

"As Superintendant Quayle reminds me at every opportunity." They shared a laugh, eyes only for each other. Hiero itched to take his Kip's hand, wishing there were a cradle near for the first time since their ordeal.

"Who would I be if I abandoned these women after ruining their one chance to offer their children a proper start?" Hiero said, returning to his favorite topic: himself.

"You did not see the orphan asylum." A coughing fit overtook Kip, but he had not spoken his last on the subject. "Perhaps for the best if you aim to rehouse every babe who gleams its eyes at you."

"I do have a fondness for strays."

"It also appears that despite many protestations to the contrary, you are a good man."

This sobered Hiero. "I have not been, in the past. Timothy, you must never forget that."

"'Timothy'? Oh, dear. Am I in for a scolding?"

"I have cheated. I have swindled. I have stolen and lied and…

well." Hiero pressed into the rocking chair, the sizzles around the edges of his back a painful reminder. "But perhaps, through our work, I might find a measure of grace. Even I can find it in me to believe in that."

Kip considered this. "Ours is not a kind, or a just, or a patient world. But it is ours, and we must make of it what we can."

He beamed at him then, and Hiero wished again they were at home alone.

A second shadow fell across Hiero, this one less familiar. Ghost of Future Perils, perhaps?

"I don't care to remind you to be quiet again, DI Stoker," Sister Zanna chided. "Bed rest and only necessary communication for at least a fortnight."

Kip nodded, chastened.

"And I expect you, as his... accomplice of some sort? To respect the demands of his health," she continued. "Understood?"

Hiero dutifully bowed his head, thinking of all the things he could do to with Kip's talented mouth to distract him from his aches.

"Your wish is my command."

Sister Zanna harrumphed but made no further protest. With her hair wrapped in a messy scarf bun—she, and many of the Daughters, had unraveled their winged plaits upon Sister Juliet's arrest—and her apron askew, she appeared in her element. She'd barreled through the events of the day with the fortitude of a war nurse and now, victorious, effortlessly led the charge.

"I'm afraid this one is due for a look-over." She pinched his golden cheek, then eased him out of Hiero's arms. "Can't be too careful at this age."

"If you must. But don't stray too far, if you please. Now he's found a home, it wouldn't do to lose him."

"Has he? That was fast work." Sister Zanna clicked her tongue as the babe began to fuss. "I'll see he gets a bath. Have him smelling fresh for his new parents." She scrutinized Hiero as she bounced him. "And you, Mr...?"

"Bash."

"Ah! How fitting." Her lips curled into a cautious smile. "Your back, I'm told, suffered some abuse. If you'd care to join me in the examination room?" She misinterpreted Hiero's scoff as condescension. "Or we could summon your personal physician."

"No need," Kip interceded. "The only victim of the blast was Mr. Bash's jacket, the shirt beneath quite intact."

"And the smoke." Sister Zanna sighed, unimpressed. "Let me fetch you a poultice."

Hiero shook his head, letting his distaste mask his worry.

"Another brandy would be capital. Otherwise I'll continue my vigil until the Yard requires me."

"'Vigil.'" Kip snorted. "Not rid of me yet."

"Necessary communication only," Sister Zanna reminded him before taking her leave.

As soon as she'd disappeared into the examination room, Hiero slid—well, staggered—over to the cot and perched on the edge. He adjusted his posture until it felt like only his sides scraped like a knife over sharpening leather. He angled his legs to conceal how he twined his inner hand with Kip's. He brushed his thumb over callused knuckles, wishing they could speak freely, and not just for medical reasons.

"Promise me you'll have someone see to your back," Kip murmured. "And not Han."

Hiero nodded. "I'll have one of Apollo's old acquaintances call when we return. He is discreet. Of our tribe."

"Good." Kip exhaled a wheezing breath. "Hiero—"

"Shh. Be a good boy, and you'll have your treat."

He stroked the underside of Kip's hand, then turned it over. A whirl of Hiero's wrist, and Sister Juliet's necklace dangled from his fingers. The diary key swung like a pendulum until it landed in Kip's palm.

Kip coughed around his squeak of delight. He pointed to his discarded jacket, from which Hiero retrieved the diary. A click of the lock, and the pages were laid out before them, a buffet of secrets for Kip to feast on until he was hale and hardy once more. Hiero, enacting the part of podium, canted the book toward the light as Kip searched for the answer to the one mystery left to solve. His skimming finger came to an abrupt halt, underlining a certain entry as his mind checked and double-checked its facts.

Hiero could have eaten the resulting smile with a spoon.

"Fetch Sir Hugh," he urged with the last of his voice, sending Hiero off with an affectionate squeeze.

Callie caught the tiny hand that threatened to tug off her wig, kissed it to mask her annoyance. She couldn't blame the little mite—the recent purchase, a spring-curled flaming red to contrast with her wavy blonde society persona, itched like mad. Coarse and overly perfumed, she resisted the urge to scratch the back of her neck rawer than it already was. If the heat flush that spread over her shoulders was any indication, her skin probably matched her wig. If only higher collars were in fashion.

She stifled a growl when the boy sneezed into her shoulder. Shahida, sensing how close Callie was to breaking character—and the obsequious smile on Mr. Crook's face—rushed to scoop him out of her arms. Callie mined the last reserves of her patience as she petted his scraggly head and gazed adoringly at the son the philandering Sir Hugh did not deserve.

Not that she wished this boy, or any child, dead. But she kept the memory of the babe who had died close to her heart, having the previous day delivered the news of Sister Merry's cruel treatment of him to his harried and dismissive father. They hadn't been able to locate his mother. Callie privately thought this a mercy. Shahida had suggested knowing what became of her son might only crush what was left of her spirit, and Callie could not disagree. She wanted to be glad of Sir Hugh taking responsibility for his child, since so many others did not, but could not overlook the actions that had led them to the orphan asylum that afternoon. Could not help but wonder if a creature like Sister Merry was born out of the impulses of rich, callous men.

Then she recalled Sir Hugh had offered Amos Scaggs a position on his gardening staff, where by all accounts he was settled and content, and found the poise necessary to take his arm as they left the asylum.

As soon as they'd rounded the corner where the carriages were parked, Sir Hugh cleared his throat. Not once but four times. He released her to seek out his handkerchief, turning his face away. After a flurry of sniffling and dabbing that had Callie clutching to her antipathy with strained fists, Sir Hugh reached to Shahida.

"Give him here." He crushed the boy to him.

Looking at them, no one could doubt their similarities, even if the little lad favored his mother's coloring. A spark of hope lit in Callie's chest, for which she was grateful. These errands of Tim's, which she'd brashly taken on whist he convalesced, had given her a greater respect for the demands of his position. Little wonder he preferred chasing down possessed fangs and cracking codes to playing nurse to society's troubled.

"Miss Pankhurst, I am in your debt." Sir Hugh, having collected himself but not relinquished the boy, bowed in her direction.

"If you feel you owe me anything, let it be allegiance to our mutual friend. Protect him, that our work may continue."

"You have my word of honor."

"Then I wish you and..." She smirked at the boy, already asleep on his father's shoulder. "What will you name him?"

"Jonah, after my bother."

"Spat back from the bowels of a whale. Perfect."

They parted ways as they reached the carriages, Sir Hugh spiriting Jonah off to his new life. Shahida fell in beside her as they watched them go, a wry expression curving her lips.

"You could do worse."

Callie scoffed. "He'd have me hosting soirees and serving as some duchess's lapdog before I could blink." She pried out one of the pins holding her wig in place, then scrubbed the end under her ear.

"He's gentle. Righteous. Well placed but not too well placed."

"Do pass the cyanide."

Shahida laughed, but it didn't meet her eyes.

"You've been granted many liberties. Many in lower circumstances would envy that. Mind you don't forget it."

Callie, chastened, hooked her by the arm. She glanced down at Shahida's belly, just beginning to round out, and made a silent vow.

"Never."

The door to their carriage clattered open, and Han poked his head out.

"Though I do agree. You can do much better," Shahida whispered when Han hopped out onto the street.

Callie elbowed her in the side as they moved to join him.

"All's well that ends well?" he asked.

"For wee Jonah Winterbourne, I daresay yes," Callie replied.

"Then all is as it should be." He broke into an uncharacteristic grin, one Callie found she couldn't move away from. Until she heard Shahida's snort. "Where to?"

"Hyde Park." She took Han's hand as she climbed into the carriage, wishing she could ride up front with him.

But then Callie spotted her mother's elated face and settled in beside her.

"I'd have thought you'd had your fill of gardens," Han remarked, lingering in the doorway.

"I'm not as partial to them as some." She glanced at Lillian, rosy cheeked and restored from her ordeal. "But it would do us all good to take a bit of air."

"I bow to your wisdom." Han spared her a wink before taking the carriage reins.

Callie avoided Shahida's knowing stare, kicked her ankle to stop her snickering.

Chapter 24

ONE MONTH LATER

*T*im turned his face to the sun as the carriage rounded Berkeley Square. So many people relaxed on the lawn on this rare sunny day it was difficult to tell the grass was green. Not so the trees, which shed their pink spring blossoms in spiral showers, dappling the dresses and hats of ladies *en promenade*. Han, at the reins beside him, waved to Angus and Jie, strolling with their new, renamed son Feng in the pram as Ting skipped ahead. Tim inhaled deep, relishing the stretch of his recovered lungs, if not the overripe London stench. Not everything, as they said, was sunshine and roses.

Though on this day of all days, Tim could be forgiven some optimism. And trepidation.

When the carriage came to a halt at the front steps of 23 Berkeley Square, Tim stared up at the grand old townhouse, still not quite able to reconcile that this was now his home. He remembered his first glimpse of the place only eight or nine months earlier, half-hidden behind one of the trees across the street, searching for clues as to the dastardly deeds of the notorious Hieronymus Bash. To say he had found something unexpected behind that silver knocker was no exaggeration. But the true marvel was the discovery of the bit of himself he hadn't known he'd been missing.

He hopped down from the front seat just as Angus jogged over to help them unload the boxes. Tim cringed when Han propped open the door, still embarrassed the entirety of his worldly possessions didn't quite fill the carriage compartment, especially when compared to the five-story colossus behind him. But he reminded himself every one of the current inhabitants had come to Berkeley Square with less, even Lillian and Callie, born into nobility, and most, if they left, would bring no more with them. His ego appeased, he reached for one of the boxes...

Only for Angus to shoo him away.

"Dinnae fash, Mr. Stoker. We'll see to it. You're still mending."

"I'll not have you wait on me, and I need the exercise."

Did two half truths make a lie? Tim couldn't be bothered to do the mental math. He grabbed one of the—lighter, it must be said—boxes, ignoring the screech of his biceps and the groan of his back. Three weeks of bed rest and another of minimal activity had shrunk him down to skin and bone, or so it seemed every time he glanced in the mirror, where he'd also spotted the leg rash that bit deep enough to leave permanent scars. Though his physician forbid him from training at his sports club or resuming work for another fortnight, Tim would not play the invalid a moment longer.

Until felled by a coughing fit halfway up the stairs.

"A wise man once told me," Han counseled as he eased the box out of Tim's hands, "not to wait on chasing happiness, else it might escape you."

"And here I thought we were done with false prophets."

Han chuckled. "Well and done. My uncle aspired to many things, but godliness wasn't one of them."

Tim cast a fretful glance back at the carriage. "You're certain?"

"Go. Or he'll dig a trough in the floor with his pacing."

With a grateful smile, Tim climbed the rest of the steps. The door opened before he could knock, Aldridge stoic as ever. He started to perform a bow, but Tim extended his hand. Aldridge clasped it between his own, eyes twinkling as he directed Tim toward the grand staircase to the upper floors.

Though he had dressed and groomed in the cozy third-floor room just that morning, Tim felt a crackle in the air as he entered. The smallest and humblest of the bedchambers at Berkeley Square, it still doubled the size of Tim's Kensington apartment. Never one to miss an opportunity to redecorate, Hiero had taken inspiration from the forest. Pine greens and lichen yellows accented the furniture's earthy browns. The leaf motif of the wallpaper gave the illusion of a canopy of branches over the bed, with linens and pillows in lush, mossy textures. Secluded at the far end of the room, his writing desk curved invitingly around the wall of majestic mahogany bookshelves, which awaited population.

The most notable piece, a pop of chartreuse tucked under the window, was, of course, the fainting couch, formerly of Hiero's dressing room. Tim didn't imagine he'd while away too many afternoons lounging on it, but he took it in the spirit it had been given—a reminder of the attraction of opposites that forged their undeniable connection. That had led him here, to this new life with the man he adored.

A man who threw open the hidden door that just so happened to adjoin onto the master bedroom. Hiero paraded in as if he'd recently been beatified, his red-and-gold dressing gown over violet silk trousers evoking the papal robes. The scent of him, smoke and spice with a hint of nervous sweat, fanned the flames of Tim's desire.

He locked eyes with his sleek, suave, faintly ridiculous Hiero. How Tim longed to worship him.

"Welcome home, dear Kip."

Tim noted the tremor of hesitation in his voice and hastened to silence it. "You've made it so," he whispered, quieting their doubts with a lingering kiss.

Hiero drew him into an embrace that did not break until Han and Angus burst in with the first of the boxes. Tim let Hiero take charge of directing them, knowing it would calm him to make sure Tim's possessions were in order. As much as his Hiero thrived in chaos, Tim had noticed one of the ways he expressed his care was in settling things for others. So Tim nodded when consulted and otherwise enjoyed being able to stand in a room full of friends with his arms around his lover without judgment or censure.

Perhaps he truly was home.

"This was once my boudoir," Hiero remarked as they set the last of the boxes by the desk.

"So you've said."

"A lifetime ago, it seems now."

"Hardly a revelation. You've had so many."

"Even so." Overtaken by a pensive mood, Hiero retreated a few paces to observe Tim in this new environment as a painter might an unfinished portrait. "It suits you. You complete it in a way I never could."

Tim smirked. "The room, or the household?"

This drew out his smile. "The household is an ever-changing thing. It grows new members as we speak. Others might come to tire of it, seek out new adventures or families of their own. But this room, I feel, has found its person."

Tim heard in his words what neither of them was yet prepared to say. Too many things between them remained uncertain, including how they would acclimate to living in such close quarters. But he ignored any reservations he felt in favor of kindling the flicker of hope in his heart. That he had found his place in the world, his people, and, more importantly, his person.

"Pity that."

Hiero started. "Oh?"

"I fear I've already betrayed her. In that I've become rather partial to the bed next door. And it's... delicacies."

Hiero clicked his tongue. "Careful. The fainting couch is easily wounded, if you'll recall."

"Really? I always thought her quite sturdy."

"In construction, yes. But even those of us made of stronger stuff can wobble when it comes to matters of..."

"Personal history?" Tim closed the distance between them, weaving his withy arms around him. "Echoes of another lifetime?"

At first Tim thought Hiero might offer up his usual evasions. But he gazed down at Tim with open, if timid, eyes. He felt a shiver skitter through him.

"Come join me once you've settled," Hiero murmured, "and we'll speak of things long forgotten."

Tim caught him as he made to retreat. "I'm quite settled for the moment. Tell me now."

"Nonsense." Hiero's solemn stare regained some of its normal sparkle. "You haven't even noticed your gift."

"My gift? You mean besides the refurbished room let to me at negligible cost?"

"Oh, I will exact a price." Hiero steered Tim toward the absurdly oversized wardrobe.

In which he feared he would find a row of suits and finery of a cost he could never hope to repay, even in flesh. But instead found only a dressing gown, monogrammed and matching Hiero's own, but in silver and blue. A pair of burgundy silk trousers completed the set. Tim lifted up one of the cuffs to rub it across his cheek.

"Thank you. For the warmest welcome." He turned to see Hiero disappear through the adjoining door.

"Dress. I await you."

"As you wish," Tim shouted after him, already through the buttons of his waistcoat.

Some time later, the decadent scent of rose and musk lured him into Hiero's bedchamber. Thick velvet curtains had been drawn to block out the sunlight. The flicker of candlelight enhanced the intimate atmosphere, gilding the playful murals and bawdy statuary. A basin of steaming water had been set before a thronelike armchair, beside which Hiero tinkered with a tray of creams and elixirs. He'd shed his papal robe for an apron over his loose silk shirt and trousers.

Seeing him barefoot and kneeling, Tim's mind bloomed with possible scenarios for their afternoon of leisure.

He reminded himself—especially his eager prick—to await Hiero's instruction.

"Ah," Hiero greeted him with an anxious glance. "Come. Sit."

Tim stopped to card his fingers through the glossy waves of Hiero's hair before obeying, concerned. He massaged his hands down the nape of his neck and over his shoulders. As soon as he worked out a knot of tension, another coiled in its place. Hiero pressed his face into Tim's hip, uncharacteristically silent. Tim dropped a kiss to his crown, attempted to draw him up to his feet, but Hiero resisted.

"Sit."

Tim sank into the luxurious armchair, its buoyant cushions and cradling cant almost erotic. He could not help but spread his legs wide, which only encouraged his burgeoning erection to sprout higher. Its arrogant twitch caught Hiero's eye; he licked his lips. Tearing his gaze away, Hiero snatched a bottle of indigo liquid from the tray, poured three careful drops into the basin. As he swished the waters, another waft of spicy, woodsy scent enticed Tim's senses.

"That fragrance," he purred. "Eau de Bash. What is it?"

"Oudh." Hiero offered him a sniff of the bottle. Tim inhaled, the smell so deep, so rich, so raw it was as if they were already entwined. Or so his throbbing cock was persuaded.

"Touch me." Tim reached for him.

Only to be smacked away. "Patience."

He wanted to bite the smirk off Hiero's mouth but decided to behave. Despite the intensifying simmer of his desire, Tim was curious. Especially when Hiero folded Tim's trouser legs up over his knees.

Hiero painted a generous stripe of cream from Tim's ankles to his toes, then his magnificent hands set about massaging it into his left foot. Tim fought to relax and give in to his ministrations, to forget his concerns and let Hiero care for him. He let out a soft moan as Hiero eased his leg into the soothing waters of the basin, wishing his magical hands would hurry with his right foot so they'd be free to travel higher. Glutted by sensation, Tim only hungered for more: to be jerked and sucked, bent over the chair and fucked, to feel Hiero atop him, inside him, possessing him, melting into him.

Tim woke from sensual reverie when Hiero lifted his first leg out of the basin, propped it on his thigh, and proceeded to scrub. He used a firm brush, tending to every inch of Tim's cracked and callused foot with a concentration rarely glimpsed in him. This focused tenderness bubbled through Tim like the headiest champagne, leaving him fizzy with affection. He gave all his attention to watching Hiero, his master thespian giving the humblest performance of his career. And all for Tim.

Hiero didn't once look up, not even when he switched feet.

"I learned this custom at my father's table."

Shocked, Tim almost yanked his leg away. But he forced his body to soften. Opened his mind and his heart to what Hiero would confide in him.

"He invited so few guests into our home that those he trusted were treated like kings." Hiero placed Tim's second foot back in the basin, then poured in a fresh rush of hot water from a covered pitcher. "Always he washed their feet when they arrived. Some were surprised, I think, even those of our culture. I've long thought of doing the same here, but feared it would be too…"

"Revealing?"

A hint of a smile. "But you… You, Timothy Kipling Stoker, are most welcome indeed."

Hiero's starburst eyes flicked up. Their gazes locked. Tim marveled at all he read there, more than a simple verse or letter could ever convey. More meaning than could be uncovered in an entire library.

Hiero unfolded a towel, slipping the basin to the side as, one by one, he patted Tim's feet dry. Tim stifled a moan at the sweep of the fabric across his soles, refusing to be distracted from the banquet of information being spread before him.

"I am my father's only son, his youngest child. With all the privileges and all the expectations that entailed." Hiero paused his ministrations, lost to memory. "I remember sleeping in a nest of pillows as a young child while my parents and my sisters worked around me. I remember their sad eyes when he would invite me to accompany him on some errand. They weren't permitted to leave the shop or guard the register, but I learned to tally the accounts on my first day. My father gave me everything of himself from the day I was born until..." A heavy sigh. "Until he discovered who I was."

Tim, having moved to the edge of his seat, hovered over Hiero, unsure whether to gather him up or drop into his lap or wait on his signal. He wanted so many things, but most of all to hear the full span of Hiero's tale.

"You must understand he forgave so very much in me. My complete inability with sums. My tendency to pass the afternoon chatting with our regular customers. The time I mislaid a week's worth of inventory whilst transfixed by a Punch and Judy show."

Tim chuckled. The noise startled Hiero out of himself, earned Tim a fond look.

"Much the same as ever, then." He scooted over to the left side of the armchair—room enough for a small family beside him, really—and invited Hiero up.

Hiero cast off his apron and slunk into the space beside Tim.

"I was no one's idea of an ideal heir, least of all my mother's, but Baba... He believed in me. Trusted I would find my way, even if it differed from his. And I did. But not how he expected." Tim twined their fingers, anticipating the turn. "The first time he found me with a friend, we did not speak for five days. Mama shouted the house down and forced me to pray night and day, but Baba locked himself in their room. His disappointment cut so deep I kept away from anyone for a year. Dedicated myself to work and study and family...

and thought about hurling myself in the Thames almost every night. But at that age, already prone to distraction and in a constant fever..."

"You found someone new."

"I found them. They found me. I learned caution, but authority chafed. The strictures, the responsibility, their expectations..."

"You provoked an incident?"

"I tested my boundaries. Repeatedly. Until."

"Your mother."

"Alas." Hiero heaved in a stuttering breath. "A devout woman. Disciplined, cold. Never touched except to strike. Near the end she considered me a plague upon our family. She would never have breathed a word of our troubles to anyone, but I became involved with a family friend's son. His mother knew of a doctor who smote out that kind of sinful behavior. And that, the promise of me being reformed, was what convinced my father to send me away."

Hiero withdrew his hand from Tim's clasp, peeled back his sleeve to reveal the scar around his wrist. Tim didn't hesitate to curl a possessive hold around Hiero's arm, caress the scar.

"Monsters."

"If only they'd had claws and horns instead of vile machinations, I might have stood a chance."

Tim let out a soft growl. "How long?"

"Two years."

His cursed response earned a weak chuckle from Hiero. "Names. Any details you can remember. I will hunt them. I'll see to it—"

Hiero pressed a hand to his chest. "They've been dealt with. I have become, as you might recall, a man of means."

Tim blew out his anger. "You're a treasure."

His stomach did a little flip at the faint blush that colored Hiero's cheeks. Possibly the first time in recorded history they'd taken on a bashful tint.

"Go on."

"Not until we have all the poison out." Tim drew him into a half embrace. "Your parents."

Hiero grimaced. "My father visited every month. At first I strived to hide my wounds from him. I wanted to be well again. I wanted to return to them. I would have done anything to leave that place. Even obey. As time wore on, it became... impossible to hide what was being done to me. I begged him to stop it. Promised to go away to school, promised to marry..."

Tim steeled himself against where he knew the dread tale would lead.

"But he did nothing. My baba, who used to carry me on his shoulders until his arms shook, left me to be..." A sniffle was all Hiero allowed himself, and a strenuous clearing of his throat. "Visiting me was his penance. The price he had agreed to be rid of me. I was never getting out."

Tim cinched him in closer. "They underestimated your resourcefulness."

"So they did. Though I was not yet the wily wonder that sits here with you, I was not, as you say, without options. Indeed, I held on that last half year under the delusion I was close to the end of my tenure. After the worst of the floggings, I was certain I'd earned my way to absolution. I'd even made a friend."

Tim smirked. "Han?"

"Well, if you mean to spoil all the secrets, I don't know why I'm bothering to tell it."

"My apologies. Please go on."

Hiero sighed. "Yes, Han. We escaped. On our first attempt."

"To considerable renown among the inmates of the asylum."

"One can only guess."

Tim hugged him fiercely. Felt for the first time like he could draw an accurate sketch of the man he held, one with a history, a family, a youth not dissimilar to his own. Though he had not suffered anything like the abuse and rejection Hiero had known, Tim marveled at how alike their childhoods were. Both sons of merchants, not rich but not poor, with two sets of stable parents until their respective tragedies struck. He'd often wondered how his beloved mother and father would have reacted to learning of his proclivities. Now he understood their ignorance to be the one blessing to come of their early deaths.

"I cannot be thankful you knew such pain, even if it led our paths to cross. But I am grateful to know something of you at last."

"My dearest Kip," Hiero murmured into his neck, "you know me as no one ever has nor ever will." He angled his face that they might gaze in each other's eyes. Hiero caught him in a look more unguarded, more honest, more real than Tim had ever perceived there before. A breathtaking look aimed at him alone. "You hold my heart."

Tim smoothed his fingers along Hiero's cherished visage, claimed his kiss. Rested their brows together that they might simply be, two lovers with their limbs, lives, souls entangled. Guided Hiero's arms around him to let him take what he wanted, he who had given so much. Met his lips in a crushing embrace, shifted into Hiero's lap that he might manhandle Tim at will.

As Tim desperately hoped he would.

In a rare show of strength, Hiero hoisted Tim up and carried him over to the bed. Tim wasted no time spreading himself across the coverlet, snaring Hiero by the hips with two nimble legs. Tim made quick work of his shirt buttons, parting the satiny fabric to expose his chest, should Hiero wish to sup or fondle. He teased down the waist of his bed trousers, inviting Hiero to aid in their disposal, eager, so eager now for his touch and his taste and the hard thrust of his prick. To strip his body bare as Hiero had stripped himself naked in spirit.

When no sensuous hands traveled the length of his frame, Tim glanced up to see...

Hiero struggling with the clasps of his shirt. Brow wrinkled, fingers fumbling. Tim leapt up, caught them in his own.

"You owe me nothing. You've laid yourself as bare as—"

Hiero silenced his concerns with a chuckle. "Seems I'm out of practice. Will you help?"

"If you're certain."

"I would give you all of me. Of that I am certain." Their heated breaths mingled as Tim unhooked the meddlesome clasp. "Ah! There." Hiero shrugged out of his shirt and unlaced his trousers, which flopped to the floor. "Freedom at last."

Tim only had eyes for Hiero's radiant smile, but his hands, less prone to distraction, hastened to grab their fill of Hiero's plump buttocks. Too riled by recent events and conversation to take his time, though he whispered a promise to every inch of Hiero's satiny skin that he would devote the evening to its exploration, Tim stopped his mouth with a deep, delving kiss.

Hiero crushed Tim to him; they moaned at the first thrilling press of their naked bodies, chest to furry chest, hip to bucking hip, prick to jutting prick. But all that glorious contact wasn't enough for Tim, who collapsed back so Hiero could climb atop him, taking the full weight of his sleek form. Tim laughed, dizzy with joy and arousal as Hiero licked down to his collar, sucking on the fleshy notch found there.

"No niceties." Tim rubbed the head of his cock up and down the coarse trail of hair that bisected Hiero's abdomen. He stifled a scream of pleasure at the sensation. "Take me. As only you can."

Hiero lifted his head, his eyes a sparkling obsidian. "I had rather thought you might care to... sample my wares?"

"Is that what you would prefer?" Tim asked, fighting to keep the needfulness from his face. His Hiero would have whatever he desired on this day of all days, no matter how much Tim ached to be owned by him. Which was very, very much.

Tim knew he'd lost the battle when Hiero chuckled, his lustrous look brightening all the more.

"We truly are well matched."

"Some might say," Tim panted as Hiero saddled between his legs, "we flirt with perfection."

"Only flirt?"

"The day is young. And I have passion to spare."

Hiero watched the shadow play of wind-tousled branches on the bedroom wall, feeling replete. Splayed across the newly christened sheets of Kip's nominal bed, without a stitch of cover except for Kip's warm body melting into his legs and back, Hiero basked in the moment's hard-won leisure. Outside a howling late-summer storm thrashed the trees and gloomed the sky. But here, in what he privately called their apartments, a sirocco had swept across the parched dunes of his skin, raining pleasure.

His Kip had made good on his promise to worship every inch of Hiero's sinuous frame with lips and touch. He began by massaging him into a near-hypnotic state. Then with the ardor of a true explorer, he mapped every plane and curve of Hiero's body, from the coarse bracken beneath his arms to the delicate skein behind his knees to the coronae of scars around his ankles to the deep cleft between his buttocks. The mind-bending sensation of being sucked *there*, of being teased and taken with tongue—a first for Hiero—almost transported him out of his body.

Except he had very much wanted to stay tethered to his earthly frame, to ache and curse and shout and sob as Kip undid him, remade him in his image, a Hiero of light, of hope, of ecstasy. Having completed this great work, Kip now slumbered atop his creation, heavy with languor. Really, all those prudish, pious types misunderstood epiphany if they thought it could be achieved through celibacy. Hiero had never felt so blessed as in the arms of a lover.

This one in fond particular.

Which was why he groaned at himself when that old itch, restlessness, tickled his ear like a pesky fly. He should have been content to lay there well into the evening until Han summoned them to family meal. He'd conquered his fears of exposing himself to Kip, found new purpose in their endeavors, and lured his skittish paramour into cohabitation. They'd enjoyed a carefree summer of solving petty crimes and surreptitious heavy petting, their desire for each other unquenchable. Even Kip, exasperated by his inability to work long hours and annoyed by the restrictions the doctor imposed, had surrendered to their afternoons of delight.

So why couldn't he relax in kind? Had the torments of his youth and the hardscrabble years after inured him to happiness? Had he grown so accustomed to blotting out the bad with tomfoolery and drink he couldn't embrace the life before him, sober and sated? Or was it simply that the cynic in him held no faith in their togetherness despite all evidence to the contrary?

A kiss between his shoulder blades halted the carousel of his thoughts.

"Your quiet is rather deafening, my lovely." Kip snugged his arms tighter around Hiero's torso. "What troubles you?"

"Not a single solitary thing."

"Precisely the problem?"

Hiero harrumphed. Kip shifted until his stiffening cock notched into the very cleft he had earlier plundered.

"Do you require... further distraction?"

"Your attentions are always welcome."

Kip stopped the slow rotation of his hips. "As bad as that?"

"Worse." Hiero sighed, missing the decadent weight as soon as Kip slid off him to converse face-to-face. Though his moroseness lifted some—as it ever did—when he looked at Kip's concerned face. "I fear I've been infected by the plague of introspection."

"Oh, dear. Should I summon your physician?"

Hiero scoffed. "Scamp."

"Misery guts."

"Bluebelly."

"Lushington."

"Ha! A tipple would not go remiss." Hiero laughed. "Scuffer."

"Beauty." Kip tangled his fingers in Hiero's hair, drew him into a languid kiss. Rested their brows together when they parted. "I see I will have to dedicate my considerable skills to relieving you of this maudlin mood."

"Continue as you have been, and I'll soon brighten."

"Oh, I intend to." A flash of heat illuminated his green eyes. "As for my amateur diagnosis, after examining all the signs and symptoms over the past few months, I can only come to one conclusion."

"Which is?"

"You, my beastly one, miss the stage."

Hiero opened his mouth to protest, but any attempt at twisted logic died on his lips. Such were the perils, he supposed, of living with a detective. One's peculiarities, idiosyncrasies, and foibles were understood, perhaps too well.

He exhaled a heavy breath and frowned. "I do."

"Then you must return."

Before Hiero could decide how to feel about that, a knock seized the door. Hiero recognized Aldridge's particular rhythm, bade him enter. Accustomed to their afternoons of repose, Aldridge kept his eyes level as he delivered an officious-looking note. Not to Kip, as Hiero had expected, but to him.

"Royal summons, do you think?" Kip asked, sitting up.

"A bastard prince birthed at Castleside, and we overlooked him?" Hiero chuckled. "There's my knighthood gone."

After thanking Aldridge, they perched, entangled, on the edge of the bed as Hiero tore open the envelope. The contents, however, did not reflect the pomp and circumstance of the packaging.

ONE WILL FALL EVERY DAY
HORACE BEASTLY STAYS AWAY

Hiero repressed a shiver. "No signature."

"You see." Kip stole away the letter for a closer examination. "The public clamors for your return."

"And I suspect your skills, Detective Inspector, will soon be in high demand, if this blackguard has any bottle."

"Shall we rally the team?" Kip asked, thrumming with excitement.

Twinkle eyed, they shared a conspiratorial grin.

"As the toffs would say, tally-ho!"

STOKER AND BASH WILL RETURN IN...

THE DEATH UNDER THE DARK ARCHES

Notes on the History Behind the Fiction

I can't remember how I first learned of the Panacea Society and their prophet, Joanna Southcott, but they are the inspiration for the Daughters of Eden. I've used a few quotes from Mrs. Southcott's writings in Sister Juliet's preaching, and many of the small details were taken from the Society's practices.

Joanna Southcott believed she was the Woman of the Apocalypse from the Book of Revelation (a part I gave to Callie) and foretold she would give birth to the new Messiah at age sixty-four (she died instead). She indeed had a box, leaving instructions that it should be opened in a time of national crisis by all twenty-four bishops of the Church of England. The alleged box was opened in 1927 by a psychic researcher and found to contain weird bits and bobs like a lottery ticket and a horse pistol. Her followers in the Panacea Society disputed the authenticity of the box and claim it remains unopened. The last member of the group died in 2004, and you can visit a museum dedicated to Joanna Southcott and the Society at the Castleside compound in Bedford, England (and they do have a small garden). Thanks to the digital wizardry of my cover artist, Tif, that is a picture of Castleside in the background on the cover. If you want to learn more about the Panacea Society—like the fact that, for decades, they kept an entire house ready and waiting for Jesus' return—there's an excellent documentary on YouTube.

Serial murders as a result of baby farming were an all-too-real epidemic in the Victorian and other eras (and it's not a far stretch to connect them to current real-world problems). The practice first came to light in 1870, with the discovery of Margaret Waters's crimes. Later executions involved childcare workers such as Amelia Dyer, probably the most notorious female serial killer (not called that at the time, but that's essentially what they were), and Amelia Sach and Annie Walters. If you're interested in further research, a warning that the details of these cases are not for the faint of heart.

This is where I confess I cheated a bit on the pregnancy front. There was no accepted scientific pregnancy test invented until 1930. Before then the only surefire way to know was around the fifth month, when women started to show. However, since scientists rarely consulted midwives or nurses when studying pregnancy hormones, it's believed these experienced women had nonscientific ways of telling when someone was going to have a baby. I've cast my lot with in the midwives.

The list of incredible historians doing wonderful, detailed work on the Victorian era and other periods is too long to mention, but I was particularly helped by books/websites by Liza Picard, Dorothy L. Haller, Lee Jackson, Ruth Richardson, Judith Flanders, Moira Allen, Chris Payne, and Fern Riddell, and the plentiful resources at the V&A and the British Library. Any mistakes I made while transforming their sterling facts into fiction are entirely my own.

Acknowledgements

Self-publishing is kind of a misnomer since publishing a book is not really something you can do alone unless you're way more multitalented than I am. It absolutely takes a village. I am forever grateful to everyone who helped bring *The Fruit of the Poisonous Tree* to fruition and who has given their best for three books now (and counting!). My brilliant editor Nancy-Anne Davies's insights rescued the emotional arc of the book and made it sing. Anna "Tiferet" Sikorska listened when I needed it and delivered another gorgeous cover (and I will be forever in her debt for finding a model for Hiero). A wonderful group of betas held my hand through the initial feedback, namely Liv Rancourt, Francesca Borzi, Sam Higson, Day's Lee, and Judie Troyansky. The lovely Elena Meyer-Bothling gave the book a thorough sensitivity read and consulted on Shahida. The amazing Rachel Maybury from Signal Boost Promotions works her magic on the review blogs every time. And Paul Salvette from BB eBooks is the formatting wizard that keeps the books looking as sharp on the inside as on the outside.

I worship at the altar of Polly Jean Harvey, whose album *To Bring You My Love* lit the spark that eventually blazed into this book. And a special shout-out to Jordan L. Hawk, a huge inspiration whose squeeing about *The Fangs of Scavo* basically made my life.

Share Your Experience

If you enjoyed this book, please consider leaving a review on the site where you purchased it, or on GoodReads.

Thank you for your support of independent authors!

Books by Selina Kray

Stoker & Bash Series
The Fangs of Scavo
The Fruit of the Poisonous Tree
The Death Under the Dark Arches (coming Fall 2019)

Historical Romance
Like Stars

Contemporary Romance
In Wild Lemon Groves

About the Author

Selina Kray is the nom de plume of an author and English editor. Professionally she has covered all the artsy-fartsy bases, having worked in a bookstore, at a cinema, in children's television, and in television distribution, up to her latest incarnation as a subtitle editor and grammar nerd (though she may have always been a grammar nerd). A self-proclaimed geek and pop culture junkie who sometimes manages to pry herself away from the review sites and gossip blogs to write fiction of her own, she is a voracious consumer of art with both a capital and lowercase A.

Selina's aim is to write genre-spanning romances with intricate plots, complex characters, and lots of heart. Whether she has achieved this goal is for you, gentle readers, to decide. At present she is hard at work on future novels at home in Montreal, Quebec, with her wee corgi serving as both foot warmer and in-house critic.

If you're interested in receiving Selina's newsletter and being the first to know when new books are released, plus getting sneak peeks at upcoming novels, please sign up at her website: www.selinakray.net

Find Selina online:
Twitter: @selinakray
Facebook: Selina Kray / 23 Berkeley Square
(Stoker & Bash fan page)
Google+: Selina Kray
GoodReads: Selina Kray
Email: selinakray@hotmail.ca
Website: www.selinakray.net